Tim Waterstone was born in̶̶̶
educated at Cambridge University. He lives in London
and has eight children.

He founded in 1982 the Waterstone's bookshop chain,
now the largest specialist booksellers in the British
Isles.

LILLEY & CHASE, published in 1994, was his first
novel, and was followed in 1995 by AN IMPERFECT
MARRIAGE. Both novels have been critically
acclaimed.

Also by Tim Waterstone from Headline Review

Lilley & Chase
An Imperfect Marriage

A Passage
of Lives

Tim Waterstone

HEADLINE
REVIEW

First published in 1996
by HEADLINE BOOK PUBLISHING

First published in paperback in 1997
by HEADLINE BOOK PUBLISHING

A HEADLINE REVIEW paperback

10 9 8 7 6 5 4 3 2 1

ISBN 0 7472 5188 6

Printed and bound in Great Britain by
Cox & Wyman Ltd, Reading, Berks

HEADLINE BOOK PUBLISHING
A division of Hodder Headline PLC
338 Euston Road
London NW1 3BH

For my parents,
Sylvia and Malcolm,
in happy memory.

Author's Acknowledgements

I would particularly like to express my thanks to my friend Professor Sir Cyril Chantler, my distinguished, unpaid and loyal adviser in all things medical, from whose own casebook the idea for the tragic Michael came to me.

Amongst my reading on the Holocaust I would give pride of place to the coldly factual *The Buchenwald Report*, published by Westview Press, which was prepared by a special intelligence team from the Psychological Warfare Division of SHAEF, and assisted by a committee of Buchenwald prisoners. Also invaluable were Gerald Jacobs' *Sacred Games*, published by Hamish Hamilton, and Theo Richmond's extraordinary *Konin* (Jonathan Cape).

The crossword clues in chapter forty-one are quoted by kind permission of Times Newspapers Ltd. The material on the Swiss bank accounts was greatly facilitated and improved by the advice of Roger Boyes of *The Times*, and I am grateful as well to Sir Sigmund Sternberg of The Sternberg Centre for Judaism. The late Ernest Hochland, founder of the great Manchester bookshop Haigh & Hochland is **not** the model for Gareth Edel, but when I think of The Book of Job, and bald, retiring, fiendishly intelligent Jewish booksellers in hornrim glasses I wonder why he wasn't. Mrs Eileen Seymour, introduced to me as the finest Yiddische brain in Gidea Park, gave me my little phrases in Yiddish, and the Charles Ponzi story is well documented, but particularly well picked up in *Time* magazine last year, in describing the downfall of John Bennett, chief executive officer of the Foundation for New Era Philanthropy, a charity out of Radnor, Pennsylvania which Lewis Cohen himself might well have enjoyed doing business with.

PROLOGUE

1945

Joseph Hermann

The previous day, two more transport trains had arrived at Buchenwald, this time from Blechhammer and Auschwitz. The schedule thrust in front of Joseph Hermann showed that a further one, from Gross-Rosen, was due in that same afternoon.

No one had been able to keep control in these circumstances, of course. When the men opened up a railcar, scores of bodies tumbled out right there, straight down on to the ground. The road to the bath-house from the railway station was lined with corpses that no one had had the chance to clear away. The sick barracks, already too small for Buchenwald itself, was overwhelmed by this flood of prisoners arriving in from the other camps. To simplify matters, the SS had begun to liquidate complete transports right there at the bath-house, or in the tent they had erected next to it.

But now, at last, Hermann had managed to persuade the camp authorities to give them this extra space for hospital use. A horse stable. Block 61. The weakest prisoners were here and nursed with some comparatively good equipment and drugs, did the SS but realise it. Since the prisoners had not been provided with proper instruments and medication, Hermann had arranged for them to be stolen. From the SS's own infirmary.

He looked up as Senior Block Inmate Armin Gildrich came into the room, and flopped, beyond exhaustion, on to the single wooden chair in the corner. Hermann gazed at him, wondering if he was in a fit state to absorb the instructions he had for him. Yesterday's madness could not be repeated. The SS Master Sergeant, following orders no doubt, had been 'sorting' prisoners in the antechamber without allowing them to be admitted into the Block proper – a process that involved giving them lethal intercardiac injections.

'Listen to me, Armin. This is what we are going to do.' Hermann

3

held up his hand, fingers extended, palm outward. 'Absorb this, my friend. We have to achieve better control – we can't give up. We must use the opportunity we have, so we're going to change the way we operate. Five points. Here they are.

'Number one: the moment a transport arrives, you or one of your people must be there as quickly as the Master Sergeant. Ahead of him, if possible. Never let him get there first.

'Two: swap names. Take the names of the people already in Block sixty-one who are beyond saving, and exchange them for the healthy coming in.

'Three: you know the list we have of the SS informers? Use that, and immediately. We'll have to kill them, and those coming in can have their identities.

'Four: I've organised for some prisoners in danger from the SS to be smuggled into the Block today. Give them the names of the dead, and we'll get them back into the camp tomorrow with these new identities.

'Five: we're submitting the official death notifications far too quickly. Hold them back. The SS records are as stretched as our own. If we delay, we can get several thousand extra food rations, and I've already agreed with the various national leaders how these can be most fairly distributed. Slow things up, Armin. Do you understand what I'm saying?'

Armin Gildrich nodded at the young man, his fatigue such that he was falling asleep there and then. Hermann came round the table, and squatted at his feet, then took him by the elbows and gently shook him until he was awake enough to hold his gaze.

'One thing more,' Hermann said. 'It's the young we have to save. Where there's a choice, you must ensure that it's the young life you preserve. That's our future, Armin. And there *is* going to be a future. The War's nearly over. There's a new world ahead for us all.'

Mariss Steiner

Senior Camp Inmate Weisenberg ran his fingers through Mariss Steiner's hair, then led him towards the dark little room at the rear of the camp brothel, or 'special building', where he usually went when he needed some moments of privacy for this arrangement.

That afternoon, for his own protection, he had taken a bribe from a guard to deliver one of the 'doll boys' there for half an hour while he stood sentinel outside. He'd picked on Mariss because, at fifteen, he was a comparatively sturdy lad, given the privations of Buchenwald food – and Weisenberg knew the sadistic nature of this particular guard, having stood sentinel for him before, and heard some of what was going on behind the closed doors.

Of all the young boys under his informal supervision, Mariss Steiner was, Weisenberg thought, most likely to be able to keep himself out of serious harm's way. Not only was he healthier and stronger than most of the others, but he could talk. Goodness, how he could talk. And he never seemed afraid. Manipulative, obliging, confident, clever – seductive and flirtatious even, when he needed to be – but never afraid. A great survivor, young Mariss.

The Americans would be at the camp within days, it was rumoured. Hours even, some said. Mariss Steiner's war was nearly over. So was Weisenberg's. They'd both tricked and twisted and dared their way through, and they were alive, and so many thousands were dead.

They'd reached the room now. Weisenberg glanced behind him, gave a couple of quick little raps on the door, then, his hand in the small of Mariss's back, he waited for the lock to turn.

'Look after yourself with this pig,' he whispered out of the side of his mouth. 'It's nearly over, Mariss. And then we'll all be free.'

Jacob Bergdorf

Jacob Bergdorf sat on the floor of the railway truck, and nodded with pleasure as one of the men by the window called out the name of the town they were passing through. *Wahrenholz.* He'd been there. He'd passed through it as a boy with his father, when they'd gone to stay with his grandparents in Hannover. It was on that little river that wandered down to the Aller. You could see the old men and children sitting there along the banks on a summer evening, their fishing rods in their hands, hunks of bread, and sausage, and bottles of beer and lemonade beside them on the grass.

Bread. Sausage. Beer.

Bergdorf looked up at the guard on his stool by the carriage door. The man's rucksack was open, and some dried vegetables and a crust of stale loaf were laid out on a cloth on his knee. Bergdorf turned away again, unable to watch. Bread. Sausage. Beer. Chilled, crisp white wine. Bright tablecloths on café tables, and chattering waitresses bustling out from the kitchens, trays held high, the plates on them laden and steaming, laughing their way through to the young men and their girlfriends sitting outside in the village square. Bergdorf amongst them. Bergdorf waiting with the others, his arms around a girl, the tall Stein frothing over, the waitress bending as she lowered the tray on to the table, the plates so full that gravy slopped over the sides, allowing Bergdorf to reach forward to scrape it up with his finger, then put the finger in his mouth, and the taste, the taste of the gravy like . . .

A foot pressed down heavily on to his thigh as a Ukrainian struggled and stumbled his way over the packed bodies to the bucket of water beside the guard's stool, cursing and railing at the Jews as he went. Bergdorf noticed that the man squeezed up next to him, his eyes closed, his head slumped, made no reaction when he was trodden on. He stared at him more closely, and saw that he was dead. He'd been talking to him only an hour or so before, and he'd seemed strong enough then. They'd talked of food. The meals they would have. The meals they remembered. Course, by ecstatic, slavering course.

Bergdorf turned away, and looked up to the window. The light was beginning to fade on another day. How many more would they have in this train, seemingly going around the German countryside in ever-slower circles? They had been trapped in it for well over a week now. The guard clearly had as little idea as they did of their eventual destination. Bergdorf wondered if anybody had any idea. Perhaps they weren't being sent anywhere.

The man behind him screamed, the terrible, animal cry of the final agonies of starvation, and Bergdorf reached into his pocket for the last slivers of the moist potato peelings he had managed to beg from the guard the previous night, when most others were asleep.

He slipped them into his mouth. I'm a survivor, he thought. We Bergdorfs survive.

Lewis Cohen

Lewis Cohen awoke at least half an hour before the Buchenwald camp sirens sounded.

He could hear outside the muffled noises of tens of dozens of SS guards moving into position around the barrack huts. By the glimmer of moonlight shining through the cracks in the wooden doors and walls, he could see some of the other inmates stirring in their bunks, their heads raised to listen. Then the floodlights in the compound outside were suddenly ablaze. Sirens blared, and orders were shouted again and again through the megaphones: '*Juden antreten! Juden antreten! Schnell! Schnell! Juden antreten!*'

Immediately the Häftlings – the supervisory attendants – and prisoners struggled out of their bunks, and on to the floor. They pushed and jostled towards the door, those in the rear forcing their way through to the safety of the middle of the throng. Lewis found himself beside another boy of his own age, a pastrycook's son from Budapest, whose face already showed the boils and inflammations of adolescent acne. The two stayed close to each other as they were herded into long, winding columns, the SS guards' dogs snarling at their leashes, and snapping and tearing at the striped tunic trousers.

Then, as orders were screamed at the Jews to march, they could hear the drone of approaching aircraft, faint at first, then louder, then deafening as the planes crossed overhead. As they all looked up into the skies, now lightening with dawn, the pace of the march slackened, until they were standing still once more, shielding their eyes with their forearms, straining to see what was happening.

As the bombs fell on to the few remaining factory buildings of the Gustloff Works, no more than three or four hundred yards away from where they stood, the pastrycook's son threw his arms around Lewis's shoulders and shouted his laughter. Explosions thudded, and the sirens wailed out once more. '*Schnell! Schnell!*' the guards were screaming now, as they streamed away back to the supposed shelter of the barracks, gesticulating as they ran for everyone to follow them. But few of the Jews did; and the columns of men broke into a formless shambles, as they gazed across at the dust and smoke now clouding up from above the trees.

'The Americans have come at last,' said a voice behind, and Lewis and his friend turned to see the tailor from the little village outside Mühldorf, his face twisted up at an agonising angle from his sunken, bowed posture. 'They've come,' he said. 'Soon it will be over!' And he pointed across at the smoke, then shouted out once more in his joy as a single stray plane crossed above them. More bombs dropped, and the ground shook and thudded, and they could see now the buildings illumined by the flames that ate up through their roofs.

'Remember Samson!' called the tailor. 'Samson praying to God for strength – just once more – so that he could push away the columns and destroy the Philistines.'

7

'Along with himself,' sniggered the pastrycook's son, but his laughter, and the tailor's angry response, were lost to Lewis as another bomb fell, this one almost cutting the SS guardhouse in two.

Amos Bronowski and Gareth Edel

Major Dawes sat at the trestle table and gazed sadly at the shrunken, emaciated children lined up before him.

Beside him was the Rabbi. They had taken and burnt his striped prisoner's uniform, and he was now, bizarrely, wearing the clean, pressed uniform of an SS guard, from which all markings and decorations had been stripped away. His tiny, bony wrists and hands protruded from the sleeves like those of a skeleton. Only his eyes had life and energy in them.

Despite himself, Major Dawes shifted an inch or so further away from him. He was frightened of illness, and repulsed by death. The Rabbi was, all too obviously, extremely ill. Dying, most probably.

'Come forward in twos,' the Major said in his Welsh-accented German, then repeated himself slowly as he saw the frowns of incomprehension on the children's faces. 'This is to continue what we were doing this morning. I am here to help you. I want you to tell me where you would like to go, and why, and I will try to send you there. I only want what is right for you,' he said, his voice trailing away. 'Want what is comfortable for you,' he said now, wondering if that was better German, but he could see from their faces that he had succeeded only in confusing them the more.

Two boys shuffled in front of him, prodded forward by those behind them. They stood before the Major, both gazing mutely at the ground.

'Your names?' said the Major, but the boys said nothing. He repeated the question, this time leaning forward, as if to be closer to them, trying to project into his voice a reassurance of concern, and kindness. But they still looked down at their feet, and, after a prolonged silence, it was the Rabbi who responded.

'The smaller one is the Edel boy. He was barely old enough to crawl when his parents died. They had only been here in Belsen a day or so. His father was a tailor in München. There are no other relatives alive, so far as I can tell. The boy has no name that anyone is aware of. Isn't that right, Amos? He has no first name?'

He asked the question of the taller boy, perhaps six years old, who shrugged and, quite unexpectedly, smiled. Then, as if suddenly emboldened, he muttered, 'My name's Amos Bronowski. I want to go to America.'

'To America?' said Major Dawes. 'Are there relations there to help you? Whom can we contact for you? Where is it in America you want to go?'

The little boy blushed, and again the Major had to lean forward, this time to try to hear what the child was saying.

'To America,' he whispered. 'To America,' and would answer no more questions, whatever Major Dawes or the Rabbi said to him.

Sighing, the Major looked down again at his pad. He had been at Bergen-Belsen for only two days and had already exhausted the allocations he'd been given by the United States processing officer, but there was a place or two left for Canada; so he filled in the column on his form that would, if all went well, send Amos Bronowski there.

He was about to put the Edel child down for Canada as well, when he suddenly changed his mind. The little lad looked too frail for such a long journey. Get him on the short trip home to Britain as quickly as possible, and someone would take him in, and cherish him. A country family best of all. Welsh. Newbridge-on-Usk or Llantrisant people, perhaps – where his own childhood had been. Fresh air, and fishing, and gardens, and hay-making in the summer. Good homemade bread and country eggs. That was what he needed.

Edel he wrote on the allocation sheet, and then, under the various columns: *Approximately four years of age. German. Jewish. Most substantially underweight and ill nourished, but apparently in relatively sound health. Parents deceased. No evidence or knowledge of living relatives or connections. First name . . .*

Major Dawes looked up, and saw that the child was staring directly at him now. There was in his eyes a hint of trust and dependency.

'I'm going to call you Gareth,' the Major said, this time in English. 'That's my name – it's Welsh. The best name in the world. It's my gift to you Gareth.'

And as he smiled, there ran through Major Dawes's mind a prayer for the child, and for his survival, and for his life. Britain's the best place for him, he thought, as the Rabbi led him away. That's where he'll be looked after best.

BOOK I

1965

Chapter 1

The meetings of the concentration camp survivors' group were held in the upstairs room of a pub tucked away in a little alley near the British Museum. This was Gareth Edel's first attendance, and Mariss Steiner had suggested that he should arrive no later than seven o'clock, so that he would have time to introduce him to the others before the proceedings began. Edel was exactly punctual, but then lingered outside, taut with shyness. He was anonymous enough, in his businessman's suit, horn-rimmed glasses, raincoat and trilby hat, to be lost in the little crowds of men hurrying past on their way home from work, and he was just beginning to wonder whether he could simply join them, and walk away, when a hand was clapped on his shoulder.

'This is it,' Steiner said looking up at him smiling, his pleasant plump face reminding Edel, as when he had first met him, of a devious and dissolute teenager. 'You found the place. In you come!' And Edel allowed himself to be swept in, and up the stairs to the first floor.

The room, already packed with people, was thick with smoke, and deafeningly noisy. The majority of those present were men; the youngest of them in their mid-twenties, as Edel was, and few of them more than forty. Steiner's clothes were subtly more sophisticated than most – black rollneck jersey and black trousers under a black raincoat, with a duffle bag slung casually over his shoulder. Some of the others wore the suits of bookkeepers or clerks or minor businessmen, but most appeared to be students, in their corduroy trousers and sports jackets and sweaters. The few women were dressed in simple cotton dresses, with cardigans thrown over their shoulders, and Edel, frightened of contact with women but intensely romantic about them in his heart, thought that they looked uniformly attractive.

There was only one person there whom he had met before – Lewis Cohen, a tall, good-looking young lawyer – but he stood shyly apart as Steiner greeted Cohen, thinking, correctly as it turned out, that the lawyer would have no memory whatsoever of him in return. Watching Steiner, Edel thought how oddly uneasy he looked. He seemed to know everybody there, moving from group to group, slapping backs, laughing at jokes . . . but Edel, following along behind him, smiling all the time, sweating with nerves, felt the lack of intimacy and warmth in it all.

But now Steiner swung around, took Edel by the arm, and led him across the room. Here a tall young man, perhaps two or three years older than Edel, was haranguing a group. His appearance was striking. Curly-haired, olive-skinned, there was something mesmeric about the physicality and swiftness of his movements. Raising both his arms, he thumped at the air in some wild affirmative statement over one thing or another. Then, as if making a point of theatrical emphasis, he struck a gesture, Gallic perhaps, of holding his fist before his face, then exploding the fingers outwards, wide apart, to make an open, rigid palm.

Steiner waited until he had finished, then laid a hand on his shoulder. The young man, smiling broadly now, turned, and looked down at him.

'I have a surprise,' Steiner said. 'Let me introduce Gareth Edel – or perhaps I don't need to introduce him. You were in Belsen together. Do you remember each other?'

The man shrugged, and reached across to shake Edel's hand, his eyes still glittering with amusement at his own performance.

'Amos Bronowski. Too long ago. Hello, Gareth. Odd name for a Jew. Welcome.'

Chapter 2

Bronowski's pace was much too fast for Edel, and he felt his breath shorten as he tried to keep up with him. Eventually he called out, 'Stop! Slow down – or it's the last time I come for a walk with you.'

Bronowski looked back at him, grinned, and flopped down on to a bench. Edel caught up, and sat down beside him.

'You were saying,' said Bronowski, 'about the country solicitor who fostered you, and his plump, apple-dumpling wife. The bucolic joys of provincial England. Or was it Wales? I'm entranced. Continue.'

But Edel talked instead now of his memories of Belsen; of how he was to this time still frightened by certain surreal, fragmented dreams. He had no means of knowing whether he had actually experienced these as a small child, or whether he was now projecting them into a void that he felt the need to fill. He tried to discuss this, but realised that Bronowski wasn't listening.

'The problem is that you don't care enough, Gareth,' Amos interrupted after a few minutes. 'I'm not interested in the fact that you can't remember anything or anybody in detail, including your family. That's not the point. And everyone gets nightmares. The point of significance is that *you were there*. All that matters is that *you were there*, whether you remember it accurately or not. And that puts you in a very responsible position, like the rest of us. Our lives amongst Jewish people stand out now in sharp relief. We need to consider how we should handle that. What the agenda is. What the priorities are. What our moral responsibility is.'

'I *do* care!' Edel objected. 'What I don't like is the inference of what you're saying. What you really mean by "care" is that I should be dreaming of nothing but revenge and revolution. Intense nationalism. Zionism. I'm not sure that's what I am. I'd rather show that I care by being something else than that. I've already told you what that is.'

Bronowski fiddled with the bark of a stick he had picked up, then, in a sudden, destructive gesture, he snapped it in two, and threw it behind him.

'Well, let me tell you what *I* want to be,' he said. 'I want to be a chronicler. I want to hold and record the truth of what happened, so that Jews a hundred years hence can know their own history. Their *real* history. The prisoners' orchestra, out in the afternoon sun on the *Appellplatz* at Auschwitz, playing their Beethoven. A Jewish prisoners' orchestra, playing Beethoven. While a French Rabbi, tearing at himself, runs out and screams that there is no God, the orchestra, as if nothing in the world was happening, quietly plays on. Jakub, the Jewish hangman there, calmly stringing up his own people. The Christian cloth merchant, born a Jew but a stalwart of his church, denounced by his fellow Christians, and swept away to the camps. Those things. The detail. That's what matters to me. That's what "caring" is for me. It's the chronicling of the truth. That's what moral responsibility is, in my opinion. You feel the need for other manifestations of it. They're not for me.'

Bronowski became silent for a moment, scratching at the dust at his feet with another stick. Then he turned to Edel, smiled, stood up from the bench and gestured cheerily to Edel to do likewise.

'And yet we're not so far apart,' he said. 'Closer than most. It was clever of Mariss Steiner to make sure that we met, though what that man's motive is in anything is hard to know. Let's walk on, boyo.'

16

Chapter 3

Bronowski was in the second year of his doctorate at the London School of Economics, and Edel, after a year's librarianship course at Middlesex Polytechnic, was now started in his initial post at what would turn out to be his home for his entire career; working at what was then known as Burridge's Bookshop, in St Martin's Lane.

Despite their growing friendship, the contrast between them could hardly have been more pronounced. They seemed to be totally dissimilar, both in temperament and in their physical demeanour. Where Bronowski had his good looks, and flamboyant clothes, and furious energies, Edel was hunched, shabbily dressed, quietly spoken and retiring. Where Bronowski ranted and rushed, Edel pondered, and appeared to attempt very little. Bronowski had the reputation of being physically voracious; Edel had never been known to have any romantic involvement at all. Yet even in matters of love and faith, all was not as superficially appeared.

For one day, going into the Burridge's History and Genealogy Department to pick up an order, Edel saw a red-headed Irish girl kneeling on the floor, sorting the stock, a hole in the heel of her tights, piles of books around her. He had noticed her several times before in the staff canteen, and had wanted to talk to her, but never quite managed it. But here she was now, and her smile as she saw him standing there was pretty, and warm, and naive, and Edel was in love.

Maeve was eighteen, or so she said. Actually she was seventeen, and only a week into that, but Burridge's would not employ booksellers under eighteen, so she had lied about her age. And, having lied, she went immediately to Confession. For Maeve was a country girl of traditional and literal Catholicism, frightened a great deal by London, and determined not to be seduced away into a world of lying and deceit, and metropolitan lack of moral scruple. But the priest regarded the confession of her little falsehood as a barely concealed joke, and immediately comforted her, and bustled

17

her on her way, and Maeve soon found other things to feel guilt about. The aversion of her gaze from the homeless beggar outside the underground station. The wrong change given to her by the greengrocer, when, in a rush, he had confused her five-pound note for a tenner. The time she rode on the bus, and was never asked for her fare.

Edel asked about his book, and she went off to find it. They exchanged banalities about the weather, and Ireland, and where she lived, and where he lived, and then they went together to the coffee bar around the corner, and began to settle in each other's company. He took her out that night to a film, and saw her home afterwards to her bed-sitter in Maida Vale. And again the following evening. And for almost every evening thereafter, until they married in the Servite church in the Fulham Road, one wet Saturday afternoon, eleven months after they had first met. Maeve's large family of parents and aunts and uncles and siblings came *en masse* from Ireland and Birmingham and Kilburn to be with her, and her oldest brother acted as Edel's best man.

Of those of his own acquaintance, only Bronowski was there at the ceremony. He sat alone, still numbed, as Edel knew, by the realisation that his friend had for the previous four months been under instruction in the Catholic faith. Edel had told him this in a rush, at the same time as inviting him to the wedding, by that point only three days hence.

Bronowski had gazed at him, his face aghast. At first he was silent, then, 'That's . . . that's . . .' He paused, tried to pull himself together, and started again. 'She's a very nice girl,' he mumbled, and put his face in his hands. Then he suddenly looked up, shook his head, and grimaced in anger.

'For the love of God, Gareth. What on earth do you think you're doing? You're ashamed of it, otherwise—' He checked himself, but remained gazing directly at him, biting at his lip. 'Gareth – you're ashamed about what you're doing. That's why you haven't told me about it before. You knew I would have hated it, and argued with you, and shouted at you, but I do that all the time anyway, and you're always perfectly able to look after yourself. For you to go through the pretence and sham of becoming a Roman Catholic, in such an undignified hurry, for whatever reason, is shameful. For you especially. Such a stickler for moral courage and all the rest of it . . .'

'Yes. That's the point,' said Edel. 'I'm a Jew tribally, and I always will be. Actually, now that I've done what I've done, I think I probably feel that all the more. But my religious beliefs have always been untidy. You know that – we've discussed it endlessly. Of course I wouldn't have done this, were it not for Maeve. I've told her that, and I've told the priests that too. But I'm quite comfortable with what they've asked me to accept. I find myself able to put aside the detail of it, actually. And I like their Mass. I think it works. But none of that's the reason. Maeve's the reason. I did it for her.'

Bronowski fiddled with the coffee cup before him, then said, without any attempt at enthusiasm, 'Maeve's a very pleasant girl. Of course I'll come to the wedding, if you want me to. But don't expect me to . . .' He shrugged. 'I'll be there,' he said. And so he was; uncharacteristically prompt, sitting on his own at the very back of the church, fiddling miserably with the unfamiliar books of worship.

Maeve died barely five months later. Edel knew that it was coming. She had told him of the cancer within a week or so of their first meeting. The doctors had been hopeful of a little more time for her, but it was not to be. Above everything, Edel wanted his wife to die conscious and in his arms, with his words of love the last human contact of her life. He prayed, with his new Roman Catholic prayers, that this would be how it would happen.

But she drifted away one afternoon, alone. She had appeared to be a little stronger that day, and as they were stocktaking at Burridge's, Edel had gone in to help, just for the morning. At lunch-time he was asked to stay for an extra hour or two, and, in his courteous way, he had agreed. When, in the early evening, he at last reached home, he ran, panting, straight up to her bedroom. He thought Maeve was asleep, and tiptoed across to the curtains to draw them. But when he looked down at her again, he saw that she was still.

Maeve was the only family that Edel had ever known. She was the only human being he had ever in his life possessed. When she died, there passed away in him all expectation and hope of love.

Bronowski was stunned by the grief he saw in Edel. The desolation came, and all quarrels of apostasy and breach of trust were swept away and irrelevant. He remained in the hope that Edel would find his way back to Judaism. He was none too sure that he would. And in any case, unheard of for him at this time of his life, Bronowski had the delicacy and tact to leave the issue undiscussed and unresolved.

In time, as the sharpest edge of Edel's bereavement eased, their friendship resumed its course and its intimacy. Actually, it had never really been at risk; and in Edel's eyes it had now been strengthened, if anything, by Bronowski's gesture in coming to the wedding ceremony. Bronowski was embarrassed, but proud that he had made the decision to attend. He had never believed that he would.

Chapter 4

Taut with shyness, and conscious only of what she perceived to be a suffocating, provincial inadequacy, Miranda Thomson had sat in the Headmistress's study at St Peter's Girls' School in West London, and tried to hold her cup without it rattling in its saucer. Lady Phillipson had an approach to young, initiate teachers, and particularly those of indeterminate social background, and plain, unassuming appearance that was intended to put them at their ease. Invariably, however, it served only to achieve the exact opposite. As had proved the case with Miranda, whose soft Morningside accent had, in her terror, grown yet softer and more Morningside the longer the difficult session had lasted.

'You must speak up, my dear,' Lady Phillipson had boomed after some moments of this. 'Frankly, your pitch is inaudible, and I'm afraid your Scottish accent is largely unintelligible to a southern ear. You will be responsible now for some very clever children, whose one desire is to be educated and enlightened in the glories of their native literature. Little can be achieved if they are unable to hear a word you are saying. We must trust in you to amend the inaudibility. And to adjust the accent. Charming of course as it is.'

Whatever Miranda's self-confidence had suffered from this induction from Lady Phillipson, by the time of her first encounter with Amos Bronowski, she had begun to feel not only content in her job, but familiar and comfortable with London itself. She had come to St Peter's straight from her final undergraduate year at St Andrew's University, and before that, with the exception of a single weekend as a small child with her father at the Methodist Missionary Society Headquarters in the Euston Road, she had never been south at all. Her leisure time over these first nine or ten months was spent largely on her own. She went to as many plays and films and concerts as she could – particularly concerts, and particularly chamber music.

21

One evening she had been standing at the Wigmore Hall in line for a ticket since late afternoon. But once the concert had begun she found that the programme that night was overfamiliar, and the performance of it unexhilarating. By the time the interval came, she was tired and dispirited, and in need of a glass of wine to sustain her until, in due course, she would be on her way back to her little flat in Shepherd's Bush for supper.

She was standing at the bar, trying to get served before it was too late and they were called back to their seats. Bronowski happened to be beside her, and watched with amusement her flushed irritation as time after time the barman took orders from people either side and behind, but never from her. Bored, Bronowski decided to play the game of pretending to pick her up. He expected to achieve, if he could be bothered with it, a routine, immediate, effortless conquest. Thinking little more about it, he laid his hand on top of hers, and she looked up at him in surprise.

'I can't bear to watch this happening to you,' he said, and reached across the counter, tapped the barman gently on the lapel and, with courteous, silken menace, told him to serve them immediately. Their drinks came, if with a flounce.

'This is my standard seduction scene,' Bronowski told her. 'I do it all the time. I rescue young girls from this monster of a misogynist barman, and then they come straight home and go to bed with me. That's the accepted procedure. Drink up.'

This sort of chat, arrogant and brittle and amusing perhaps in certain circles of Bronowski's acquaintance, was wholly inappropriate with Miranda. She looked and felt patronised, incompetent to engage in the rituals of it, and ashamed at her lack of urbane wit and self-confidence. All she could manage was a blushing, muttered statement of gratitude, and then she turned away from him back into the auditorium, relieved to see that he was not following her.

The Tuesday after that she came again to the Wigmore Hall for a second concert in the series. Making her way into the bar for a soft drink before the performance started, she found to her dismay that Bronowski was standing there once more. She immediately spun around and went straight to her seat; to avoid him, she spent the interval in the ladies lavatory. But at the close of the concert he was waiting outside in the street.

'Supper,' he called, before she could escape. 'Around the corner – a little French restaurant. Even I can afford to take you there. Let's go.'

But again she turned away from him, and hurried off towards the underground station. He ran after her, and stood there in front of her, barring her way, thrusting his arms out in a gesture of theatrical rejection.

'For heaven's sake – what is this? Grow up. Say something to me. We're both here, we met last week, we both come for the music. Don't make a production out of it. I'm just making friends with you. Come and eat. Please . . .'

Looking around her in panic, Miranda nodded her head, and then felt ashamed of herself for the absurd, humiliating gaucheness of her response. She heard herself say, 'All right. But I have to be home very soon. I've got work to do.' She tried to think of a way to make the excuse sound more authentic. 'Essays to correct before the morning,' she concluded miserably, thinking that she sounded exactly like a missionary girl who was flattering herself, pathetically and inaccurately, that she was being propositioned by an importunate admirer.

So they ate together, and Miranda tried to fight her shyness away. But then he told her that he had been unable to put her out of his mind, and had wanted to see her again so much that he had gone to the Wigmore Hall that night on the offchance that she might be there.

She stared at him, at a loss to know what to say or think. As soon as she was able to break away, she did so. And, confused, she went out into the street to find a taxi, hoping that she would never be forced to go through such a humiliation ever again. She wanted to be left alone. Adventures of this sort were not within her compass. She had no desire that they should be. She knew what she was, and what she could manage. She was content with that. She knew she had to be content with that. She just wanted to be left alone.

Chapter 5

'The flowers you sent yourself are over there, Miranda. We've all been over to look at them. We're all *impressed*.'

Miss Clinch the Games Mistress smiled sweetly at her, then turned away with a knowing look to the others, and made an elaborate show of pointing over her shoulder to the table in the corner of the staffroom. And there they were. Not just a simple bunch flowers, but a vast, gaudy bouquet, wrapped in a most disagreeable combination of crackling cellophane and thick satin ribbon.

Miranda went over, and looked around to see who was watching. Then, realising that every single person in the staffroom had their eyes on her, she braved it anyway, and read the card inside the little envelope.

The flowers were indeed for her. The message was about love. And – horrifyingly – something about physical desire as well, and she knew the scorn there would have been for her in the eyes of any of those who had peeped inside the little envelope to read it, as some of her colleagues probably had.

She picked up the bouquet, and thought for a moment of making an overt gesture of rejection of it; throwing it into the bin with a light, sophisticated laugh perhaps, followed by the telling of a sparkling anecdote about a persistent and unwanted old flame. But she knew this would be outside her range, and certain anyway to backfire, so she simply smiled – quite unintentionally with mysterious ambiguity – and carried the bouquet out of the room.

If she had possessed a car she would have taken the absurd thing and hidden it away then and there, but she didn't. All she could think of was to dump it, as quickly as possible, in one of the outside dustbins. But here she was now, walking along the corridor, clutching her admirer's flowers, pressing herself back against the wall as the girls jostled their way to lunch. She could not have felt more foolish, and the incident gave rise, as she knew it

24

would, to a flurry of hilarity and tittle-tattle that took several days to disperse.

In the aftermath, of course, the incident served if anything to raise her profile and reputation; the girls looked at her with an entirely new eye, and Miranda, on the whole, was rather pleased by that. But she didn't want it to occur again, and the risk that it would seemed to grow more intense every day that passed. Bronowski's persistence was never-ending. He cajoled her into ever more frequent meetings and conversations. There were messages for her from him everywhere she went. And in time Miranda fell in love, as she was bound to do. But though in love, and finally, trembling with nerves, in his bed, she knew that the affair was a mistake. She was a Scottish gentile woman of plain appearance, plain tastes and plainer aspirations. Amos was an exuberant, exotic young Jew. She went with him because of his insistence, and because, in the end, she was in love with him. He went with her for reasons that she could never deduce. She hoped it was love, and he certainly proclaimed it as such, endlessly proclaimed it to be such, but she could never wholly believe that it could be so.

Good-looking men do fall in love with women of homely aspect. Good-looking women fall in love with plain-looking men. Miranda knew that it happened all the time, and it always would, and nothing could be less surprising or more natural. In her more self-confident moments she was aware that physical appearance rarely has any bearing on the incidence of love at all. But that was not the point. In lasting, lifetime relationships there is, beneath the conventional, generous interchange of courtesies and kindnesses, a frank, unclouded acknowledgement of reality. Miranda wanted to be loved notwithstanding anything and everything about her. As people do. She wanted to be loved for what she really was. She found it impossible to believe that Amos was dealing in anything else but fantasy. But if he was, then she knew that in one way at least she was what he truly wanted. Amos had an absolute disdain for unserious people. Miranda was anything but an unserious person. Miranda was one of the most serious and responsible people she herself had ever met.

So there was that; but in all other ways the relationship seemed to Miranda to be insufficiently grounded. They married in a flurry of Bronowski's enthusiasm and determination. Within days of their wedding they had begun to flounder. Miranda was terrified of physical intimacy, but hoped that she would rid herself of that by the familiarity of conjugal life. In fact, the reverse happened, though she did all she could to conceal and disguise it. But Bronowski sensed her lack of ease, and grew infuriated by that, and infuriated too by so many aspects of Miranda that he had before appeared to find amusing and diverting.

She tried to keep calm under his growing, incessant ill-patience. She assumed that what had happened was that he had thought himself in love with her because she replicated for him the only stable, wholesome period of his life so far – as a fostered child with Scottish teacher parents in the remote outreaches of Ontario. She believed there were demons in him stemming from the horrors of his early childhood that would in time, and under her support and care, work their way through to the open and be released.

'I want to have a marriage, Amos,' she said one day, turning away from him so that she could wipe the tears from her face unnoticed. 'I imagined that that's what you wanted too. Whatever happens, I hope you stay with me now for ever. And despite the things you say to me at the moment, and your impatience, and your unkindness, and the rest of it, I think you will. I really believe you will. And I believe you'll be happy. As soon as we have a family . . .'

And as she felt her voice tighten up on her, and her chin start to move once again, she turned away to the sink so that she could busy herself there, and avoid the need to say more. She was sure though that what she had said to him was true. Despite the strains in him at this moment, he did want a marriage, and he would stay. As soon as she had a baby, then he would be fulfilled and happy and so would she. As soon as that happened, everything would settle down.

She resolved to be a better wife to him. She was determined to fight and, at worst, to dissemble and camouflage better her lack of confidence. She cursed herself for being insufficiently aware of what he needed to draw from her. She was uncertain whether he wanted her to be an Ontario schoolmistress, or a Zionist freedom-fighter, or maybe something quite different from either of these. She would find out from him what he needed her to be. She would attempt anything, or be anything, to keep him. She loved him, and she wanted to be his wife. She would accept this period of unrest, and trauma, because she was determined to win through.

Belsen could not be lost in a day. That was the reason for his mood swings, and his anger with her. Belsen was to blame.

Mending Belsen would take a lifetime. But she was his wife, and that's what wives were for. She loved him, and together they would find their way through all the darkness and the difficulties.

But they never did. One rainy July morning, on their second wedding anniversary, Bronowski walked out of the house, apparently *en route* to the chemist, and she had never seen him again.

It was Gareth Edel who told Miranda some months later where Bronowski now was; back in Ontario, a teacher himself now, a junior lecturer in Economics at a small provincial college. Edel had telephoned her at home one evening, saying that he was doing so simply because he was concerned about her, and wanted the reassurance of knowing that her life had recovered, and that all was well.

Miranda might have told him that what was actually happening to her at that moment was that her labour pains were just starting, and that as soon as she was off the telephone she would drive herself into the local maternity hospital for the delivery of her baby. But it never occurred to her to do so. Bronowski didn't know what he had walked out on. She had never told him. So she did no more now than to thank Edel for his call, and to ask him, when next in contact with Bronowski, to give him a message.

That she was well, and she was happy, and she was in control of her life.

Chapter 6

The upstairs room in the Bloomsbury pub was full for him, and Lewis Cohen, who loved a gallery, was on top of his humour. His talk was billed to be on a topic which he had meant to spend time in the week properly researching, but he had been so busy with his work and his social engagements that he had not got around to doing so. This worried him not in the least. As his friends at the group knew, when Cohen was the speaker it was a knock-about affair, only tenuously related to the official subject. Mariss Steiner, however, had arrived late, looked out of sorts, made no attempt to join the general mood, and grew angry and flushed as Cohen, to hilarity from the others in the room, made fun of some question or other that he had got to his feet to ask.

As the meeting broke up, and the audience filed out, Cohen jumped off the platform, and went straight over to Steiner, who had remained sitting still, alone now in the third row.

'Don't take it all so seriously, Mariss,' he said. 'It was a joke, that's all! You made your point, and because it's a light-hearted evening, I pulled your leg a little when I replied. I didn't mean to be offensive! Showing off, perhaps. Come on, Mariss. Let's join the others, and have a drink.'

Steiner crossed his arms over his chest, and remained seated, staring silently before him.

Cohen burst out in laughter. 'Mariss! You're like a child!'

But then, instead of walking away, Cohen stayed where he was, and allowed the laughter to drain away from his face. In time Steiner spoke.

'I'm not strong enough for mockery. I'm not resilient enough to be the butt of people's wit. Some are. *You* are. I'm not. It's a weakness of course, but that's what I am.'

Cohen nodded, and shrugged. 'I know,' he said. 'I apologise again, I really do. But you're a star, Mariss, if you did but realise it. You're as good as any of us – better. You survived – we all did.

28

That's why we're here. Don't take the politics of all this business as if they were the be-all and end-all of your existence. We're just a lot of cocky young men and women huffing and puffing around and having a good time. Do the same thing. Have a go at normal life. You're a good journalist – you've run some very strong stories. So run some more. Work on your contacts – build on that. Build on normal things. That's what I'm doing. You should do so too.'

Steiner got to his feet, kicked a half-full plastic cup of coffee from out of his path, and set off towards the exit.

'Normal things, Lewis?' he called back over his shoulder. 'How do you know that I don't? How is it that you think you know so much about my life?'

Cohen watched him go, then shrugged, and went to join the others in the bar. He wouldn't let the incident bother him, though there was in him a distaste of wounding other people's feelings, particularly with the mob baying behind him in support, as they had been on this occasion, if nothing like as maliciously as Mariss had seemed to suppose. The following day he was to have his chat with old Rubinstein, and whatever the ironies of the timing of that, it was pleasant to be the recipient of a compliment in that way. He looked forward to it. He would forget about Mariss for now, he decided. Make it up to him later in the week. Feed him with a little bit of tittle-tattle which he could pass surreptitiously on to the Americans, then feel like a hero. Lewis had often done this before, when Mariss sulked. He was the easiest man in the world to please, and win around again. Once one realised what made him tick. Once one realised that the Americans were all that he was interested in.

Chapter 7

Cohen got up from his chair, and shook the hand that the senior partner held out to him. He nodded and smiled his pleasure at what was being said to him, as if it was a complete surprise, though the truth was that Mr Robert's private secretary had already given him the news the evening before. But he *was* elated about it. Of course he was! Were it not for that indiscretion five or six years ago, he would have been made a partner well before this time. But never mind that now. Better late than never. He was on his way at last.

'. . . one of the cleverest young men we've ever had in the firm,' Mr Robert Rubinstein was saying. 'Perhaps *the* cleverest. At thirty-five, or whatever you are now, the world's ahead of you, Lewis. Considering where you came from, you've done so very well for yourself. Apart from anything else, you've built up here in London the most astonishingly wide social acquaintance. And that's useful to us, of course it is. So now that we've finally taken you into the partnership, we hope you'll be introducing us over the years to some increasingly valuable clients. I'm sure you will. But it's not just that, naturally. You're a very bright young man. And I'm very fond of you. So – once more – congratulations from us all.'

Cohen nodded again, muttered something of appropriate gratitude and humility, and went on his way. Rubinstein was right: the range of social contact that he had established over the years *was* astonishing. Looking back on it, Cohen was not at all sure how it had been achieved. Given the fact that when he arrived at Beltane School in Wimbledon in 1945 for processing and clearance, he knew no one in England whatsoever. And, apart from three or four words of English, and the clothes provided by a Jewish charity – a *yarmulke*, two pairs of shoes, two gaberdine suits, underclothes, socks, and three white cotton shirts, all in a cardboard suitcase – he had not a possession to his name either.

30

He had been most unusually fortunate. The lawyer's family in Putney with whom he had first been lodged were warm people, who treated him with good humour, and made a sustained effort to make him feel at home – the daughters of the family in particular. In fact, it had been a long line of daughters from one household after another that had helped Cohen's struggle up the ladder. A schoolteacher's family in Chiswick had ensured that his education was pushed to the extent that he made his way to a place at University College, London, to study law, and this only a year or so behind conventional English students of his own age. Sarah was the daughter of that household. His first love. Was that love? Or was it expedience? Or was it a statement of gratitude to a family who took Cohen to their bosom, and did so much to help him on his way? Rather faster on his way than perhaps they had planned, for then there was the daughter of another family, Hannah; shamefully, Cohen had immediately abandoned Sarah for Hannah when he saw her across the room at a programme dance organised by a synagogue social club. He danced every dance with her that night. Then lived with her for nearly twelve months of love, and quarrelling, and poverty in a tiny bed-sitting room above a greengrocer's shop in Notting Hill Gate, until her father arrived one night, private investigator at his side, and took her home.

That had been Cohen's adolescence – Sarah, and Hannah, and all the girls in between. And the Hebrew Welfare Society cardboard suitcase and the well-meaning teacher, and the silent father, rapping on the door for his daughter at eleven o'clock at night.

The day before his twentieth birthday he enrolled at University College, a happy-looking, pleasant-faced young man with a most winning, open smile. He was clever enough too, though secretly indolent for much of the time, but his final examinations were mysteriously successful, and the day after his twenty-third birthday he arrived safely at the prestigious law firm of Rubinstein Rubinstein & Co for his first day as an articled clerk. At twenty-nine he had been on the point of dismissal for dealing in the shares of a client company on the receiving end of a takeover bid; his career was rescued only by the good offices of Mr Robert Rubinstein himself. And now, at thirty-five, Cohen was finally a partner.

But there was an irony in that, as there so often was in Cohen's life. For he was already far advanced in negotiation with a group of his friends for the establishment of a new firm, of which he was to be the founding senior partner. He resigned from Rubinstein Rubinstein & Co barely three weeks later, and Mr Robert Rubinstein sent him a handwritten note the day he left.

He gave Cohen his best hopes for his prosperity, and he wished him and his new colleagues good luck. But with the note was enclosed a little personal invoice made out to the sum of one hundred pounds, plus eleven and a half years of compound interest. This was to cover the money that Cohen had 'borrowed' from the petty cash box one Christmas Eve, and never returned. It had been subsequently replaced by Mr Robert, without comment, when he had realised who had taken it.

Chapter 8

Jacob Bergdorf sat at the window of his Vienna apartment, his wire glasses perched on the end of his nose, his waistcoat and jacket still formally buttoned from his day at the office. His plump face frowned in thought as he gazed fixedly out at the evening rush-hour traffic inching its way up towards the Schwarzenberg-Palais. He was calmer now than he had been earlier, but he'd had an unpleasant shock, there was no doubt about that. Just an hour or so before, he had nearly been caught by the senior partner of his law firm there at the office electric typewriter, typing out a letter to the Ledelheimer Bank on notepaper he had purloined from the Israeli Embassy.

There was money in those Swiss bank accounts that didn't belong there, and should be released as soon as possible. Either to the moral owners of it – the families themselves – or to a reputable third party. *Like himself.*

Bergdorf went over to a cupboard in the corner of the room, unlocked it with a key held in the zipped pocket of his wallet, and took out a large brown envelope. He removed some papers from it, glanced through them, then replaced them, and still holding the envelope in his hand, he went back to sit on his windowsill. As he settled again there was a heavy knock, and immediately another, and as he got up to investigate, the door was pushed open, and his small son rode in, seated on his birthday tricycle, honking on the horn bulb secured to the handlebars.

Bergdorf stormed into the passage and bellowed for his wife, who came running along from the kitchen and hastily took the tricycle by the handlebars. She turned the child around, and steered him away again, safely out of his father's presence.

'I have work to do, don't you realise that?' Bergdorf shouted at her. 'Money doesn't grow on trees, you know! Someone has to pay for the luxury we live in!'

He slammed the door shut after them and, muttering irritably, returned again to the window. After a few minutes he began to feel guilty that he had behaved with such anger to his little boy. He was conscious of the fact that he had been prone to that sort of thing recently. But he received such little support from his wife. She had no idea how hard he had to struggle to keep them fed and housed. None at all. Tomorrow he was going to try to see Hermann. She had no inkling of how resourceful he was going to have to be to get what he wanted from the famous Professor Hermann. He, Bergdorf, still a comparatively young lawyer, would have to pitch his wits against this truly formidable man.

'So what is it that you want of me, Jacob?' Professor Hermann said, and settled more comfortably into the corner seat of the mountain inn, where Bergdorf had 'come across' him that evening, on one of Hermann's solitary weekend hikes. 'Wild horses would not have driven you up here, were you not in search of me. I'm honoured. Now, you want something. What is it I can do for you?'

The Professor smiled at him coldly, and Bergdorf, shifting awkwardly in his chair, felt like a small boy sent to the Headmaster. Before he could get a single word out, though, Hermann had moved on.

'Don't bother to explain,' he said now, making a vaguely irritable gesture. 'You'll only make it all too complicated, and I already know what it is. You've been trying for years to find a way to ask me, so let's not beat about the bush. What you want is this: for me to introduce you to the survivors of the Jewish families in East Germany, and elsewhere perhaps, whose money and possessions have been locked away in Swiss bank accounts ever since the War, and who find it impossible to get them released. You want to help them gain access to their family possessions – or rather, your law firm does, and no doubt earn some large fees at the end of the day.'

He held up his hand as Bergdorf flushed.

'There's nothing to be ashamed of in that,' he said. 'That's what lawyers do, isn't it – earn fees, as large as they can make them. It's all one to me, Jacob! So tell me. Just be straightforward with me, and tell me. Is that what you want? Names and addresses? Personal introductions? Some estimates of what each family has got locked away there? That sort of thing? *Is that it?*'

He laughed, and shook his head. 'Why don't you simply ask me, Jacob? Why do you insist on all this subterfuge and deceit? Of course I'll help you. Or rather, I'll help the families get back their money. You want my help in meeting these people? I'll arrange it. But you mustn't let me down in this, Jacob. I'll help you, but you mustn't fail me, or mislead me. I'll give you the assistance you request, because it's possible that you're the best man for the job. But you mustn't let me down! Do you understand that? Not under any circumstances.'

BOOK II

1975

Chapter 9

The staff meeting went on interminably. Lady Phillipson, chairing the meeting that night in the Deputy Headmistress's absence, was at her most verbose and combative. She had already shot Miranda a look of venom when she caught her glancing surreptitiously at her watch, and spent several minutes lecturing her about a supposed lack of discipline amongst the younger girls.

Finally, at seven o'clock, they were all released, and Miranda ran most of the way to the underground station, trying to get there as fast as she could, despite the ice and snow on the pavements. She had promised the day nurse that she would be home before half-past seven for sure, and she didn't want to fail in that. This one was the latest in a long line of nurses supplied by the borough council; she was of a much better standard than any Miranda had had from them before, and she was determined not to lose her.

There was a delay on the District Line at Earls' Court, but Miranda muttered to herself to remain calm, and kept her eyes from the watch on her wrist. And then she was at Fulham Broadway Station. The crowd of people on the stairs up to the exit seemed to her to be moving with painful slowness, as if unwilling to reach the cold of the winter night outside. It was only five or six hundred yards to her house, once she was out in the street. And at last she was, and sprinting along on the edge of the road itself, her lungs heaving with the unaccustomed effort of it. She was nearly there. Now she would look to check what time it was. Twenty-nine minutes past seven. Just in time. Calm yourself, and settle down. Find the key in your pocket. Turn it quietly in the lock. Stroll into the house. Smile. Look casual. Make a joke of the near-run thing.

'And how is he, you say?' trilled the nurse. 'Oh, much the same, I think, dear. Nice and quiet. Nice and comfy.'

There was a little more of this, then, pulling her scarf around her neck and chattering inconsequentially and interminably about the weather, the nurse was gone.

They were alone now. She ran up to the bedroom, and there he was. There, lying on his bed, was her nine-year-old son. His mouth hung open, and a dribble of saliva ran down from one corner of it and on to his pillow. His dark, deep brown, startled eyes, fixed in their oblique cast, stared directly up at the ceiling. His arms lay stiff and straight beside his body, his hands clenched and clasped.

Miranda's first act, as she sat beside him on the bed, was, as always, to take each of his hands into hers. She gently unbent and loosened each finger in turn. Then, using the strength of her thumbs, she pushed and pressed and rubbed the back of the child's hands and the joints of his fingers until she could feel the relaxation and release easing into them.

'Michael?' she said. 'Mummy's home. Have you been waiting for me? Did you know that I would come?'

He was dressed in the clothes in which Miranda had left him that morning: cotton shirt, red Shetland jersey, blue jeans, sports socks and, despite the fact that he was supine on the bed, a brand-new pair of white trainers. Gently now she undressed him, fiddling to undo his shoelaces, chattering to him all the while as she did so.

'Well, we have to do the laces up tight for you, don't we, Michael? We can't have you pulling your shoes off in this weather, can we, my darling?'

When she had finally prised the trainers off the boy's feet, then pulled down his jeans, she took an adult's incontinence pad from a pile on the closet beside the bed, and pushed up his shirt-top so that she could the more easily deal with him and clean him. She undid the pad already there on him, then lifted his legs, slid it away, and cleaned him down with some wipes kept in a plastic container. She powdered him, and lowered his legs gently back down on to the bed. She began to massage him again, this time up and down his thighs, and then his lower legs, and then the feet, and finally the toes. She pressed and kneaded and squeezed her child, flexing and bending the joints of his knees and his ankles, talking all the while, smiling at him, complaining at the physical effort of the massage, joking, laughing. Finally, she laid the palm of her hand flat on the boy's stomach, and gently, gently, stroked him back and forth, across the neat indentation of the navel, up to the ribs, then back again, to and fro.

'Do you know something, Mike?' she said. 'In the spring, you and I are going to take the car down to Sussex. We'll have a day out at the seaside, at Rye, with a picnic lunch, and go on a long walk. We can watch the birds. I'll take that bird book I bought last year, and we'll see what we can see. I promise you – the very first fine spring day that comes along. We can look forward to it together. We'll plan how we'll spend the day, and what we'll do.'

She smiled at him once more, then looked down at his smooth, firm, ashen body, still hairless and childlike and pre-pubescent.

'You're like an angel, Michael, do you know that? Like a little angel of God.'

She remained staring at him for some moments, then went down to the bathroom below, and came back with a bowl of warm water and a face-cloth and a cake of soap.

First she wiped the child's face and neck, and then his arms, and his stomach, and his groin. She turned him to sponge down his back and his buttocks, and then, when she had wiped him dry with a threadbare towel, she went across the room to the cupboard in the corner, and came back to him with a freshly ironed set of pyjamas. She put them on him, then held him in a sitting position while she brushed his hair. Laughing, struggling, she picked him up in her arms, and carried him downstairs to the kitchen. Once there, she secured him in his special retaining seat, then stood back, panting, wiping at her forehead, smiling at him all the while.

'You're getting too big for me, Michael. Too heavy to carry. We're going to fall down those stairs one day, you and I. What are we going to do about that?'

She ran her fingers through his hair, then went to put some toast on to grill, and poured some milk into a baby's beaker. She sat beside him on a stool, holding the beaker to his mouth. He drank, and when the beaker was taken away, he gave a little whimpering, urgent cry. He was looking directly at his mother now, and the eyes, as they always had, carried a certain distinctive quality of startled, frightened melancholy.

'Do you know what I think, Michael?' Miranda said, wiping the spittle off her child's mouth and chin with a fresh cloth.

She put the cloth down and stared at him now, a smile in her eyes, stroking the boy's head, then, in playful mime, pinching at his ear.

'Do you know what I think, my little Mike? I think you tease me. A fool like me, spending my whole life running around after you, while you're having a little game with me.'

Miranda laughed, and spooned now into the boy's mouth some oatmeal, and some tiny cubes of toast, wiping every so often at his lips and chin. As she did so, Michael's gaze came on to her again, unwavering, like that of an animal caught in a trap. Miranda stared at him in return, then put down the spoon, and stroked the side of his head with her open palm.

'You're a clever boy, my darling. In there somewhere you're a clever boy. I know it's true. We'll find it, Michael. We'll find the key. You and me, my little Michael. You and me.'

Chapter 10

Amos and Miranda had lived their short married life together in a little terraced house on the Moore Park Estate in West London, and, when Michael was born, she made her home there with him.

The Victorian cottages stood in a grid of tree-lined streets to the north of the King's Road. They were not in a fashionable part of London, nor a particularly expensive one, compared at least to some of the streets in even the most western reaches of Chelsea, no more than a few hundred yards away. But the small, neat houses were pleasant, and the gardens pretty, and the ambiance of it all agreeably peaceful and reclusive. It would have been difficult, with Miranda's very moderate income, for her to have found anywhere else in London very much better to be. As Miranda took a thick woollen coat off the hook behind the door, and put it on her son, arm by arm, she thought, as she so often did, how contented she was in her home. It was just that. It was a home. A place of refuge and familiar comfort, and there was nowhere she would rather be. She buttoned the coat up and pulled a balaclava helmet over his head. Then she squatted in front of the wheelchair and smiled at him, rose to her feet, and felt in her pockets for the doctor's appointment card. Rechecking the time they were due to be there, she wheeled the chair out of the room, and made her way through the cramped hallway to the front door.

There was a much-practised, tight manoeuvre to swing the wheelchair around at such an angle that it would fit through the door, then Miranda pushed the child across the ice and snow out to where her little car was parked, next to the overflowing dustbins of the house next door. There were special retaining straps fitted on the front passenger seat to enable her to secure Michael firmly and, with these in place, Miranda folded the wheelchair and stored it in the boot. She made her cautious way around the kerb, waving to an elderly neighbour who stood there outside his house watching her leave, his snow shovel in his hands, then climbed into the driver's

43

seat, turning to tug one last time at the straps to ensure that they were safely engaged.

It was a half-hour drive to the surgery in Devonshire Place. The whole way there Miranda talked to Michael without ceasing; pointing out the landmarks as they went, and the fire engine as it rushed past them, and the soldiers marching down through the icy roads of Hyde Park.

She parked in the special spot she always aimed for, right up outside Dr McCready's house, then unloaded the wheelchair, settled Michael in it, and made her way through to the familiar surroundings of the waiting room. It was only a few minutes before the amiable, rubicund figure of the doctor was in front of them. He pumped Miranda's hand, then led them into his surgery.

He motioned Miranda to sit down, and she settled herself beside Michael, who gazed fixedly at the ceiling, hunched and motionless in his wheelchair. McCready explained to Miranda the results of some routine tests that he had taken on her previous visit, then, unexpectedly, he pulled his chair around to join the two of them on the other side of the big desk. They sat together as if they were old friends, exchanging comfortable small talk in a street café.

The elderly doctor, now in his early seventies at least, took off and polished his glasses with meticulous care, frowning in concentration as he appeared to be thinking through whatever it was that he wanted to tell her. He finally replaced the glasses on his nose, then smoothed his hand across Michael's hair, in a gesture of almost over-emphatic tenderness.

'We've known each other for such a long time, Miranda,' he began, 'that I can say things to you in friendship and respect, and know that you will understand where I'm coming from. Isn't that right?'

Miranda nodded obligingly, but inside she was already beginning to feel the familiar prickles of irritation. There was something about his manner to her ... the elaborate courtesy ... the patronising sense of painstaking simplicity in his speech, almost as if she were a child.

At that moment Dr McCready spread his arms in a theatrical gesture of enquiry. 'Otherwise, what's friendship for?' he asked. 'Do you agree with that, Miranda?'

As Miranda was giving her ritualised response to this, Dr McCready reached over for Michael's file. He leafed through the various documents in there until he found whatever it was he was looking for, read quickly through two or three papers, then threw the file down on the desk, and faced Miranda once more.

'My dear – what I want to do is to remind you first of all of the basic facts regarding Michael's condition. Then we can discuss your understanding of what I've said, and finally you'll tell me what you think about some suggestions that I'm going to make to you. Is that all right?'

Miranda nodded, willing herself to play the part that he wanted her to perform – that of the simpleton, the over-protective mother. She would do that and anything else, if the result of it was some new information that might help her decide what she could do next for her child.

'So let's cover the facts of the case first of all. You know by now as much about Michael's illness as I do, I expect.'

Miranda forced a warm, compliant smile on to her face, and sat there nodding continuously.

'Now then – the term cerebral palsy is used sometimes as a over-generalised catch-all, covering all manner of motor disturbances arising from early brain damage. But we'll use it here anyway, and you and I both know what is implied by it in Michael's case.

'We classify cerebral palsy according to the type of dysfunction there is in the muscles, and the extent of that dysfunction as it manifests itself. There are five types that can occur. By far the most common – perhaps eighty-five per cent or more of all cases diagnosed – are the first two that I'll mention. First of all spastic, when the muscles contract. And secondly athetoid, when the muscles make continuous uncontrolled and uncontrollable movements.

'Spastic and athetoid – these are much the two most common dysfunctions. But then we have three others. Ataxic, when the patient constantly falls over, due to an impaired sense of balance. Tremor, when there is a constant shaking of the limbs. And finally rigid, where you get these tight muscles that resist to a greater or lesser degree all or most forms of movement. Those are the five. Spastic, athetoid, ataxic, tremor and rigid. And Michael suffers from the last. His dysfunction is that of rigidity, perhaps the least common of all.'

Miranda had been given this particular briefing by Dr McCready several times over the years, and increasingly had difficulty remaining mute through it. He seemed to her to delight in the lecturing of his patients. He not so much imparted information, she felt, as wore one down with an exhaustive, painstaking demonstration of his professional knowledge. He talked textbooks at you.

All she was interested in was how her child might be helped. Not healed exactly, for even Miranda accepted the fact that healing Michael to the point where he was conventionally whole was not a likely possibility. Maybe he couldn't be 'cured' in that way at all. But he could be helped. And released, from the entrapment of his soul and intelligence in this cage of silent, expressionless remove.

'So that's how we classify the dysfunctions themselves,' Dr McCready was continuing. 'But having done that, we then have to measure the extent of it, and classify that too. And we use four grades for that. Monoplegic for one limb. Hemiplegic for one side. Diplegic for both upper and lower limbs. And finally quadriplegic, in which all four limbs are affected. And again, with Michael, we are looking at something very severe. His is a quadriplegic condition. All his four limbs are affected. Though one could say in mitigation of that perhaps that there is a diplegic differential between the upper and lower limbs. At least to a very marginal degree.'

He paused at that, turned to Michael, watched him for a moment, then again faced Miranda. He smiled, gently and momentarily.

'Sometimes, though not very frequently,' he went on, 'the causes of cerebral palsy lie in heredity. Incompatibility of parental blood types can be the roots of it, but not in your case. It can also happen if the mother incurs an infection during pregnancy – that can do the damage to the brain of the foetus that shows itself in this condition. But with Michael it seems certain that the cause of the damage was the prolonged lack of oxygen during labour. As simple and as tragic as that. We know you had a very difficult labour indeed. The oxygen lack went on for far too long.'

Again Dr McCready paused, and this time his hesitation lasted for some time.

'I've known Michael almost all his life,' he said. 'Nine years. Ever since he was a few months old, and my friend Dr Bernerd suggested you bring him to me. He's a beautiful child. I've known him so long that I feel I love him as I would one of my own family.

'Miranda – you bring him here to me so regularly because you think that somehow I can perform a miracle for him. I let you do that, because I know it brings you reassurance. I send you to people who can help make him superficially more comfortable – physiotherapists and so on – but you always come back to me, in the belief I can do something for him. Something miraculous.

'I've tried on other occasions, but this time I really do have to succeed in helping you come to a real understanding and acceptance of what is possible. I've tried to tell you before about the nature of Michael's condition, and the prognosis for him, but I believe that either deliberately or subliminally, you lock out the truth from yourself. I admire you very much for your love and protection of your son. But this time I'm going to strive again to get you to accept the truth, because if you do accept it, you can help Michael more.

'Miranda – Michael is one of the most severely damaged children of this type that I have ever seen in a lifetime of specialisation in this area of medicine. The paralysis is comprehensive. He is not entirely rigid, as we know, and his limbs will, to differing degrees, adjust and bend and resettle under massage and manipulation, for which you yourself seem to have developed a special and wonderful facility. But nonetheless the rigidity is still severe.

'Barring something unforeseen, his expectancy of life is comparatively good, as far as we can tell at this stage. But – and here is the real issue perhaps – his mental subnormality is profound. In many cases there is no mental subnormality at all for those who have cerebral palsy. I'm afraid we both know that that is by no means the case here. No treatment can help Michael. There are almost no motor or intellectual assets in him that we can reach. Your son is very severely mentally retarded indeed.'

Miranda was nodding still, but her eyes were dull, and Dr McCready, gazing at her, knew what he was seeing. It always had been so in these conversations. She was pretending the courtesies of attention and respect and comprehension. But she would never, as long as she lived, hear and accept the truth of what she was being told.

He concluded sadly, 'There is nothing more I can say to you, Miranda. I wish with all my heart there was. And there's nothing more that I can do for Michael either. There's nothing any of us can do, except you. And that is to love him, and to care for him. And, in due time, to find for him an institution in which he can be maintained in as much comfort as is possible for someone in his condition. That's what he will need. In the fullness of time he'll require institutional care, for the rest of his life.' He looked at her more directly now. 'That's what I wanted to tell you. That's why I asked you to come here today. That's what I want you to accept.'

And now, at last, Miranda stopped her persistent nodding. Her face dead, she suddenly got up from her chair to prepare Michael for departure; straightening his coat into place and buttoning it up to the neck, pulling on his balaclava, struggling to lift him into his seat to adjust his position more comfortably, folding his hands side by side in his lap. She went to the rear of the wheelchair to take the handles, then stopped with it on her way to the door, and looked back.

'I don't believe you, Doctor McCready. Institutions . . .' She shook her head repeatedly, grimacing with disgust. 'I know Michael's got problems. Of course he has. Severe problems. But there's something there in him, and you don't understand what it is, or how I can see it. But it's there! You could see it if you knew him as I know him. Perhaps it's beyond doctors. I shouldn't expect it of you or anyone else. But *I* can see it! And I know that he and I together will bring it all out one day. Into the light. I don't know how that will happen, I just know that it will.'

Miranda turned now so that she was facing the doctor directly, her voice so quiet that the old man had to strain forward to hear her. Tears started to show in her eyes, and run down on to her cheeks, and she brushed them away quickly with the back of her hand.

'You seem to think that I'm too stupid to understand what you're saying. You talk to me as if I'm an imbecile. You think I'm so sentimental and emotional about Michael that I'm unable to behave like an adult over him. Well, that's not the case. I'm as adult as you are. I know as much as you do. Of course I understand what you're saying! But you're wrong. That's all it is. You're wrong.'

Both stood there, white and shocked and shaken by what was being said. Then, so quietly that Dr McCready could now barely hear her at all, Miranda spoke again.

'None of you knows what you're talking about. However much you posture and patronise, not one of you fully understands what happens to the brain. One Harley Street neurologist told me that he wasn't sure of correctly identifying the illnesses of as many as half the children that he sees. He had the self-confidence and the humility to tell me that. Why haven't you?

'There's no need for help from anyone, Doctor. From you or from anyone else. Michael's mine. I know what he can do: he knows what he can do. And he'll do it, too. He'll do it with me.'

Chapter 11

The weather forecast on the evening news had been fairly encouraging, and Miranda decided, as soon as she awoke, that she and Michael would definitely have their trip to Rye that day. It was still a little early in the year, and April weather was notoriously unreliable, but she and Michael hadn't been out of London since the previous summer. It would do them both good to have some fresh, sea air. And if she could get them out of the house and on their way by half-past nine at the latest, then they would be able to have as much time at the seaside as they needed. They could walk along that lane across the side of the golf course that led out to the dunes. If she remembered correctly, there was a path lined with railway sleepers for the few hundred yards from the end of that. Sufficiently firm for her to be able to push Michael's wheelchair out to the little promontory overlooking the sands on one side, and on the other the tidal inlet leading down to Rye Harbour. That would be where they would have their picnic lunch perhaps. Perfect! But she must get them both going and on their way.

She bathed and dressed, drank a mug of tea, then went up to Michael's room to wake and dress him. He was still asleep. She pulled back the curtains, and as he stirred and opened his eyes she sat on the edge of his bed, and smoothed the hair back from his forehead.

'We're going to Rye,' she told him. 'Today's the day. We must get you up, and give you your breakfast, and then we'll be on our way. It's a lovely blue day.' But as she glanced out of the window, she saw that the pure texture of the sky had now begun to cloud. She tried to remember what the weatherwoman had said. *Fine at first, then the chance of the odd shower*. Was that it? *Average temperatures for the time of year*. It should be all right. Good enough to risk it.

She pulled him up to a sitting position, then struggled to get his arms through the sleeves of his shirt and his sweater. Something in the action of this turned her mind back to the comments Dr

McCready had made. 'In due time you must find him an institution, in which he can be maintained in as much comfort as is possible for someone in his condition.'

Never, Miranda shuddered. Although . . . it was going to be more of a business, of course, as he grew heavier and bigger. She should start to plan now how she was going to deal with that. Already, the lifting of him up and down the stairs was becoming much more difficult. And dangerous. They would probably have to move, and sooner rather than later. Miranda's spirits dropped at the thought of a flat. The dark corridors and gloomy stairwells of one of London's less agreeable Victorian mansion blocks. The smell of other people's cooking always there in the air. Other people's milk bottles standing around on unswept landings. The shouts and noises of other people's domestic lives coming through at her from the walls and the ceilings. And then there was Michael's general health. He wasn't well enough for an institution. No one else could look after him as she did, or understand his needs. No one.

She pulled on his jeans, and buckled the new leather belt she had bought the previous day. Groaning in jest with the effort of it, she lifted him into her arms then, her back taut against the strain, she looked into his eyes and smiled. She would start thinking about a flat this year, so that there was plenty of time to find somewhere comfortable and clean and quiet before she had to rush at it, and do it all in too much of a hurry. Though she would hate leaving her Fulham house. Michael and she had been alone there together for all the nine years of his life. He'd known no other home. She hoped he could manage a separation from it. She so dreaded the thought that he might be unhappy and dispossessed by the change, and she might then fail to grasp fully what he was going through.

She cut sandwiches for their lunch, and packed them away in a Marks & Spencer carrier bag, which she knew would fit into the container tray underneath the seat of the wheelchair. She remembered to put in a knife to cut Michael's apple for him, and paper cups for their orange juice. Then, at the last moment, she went into her sitting room at the back of the house, and picked from the bookshelves a paperback copy of *Moby Dick*. She waved it at him as she went back into the kitchen.

'*Moby Dick*, Michael,' she cried. 'Captain Ahab, and his search for revenge on the white whale. We'll start it this morning at Rye. You can look out to sea, and pretend you're searching for the white whale as well.'

Miranda taught all her pupils *Moby Dick*. It was something of a masterclass by now; one of the great moments of their year with her. She always opened the lesson with the Epilogue; the young narrator Ishmael, surviving all alone the destruction of the doomed whaler *Pequod*, clinging by himself on to the harpooner's coffin. '*And only I am escaped alone to tell thee*,' Ishmael says, quoting the Book of Job, and Miranda would see the children's eyes stare at her in their concentration, and in their immediate recognition of what was going to be a good, gripping, dramatic story. She had never known a single occasion of failure with it. Oh, she cheated a bit, missing out the dissertations and soliloquies, or dramatising them herself. But it was always a star point of her class's year. *Moby Dick* never missed, in Miranda's hands.

Chapter 12

The tide was so far out, and the wet, flat sand leading to the distant shoreline appeared so firm and solid, that Miranda was in two minds as to whether she might take the risk of pushing Michael's wheelchair on to the beach. She would need help from someone in carrying him over the first few yards of the soft sand, of course . . . and Miranda abandoned the thought, and settled him more comfortably into his chair. She pulled off his quilt anorak so that he could feel the fleeting warmth of the sun on his neck and arms as it broke through the clouds, so threatening until just a few minutes ago.

She felt pleased that they'd come, happy from the moment they had turned out of Britannia Road. She had spent the drive chatting inconsequentially to Michael; pointing out some building or view that caught her interest, or a farm animal in a field, or a burst of spring flowers in a cottage garden. Miranda liked this part of England, and had long promised herself that one day she would buy a cottage for them here, in some agreeable village or another. This fantasy carried them along that day, and she stopped to show Michael a particularly attractive little house she had noticed on the previous occasions she had driven this route, and talked away about the life they would lead there, and the times they would have. It was a nonsense of course, and she knew that. She would never leave London now; not even after she retired. She had few enough friends as it was. Outside London she knew no one whatsoever.

They drew nearer to Rye, and Miranda, her mind elsewhere, found that she was singing to Michael, as she had from his infancy, some of their long repertoire of familiar songs. She gathered herself together, thinking that these days she should try something less childlike. She tried to recall some of the music-hall songs she had heard on her parents' wireless in the immediate post-war years. 'Underneath The Arches' she sang, and

52

then once more, in an attempt at a simultaneous impersonation of both Flanagan and Allen. Then 'Umbrella Man', again several times over, remembering only the odd word of it. 'The Boy I Love Is Up In The Gallery' she sang in full voice now, the primroses and the buttercups starring yellow on the banks of the lane. How happy I am, she thought, then glanced quickly at Michael beside her, and saw that he had turned his face to her as well, staring straight into her eyes, expressionless, solemn, unflinching in his gaze.

Miranda smiled at him, then sang on.

> 'There he is,
> Can't you see,
> Waving of his handkerchief,
> Happy as the robin,
> Who lives in the tree.'

Lives in the tree? Sits in the tree? She took one hand from the wheel, and touched Michael for a moment on the cheek. 'The boy I love is looking down at me,' she said in a matter-of-fact voice, tired now of the singing, her eyes back on the road.

How odd my life has become, she thought. That short period with Amos was just an aberration. I was born to be a dutiful daughter and a devoted mother. Those things – not, it seems, a wife. I've never been able to see myself as someone for whom romance is a possibility. I told myself that it might be, when I was with Amos. But I never wholly believed it, and I was right in that. It's me and Michael now. That sort of love. That's what I'm good at.

She had turned the car up the narrow path out on to the dunes, stopping it when she could go no further. Then she settled Michael into his wheelchair, and pushed him another two or three hundred yards along the line of railway sleepers. She laid the rug down on to the tufty grass, arranged the picnic around her, and *Moby Dick*, and her glasses, and stared out across to the great reach of sands away to her left. In the distance a family group stood quite motionless, oddly theatrical, as if in pose, each a yard or so apart from the other. There were two little girls amongst them, both in loose white dresses that billowed and flapped around their legs. Put them in wide-brimmed straw hats, with a stick and hoop in their hands, Miranda thought, and they could be children in an Edwardian tableau, photographed at Biarritz.

There was a sudden shriek of laughter from the beach immediately below them, and some children came running out from the cover of the dunes, a yapping, leaping dog at their heels. Amongst the children was a boy, ten years old perhaps, much of Michael's age, hurling a stick for the dog, then attempting to do a handstand, and, failing, toppling down on to the sand, screaming his laughter. Immediately he was on his feet, and sprinting away from the others, the dog in pursuit of him.

That should have been Michael, Miranda thought. All that energy and vitality and life about him. Amos must have been like that as a boy. Running through the corn of the Ontario fields, his hair flying, the farm dogs running and jumping at his heels, the blue skies of the Canadian summer cloudless above his head. That boy is Michael's age. If everything had been different, that child would have been Michael now. Michael would have been like that.

She sat for a moment, gazing out across the sands, then shook her head, turned, and laid her hand on his arm.

'Time for lunch, Mike,' she said. 'Then *Moby Dick*. Captain Ahab and the white whale.'

Chapter 13

By the time they arrived back home from Rye that night, Miranda was certain that Michael had become suddenly extremely unwell. However, their local doctor was not available for call-out on a Sunday night, and she was reluctant to put Michael through the discomfort and delays of the casualty department of the local hospital, so she put him to bed, and gave him aspirin in the hope of making him more comfortable, trusting that by the morning he would be improved.

The day nurse arrived at half-past seven, and there were only a few minutes to spare before Miranda had to rush off to St Peter's. She was able to do no more than ask the nurse to watch Michael carefully, to check on his temperature at regular intervals, and to call her at the school at the least sign of his being in distress.

She had hoped to be able to leave school early that evening, but a staff meeting was called unexpectedly in the late afternoon, and it was half-past six before Miranda could get home. Immediately she saw Michael she was concerned at his appearance. She started to cross-question the nurse about how he had been during the day, but the woman grew angry with Miranda for what she perceived to be criticism of herself. He had no more than a simple chill, she said. Mrs Bronowski should calm herself down. Miranda drew a deep breath and made an effort to do so, lest she alienate the one person in the world who was available to assist her in Michael's care.

The next day, Miranda was again delayed at school, and it was the same situation once more when she arrived home at Britannia Road. The listlessness in Michael's eyes was immediately apparent to her. She asked her local doctor to come that evening, but he telephoned later to say that he was unable to arrange it until the following morning, and gave an approximate time for the visit that Miranda knew she could not herself be there for. So the nurse gave Miranda the doctor's message to her when she returned home. Nothing to worry about, he had said. Lots of this sort of thing around. It was a straightforward infection that would be dealt with by the antibiotics he had prescribed. Miranda could give him a call again in three or four days if she wanted to, but Michael would be better by then. She mustn't worry at all. There was nothing whatsoever to be concerned about.

But she *was* concerned. She had never seen Michael unwell in this way before. If Miranda had been a woman of less professional conscience and responsibility, she would have taken a day or two off work, to be with him herself. But there was the special coaching programme for the University-entrance girls she had promised she would help with that week, and staff sickness too, and it was just not a time when Miranda felt she could absent herself. So she didn't. And by the Saturday afternoon, when she took Michael into hospital, having rung Dr McCready in tears at the sight of him when she got home after the morning's staff meeting, it was already too late.

McCready came in especially from his country house when the hospital called him with the news. He sat alone with Miranda in a tiny, cluttered waiting room, and explained to her what had happened.

'You know about Michael's general health, Miranda. The cerebral palsy of course, but the kidney disease and the consequent high blood pressure too, which we've been able in the past to control with drugs. But now . . . I'm afraid we're looking at something very much worse.'

He hesitated for a moment, fiddling with a ballpoint pen that had been left on the table beside him. Then he turned to her once more.

'It's one of those things. Most unfortunately, the infection was not reactive to the particular antibiotic prescribed. But that in itself is not the problem. It appears your doctor may not have fully realised the degree of dehydration that Michael was going through, although we mustn't blame him for that. The dehydration, unfortunately, became very much more severe in the following days as the infection and the fever persisted.'

He hesitated again. 'And with the problems with the kidneys, and the blood pressure . . .'

'Michael can't speak, Doctor,' Miranda said, interrupting him as if deliberately, sitting bolt upright and still on her plastic chair. 'So he wasn't able to tell the doctor what he needed. Or the nurse. Or me. It's my fault. It's my—'

She closed her eyes, and bit at her lip, and willed herself to keep calm. All those days away from him while she was at St Peter's. The council nurse telling her that she was giving him all the fluids he could possibly require; so insistent in this, and so irritated by Miranda's questioning. She had concentrated on sponging him down, to reduce his temperature and make him more comfortable. She gave him sips of water sometimes – of course she had. What was she being accused of, for heaven's sake? A trained nurse like her . . .

Miranda bit at her lip again, so hard this time that she could taste blood in her mouth. Dr McCready was gazing straight at her, trying, it seemed, to smile at her in comfort. But behind the smile, and the silence while he gave her a chance to settle, he was willing himself to find words that would give her the truth of the situation, but in a way that she could accept.

The dehydration was extremely severe; he had told her that. The child had been dehydrated to the extent that the sodium content in the blood had risen to a level that had pickled, literally, his brain in brine. The brainstem in particular. Did she know what damage to the brainstem meant? He reached inside his jacket pocket for his propelling pencil, glad to break the spell by the demonstration of a little show of technical knowledge. He took a sheet of paper off the desk behind him, and started to draw on it.

'Here we go,' he said. 'Here's the spinal cord . . . and this is the forebrain . . . and between them, running transversely, is this thick bundle of fibres. The *pons*, as we call it. The midbrain . . . there . . . is above the pons, and the *medulla oblongata* there, below it. On the rear surface of the midbrain are these four rounded projections called the *colliculi* – these receive and transmit impulses for the reflex rotatory movements of the eyes, head, body, and limbs, away from or towards light and sound stimuli. But here, in the *medulla*, the vital physiological centres are located. You know what they are. The cardiac, respiratory, and vasomotor functions.'

He glanced up at her. 'Sorry. Vasomotor means the processes of constriction or dilation of the blood vessels. Cardiac and respiratory you understand, of course.'

She nodded, having known perfectly well what vasomotor meant as well, and recognising that the familiar drone of his voice in his lecture mode was, at this moment, acting, bizarrely, as a source of comfort and calm for her. It was like old times. He was shading in his drawing now, correcting the proportions of it here and there, satisfied to be teaching, as if the drama with Michael was in the abstract.

'In dehydration as severe as this, the brain becomes damaged by the increased levels of sodium in the blood. The brainstem particularly. And it's the brainstem, as I've told you, that controls the vital functions. The breathing function amongst them. That's what you heard and saw in Michael when you rushed him into hospital this afternoon. His breathing has become irregular and intermittent. Strikingly so because of the shrinking of his brainstem, which is no longer sending out the necessary messages.'

Miranda could hear and feel the shallowness of her own breathing, and her heart was feathery and light. She told herself that soon she would be alone, and able to settle down to her private, unorthodox rituals of prayer. But she had to hear this out.

'What can we do?' she said, and the quiet calm of her voice sounded to her as if it was emerging from another woman; an observer, no more, of this deathly, deadly scene. 'There must be some way we can help him. The brainstem is damaged – shrunk by the dehydration. But he's on a drip now, to correct that. We can bring the sodium level back to normal. So, surely the condition isn't irreversible?'

She knew perfectly well that it was as irreversible as could be. But then she was irritated by the length and verbosity of McCready's response, and, slapping her hand on her knee, interrupted him in mid-sentence.

'Well, we must put him on a ventilator then. If it's all hopeless, clearly he must go on a ventilator. Immediately.'

'My dear . . .' McCready shook his head. 'This is a big decision. Too big for tonight. I think we should talk around this a little before we decide anything of that sort. Sleep on it, per—'

'No. No sleeping on it. What do you mean, the decision's too big for tonight?' She heard her voice rise, a shrill note of tension in it. 'I want him on a ventilator now. *Now!* Before it's too late.'

'We're a different generation,' McCready tried, looking away from her, 'and it's possible that I have never managed to communicate with you in a fashion that would have helped you through these years with Michael. But this time, I *mustn't* fail you. Because my inability to reach you over the years has been a failure. Of mine – not of yours.'

Miranda attempted this time to speak more calmly, but the more the words came tumbling out, the less control remained.

'There must be something you can do, Doctor McCready. I appreciate the fact that you are trying to be frank with me, but Michael must certainly go on the ventilator. There must be something more you can do more for him beyond that. I can't believe you're trying hard

58

enough. You never have done! Perhaps I ought to have a second opinion.'

Dr McCready grimaced. 'A number of the medical staff are going to be dealing with Michael over the next few weeks, Miranda,' he said: 'You will have the chance of talking with . . .'

And as he spoke on, Miranda's breath fluttered at the words 'over the next few weeks'. So that meant he didn't expect Michael to die. It meant that nothing much was really going to change. Michael would still be alive. In a coma, of course, at least for the moment, but he had been in a coma of sorts all his life. And the longer he lived, the longer she would have to pray for him. That was what she needed. She needed time to pray. She would *pray* her son out of this danger, and back to where he was. She wanted this conversation to finish now, so that she could go away and get on with it. Prayer would do it. She longed to be on her own to pray.

Dr McCready was still talking when Miranda got to her feet and started to move towards the door. He rose too, halted in mid-sentence, and stood there, silent. Conscious of her rudeness to him, Miranda started to mutter some words of gratitude, but he ignored them.

'Let me say it again, Miranda,' he said instead. 'Your comment to me was: "there must be something you can do, beyond the ventilator." And yes, there is something. And we're going to do it. We're going to make you understand. However long it takes, *we're going to make you understand.*'

'Understand what?' Miranda snapped. He was wasting her time. But as she went out into the corridor, McCready called after her, and she paused.

'Do you know something, Miranda?' he said. '*Treating* children when they're dangerously ill can sometimes be the easy option. Any fool can look busy, stuffing modern-day drugs down the unfortunate children's throats, and plugging them into state-of-the-art machinery. Treating's the simple option. Most of us adopt it through sheer bloody indolence. I do it myself sometimes. And when I do so in cases like these, I recognise it not only as indolence, but as cowardice. Moral cowardice.

'Because the difficult way to go, and the real responsibility we have, is to give those desperate children what they actually need. Not just treatment alone. Not just strapping them on to machines. Not that. It's care that they need. That's what takes time and commitment. Care. Dignity. Respect. And that's what we're going to give you both, Michael and you. Those things. You have my promise for that.'

59

Chapter 14

Dr McCready leapt to his feet when Miranda walked into his office the following morning. She shook his hand, but had already turned to glance down at his desk to see what was on it, and what the conversation was going to be about. Nothing was there, and realising that she was showing her impatience she tried to smile, but longed to get out of the room and back to Michael. She had left him there tucked away behind his screen in the children's ward, under his intravenous drip, lying in his coma, gazing at the ceiling. He was alone, and she wanted to be with him.

Never before in his life had Michael been subjected to the trauma of peer exposure as immediate as this. There he was in a ward, hidden away it was true, but still side-by-side with noisy, articulate, 'normal' children of his own age. Miranda recoiled from the prospect of the stress of that for him, but had no idea whether he comprehended it or not. No one else would think for one moment that he could possibly be aware enough to feel any stress, but she rejected the certainty of it. Miranda didn't know for sure what Michael felt, and no one else did either.

As if reading her thoughts, Dr McCready said, 'I'm sure you want to be with Michael, my dear, rather than talk all over again to someone like me. But just allow me to say one or two things that might help. Not as a doctor, but as a friend. I'd like us to have a different sort of conversation from the one we had yesterday. Can we do that?'

Miranda felt anger building within her once more. He should have known her better than this. She didn't want the 'comforts' of religion served up to her, if that was what 'a different sort of conversation' was all about. She had her own, idiosyncratic, intensely private way of reaching for God, when she needed that. At no point in her life had she been able to stomach conventional, churchy religion. And she absolutely didn't want to be subjected to it now.

'I'm not a religious woman, Dr McCready,' she stated. 'I warn you of that before you start. In my own way I have certain instincts and beliefs perhaps, but they're my own and . . . I particularly dislike being put in a position where I'm obliged to talk about religion with other people. I don't want to have that sort of conversation at this moment, under any circumstances. And to be frank with you, I don't want to waste time on the hypocrisy of it; I've too much on my mind. I'm not in the mood for homilies, and false comfort.'

Dr McCready laughed, with such good humour and enjoyment, or so it seemed, that his dentures were exposed top and bottom, to the extent that the join with the gum was clearly apparent. Miranda found herself staring at his mouth too directly, and hastily turned her gaze away.

'You have nothing to fear from me in that regard, Miranda, I can promise you that. I find it well-nigh impossible to talk about religion with anybody, and always have done. Even as a father I could never do more than teach my children the elements of simple religion, and leave them to find the rest. That, and show them I was happy, and trust them to deduce something from that. No, you have nothing to fear from me.'

Miranda wondered once more how soon she could get back to Michael. As discreetly as she could, she glanced down at her watch.

'Five minutes, Miranda,' he said, seeing her eyes look down. 'That's all I ask of you. First, let me say this. Michael's breathing is intermittent, but he's in no real distress, as far as can be told. The intravenous drip has corrected the dehydration, but the damage to his brainstem is there, and nothing can be done to correct that. You still want him to go on to a ventilator, and I can understand that. But I have already told you, as clearly as I know how, that putting him on to a ventilator is not going to solve anything whatsoever. Once he goes on to the machine he may live a little longer. Perhaps. No one can tell. But that, I'm afraid, is all it is. He may struggle out a few more days of life, even a few more weeks. *If* we can call that life.'

'It's life, Doctor McCready,' she said. 'We've covered all this already. I'll say it to you again. Michael has never had life in the way that others have. What he's always needed is more time. I know that to be true. I look into his eyes, and I know that in there somewhere is the spark of understanding. It's all just waiting to come out. I can see it there because I'm his mother. To me, it's unmistakable. It's there. We're not going to talk about religion, but I know that God has allowed me to look into Michael's eyes

61

and to see . . . to see his soul. Oh, Doctor McCready, I can see it there. Michael's a child of God. He's an angel of God.'

Dr McCready smiled at the mention of God from Miranda's mouth, but said nothing as she talked on.

'I'm not going to let him die. How could I? Who can tell what will happen if we can keep him going? Who can say how long he can be kept alive on the machine? You don't know the answer to that, no one does. But as long as he can be kept alive, then he must be. There's no choice in the matter. He goes on to a ventilator. How many more times do I have to say the same thing to you? He goes on to the ventilator.'

She started to move in her chair in such a way as to indicate that the interview was over. But Dr McCready stayed where he was. He shook his head slowly, and said, with a new definition in his voice: 'No, Miranda. That's not how it's going to be.'

She looked at him. What was he implying? What did he mean? Had she misunderstood her legal position in all this? Surely it was for *her* to decide in law whether or not Michael's life was to be prolonged by going on to the ventilator, and not the doctors? What was he saying?

'Michael has had too much pain in his life,' the elderly man said finally. 'The pain of being locked away in his private world, with no means or hope of ever breaking through into a real life. You tell yourself that a miracle will happen. Michael knows that it won't. It can't. Michael's condition is the will of . . . it's the will of things that that is how it's going to be for him. He'll die anyway. One way for that to happen is for him to be plugged into a machine. It will pump and force breath into him, until the point comes when his body can no longer take it. To my mind a death of that sort has as much dignity and grace in it as the death of a drunk, choking on his vomit.

'Consider the alternative,' he said more quietly. 'As it is, Michael's in no pain, no discomfort. He's fading gently away. Pneumonia will quietly and peacefully allow him to drift to sleep. It's happening now. It's happening already.'

Dr McCready held up his hand to stop her as Miranda started to speak, and immediately continued: 'Michael's had a crippled life. Despite the love you've given him, he's had to suffer far too much. Alone. But now, at last, he's been given a great gift. The most marvellous gift of grace. The unexpected chance to die in calm and dignity, no more than nine years into his life. Wrapped in his mother's arms. Surrounded and held by love.'

They sat there without speaking. Miranda leant forward with her elbows on the table, her face held concealed in the palms of her hands. After some moments, Dr McCready spoke again.

'It's in your power to deny him that gift. Legally, without any doubt, you could insist that Michael is subjected to that ventilator contraption. As you know, all of us here would have to agree to your instruction. Even though we know the cruel futility of it, we would have to let you have your way. So you could deny him the gift of a death of calm and grace.'

He paused, then moved forward in his chair, and said, 'It's just that you won't. I know that to be the case. You're too intelligent. And you're too brave. You won't do it.'

There was a long silence, then Miranda said, her head still in her hands, 'All I wanted was more time. More time for him to come through to life. More time for . . . for a miracle, I suppose.'

Dr McCready reached out, and held both her elbows in his hands.

'We know what it is, Miranda, you and I. We know what it is – you told me. Michael's an angel of God. He's in God's hands. I couldn't say it to you the first time, but I'll say it now. His life, his death, your love for him; it's all one thing.

'It's the love of God, Miranda. It's the will of God. Accept it now. Let him go. Let him go to his peace.'

Chapter 15

Dr McCready was right. Only a few days after they had spoken together, Michael did die, wrapped and secure in Miranda's arms. And it did seem to her, as McCready had said, that he had in him at the moment of death a quality of peace, and dignity, and awareness, that she had never seen in him before.

Perhaps, Miranda thought, the way of Michael's passing really was a final gift to him. A gift of grace. Perhaps, at last, he really was going home.

He died at eight o'clock in the evening, as the final light of the day was fading away. Just a few minutes earlier, Miranda had thrown open the curtains, and then the windows themselves, determined, on an impulse, that Michael's last contact with the world should be one of sunset colours, and evening birdsong, and the sound of laughter, as the children in the park finished their games and set off for home.

She turned away, and knelt beside Michael's bed, her arms around him. His breathing was now so intermittent that she wondered at his lack of struggle against it. But then he sighed, and opened his eyes, and turned to Miranda, and stared deep into hers. She held her gaze in his, and they were together. Then, at last, she saw the life in him dim, and he was gone.

Chapter 16

Felix Rosenberg was a man of great standing, both in the country and, of course, in the Jewish community. As the more vulgar commentators on the affair would have it, for Lewis Cohen to secure his daughter as his bride was fortunate for him indeed.

But there was no hypocrisy in Cohen. Elizabeth was a beautiful girl, but there were plenty of them around, and at the age of forty-five he had known a number of striking women. That she was Lord Rosenberg's daughter hardly lessened her attractions for him. But Cohen, unaffectedly, was in love. He was in simple rapture. Every cliché of besotted romance was his. He adored this girl, twenty years younger than himself, who appeared to love him as much in return. He worshipped the ground on which she trod. His open arms, each time he came to her, were weighed down with roses. She was a little extravagant, perhaps, but that was charming. A skittish, feminine disregard for the orthodox and the boring – that's all it was! And her delicious, little-girl sulkiness when things went wrong, so quickly dispersed by his kisses!

The first time he had touched her it had been like an electric charge. To that point he and Elizabeth had only been in each other's company on two or three occasions, surrounded by mutual acquaintances. Then he had invited her to lunch with him alone, and as he watched her walk over to his table he had found himself near-breathless with the excitement of what he was doing. He was crazily, hopelessly in love. Soon, he was determined, Elizabeth Rosenberg would be his. And soon, very soon after that, she would be his bride. And with his ecstasy at the thought of that, and the joy within him as he looked at her, Cohen laid his hand, concealed by the tablecloth, on the inside of Elizabeth's thigh. As he did this two thoughts came into his mind. Firstly, and guiltily, that each woman he had ever touched or made love with, dozens though they might be, felt and looked and behaved, in their nakedness, entirely different one from another. And secondly, and so proudly that he could have burst, that the shape and texture of Elizabeth's body he now knew to be as sensual and lovely as anything he had ever experienced.

A month or so later it was clear that Elizabeth was pregnant, and by the time she miscarried a few weeks subsequently in the Ladies lavatory at Harvey Nichols, the wedding had already been arranged by a less than ecstatic Lady Rosenberg and her puzzled, and ill-briefed husband.

Mariss Steiner saw the announcement of the engagement in *The Times*. He had always been an avid reader of the broadsheet newspapers, which he either stole, or read, cover to cover, standing at newsagents' shelves. He had been reading the newspapers that day at the newsstand in Paddington Station, and when his eye caught the listing of the forthcoming marriage between Lewis Cohen and Elizabeth Rosenberg he almost dropped the paper in his astonishment. Then he laughed out aloud. It was too good to be true. Lewis was always the *arriviste*, but a daughter of the Rosenberg family . . . !

Still chuckling, Steiner actually for once paid for the paper, then bustled on his way. He would add the engagement notice to the cuttings on Cohen's career he had pinned up on the noticeboard in his room. He could hardly wait to get home and on the telephone to him.

But Cohen, as usual, was too busy to speak to him, and the call was not returned for some days, and when it did come there was such an absence of warmth and friendship in Cohen's voice that Steiner immediately took offence at it. So instead of doing what he had meant to do – congratulate Cohen, tease him at his good fortune, and charm his way into an invitation – Steiner had lost his temper at him, and shouted his insults, and Cohen, muttering some vaguely conciliatory remarks, had quietly put down the telephone. And never, of course, subsequently asked Steiner to the wedding ceremony or to anything else, including the magnificent reception held in the Louis XVI Restaurant of the Ritz Hotel, so lavishly reported upon in every fashion and society magazine.

Steiner came to both, notwithstanding his lack of an invitation, dressed for the occasion in the better of his two suits, and his shiny black shoes, and his crispest, whitest lawn cotton shirt, with a pearl-grey tie and a brand new purple *yarmulke*. But he was turned away from the synagogue, protest as he might, then rebuffed again when he tried to make his entrance at the Ritz Hotel.

But he did acquire a keepsake to put with all the other artefacts he stored in his bedroom. As a woman had stepped out from her Rolls-Royce at the entrance to the Ritz, an embossed invitation card slipped from her grasp. Steiner waited until she had gone inside, then picked it up, wiped it down with his handkerchief, and carried it home. That, at least, was his.

Chapter 17

Suddenly they had broken through the cloud, and as Jacob Bergdorf leaned across the woman next to him to peer out of the window, the vivid green fields below them looked most uncomfortably near. The ground seemed close – too close – and the plane, to his perennially anxious mind, seemed in the last few moments to have lost height unusually quickly. This was what he was waiting for. This was it. The pilot had made an error in his approach. They were going to die.

But he didn't really believe that; it was part of the game. He was used to terror, and knew how to deal with it. He clenched his fists and toes up as tight as he could force them, and was still deciding who it was in his entourage back in Vienna who was to be blamed for the fact that he hadn't made the journey by rail, when the wheels touched and bounced on the runway, the air brakes roared, the plane settled and slowed, and Bergdorf was safely landed at Heathrow.

Quite instantaneously he recovered his spirits. Once again he had escaped all the perils that each time terrified him so. He turned to the woman next to him and, garrulous in his relief, chattered away like a schoolchild, despite the fact that he had not exchanged one single word with her during the flight or before it. The smoothness of their flight; the skilful completion of their landing; the inclemency of the weather that greeted them; the prospects, however, of sunshine over the weekend . . . she smiled at the banal flow of it all.

Now they were safely on the ground once more, and the plane had taxied up to its parking bay. The whole terrifying business of it was over, until the next time. Bergdorf got to his feet, took out his folded handkerchief, patted the little beads of perspiration from off his upper lip and forehead, looked down at the reassuringly familiar grip of the ancient brown leather attaché case that he had in his hand, and reminded himself of his programme for the rest of the evening. A stewardess had already announced the local time over the Tannoy, but Bergdorf never trusted a woman to be capable of accuracy in matters of that sort, nor indeed in any matters at all beyond those of the simplest tasks of child-rearing and domestic maintenance, so he consulted his watch. Five past five. That idiot of a woman had said five o'clock.

There was time enough for everything that had to be done, as long as the traffic into the West End was not so heavy that they were seriously delayed. The reception at Marlborough House was at seven, and the dinner at the United States Embassy at half-past eight. It should be a most useful evening. There were good people over in London this week for this conference. Plenty to get his teeth into.

Lewis Cohen finished tying his black bow tie, and seeing Elizabeth bending over beside him, replacing in her cupboard a pair of shoes in a line of apparently identical ones, slapped her lightly on the bottom.

'I'm still furious with you,' he said playfully, and made as if to smack her once more, then desisted as she stood up, and moved across to the basin. 'You leave me to go to these things on my own, and we've only been married six or seven months!'

But privately, the banter concealed a hurt. A quarrel with Elizabeth was the last thing he wanted. She was still so far from understanding what actually made up his personality – particularly his bouts of self-doubt. They were rare, but he wasn't as used to functions of this grandeur as Elizabeth might have supposed, and he was nervous of what lay ahead of him that evening. He would have liked to have had his wife with him – indeed, he would like to have her with him at all of the engagements he was obliged to attend. No doubt because of the age difference, Elizabeth assumed that there was no need for her to be a support, and a prop, and a friend to him – the things a wife does. Instead, she seemed to want to be treated as the charming little adored one, but without the responsibility of being a real partner. Odd that she didn't have enough self-regard to realise that much more was within her scope and scale than that.

But nevertheless he went to embrace her now as he left, and her arms went around his neck, and his heart melted for her, as it always did, and the little butterfly kiss she gave him was as sweet and delicate as a child's. But Cohen suddenly felt alone. He was a man of forty-five, with a good career developing, and the public recognition to go with that, and contacts and responsibilities in a number of different spheres . . . amongst them – though Elizabeth could hardly

Tim Waterstone

be expected to know this, of course – with certain international Intelligence agencies. He did love Elizabeth, and he had no doubt about that. But she was more now than Felix Rosenberg's daughter, and he wished she could think of herself in that way. Primarily, she was his wife. His wife first, and Rosenberg's daughter second. As it was though, she not only called herself Rosenberg still, but she meant it, too. She remained Felix's daughter, and Cohen's adoring little girlfriend. That wasn't what he wanted. That wasn't what he wanted at all. That wasn't what he needed.

Cohen arrived in St James's exactly on time, but decided to sit in the car for a few minutes before going into Marlborough House, overcome by a sudden shot of nerves. He timed it on the car clock. At twelve minutes past seven precisely he would get out of the car, and go in, and get on with it.

How absurd it was that a man in his position should feel like this! For all the *arriviste* style, and the Daimler, and all the other trappings of his insecurity, inside him he was always what he had been. Lewis Cohen. Son of Isaiah Cohen. Child of what he had learnt in recent years had been a great extended family of Cohens. Merchants of Warsaw. All now dead. All dead. Everyone.

Thirteen minutes past, and still Cohen had not gone inside. He'd give it one minute more, and then he would get out and get on with it. Smiling, and confident, and ready to work the room, like everybody else there would be doing.

And then he saw Jacob Bergdorf, strolling up to the entrance with some friend or other, raising his hand in greeting to someone else, his black evening clothes so nonchalantly crumpled and short in the leg, his tie drooping, his hair unbrushed, his patent leather shoes gleaming, but old and worn. Cohen cursed the newness of his own. The cowardly, insecure newness of them, and that of the dinner suit he had ordered from his tailor especially for this occasion. But the sight of Bergdorf roused him, and he found that he was now getting out of the car, and waving his hand too, although Bergdorf turned away without acknowledging him, perhaps failing to see in time that it was him.

So Cohen went on into the reception, first circling the room, keeping moving, waiting to see who was there and whom he could talk to. He saw an Israeli politician in the corner whom his firm represented, and chatted to him for a little, then an American banker who had come to his wedding, and Cohen, listening to himself, wondered at the immediacy with which shyness had turned into

70

his comfortable, familiar patter of charm. Then Bergdorf came up to him, arm in arm with a concert pianist so old and so famous that Cohen felt as he was introduced to him like a star-struck, inadequate schoolboy, the more so as the man immediately turned away and went to talk to somebody else. Bergdorf asked pleasantly after Elizabeth, and congratulated him on a success that his firm had enjoyed in a Brussels law suit that he must have known full well was nothing to do with Cohen, then he too turned to observe where he might go next, his eyes on a United States Senator across the room.

As he moved away, Cohen blurted out, 'I heard a rumour about Joseph Hermann, Jacob. I wondered if I should share it with you, as I know you have an interest in these things. He has many files, apparently, of names and addresses and numbers – Swiss bank account numbers. He's looking for a good lawyer with the right contacts to help him sort them out. Perhaps you should get in touch with him.'

Bergdorf turned back and stared at him. For a moment there was real, unmistakable anger in his eyes, before a smile replaced it, and he nodded and went off on his way.

Chapter 18

Hermann thought that the man he had seen sitting in the hotel lobby looked vaguely familiar, but he couldn't quite place him. He hoped he wasn't a journalist, or, worse still, a fellow historian wanting to have a gossip. It had been a most uncomfortable flight across from Vienna, the drive in from the airport had been cold and snowy, and Montréal, at the best of times, was far from Hermann's favourite town. What he wanted to do most of all was to go safely up to his room, have a drink, have a bath, and work through his papers for tomorrow's address. What he did *not* want in any circumstances was to be waylaid by a stranger.

But it was too late. Hermann failed to manoeuvre himself in time into the first elevator car that arrived, and now a hand was touching his arm, and he could do no more than turn to acknowledge it, an expression of barely adequate amiability forced on to his features. The man smiled at him in return and put his hand out for Hermann to shake, which he had to place a suitcase on the floor to do.

'Amos Bronowski,' the other said, and still Hermann had no idea at all who it was. 'Amos Bronowski,' he repeated. 'You don't remember – I do apologise. I came to talk to you once in Austria to see if we could get you to do a television programme. You wouldn't! I didn't mention it then, but we did in fact have a common point of contact. From the war. We were both in concentration camps. I was at Belsen, and you were at Buchenwald.'

Hermann winced, and caught the eye of a woman next to him, who looked up the moment she heard the names of the camps. Now the doors came open once more, and as Hermann picked up his bag and moved forward he found that Bronowski was still beside him. The doors closed on them, and Hermann, pressing the number for his floor, wondered how he was going to shake this man off. To his horror, Bronowski was still talking on.

'Yes. You at Buchenwald, and me at Belsen,' he said loudly, and Hermann flinched again as the woman stared now in rapt fascination at them both. Hermann realised that Bronowski knew perfectly well what he was doing, and wondered why.

'Somewhat different age group, of course,' Bronowski continued, as cheerfully as before. 'You were a man approaching thirty, I suppose, when the war ended, and I was six when the English arrived to get us out. A small boy. And you the great leader, of course. The *Communist* leader.'

This time Hermann jerked back as if he had been hit, and he grimaced with open anger as he stared at Bronowski. The doors opened at his floor; Bronowski accompanied him out into the corridor, and as the elevator closed behind them the two men stood face to face.

Pink in the face, Hermann said: 'Why did you do that? What's the meaning of it? Who are you anyway?'

Bronowski smiled. 'Let's go into your room, and have a chat for a few moments,' he suggested. 'I'm not here to threaten you. Buchenwald was—'

At that moment, a bedroom door opened beside them and a man came out into the corridor. Hermann irritably motioned to Bronowski to follow him. He fiddled with his own key, went inside, then flung his cases into the corner of the room and turned to face his unwelcome visitor.

'Right,' he said, his voice quieter, but still shaking with anger. 'What do you want from me?'

Bronowski motioned to a chair, and asked if he could sit, and as he did so Hermann sat too, on the edge of his bed, running the fingers of both his hands through his thinning hair in a repeated, combing motion, as if this was a means that he habitually used to calm himself when he was under stress. Hermann asked again, the anger now apparently under control: 'What is it you want?'

Bronowski started to reply, but Hermann immediately held up his hand.

'No. Let's start again. First of all – who are you?'

Bronowski nodded, as if in acknowledgement and approval that Hermann was trying now to have a sensible, level-headed conversation.

'I'm an economist,' he said. 'I teach here in Montréal, at McGill. I also do some journalism, and some contemporary research . . . into Jewish affairs.'

He stopped, and there was a silence as the two men stared at each other.

'And Buchenwald,' Hermann prompted. 'From your insistence on bringing up the name of the place every five seconds, I imagine that it's Buchenwald that you want to talk to me about. Am I correct?'

Bronowski nodded.

'Well – fine,' Hermann nodded. 'I have no objection to that, if that's what you want. Buchenwald it is. What do you want to know? Or, now that I come to think about it, what is it you want to *say*? There can't be anything you want to know. You had as much experience of the Nazi camps as I did. You look like a man who enjoys making speeches. So – make one.'

'You say I had as much experience of the camps as you did,' Bronowski replied. 'Hardly. As I told you, I was a little boy, three years old when I first went to Belsen. Six when I came out. I was just a child. You were a man – and not just a man. You were one of the people at Buchenwald who ran the place. That's a rather different level of experience. And . . .' he smiled as he spoke, as if to take the edge of aggression off his words '. . . and responsibility too. Quite a difference.'

Hermann looked at him. 'I repeat,' he said. 'What do you want?'

Bronowski shrugged, and said nothing more for a moment. Then, 'I wasn't there at Buchenwald at the thirtieth anniversary ceremony two months ago, and you may say that I should have been. *I* think I should have been. Thirty years of the Jewish prisoners' release from that place is an anniversary worth commemorating. But I've read the reports in the Press, and I have to tell you that I believe that what you said there was disgraceful. Utterly disgraceful.'

He shrugged again, and moved in his chair, as if about to be on his way.

'That's all I have to say, really. Your speech was a travesty. You Communists were collaborators. Worse than collaborators! You took the opportunity to use Buchenwald for your own ends. You were shits! I hated that speech of yours, Professor Hermann, and I wasn't going to allow you to come here to Montréal without hearing that from me. That's all. What you were trying to do was to shift the limelight off the Communists and on to an easy target. Anyone can attack the German authorities in terms such as the ones you used, and know that they will get a standing ovation for it – from the Germans themselves, as much as anybody else, they're so shot through these days with guilt and self-blame. But to say what you did is dishonest. It's cowardly. It's also historically incorrect. And you're a historian. You're not going to be allowed to get away with it. *I'm* not going to let you get away with it.'

'*You're* not going to allow me to get away with it?' said Hermann mockingly. 'Get away with what?' He went over to one of his suitcases and started rummaging in it. Still bending down, facing away from Bronowski, he went on, 'I said what I meant. You pointed out yourself that your recall of life at Belsen could only be that of a child. How could you know anything about Buchenwald?' Then he straightened up, holding in his hand a slim blue file.

'Here's my speech,' he said, and threw the file into Bronowski's lap. 'Read it. Read the original, and not the newspapers. I stand by every word I said. Why don't you sit here, and read it now.'

Bronowski hesitated, then pulled the papers out of the file, and leafed through them quickly, then muttered some comment which Hermann failed to catch, and started to read them again, this time with intense concentration. Hermann sat on his bed watching him, then got up, put both his suitcases on the bed, and started to unpack, as if flagging to Bronowski his lack of concern.

'It's what I expected,' the younger man scoffed finally, throwing down the file. 'You've taken a seductively easy line in order to get cheap applause. You say just one thing – that the German authorities are trying to divert attention from the behaviour of the Nazis at Buchenwald by putting out false propaganda about the Communists there. The "Communist resistance" as you put it, though I would call it something else.

'Here are two typical passages. The first to set the thing up, and make our flesh creep:

'". . . No progress is visible. None. The same gentlemen who created and ran Buchenwald and the other camps, now sit on Boards and committees and councils and pat their bulging wallets. The same people. Thirty years on from the day of our liberation, and they're all still there. They made Hitler possible. And they're all still there. The men who murdered us. They're all still there."

'Now the second, after a lot of further blood-curdling stuff about the German military bombing innocent children, and these days spending their time strutting around with their Hitler medals on their chests. Here – this section. This is the sort of lying nonsense that I'm not going to let you get away with – not now; not ever.

'". . . Lies about the Communists at Buchenwald are told for political purposes only, and the perpetrators of those lies should hang their heads in shame.

'"The facts are these. The Communists took control of Buchenwald for one reason – the protection of all the prisoners there. Every man, every woman, every child, whatever their race and whatever their creed. Because we were strong, and because we were united, and because we *had discipline, we Communists saved Buchenwald from the extremes of anarchy and destruction that at one stage looked inevitable.*

' *"There was no collaboration with the Nazis. None whatsoever. What there was was* control. *Unless the Communists had taken the reins of power from the common criminals who ran the camp in the early days of the war, then Buchenwald would have been an even greater tragedy than it was. We took control, and I tell you what happened.*

' *"Twenty-one thousand comrades who otherwise would have died at Nazi hands were saved. Nine hundred children, who would have been shipped away to the gas ovens, were saved. We saved lives. We saved our comrades. We put a protective shield around inmates too helpless to fend for themselves.*

' *"The world knows the truth. The plaque at Buchenwald commemorating the four British airmen who owed their lives to Communist protection in the camp tells the truth. We did it for them. We did it for so many others. We shielded the innocent. We protected the sick. We staved off catastrophe. At a moment of horror, and darkness, and evil, the Communists of Buchenwald were all that stood between annihilation and the light of another, better day. I'm content in that. I'm proud of that."'*

Bronowski took a deep breath and glared at the older man. 'That's what I'm going to stop you from ever claiming again. Because *it's not true.* The Communists gained control of Buchenwald because you were an organised body, and you were used to strict Party obedience. Also, you'd been in the camp for longer than most. You were better grouped than the others, so you were able to step in and take what was going. And once you got control, you sat on it. This stuff of yours about "taking the reins of power from the common criminals" . . . What you did was share it with them. You did a deal! You did a deal with the criminal groups, and you did a deal with the SS.' His voice was bitter. 'Collaboration is too soft a term for that, Professor Hermann. You weren't collaborators with the Nazis. You were partners.'

Hermann threw up his hands. 'What's the point of this?' he said. 'Why come here and threaten me in this way? I don't want to quarrel with you. I don't even know you. You teach at McGill, I teach in Vienna. We're both of us respectable, intelligent, professional men. You have your views about Buchenwald, from whatever you've read about the place, and I have mine. From my own experience. Neither of us was exactly fortunate to have been in the camps at all. But we were, and you were a child, and I was a man. We both survived, and we're both now busy making something of our lives. Let's live, and let live, and do that. Make something of our lives.'

Bronowski paced restlessly around the room. 'Live and let live? How is that possible? You're a Jew, for the love of God. You were the leader of the Communist group that controlled the camp. And specifically, *controlled the camp infirmary*. The infirmary was run by *Jewish* Communist trusties, under *your* control. And those trusties chose which of the so-called patients should be given the lethal injections, and which should be allowed to live. Your people did that. Jews did that to Jews, Professor Hermann. You chose which Jews should live, and which should be murdered. I've researched it. I know what I'm saying is true. You did that. And thirty years later you can sit down and write a speech all about—'

'STOP!' shouted Hermann. Then again, more quietly: '*Stop!*'

The two men gazed at each other, both shaking now, and there was a silence. Then Hermann got up and stood in front of the younger man. When he spoke his voice still trembled, but he had himself under control.

'Please leave me now, Mr Bronowski. I wish you no harm. Indeed, I wish you peace. But I want you to leave me. One more time: this all has to be put behind us. It's over. We have our lives to lead. We both of us have our lives to lead.'

Mariss Steiner made another entry into the lobby at The Grosvenor House, and this time he saw what he had been looking for. He had made three previous sorties into the place without success, but now it was perfect. A large party of men and women in evening dress had all come in together, some of whom Steiner recognised from their press photographs. He swung in amongst them, his dinner jacket and black tie entirely in uniform, and laughed immediately and uproariously at a joke he couldn't hear from a man over on his right, then blew a kiss and winked at a middle-aged actress beyond him, who was looking as if she first had thought he was someone she knew, now couldn't place him, but anyway returned his kiss, and his wink, and added a charming little wrinkling of her nose as a bonus.

'She's looking marvellous, darling – don't you think?' said another woman, pressing against him as they all, radiant with delight, tried to squeeze into the lift together. Steiner, laughing and chattering, allowed himself to be pushed up against the back, whence he was swept out with the rest of them when they arrived at their destination, which Steiner saw, as he emerged, was the top floor. The doors beside them opened, and the others of the party emerged from the other lift, and there was a new little interlude of shrieks and embraces as they all met up with one another

once more, then swept along to the double doors at the very
end of the corridor. There two burly figures in dinner suits stood,
broken nosed, muscle heavy, hands folded across their groins, a
type-written list lying before them on a little green-baized table.

Names were given, and ticked, with thin, mirthless smiles from
the bouncers, then one by one the group went on into the suite, and
seized their champagne flutes, and embraced each other all over
again, and the clamour and laughter and shrieks of joy rose into a
bedlam of theatrical ecstasy. Steiner caught a fleeting moment when
both the checkers had turned away, and hurried through alongside
the women with whom he had exchanged the blown kisses. 'There
they are!' he cried, and took his glass from the waiter, gulped at it,
then, calling out, pressed his way across the floor.

The timing was absolutely perfect. Elizabeth Taylor and Richard
Burton were standing together, but two or three feet apart, laughing
delightedly at some remark or another. Just at the very moment
the press photographers flashed their bulbs, Steiner had stepped
between them, chuckling as joyously as they did, his two palms
resting intimately in the small of their backs.

As they turned to him the bouncer was already at their side, his
arm locked through Steiner's as he pulled him away, and marched
him out once more into the outside corridor. Steiner could not
have minded the indignity of it less, and as he was pushed on
his way towards the lifts, he stumbled, picked himself up from
the floor, dusted himself down, made a cheerfully obscene and
explicit invitation to the more handsome of the two, and set off
on his way.

And he was fully rewarded. The morning following the photograph of him with the Burtons was on the front page of the *Daily
Mail*. 'Liz and Richard have a ball with their friends', was the
caption, and Steiner bought or shoplifted every copy he could find
on the shelves of the news-stands in his neighbourhood. One copy
he cut most carefully from off the page, and stuck it on his bedroom
wall. Beside his other pride and joy. A *Daily Telegraph* photograph of
him standing by the shoulder of the Chief Rabbi as he shook hands
with the Pope, and looking for all the world as if he himself was the
next to be presented.

Chapter 19

Tuesday was the one night of the week that Burridge & Edel stayed open after half-past five, and it had been that way for as long as anyone could remember. The practice seemed too rooted now to change, though the other bookshops around Cecil Court tended these days to stay open late each night of the week, in response perhaps to the unpleasantly aggressive tactics of the new people further up Charing Cross Road. But old Mr Thomas Burridge had been in his time a five-o'clock-train-home-to-Weybridge man, and young Mr Thomas who succeeded him was most certainly that in his turn, and when Gareth Edel, for so long the Manager, borrowed the money and bought out the bankrupt Burridge's from the Receiver, he was respectful enough of the past to continue the tradition. And respectful enough too to call the new business Burridge & Edel, though it had to be said that no trace whatsover of the two Mr Thomases' ineffective ownership of the bookshop had survived five minutes of their retirement.

Edel was thirty-four when he bought the business, but looked years older; already a man who had assumed, quite deliberately, the mantle of middle age. Of full middle age, and of particular lack of presence. His clothes were a caricature. He wore at all times, including weekends, a baggy, grey pin-striped suit under a gaberdine raincoat. The suit was habitually marked, as a teacher's might have been, with what looked like smudges of schoolroom chalk on the flap of one of the pockets and on the inside of the sleeves. His shirts were of nondescript white cotton; his ties patterned homeknits of indeterminate shades; his socks, even in the warmth of summer days, thick and grey and encased in elderly black walking shoes.

With his pipe cupped in his large, clumsy hands, and his balding, shiny head, and his oval, brown hornrim glasses, Edel resembled a character from a J.B. Priestley novel. A mild, gentle, solitary man. And so he was. Solitary, certainly. Gentle, too. Gareth Edel was both those things. But he was also a spy.

The original approach to him had been made one evening six or seven years before as he was tidying up some books in the storeroom at the rear of the shop. It was well past half-past six, and when Edel heard a rap on the door his first action was to come out on to the main part of the floor so that he could be seen, and signal that the shop was closed. But the man there held up his hand to halt him, and, taking out his fountain pen, printed a message on to the back of an envelope, which he then pressed against the glass for Edel to read. FRIEND OF MAEVE it said, and Edel, seeing an amiable face and a pleasant, open smile, went back into the storeroom to retrieve the keys and let the visitor in.

Edel took him to be about the same age as himself, though his jeans, cheerful plaid shirt and curly hair gave him the appearance of someone at least ten years younger. The accent, which in his first few words to him Edel concluded to be as Dublin as could be, became as their conversation ran on more obviously touched with American. Perhaps Boston American, Edel thought, though he knew very little about such matters. He searched around in the back office for the ornamental corkscrew and the bottle of wine, which a book salesman had brought in at Christmas-time, hoping some member of the staff had not since purloined them. He wondered how it could be that Maeve had had an American friend of that age. The visitor was too old to have been a schoolfriend, and she never went to college. Perhaps he was a friend of one of her brothers . . . yet he had been very direct about it. He said he had been a friend of Maeve.

'What can I do for you?' Edel said, and poured the man his helping of bottom-of-the-range Bulgarian red.

But the American's conversation was unfocused now, if charmingly fluent, and, in its opening exchanges, oddly, jarringly, overemphatic about the Jewishness of them both. The point seemed to Edel to be at that moment blindingly irrelevant. Moreover, it had no connection whatsoever with Maeve. It was on an appeal about Maeve that the man had arrived, and now he seemed to have no intention of following it up. Edel had no idea what he could want with him. For a moment he was physically uneasy about the fact that he had allowed him access, but then put the thought out of his mind. The stranger was not that sort of man. The Irish/American/stage-Jewish performance was not without its *longueurs* and artifices, but it was pleasant and intelligent enough, and there was no threat in him.

No threat, but certainly an oddness. There was a pre-planned deliberateness about his conversation that was too obviously set to intrigue. The man knew what he was about. He had prepared himself. There was something he wanted.

An Old Testament lay on Edel's desk, open at the Book of Job. He had been reading this intermittently over the last few days, absorbed in his reflections on the enigma of suffering, sparked off for some reason or another by a visit he had made to a retrospective exhibition of John Minton's work at the Hayward Gallery.

The American picked it up, flicked over some pages and read, '"The Lord gave, and the Lord hath taken away; blessed be the name of the Lord." Chapter 7. Verse 21. Pretty much what happens – don't you think? The people we love most are removed from us, and then we're supposed to say thank you for it. An unsatisfactory deal, in my view. But, oddly, it's true. We're actually grateful when they die, partly because we sense, despite ourselves, that they're moving on to something else, and that where they're going is *home*, whether we like it or not. Is that how you see it? Is that what you felt about Maeve?'

'No,' said Edel shortly. 'It's not how I see it. And it's not what I feel about Maeve. I miss my wife too much to be able to console myself with that sort of stuff. I'm not at all grateful that she's dead. I *hate* the fact that she's dead – and I hate God for killing her. I miss her. I long for her every moment that passes.'

And so they talked on. Edel doubted, as the three or four hours passed, whether the American or Irishman or whatever he was had ever laid eyes on Maeve in his life; yet as he came to the thought, he realised that he didn't very much mind. Someone had briefed him, and the fact of that gave Edel a sense of belonging. Someone cared that Edel should feel comfortable and reassured and part of a family. And it had been done overtly. Maeve. The prepared debate about loss and suffering. The fortunate coincidence of finding The Book of Job open there on his desk. And then what was happening, now. The address on belonging, on membership, on loyalty, on pride.

That's all it was. There were no great theatrics of initiation rites, or moments of decision, or the turning of the screw. Not very much persuasion of any sort. The man didn't seem to want very much. Just an eye kept on the activities of X, and some assistance in getting access to the papers of Y. 'We'll just take it from there', he had said. 'You know what we're about. You've probably guessed anyway that we have fingers in rather more pies than we publicly profess. We're there to help the world along a little – that's all it is. Give a little push and a shove when things get stuck. Or when they become a nuisance. Or when they're not in the interests of our people.'

And so Edel did it. He did the one or two simple tasks that the men from the World Jewish Council asked him to, then more, then some others, which gave him a moment's glimpse into a wider, more violent world. He enjoyed it. He was good at it. It became in time the centre of his life.

Burridge & Edel developed over the years as the posting point for certain initiatives that, had they known about it, would have made the old Mr Thomas and the young Mr Thomas incandescent with rage. And turn in their suburban, little-Englander, anti-Semitic graves.

BOOK III

1995

Chapter 20

All of Miranda Bronowski's professional life had been spent at St
Peter's. Thirty years of it in the same school, with the exception
of one single period of fifteen months, when, eight years after
Michael's death, and just past her forty-third birthday, she went
as a special exchange teacher to mission schools in Zaire. But after
four terms of it she was back at St Peter's, and glad to be so.

By no means had she grown into an ambitious or adventurous
woman. She knew that her younger colleagues regarded her career
as one of seamless and progressive nonentity, and on the whole
she agreed with them. In her fashion, however, Miranda had
coped rather well over the long span of her working life. There
had been a brief and unhappy period as Deputy Head of the
English Department, during which she had been obliged to teach
an older, and more cynical age group, and it was this experience, as
much as anything, that had decided her to go to Africa. But now she
had returned for good to her class of twelve and thirteen year olds,
and with these younger girls she had become an effective as well as
a kindly teacher. There was a sincerity in Miranda's constant, shy,
awkward smile, and most of the children in her first-year class did
move on up the school at the end of it stimulated by a full and new
range of enthusiasms, and half-grasped opinions, and prejudices
too. It was with Miranda Bronowski that they took their first
halting steps into the realisation that fiction could actually signify
something beyond the strictly narrative, and that Shakespeare could
be made intelligible, and Oscar Wilde funny. And, for ever after,
succeeding generations of St Peter's girls, on passing through
Nottinghamshire, would remember D.H. Lawrence, and *Odour of
Chrysanthemums*, and Mrs Bronowski's famous class to her girls at
the end of each year, on the nature of human isolation, and love,
and loss.

There was still a degree of gossip among the staff and pupils
about Miranda's personal history, but as the years went by, the lurid

myths of romantic abandonment and tragic bereavement seemed too remote from the credible to those who only in recent times had made her acquaintance. Very few of the staff at the school at the time of her marriage to Bronowski were still there. Lady Phillipson had some years past become head of a glamorous international charity; Miss Clinch had left in a huff, and joined the WRNS. Other dramas had happened, and other lives exposed to scrutiny. Teachers had come, and teachers had gone. Miranda was there still, one of the anchors of the school's continuing achievement; reliable, kindly, honourable, contained.

And yet glimpses of what was there in her might, to the most perceptive, occasionally show through in her teaching. A Katherine Mansfield short story. Graham Greene's *The Heart of the Matter*. *Anna Karenina*. Stevie Smith. In her classes on these, there was in Miranda a certain chilling definition in her treatment of the way that death can serve to enrich and feed the human soul. And, in its passage, plant in the scarred hearts of those left behind a curious, unexpected, privileged glimpse of the transcendent.

'Watch someone you love die,' Miranda once said to her class of new girls, '. . . and when you do that you'll see the soul within them rise up and float away and find its peace and its resolution. It's true. You must always believe that; always, always believe that. It's true.'

One year, early in the autumn term, only a week or so after she'd returned from a walking holiday on the island of Vis in the Adriatic, she had suddenly turned at that point in the lesson, and wrote up on the blackboard an inscription she had seen there on a plaque in the British War Cemetery.

'*Life to be sure, is nothing much to lose; But young men think it is, and we were young.*'

'Be moved by the genuine statement of self-sacrifice in that,' she said, 'but be comforted by the truth. Young men, with their lives before them, don't in the least want to die. Who can blame them? Life is precious – yes. Certainly it is. But the preciousness of it is illusory. At the moment life is lost, the soul is freed. It isn't death at all. It's life! When you witness it, you know the fact of it.'

After years of silence, there were the letters. They came from Bronowski now in a constant flow, every two or three weeks; more often in recent months, and progressively more insistent and heartfelt in tone, with their pleas to Miranda that she should allow him a fresh chance, and a renewal of life together once more in the Britannia Road house, from which he knew she had never moved.

Miranda could recognise his handwriting on an envelope from a range of fifteen feet, which was the distance from where, as she came down the stairs in the morning, the letters on the doormat came into view. And each time a letter was there, her heart would lurch at the sight of it. She dreaded all those appeals to her for forgiveness; recollections, or the pretence of recollections, of bygone moments of happiness together; promises of peace in their fading years. All fantasy. All dangerous.

That particular autumn night, back late from school, Miranda came into the house so wet and cold and tired that she had half a mind to do no more than have several glasses of white wine, a hot bath, and an egg on a tray in her bedroom while she corrected the first-form essays. But there, under her feet, was the second letter she had received from him that week.

She groaned aloud as she saw it. 'Christ, oh Christ, oh Christ,' she said, her voice rising in a crescendo. Then she picked the envelope up, and ripped it open. She was anxious and impatient to be rid of it, then get her wet clothes off and run her bath and pour in the scented oil, and lie there with her drink.

She quickly skimmed the letter to get the broad sense of what he had written, as she always did, usually to do no more than this. But this time she found that it contained news of a particularly dramatic sort; this placed, as if dealing with a matter of comparative inconsequence, halfway down the second page. Her dismay at what she read was such that for a moment she felt faint. She cursed herself for her weakness, but she recognised that her alarm was tinged with a certain indefinable excitement.

'So I'll be in London on the Friday night. Assuming that my flight is on time. And it's been so long since I flew to England from New York that I've forgotten whether these things normally arrive on time or not. But, unless there's something untoward, I should be at Gareth Edel's house in Chiswick at around ten or eleven, and I'll telephone you then, Miranda, if I may. I'm so longing to hear your voice. I've been writing to you too long, and speaking to you too little. And I hope so much that you will then agree to see me.

Neither of us has ever married again. We're both too loyal, in our different ways. And – I'm certain I'm right – too fond of each other as well. We made mistakes, of course – no, I made mistakes. But nothing of that sort really takes away love, I believe. You can fall out of love, but you and I didn't. For all my behaviour, we remained in love with each other. The Christian goyim, normally so dim, understand it well. "From this time forward," as they say. "Till death us do part. In sickness and in health. For richer, for poorer." They're right.

That's part of the reason why I'm coming to England. It's time that the mistakes of the past were buried. We must both of us move to the present, and live there. Before our lives are over. Along with the chance for us both to find our peace. That would be tragic. Needless too.'

Miranda sat at the kitchen table, her wet clothes and her cold feet and the ache of her fatigue forgotten now as she absorbed what she had read.

This is all some cruel, manipulative fraud, she thought. I've no idea what he really wants from me. There's a self-absorbed and self-seeking quality about him, and there always was. All this insistence about love, and yet I know perfectly well in my heart that there's something else he wants from me, although I don't as yet know what that could be. A game of some sort, in which I'm the quarry? It could hardly be money, given my circumstances. He's had a far more successful career than me, and on a North-American salary as well. And he's not a man of any extravagance – the reverse of that. So it can't be money . . .

Miranda went over to the fridge, and took out the single bottle of supermarket Frascati that was still there. She noticed, gloomily, that the previous night she had drunk more than half of it, and that tonight she would only get a helping and a bit out of what was left. She poured some of the wine into a glass, and added to it, from an inadequately closed plastic bottle, a small amount of mineral water, which she then realised was almost completely flat.

'Fuck,' she said, an oath which she very occasionally allowed herself when on her own, but absolutely only then. Pushing her glasses more firmly up on to the bridge of her nose, she set off up the stairs for her bedroom. 'Fuck,' she said again, relishing the sound of it on her lips.

She went to run her bath and, straightening up, caught sight of herself in the full-length mirror that hung on the bathroom wall. As she studied the image, a familiar weariness of heart came to her. She smoothed back her brown, dull hair with both hands, in an attempt to give herself a sleeker, more sophisticated look, and turned her head from side to side to assess the effect of it. Then she took off her glasses to check, for the millionth time in her life, what change it made in her appearance. She was as disappointed by the experiment as always. Taking off all her clothes, she threw them into a pile in the corner by the laundry basket, then bent down to turn off the taps, and stood facing the mirror once more.

One quite extraordinarily plain Scottish lady, she thought, and, for no particular reason, pinched and rubbed her nipples for a moment to make them stand out. Then she abandoned that, and gazed first at her almost completely flat breasts, then down across the white, curving belly towards the abundant pubic bush, and the thin, slightly bowing legs. Below them were the bony feet, with the toes bunched up, as they always had since early childhood. The toes contributed to her oddly staccato walk, much mimicked, as she knew, by succeeding generations of St Peter's schoolgirls, and she smiled at the thought of it.

Turning sideways to look at herself in profile, she saw yet again the pear shape of her body, accentuated now by her nakedness, and the consequent lack of that camouflage and enhancement that, when dressed, she had from the assistance of her brassiere. The nipples stood out from only the barest of hillocks; the stomach curved out and down to the pubic area in an abrupt and prominent swell; her buttocks, quite disproportionately large, sagged downwards towards the back of her inadequate, spindly thighs.

Miranda reached down for her glass, drank from it, and stood there for a moment more. Suddenly feeling emphatically more cheerful, she put her foot over the side of the bath to test the temperature, then climbed into it and lay there in the water, sinking her neck deep down to enjoy the pleasure of its warmth.

'Well, one's thing for sure,' she remarked to herself, as she so often did when she was alone, enjoyably and consciously speaking out loud, and by no means quietly. 'One thing's certain. It's not my body he's after.' And Miranda laughed, her contentment restored, and reached out for her wine glass. But found, to her irritation, that it was empty.

Chapter 21

Mariss Steiner looked over the centre aisle towards the cashier's desk. He saw that the Indian owner was preoccupied there talking to a customer, so he slipped the box of ginger cakes into the inside pocket of his overcoat, and went up to stand in line at the counter. He took a copy of the *Daily Telegraph* from the rack behind him, and opened it up to read the centre pages.

'Yes? Is that it?' said the Indian.

Steiner stuffed and scrumpled the newspaper back into its rack, and reached into his pockets to pay for the milk and the packet of sliced bread. He first laboriously checked and re-checked the change handed to him, then complained about the dirtiness of a five-pound note.

'Always you are complaining,' the old man replied. 'Always you are disagreeable. Now it's the change you don't like. Yesterday you wanted your money back on a can of soup you'd drunk already. A dent in its side! Last week you only noticed that all the eggs were broken when you got them home. The week before that the ginger cakes you bought were stale. What next tomorrow? What next?'

Normally Steiner would have responded at that point with a stream of invective, but the mention of ginger cakes rather put him off his stride, and in the circumstances he contented himself with no more than a single muttered insult. Then he snatched the white plastic bag from the counter and stumped off for the door, his dirty, oversized coat brushing against the face of a small child coming into the shop, whom he pushed out of the way with his walking stick.

Steiner was a familiar sight in Gloucester Terrace, with his grey head, the *yarmulke* on its crown, bending low over the stick on which he leant, and his overcoat, stained and long, hanging almost to the ground from his small, plump, arthritic figure. The coat flapped open as he walked, and when he raised his stick to stop the traffic at the intersection with Ranelagh Bridge, he revealed a dirty white cotton shirt, buttoned up neatly both at the sleeve and the neck, but half hanging out from his trousers. Pausing only to curse and wave his stick at a taxi-driver who had hooted at him, he continued on his way, and turned at last up the steps of the house where he had lived for the last thirty years. He walked in through the open front door, then straight across the hall, ignoring a squatting woman swabbing at the floor. His dirty footmarks trailed straight across the shining wet surface, but he made an abusive sign with his fingers at the woman's protests, and went on up the staircase to the bed-sitting room that he occupied on the top storey.

He kicked the door shut behind him, then put the milk into a tiny fridge standing on its own in the corner of the room. Dropping a loaf into a cardboard box by the sink, he picked up a crumpled white bag of biscuit fragments, and went to the window to scatter them outside on the sill. A pigeon immediately alighted and began to peck at them. Steiner stayed where he was, barely a foot away from the bird, his watery, red-rimmed eyes softening as he gazed at it. 'Ess gezunder heit!' he said in Yiddish, his voice soft and low. 'Feed well, my friend.'

He stood there for a moment longer. Below him were the railway lines, and he watched the familiar sight of a train straining to gather momentum as it pulled out from the goods yard of Paddington Station. The driver blew his horn and the pigeon flew away, so Steiner went over to the bed pressed up flush against the wall in the corner of the room, eased his way on to the grey army blanket, and lay flat on his back.

Reaching behind him, he fluffed up a grimy pillow to support his head and neck, and wriggled himself into it until he was satisfactorily comfortable. He fussed with the movement one more time, then picked at his teeth with a sharp, overgrown fingernail. Suddenly, he remembered the ginger cakes hidden away in the inside pocket of his overcoat. He reached in, took the box out and laid it on his stomach, then unwrapped and ate first one cake, and then another, the dark, rich crumbs falling into his grey beard, and down on to the lapels.

He gazed around the room, munching, liking what he saw. A single table stood in the middle, large enough only for the four wooden chairs which surrounded it. On it were piles of magazines and books and pages torn from newspapers. Under the table was a threadbare, mottled carpet, and the rest of the floor was covered by green linoleum, holed in places, and greasy with old dirt. A sofa stood against the wall opposite the bed, and draped over the back of that was a lace cloth, its original soft cream colour now darkened and coarsened with age into a dull brown. A gay magazine, folded open at the contacts page, lay on the seat of a small armchair. Beside the chair was a telephone, and beside that a large silver frame, holding a faded photograph of a family group in formal 1920s' pose. On the bottom corner of the frame was the inscribed name and address of the photographer – *Isaac Levronski, 33 Invaliden Strasse.* Next to the frame was a porcelain Star of David, and a large glass ashtray, overflowing with cigarette and cigar butts.

It was the walls, though, that gave the room its real character, such was the quantity of material attached to them. Photographs, newspaper clippings, registration forms, certificates, letters – the whole collection clinging together with shreds of adhesive tape, paper clips, drawing pins and picture hooks. In one corner, a magazine cutting had slipped from its position, and in doing so had partially dislodged several flimsy-looking sheets of paper, heavily lined and folded, torn from a notebook, as could be seen from the remains of the perforations along their top.

Noticing this, Steiner levered himself off the bed and restored all the material to its previous position. Then, tucking in the final sheet, he took from the pocket of his overcoat a small magnifying glass, and, securing it into the socket of his eye, he read what was there.

Tiny, compressed words were written in pencil, each line of text precisely utilising the minimum space available and succeeding, for there must have been as many as seven or eight hundred minuscule but painstakingly legible words written there.

Steiner read the script, his lips moving as he did so, then tucked the paper back once more on the wall, and turned back to the window. *'My God, my God, look upon me: why hast Thou forsaken me: and art so far from my health, and from the words of my complaint?'* he recited in a soft whisper, and continued on, from his memory, the text of the Twenty-Second Psalm.

'Our fathers hoped in Thee: they trusted in Thee, and Thou didst deliver them.

'They called upon Thee, and were holpen: they put their trust in Thee, and were not confounded.

'But be not Thou far from me, O Lord: Thou art my succour, haste Thee to help me.'

After a moment or two he paused, and took a long, pensive look at the sheets of paper he had pinned all over the walls.

'There are so many years gone, and so little done,' he muttered, and then, as he stood there, silent now, the telephone rang behind him.

'Mariss Steiner,' he barked in English, his accent and idiomatic fluency incongruously those of a middle-class, native-born, Gentile Londoner. Steiner had a parrot-like imitative ability with languages. After fifty years of living in England, what he had absorbed was the accent that he had selected for himself. To present himself as a middle-class, gentile Englishman was a good joke. It had stuck.

'Gareth,' he said. 'You said you would call, and you didn't. I tried your number several times and couldn't get a reply. I'm concerned that we don't leave things too late. You know that.'

He listened to what was said in response, then grimaced in irritation.

'No. I don't accept that. I want to move forward as fast as possible. We've fiddled about with it for too long, and actually done too little. I want us to meet again as soon as possible and agree a proper plan of action.'

For some moments he stood there listening, occasionally interrupting, once or twice vehemently and emphatically disagreeing. And then, replacing the receiver, he stood still and silent, staring without seeing at the trains coming and going from Paddington Station, his face dead-eyed in thought.

On most days Steiner would stay in bed until lunch-time, not so much from laziness, as because during the night he only slept fitfully, if at all. The pains in his stomach were at times almost unbearable, and they seemed the more intense in the night. It was also much warmer and more comfortable in his bed than outside it.

But today was summer, if a cool and windy example of it, and Steiner had slept comparatively well. It was barely a quarter past ten when he arrived at the corner store for his pint carton of milk and a packet of sliced processed cheese and some muffins. He had intended, in his usual fashion, to pay for the milk, and steal the cheese and the muffins, but the old man's grandson had made a point of following him shoulder to shoulder around the shop, stopping where he did, going wherever he went. Eventually, muttering, Steiner gave in, and limped up to the till. He paid for the goods, laboriously and insultingly counted the change that he was given, and went on his way, shuffling and tapping his way up the paper-blown, unswept street.

There were callers due that afternoon, but first there was the letter that he had written the previous evening to the Israeli Ambassador, denouncing a well-known London Jewish banking family as Palestinian spies. He had brought it with him rather than leave it in his room, where anyone who forced themselves into the place would be able to find it. It was all so many years ago now, the work with the CIA, but you never knew. Maybe someone still wanted to find out what he had in his possession. They'd be fools if they didn't. Most of the material in the files was relevant and up to date. Everything was still there, under the bed and on top of the wardrobe. Not the Agency's files, of course, since that search they did the day after they'd thrown him out, *and* confiscated two or three of his most precious little boxes . . . But since that time he had compiled new files for himself, put together from press cuttings and letters to and from various contacts and acquaintances of his. Some photographs, too. Very valuable for those who knew how to use them . . .

He turned into the hallway of his building, shouldering his way past an elderly woman struggling to lift her wheeled shopping basket down the front steps. The two of them exchanged ritualised insults, having been enemies from the day, twenty years before, when she had complained about the condition in which Steiner habitually left the bathroom that they shared with four other tenants from the floor below.

A pile of mail stood on the huge old radiator in the corner of the hall. Recognising the handwriting on one envelope, Steiner stuffed it in his overcoat pocket, then went off up the stairs. Checking, as every time, that the sliver of wood was still there undislodged in the doorjamb, he unlocked his door, threw the plastic carrier bag on to the unmade bed, then sat there and tore open the envelope. He read it through once, then got up to find his glasses, and went through it all over again.

There was no address on top of the letter, and no date, and the script was small and fine. The envelope had been slit open, then resealed with tape. Paperclipped to the top of the letter inside was a second note on a torn-off sheet of paper. It read:

Mariss,
If I could have faced climbing up your impossible staircase I would have done so, and pushed the letter under your door. Purposely dislodging that absurd wooden telltale you always set there, like a le Carré character, to show whether the great secrets you conceal in your disgusting room have been disturbed.

*To have gone up there myself to deliver the letter would certainly
have been more secure. But as I was arriving a few moments ago I
saw you going down the street, and guessed it was only to that corner
grocery store of yours. Just in case, I have been waiting for your return
in my car, parked on the other side of the street, from where I can see
the place where I have put this envelope out for you. I shall watch
you safely take it, before I drive away. To protect your security.
Although I have to say that I am not all that concerned about your
security in this affair one way or another. In fact, I would welcome
a good, old-fashioned leak, before any real harm is done. Only some
vestiges of loyalty and affection for you prevent me from leaking the
whole business myself. I'm not sure I would know what I was leaking
I suppose. But it would certainly be for the best.*
    Lewis

The main letter it was attached to consisted of four, tightly written
sheets.

Dear Mariss,
*Some friends we share in Vienna thought it right to tell me of your
recent interest in Joseph Hermann. You've been making enquiries
about his movements and other specific details and I'm worried about
that, and they are too.*
    *I've known for some time what Amos Bronowski has been pre-
paring, and I admire him for it. It should have been done before.
Those of my sources who have seen his work – and I shall myself, very
shortly – tell me that it's been carried out with such thoroughness and
accuracy of detail that the consequences of exposure will be severe.
Bronowski is a tenacious opponent. Those in his sights may well be
greatly uncomfortable.*
    *And so, Mariss, what is it that you want? What more are you
looking to discover that Bronowski has not already found? What could
you possibly be up to?*
    *There are certain specific rumours that I have heard in connection
with you in recent days that cause me great disquiet.*
    *If it's violence that you're after, if it's mischief and barbarism
that you're after, then you're wrong in it. And you're evil in it,
and you're cursed in it, and I despair for you, and I despair for
those with you, whoever they are . . .*
    *Unless you're on your own, I suppose. Because, my dear Mariss,
and thank God that it's so, you're wholly incapable of yourself
completing an action of that sort and complexity. Totally incapable.*

*You always have been. You bungle everything. You even bungle being
a survivor of the concentration camps. Mariss, we're the heroes of
the world, we camp survivors, if we play our cards correctly. We're
the innocent victims of the world's greatest atrocity. Everyone is
instinctively on our side. But you even bungle that, you clown. You
even bungle being a Buchenwald survivor.*

*Forget about any more battles, Mariss. Live your life out now in
peace. I do. I get on with all the other things that have to be done, and
I carry my memories with me, as much as you carry yours with you.
All of us who were there in the camps do so. How else could it be?*

*But your sort of fight is over now. I accepted that fact years ago,
and with a lightness of heart. I never believed in any of it in the first
place. It was a game. A young man's game. Revolution and tribal
revenge and all those other team sports are fun to play around with
when you're that age, but only as an alternative to football. Then one
gets on with one's life. And that's what you must do. Even now, it's
not too late.*

*Bronowski has it right. If at your age you still want to spend your
life hauling over the past, and personally I don't, then his approach is
the correct one, and the civilised one. Violence, Mariss, is the answer
to absolutely nothing whatsover. Leave it alone. You'd make a mess
of it anyway.*
With – I suppose – my love,
    Lewis.

Steiner put Lewis Cohen's letter down on the table, and went over
to the single window to gaze at the railway tracks below, as he so
often did when he wanted to think.

For a moment he thought he was going to cry. He was a man
accustomed to being an outsider, and these days he presented
himself quite deliberately in that mode. His clothes, his aggression,
his anarchic contempt for convention . . . it was how he lived. He
never these days sought out friendship, and he was suspicious
and resentful of courtesies. But Lewis Cohen . . . a letter like that
from him. He hadn't seen him for six years. A letter like that from
him . . .

Steiner watched the trains. They calmed him. They quietened his
soul. Thinking of Lewis Cohen quietened his soul, if it came to that,
though he would never even hint at the fact of that to him direct.
Not after their last conversation together.

Chapter 22

The street in which Lewis Cohen lived was expensive, quiet, and conservative, and his neighbours were all wealthy and well-placed people. Of those of his background, it was only Cohen who had forced his life through to a position of such standing in the London community, and the house he had bought was a statement of this.

The two decades that had passed since he set up the new partnership with his friends had gone well for them. The firm remained small, but their clients were enviably exclusive. Cohen himself was a Trustee of a London museum, and had become a conspicuous donor to the better known Jewish charities. He was also the Founder and Chairman of a substantial and growingly admired charitable Foundation. He appeared to the world these days to be a distinguished and accomplished man, and for that very reason Steiner would normally have despised and dismissed him as an establishment *poseur*, and done whatever he could to denigrate him. But Steiner, despite himself, was rather proud of Cohen. He was rude about him behind his back, but the malice, most of the time, was only skin-deep.

These days, however, their lives could hardly have been spent more apart. Steiner calculated it once more. It had indeed been fully six years since he and Lewis Cohen had last spoken. Some time before that there had been a difficult little scene in Cohen's office when Steiner had arrived there one day unannounced. Following this, he had been instructed not to go there again. Most unusually, if briefly, he had done what he had been told, primarily because his energies had been diverted at that moment to a personal hounding of a Jewish politician rumoured to have been involved in a child abuse case in a boys' orphanage. But soon that was all over, and the tabloids engaged in something else, and Cohen was back in Steiner's mind. Particularly because Steiner decided that he was being followed and watched, and suspected that Cohen had something to do with it. So it had been a peculiar pleasure to disobey Cohen's instructions and make a call to his office. Cohen had not been there to take it, but his assistant had telephoned back some hours later, inviting Steiner to go to Cohen's house that evening, if the matters he wanted to discuss really were as urgent as he had insisted.

He had slept heavily and pleasantly that afternoon, the evening was fine, and, by the time he arrived in St John's Wood, Steiner's truculence had dissipated into a mood of soft nostalgia – bonhomie, almost. But, to justify the visit, he tried to sustain some simulation of anger as he clumped his way through the hall. Cohen's young daughter emerged from a side room to say something to her father, but Steiner pushed, glowering, straight past her, and into the drawing room at the end of the corridor, standing in wait for Cohen to follow him in there.

'For the love of God, Mariss,' said Cohen as he joined him, softly closing the door on his daughter, 'you have a genius for histrionics. Whatever it is you've come here for, quieten down. Now, have a drink and tell me what it is.'

He took Steiner by the elbow, and placed him in an armchair. Pulling an ottoman out from the wall, he sat there in front of him, his eyes calm and amused, waiting. Steiner stared at him, then shrugged, and fiddled around with his stick.

'You're having me followed, Lewis,' he burst out finally. 'I've been aware of it for the last few days. You did it before, and you've done it again. I recognised that lad of yours from the office. He's been at my heels every time I step out of the door. He's following me everywhere. What's going on? What do you want? Why don't you leave me alone?'

There was a silence for a few moments, then Cohen replied, 'He's not so much following you as protecting you. That's all it is. Someone to watch over you.'

Steiner looked at him, and had difficulty in maintaining his semblance of anger. The comfort of the room, and the Jewishness of it, and the sound of the child's laughter from upstairs, and Cohen's familiar, soothing voice – all this served to calm him, and please him. But it was too soon to show any of that.

'What nonsense is that?' he said. 'Protecting me from whom? And what?'

Cohen got up from the ottoman, and without asking Steiner what he would like, poured him a glass of whisky and soda from a silver drinks tray on the other side of the room, and came back to hand it to him. There was the compliment of intimacy in this – pure Lewis, Steiner thought. Pure charm. But he reached immediately for the drink, and downed it in one draught.

'Protecting me from what, Lewis?' he repeated. 'From things that go bump in the night? From Syrian assassins? From Assad's hit men?'

Cohen smiled, and glanced at his watch. 'One or two of the Jewish establishment perhaps are on some sort of list of marked men. Not you I think, Mariss, although I'm sure you'd like to be. But that's not why I was looking after you.'

He stared down into the drink he held in his own hand, still untouched, and swirled it gently. Then he said, 'I was protecting you from yourself, Mariss. I wasn't sure if you knew, but Herbert von Karajan has just been in London on a private visit, staying at Claridge's. He was here for about a week, before flying back to Vienna today at noon. I awoke one night a few days before he was due to arrive, and thought of you, and remembered that rumour some years ago that you were planning some sort of personal violence against him. I didn't want to run any risks of that sort whatsoever – as much for your sake as von Karajan's. Probably more so.' He shrugged. 'I made sure that it wouldn't happen.'

'How did *you* know that von Karajan was in London?' Steiner asked suspiciously. 'I thought you said it was an entirely private visit.'

Cohen hesitated. Then: 'I can tell you precisely how I knew. My firm acts for him. One of my partners gives him legal assistance on certain matters here in England. I've met von Karajan. I know him. In fact, I know him rather well.'

Steiner stared at him, complete incredulity on his face.

'*What*? What did you say? You're a Jewish firm, and you act for a man who was a registered member of the Nazi party? A Jewish firm and you—'

Cohen held up his hand to stop him. 'Wait a minute now, Mariss. Hold still. First, we're *not* a Jewish firm. We are five partners, who work together in rather specialist areas out of a sense of common respect for our mutual abilities in the law. We enjoy each other's company, and we respect each other's abilities, and we have formed ourselves into a partnership. As it happens, four of us are of Jewish birth, and one is not.

'I don't think of my firm as being Jewish or not Jewish, or our clients either. I'm proud to be a Jew, and I know the responsibility I bear because of it. Just as you do, although we look at it in rather different ways. But my work takes me into a wider world than that. I'm an Englishman now, a leading practitioner of English law. My partners and I take the cream of all the work that is offered us. Of course my partners and I accepted Herbert von Karajan as a client! He is a considerable international figure. My firm was naturally delighted to accept his invitation to act for him and to advise him.'

'Have you lost your senses, Lewis?' Steiner asked him simply.

'I've explained it to you,' Cohen said. 'I've told you what I feel.'

Pink in the face, Steiner started to interrupt once more, but Cohen raised his hand to stop him.

'No, Mariss. Listen to me. I repeat – we are *not* a Jewish law firm. We're simply a law firm. As and when more partners are brought in, it'll be a matter of complete indifference whether they're Jewish or not. We'll simply take the best. I know you must find that difficult to believe. And even more difficult to accept. But it's true.'

Steiner frowned, and shook his head. Then he started on the extended business of finding his stick, and pushing and heaving himself upright on it, and standing there to gather his breath before setting off for the door. Cohen got up to help him, and put his hand under his elbow. But instead of leading him back into the hall, he took Steiner across the room, and around the corner to the formal dining room which adjoined it through a great pair of double doors.

There a mahogany Victorian writing table was pushed up against the window, and Cohen reached down to pull out a file from its centre drawer. Undoing the ribbon tie he opened the file, searched amongst its contents for some moments, then laid down on the surface of the table a fading snapshot of two young men. They were smiling broadly at the camera, arms around each other's shoulders, their short-sleeved shirts wide open at the neck, their baggy trousers and heavy shoes and the ambience of the scene suggesting a summer afternoon's walking in the country, and pints of beer and hunks of cheese afterwards in a village pub.

'The South Downs, if I remember correctly,' said Cohen. 'Our hiking holiday – about 1955, I suppose. That would make us both about twenty-five.' He smiled at Steiner, and pointed down at his stick. 'And fit and healthy,' he said. 'Not a twinge of arthritis between us.'

He picked the photograph up, and looked at it more carefully under the evening light from the window.

'Do you remember those short-sleeve shirts we always wore in the summer, Mariss, so that the camp tattoo marks on our arms would be sure to be seen? The famous blue numbers. Sitting there together at pub tables with our sleeves pushed up well above the left elbow, so that everyone could see. Do you remember that, Mariss?'

Steiner took the photograph from him, and held it close to his eyes, squinting one of them to give him better focus. He stared at it for a minute or so, saying nothing. Then he gave it back to Cohen, and wiped his nose with the back of his hand.

'Of course I remember,' he grunted. 'That's why I'm here tonight. That's why I was angry with you.'

'And that's why we were watching over you, Mariss,' Cohen cut in immediately. 'If you'd tried to reach or damage von Karajan you would have landed yourself into considerable trouble. I didn't want that to happen.'

Cohen put the photograph back into the file, retied the ribbon, and pushed the drawer shut. Then he steered Steiner through the dining room, and back the way they had come towards the front door. As they passed through the hall, they could hear from the floor above them the sound of the child once again, and a woman's voice calling something or other out, and then her laughter too.

Cohen opened the front door, and the two men stood together on the doorstep, gazing out into the warm summer night. He slipped his arm through Steiner's once more, and left it there for a moment.

'I'm sorry life has turned out the way it has, Mariss. That photograph of the pair of us together, and the memories of all that period in our lives. And now . . . and now . . .'

'You in your law firm,' said Steiner. 'You in your non-Jewish, only-the-cream, international law firm. The famous giver to the smarter Jewish charities of course, just so no one can say that you're trying to run away from your people. And you haven't actually changed your name from Cohen to Cowan or Coney or one of those tricks. But when you were young . . .'

He started to make his hesitant, groping way down the steps, free now of Cohen's hand. When safely on the pavement he turned, and for a moment stood there still, looking up again, staring back at Cohen.

'In your early days you looked as if you would be such a leader,

101

he said. 'When we were all young. But it never turned to much, did it?' He hitched his trousers up, and flicked with his stick at a stone that lay in front of him on the pavement. 'It hasn't been true for years. You showed me that photograph as a way of patronising me. The great man and his roots. That's all it was. That's all you feel. Do you know something? You've been married for twenty years, and I've never even met your wife. Do you call that friendship?'

Steiner turned, and started to make his way up the road towards the underground station, tapping and prodding at the pavement with his stick as he went. Cohen called after him, offering a lift in his car, but he neither turned, nor made any other response.

He either failed to hear me, or he affected not to. Probably the latter, thought Cohen, as he shut the door and went off to find his daughter.

Chapter 23

Professor Hermann was tired, and the pain of the arthritis in his wrist and fingers had finally defeated him after the two or three hours he had spent that evening working at his desk. But outside in the quadrangle he could hear groups of students laughing and chattering in the fading light, and he went limping across to his window to watch them.

He was so familiar a sight up at the window that the students would glance up automatically as they passed below, as if casting their eyes up to Mount Rushmore. It had become a joke, and he knew it, but it was where he wanted to be. He liked to stand there looking out at the young people together. This was the new generation. This was the future.

These days, Hermann was so remote from the real action of the University that few of the students knew him, and fewer still with any intimacy. Hermann had taught very little over the last two or three years; partly because of increasing deafness, and partly also because of a persistent, deadening fatigue, of which no medical practitioner seemed able to diagnose the cause. But, most of all, because he didn't have very much choice in the matter. Pupils were being eased away from him. He had made too many enemies amongst the younger generation of the University staff. Hermann's world – Buchenwald, Communist leadership as a very young man, austerity, astringent economic and political didacticism – all that had slipped away out of fashion and out of mind. He was persistent and unrelenting and unchangeable in his views and his teaching, and the new men couldn't see the point of him.

Their chance came on his seventieth birthday, five years before. A statutory retirement age was suddenly invented, and Hermann was pushed on his way. His Chair of modern political and economic history went, without his advice or his blessing, to a man in his thirties whose work Hermann thought very little of. His papers and books had become difficult to publish, and infrequently reviewed.

His career, once so publicly renowned, was fading away into indifference.

He'd been thirty-four when he'd arrived there in 1953 – a famously contentious figure, with his political past as a Communist cast in the sharpest relief in the light of his towering prominence at Buchenwald. The appointment to the University lectureship was the subject of what might well have been a vigorous and probably unpleasant public debate, were it not for the fact that in Austria in those early post-War years there was a certain reticence in publicly stating any opinion that might be taken as anti-Semitic. In any case the appointment was made, and the flow of papers and articles and books began. He made enemies then, as he had before, and continued to do. He was a humourless man, rigorously ethical, direct to the point of cruelty in his assessment of others' work. It was easy enough to admire him, but not to like him.

Shortly before his enforced retirement there was a scandal of sorts, or so the popular press decided it to be, when a young student of his committed suicide. Three weeks before, Hermann had expelled her from the University for plagiarism in one of her weekly tutorial essays. He appeared to the world to be entirely unmoved by the criticism of him that followed. Indeed, he was so dumbfounded, not by the views of the Press, for which he had contempt, but by those of some of his colleagues. He was sorry for the girl, he supposed, but she was a moral lightweight, and her behaviour was beneath contempt. That sort of thing could never be condoned. Allow it once, and the floodgates opened.

Eventually, the dust from that had settled, though the effect of it was to confirm Hermann yet more firmly in his isolation. But that didn't matter. His mind was full of something else. His Foundation. The Joseph Hermann Foundation.

For many years he had secretly helped to channel private and public charity to needy Jewish families within the new Communist nation states of Europe. Now, best of all, he had established this Foundation, in his own name, with capital sufficient to provide in perpetuity scholarships for Jewish students from the old Communist bloc countries to read for their degrees at Cambridge and Harvard.

Hermann Scholars. In time to be as renowned and as numerous as Rhodes Scholars. Hand-selected by Joseph Hermann himself, for the remaining days of his life, and then, no doubt, by a distinguished committee. *Hermann Scholars. The Joseph Hermann Foundation. The Herman Prize*, perhaps, in due course. The final seal of achievement on Professor Hermann's life.

Chapter 24

Miranda was already in her bath and just drifting off to sleep, when she awoke with a start to hear the hammering of the front doorknocker.

Cursing, and calling out that she would be right down, she dried herself in a rush, put on a towelling robe, and started for the stairs. Then, halfway, she suddenly had the sensation of being uncomfortably exposed, so dashed back up to her room again to put on some underclothes underneath.

In her embarrassment at the delay, she took no more than a perfunctory glance through the spy glass before opening the front door. But even the mere second it took for her hand to release the latch was enough for her to realise that it was Bronowski there on the doorstep. His appearance, after so many years, was an immediate shock. Miranda had retained in her memory an image of what he had looked like as a young man, but Amos was fifty-six now, and he had not aged well. It was the thin mouth, and the intent, chestnut-brown eyes that she had immediately recognised. But the skin of his neck and cheeks was tired and flabby, and the nose, once so sharp and high-boned and proud, was now thickened and coarse. His hair was grey, and his shoulders stooped. Bronowski looked unwell, and he looked old.

Miranda forced a smile of welcome on to her face, and realised in doing so that the brightness of it came from compassion, which was the last emotion she had expected to feel. She wasn't frightened of him at all now that he was here on her doorstep. She was sorry for him.

Realising that she had clutched her dressing robe around her so tight that she appeared to be in fear of assault, she stared at him, unable for a moment to say any word at all. Then she realised how awkward her gesture must appear, particularly to Bronowski, with his contempt of old for her lack of physical confidence. So she released her fingers and smiled again. But it wouldn't hold, and the pity for him faded as she became accustomed to the change in his appearance and demeanour. Charity had given way, at least for the moment, to caution. Don't let me chatter too much, she thought. Don't let me make a mess of this.

But, for all that, Miranda found she was mouthing a banal phrase of welcome as she ushered Bronowski into the kitchen, irritated that he should have caught her so unprepared. She hated the business of dressing gowns and unrouged mouths and open necks and bare legs and exposed bodies. But she was beginning to calm down now. She offered him a drink, and went to pour it.

Bronowski said nothing while all this was happening, but sat at the table as she talked, leaning back in his chair. His gaze had an odd lack of concentration and focus in it, and she wondered if it was possible that he felt as nervous as she did, for all his persistence in coming to her house unannounced. But then he gestured to the chair opposite, and Miranda immediately sat there, knowing she was doing it out of curiosity rather than subservience. Those other days were past. Tonight she would pretend respect and obedience to his male dominance in these trivial ways, if that's what he wanted, but she would do so simply out of good manners. Bronowski's edge had gone. His power had gone. He had become an ageing and weakened man. So she sat down as she was bade, and waited for him to say his first substantive words to her.

'Miranda – I came here tonight because it's the only way to break the ice between us. I can understand why you feel awkward to see me. I feel a little awkward too. But my belief is that we're still, in our hearts, man and wife. Neither of us has ever married anyone else. The divorce was meaningless. Neither of us even bothered to attend the hearing. The marriage was what mattered. It certainly mattered to me. I think it mattered to you as well.'

He made an attempt at a laugh, as if his comment had been a joke, then held his hands open for a moment in a gesture she remembered well.

'It was my fault that it was lost,' he said. 'We both know that. Well, I want to make it good for both of us, before it's too late. The years roll on, and one day it *will* be too late. It isn't yet. That's partly why I've come here to England.'

He stared at her. Even his voice had changed, thought Miranda. His words of love, if that was what they were, meant so little to her at that moment that her mind was more occupied by the difference in his accent since he had lived abroad, and the balance of his pitch. It was higher than she remembered it. Less masculine, perhaps.

'Of course I'm glad to see you, Amos.' Out the words came, in a rush of nervousness. 'I tried to stop you from coming here, because it's too late for us to be together again, and that was apparently what you wanted. But now you're here, I'm glad to see you. And of course the marriage mattered to me, brief as it was. But it's over now. Absolutely over.'

She shrugged, and smiled brightly at him, wondering whether her statement had been too definitive and unkind. Oddly, she noticed that there was irony in Bronowski's eyes now, or so she thought. Inexplicably, he seemed to be amused.

She got up from her chair, then went over to the open bottle of wine on the dresser, and poured herself another glass. Her voice was thickening a little now with the amount that she had drunk, and she knew how Bronowski would despise that, and told herself only to sip at it until he had gone.

Then Bronowski said: 'I'm here because I need you, Miranda. You're still my wife, and I need you.'

And every time you say that word, Miranda thought, a knife goes through me. Guilt, perhaps. Nostalgia, possibly. Pure sentimentality, most likely of all. But whatever happened, you were the only man who ever loved me.

His hand was moving slowly across the table towards her; slowly, but confidently. And on his hand was a wedding ring – their wedding ring, for the love of God! She'd put hers away years ago. He still had his. He was wearing their ring.

Her hand was resting there on the table, and his was approaching it. But just as he reached her she jumped up, her arms wrapped tight around her chest once more. Bronowski got to his feet as well, and she noticed for the first time the hint of a limp in his movement as he went over to open the latch of the door.

'We're a family, Miranda, you and I,' he said quietly. 'We're husband and wife – we always will be. These things are set by God. They're inescapable.'

He raised his hand, and walked out into the street. When Miranda went up to her bedroom to look from the window, she was in time for only one final glimpse of him before he was gone, around the corner into Moore Park Road, the light from the street-lamp pooling down on to his head.

He talks of us being a family, she thought. He doesn't realise how much of a family we could have been. He never saw his son. He never even knew Michael existed.

She knew Bronowski would come round again. He was there shortly before ten o'clock the next evening, and Miranda, shaking with nerves in the anticipation of his arrival, was in the kitchen working on a great pile of first-form essays. She hardly greeted him as he came through the door, this time the chatter quite gone from her. She waved him to a chair, went into the sitting room to fetch the newspaper, put it in front of him and asked him to read it for a few minutes while she finished what she was doing.

He pretended to read, and skimmed one or two pages while watching her at work, writing comments in the margins in red ink with her neat, firm hand, biting at her lower lip in her attempt at concentration.

In a quarter of an hour or so she had finished. 'Clever children, on the whole,' she said. 'I love having the first go at the new girls each year. They're always the same. I'm able to fill up their minds with all my own views before anyone else has a chance to get their hands on them.' She stopped at that, and bit her lip.

'I'm not surprised you're suspicious of me, Miranda. Fearing traps and all the rest of it. But there really is nothing there. I want you back. I'm feeling older, and I miss you, and I want you back. That's all there is, and it's what I've been saying to you in my letters all the time over the last few months.'

She looked down at the last essay in the pile, still there on the table before her, and said, 'You know what I feel, and it's hardly surprising, is it? I don't even know what you're really doing in London. I feel uncomfortable about that. There you are, staying at Gareth Edel's house, and I feel that whatever it is you're planning, it's a plot against me somehow.'

'I'll tell you why I'm here in England,' Bronowski said. 'I've completed the research which I've been working on for the last few years – on the concentration camps, and particularly on Buchenwald. I'm at the point of releasing it. It's going to be a considerable moment. There are some important revelations in the material. The *Sunday Times* will be running it. It feels . . . it feels like the closing of a circle.'

There was a silence. Then, 'So that's why you're here,' she said.

'Yes. That's why I'm here,' he replied, and gazed at her. 'But there's the other reason too. I've told you what it is. I want you back. I want you to be with me now. And I'm here now, and I'm telling you that in person.'

She placed the final essay back on the pile with the others, and said imploringly, 'For God's sake, Amos. For the love of God . . .'

'Yes,' he said, and they looked at each other.

Don't fantasise, panicked Miranda. No man has shown the slightest interest in you for years. Say it to yourself: *It's not really possible that he could want me still.*

And Miranda knew that the expression in her eyes had changed; the old panic and alarm had come back into them, and her confidence had gone. And the tears were there now too, and she must hold them back. No tears in front of Amos, of all people. For God's sake – no tears.

He was looking at her too, and he frowned as he saw her eyes. Then he stood and, so quickly that she had no time to protest, he picked her up like a child, and walked with her to the stairs. As they went her eyes were tight shut and her mouth clenched and her arms and her body were shaking.

Bronowski laid her down on her bed. Thank God, oh thank God, the lights were out and it was dark and he wouldn't be able to look at her. Her hands spasmed into tight fists as she allowed her dress to be pulled off over her head, and her underclothes eased away.

Chapter 25

At last Edel crossed the street and went towards his house, feeling in his inside pocket for the key. For the last few minutes he had been standing watching Amos Bronowski through the window. He was arguing with someone, gesticulating and stabbing at the air, but his posture had lost its arrogance and its bearing, and he looked . . . well, *petulant*, Edel thought. In his youth, Amos had been famously daunting to those who didn't know him well. That could no longer be so.

It was Mariss Steiner there with him in the room, Edel saw, and went on through the little hall. This was the third or fourth time since Bronowski had arrived from Canada that Steiner had come around to Alexandra Villas, and each time he was hardly in the door before the two of them had started quarrelling.

'That's not what's going to happen,' Amos was saying emphatically. 'What you suggest is insane! The work's done, I'm in a position now to bring these people down, and that's exactly what I'm going to do. I'll expose them. Print a public account of what they did. They'll be destroyed by that, which is what I intend. They'll be destroyed by contempt. As for pursuing people around the world with machine guns, or whatever absurd nonsense you suggest, Mariss, I don't need to, do I? I've got them where I want them. There'll be no violence, or any of that. It wouldn't do the job anyway. Violence creates martyrs. It's *contempt* that destroys. And ridicule. I want these people destroyed. *We* want them destroyed.'

Edel had sat himself down in the corner by the window, but now he got up to go into the kitchen. He took an iced bottle of Stolichnaya from the fridge, three little glasses from a row of several that were stacked in the freezer to frost, and then put them all on a tray and carried them back into the sitting room as Steiner was replying.

'You don't have the same dreams, Amos. Or rather nightmares,

110

I should say. Of corpses, thousands of corpses. I remember exactly how it was. I was a boy, and I slept amongst those corpses.'

Edel poured the vodka into the three glasses, then handed one each to Bronowski and Steiner, both of whom took them from him without acknowledgement. Steiner threw back his head, downed his immediately in one swift draught, and continued.

'And other matters too. I have an exact recall. I remember the precise colour of the eyes of the *Kapo* who pushed an old man beside me down to the ground, and kicked him as he lay there. I remember those eyes more clearly than I can picture my own, or anybody else's. I remember their exact colour, and their exact shape, and the way the eyebrows met above them.'

Bronowski was silent for a moment, then lowered himself into a chair opposite Steiner. He said, 'I know about your memories, Mariss. You were older than Gareth and me, and that makes a difference. We were just small kids, and you were a teenage boy. I know what you must have been through. What you understood. The responsibility you took. I can imagine that. Your suffering was of a different order to ours. Gareth and I were just . . .'

He shrugged, and looked across at Edel, then back again to Steiner.

'Look, Mariss. There are no secrets between us. You know how long it's taken me to get this research done, and the evidence all into place. Hermann's visit to London gives us the perfect opportunity to run the story. Join me: we'll do it all together. I haven't finished with this. You know so much, and could introduce me to new material. Forget all these blood and thunder dreams of violence. Come and help me. *Please.*'

Steiner put his empty glass down on the floor beside him, then staggered his way upright, leaning heavily on his stick, and dabbing at his forehead with a crumpled, filthy handkerchief. He smiled at them both, his small yellowing teeth showing disconcertingly clearly against the red of his lips.

'I agree,' he said, his accent suddenly that of a cringing, stagey Shylock. Edel looked up alertly, wondering what he was about. 'Of course I agree,' he went on. 'How could I do anything else? We all have the same objectives – how could they be different after the experiences the three of us have shared? The same objectives, the same quarry, the same hunt. How could it be different?'

Edel watched Steiner carefully as he limped towards the door, then got to his feet to help him. Bronowski remained where he was, his hands still deep in his pockets, and his face now frowning in thought.

Edel opened the front door for Steiner to leave the house. 'Work with me, Mariss,' Bronowski called out after him. 'I'm so nearly there. Work with me, not against me, and there's so much more we can achieve!'

But although he could hear Steiner's chuckle as he was helped out into the road, Amos could distinguish no more than a few words of what he said to Edel before he struggled off up the cul-de-sac, retracing the way he had come, back past The Princess of Wales and on through the dingy little Edwardian side streets towards Chiswick High Road.

Chapter 26

Jacob Bergdorf looked across the café table at the young man, and smiled.

'Don't take it too hard, Bernie. It's best that you know these things, so that you can mourn your father properly. I know what a private, dignified man he was, and we all loved him for that. He would never talk about his Buchenwald years at all, although there was so much pain in him that it would have been better if he had. The same applies to all of us. Those memories are too dreadful to coop up inside. We need to talk so that it's all released. Your father needed that as much as any of us.'

Bernie Levinstein nodded his handsome head in agreement. Bergdorf watched him, and thought, as he had in the past, how like the young Gary Cooper the boy was in profile. Darker of course, but there was the actor's fullness and curve in his lower lip. And the eyelashes too, he noticed, were long and lush as Cooper's had been, and as pretty. But there the resemblance ended. The hair, of course, in its modish ponytail, but it was more than that. Instead of gentleness, and calm resolve, however contrived the actor's persona might have been, one saw in young Levinstein an intelligence of a sort certainly, and resolve, but something else too. Corruption? Psychotic tendencies? Levinstein was dangerous, and that was for sure. Loyal in his way – Bergdorf was convinced of that – but dangerous and unpleasant. And one hundred per cent suited to the rôle that Bergdorf had devised for him.

He waved at the waiter for his bill, then leant across the table and patted Levinstein on the arm. 'Enjoy the rest of your stay in Vienna. Put all this behind you. You look so disturbed that it makes me wonder now if I was wise to have told you these things. But I wanted you to come to terms with your father's past. I know what you meant to each other. I loved him like a brother, and . . . I wanted you to realise what he had been through. And the burden he carried with him.'

Levinstein withdrew his arm, and brushed at his sleeve. 'Yes, well, we must do something about it, mustn't we? My father was a fool. He should've told me about it. We should've sorted this one out a long time ago. But it's not too late. I'll fix the old bastard now. In Dad's memory.'

Bergdorf shook his head, and allowed a wise, dignified smile to cross his features.

'Now Bernie, we must have no more violence. What's past is past. It wasn't only Joseph Hermann who was involved. There were thousands of Communists at Buchenwald.'

'But he was the leader, wasn't he, Mr Bergdorf?' Levinstein cut in. 'The Communists ran the Infirmary, so Hermann himself had control over it. And now you tell me that my father was one of the people that Hermann put up for the test inoculation programme. He may have seemed lucky to survive, as most of them died, but it was only to go through years of pain and illness because of it. Well, that's enough for me. Hermann's a cunt. And when I see him I'll tell him so. Shortly before I—'

Bergdorf put on an appearance of emphatic disapproval.

'No more talk like that, Bernie, if you please. Hermann has had a most distinguished career, whatever he may or may not have been at Buchenwald. I simply wanted you to know what a brave man your father was, and what he had been through, then to put it behind you, and move on. We all have to know the past, and understand the past, and then let it rest. For the good of us all. What's done is done. Goodbye, Bernie. Thank you for coming all this way to see me.' He shook Levinstein's hand, gave him a reassuring, paternal smile and went on his way.

That did the trick, he thought, and congratulated himself on his subtlety. All that sentimental twaddle about that old woman of a father of his. But it did what it was supposed to do. He's a most unpleasantly vicious young man, and it certainly did the trick.

Chapter 27

Miranda looked across the classroom, saw that the members of her adult literacy class were all bent over their desks in concentration, and wondered if it was yet time. Glancing around once more, to be certain that no one was watching her, she looked quickly at her watch, then pulled her sleeve down again over it. She would never had dared to do this if the class had been observing her, for she was always conscious of her responsibility to appear to them as the enthusiastic, unpaid, volunteer friend and helpmate. One hint that she was bored by them, and all the good work and the months of her time and patience would be spoilt and lessened in their eyes. She knew that. But she'd never known one of these Friday evening classes to go as slowly as this one had tonight. Never.

Eight thirty-two now, and still almost a quarter of an hour to go. She could break off in five minutes or so, with the excuse of a headache or something like that, but these people knew her so well that they wouldn't believe her, and would be hurt, and puzzled, and fearful of her disapproval and lack of interest.

So Miranda shook her head to clear her mind, and got up from her desk, and went to walk around the room. She usually did this anyway in the last part of the class; leaning over each desk in turn, correcting the spelling, straightening the handwriting, reading out again aloud, word by pedantic word, the simple text of the story that the class were attempting to précis.

'Well done, Miss Webster,' she said. 'Well done. I'm so pleased for you. That really is so *very* much better. You can manage so much more than you could even a month or so ago. You must be absolutely delighted.'

And as Miranda laid her hand in comfort, for that is what it was, on the scrawny, sharp little shoulder of the fifty-year-old spinster, she hoped that Miss Webster was not calculating the same mental arithmetic as she was. For if it was going to take a month of Miss Webster's fading life for her to master – what? – ten or twelve more simple single syllable words, then the best that she could achieve in her remaining lifespan, before the cancer in her bowel finished her, was just enough literacy to perhaps have a chance of tackling competently a four-year-old's first reading book.

Cat. Mat. Cup. Dog. Ball. Bat.

Dad. Mum.

Miranda's stomach turned and she looked back at Miss Webster. If she could have reached her without the histrionics of stepping back to do so, she would have laid her hand on her shoulder once more, and tried again to reach her in her loneliness.

For the *Dad* and the *Mum* were the point of it all, Miranda thought. Miss Webster, in her fear of dying, was as a little girl once more; a crippled, inadequate child, reaching out across the years to her dead parents, her cry to them the terminal shriek of a wild animal caught in the meshed jaws of a man trap, its life ebbing and pulsing away.

'Miss Webster . . .' she began, and then could think of nothing more to follow with, and no words of succour, and she stood gazing at her, her heart full of a sudden wave of pity. After a moment she shrugged, and smiled, and said, 'Miss Webster. It's all right. Good luck, Miss Webster. It's been such a privilege . . .'

And, as Miranda turned away, she knew that the tears running now down her face were the tears not only of compassion for a dying, inadequate middle-aged woman she barely knew, but for herself too. It suddenly felt all too much. Everything for too long had been held back and retained. There was too much pain in her. Too much longing for what might have been. Too much grief. Too much loneliness. Too much loss. Too much love.

Chapter 28

A week or so later, back in London, Bernie Levinstein phoned Bergdorf in Vienna.

The older man had given him a false name to use if he needed to contact him and he'd done so, not realising that the number he had rung was Bergdorf's home. He was so taken aback when Bergdorf's wife picked up the telephone that he nearly forgot his instructions, and stuttered so oddly that he was obliged to repeat the name twice, sounding embarrassingly unconvincing each time.

'Mr Elliott?' Bergdorf said. Levinstein heard the mouthpiece being muffled, presumably by Bergdorf's hand, as an instruction was given to someone or other, and then he came through once more, this time loud and clear. 'I'm so sorry to keep you. What a surprise, Mr Elliott! And what can I do for you?'

Levinstein felt his confidence flow back in him again at the juvenile duplicity of it all.

'You told me to ring you on this number if I had any more questions to ask after our conversation in Vienna the other day,' he began smoothly. 'Well, I do have. Not a question to ask, but something to report. A really strange coincidence has occurred. Do you know a Mariss Steiner?'

'Steiner . . . Mariss Steiner. Yes, I remember him very well indeed. I haven't seen him for many years, I'm afraid, but certainly I recall him. What about the fellow?'

'Well, he got in touch with me,' Bernie said. 'Why me, I've no idea, because I hardly know him at all. My father did, but that's hardly a sufficient reason for what happened next. He rang me, said who he was, and asked me to get him a gun – as if I was a fucking arms dealer. And you know what? He told me why he wanted it, too, as bold as brass, right there on the telephone. He said he wanted it to kill Hermann. And could I make sure I got it to him in good time for Hermann's visit to London in two and a half weeks' time. The man's a fucking lunatic. But I did want you to know what he—'

'Mr Elliott, I tell you what you must do – and straight away. You know Lewis Cohen through your father. You must go to him immediately and tell him what has happened. I'm too far away, and you need someone there for you in London. There's no one better than Lewis Cohen to have with you at a moment like this. Go to him, I urge you! As fast as you can! He'll look after you.'

Chapter 29

Lewis Cohen emerged from his front door, and settled himself into the back of the Daimler. As Elizabeth and his eleven-year-old daughter came out of the house just behind him, he waved with furious vigour at them out of the back window.

'Goodbye, Rachel!' he called. 'Enjoy yourself at school, my darling!' As the driver pulled away down the street he turned to wave once more. But they were looking in the other direction, talking animatedly to each other as they climbed into his wife's car, and Lewis had to force himself to put aside the flicker of hurt he felt at his daughter's indifference that day to his departure. And, it had to be said, at the vitality and ease of conversation she had, as usual, with her mother, which Cohen, try as he may, was never able to match. He was jealous, and he knew it, and the more so as he no longer, he reflected sometimes, very much liked his wife; but then, as the guilty thought came to him, he would as quickly thrust it away. In a relationship as long as theirs, liking someone was not as easy as loving them, and that he certainly did. Affectionately, possessively, and in a pleasant, easy way. They had been together for so many years. But he was also disappointed. What had appeared in their courtship to be a charming disregard for money, had become in their marriage a tendency towards acquisitiveness. The delicious, little-girl sulkiness now felt to him more like the tiresome petulance of a spoilt, immature egotist.

Cohen had always been intensely proud of her, of course, and remained so as each of the twenty years of their marriage passed. So he suppressed this irritation, for the last thing he wanted was for the marriage to break apart. He was content to accept the way matters stood. Perhaps he had been a little less than lucky in whom he had placed his affection. The same, of course, might well be true for Elizabeth. Perhaps neither of them was as suited to the other as he had originally thought. But that was all it was.

With his daughter, however, it was a very different matter.

Rachel was his pride and joy and the essence of his life. All his capacity for love was now focused on to her. And the fact that she was a bright, clever child, with a quickness of mind and humour that he imagined were just like his own, gave that love an added edge of pride. He adored her, his only child, with the particular intensity of a father of an unconventionally advanced age. He was ambitious for her. Wildly ambitious. He longed to heap on her every advantage that money could buy. He had never seen anyone more beautiful. His study was lined with photographs of her, and of her alone. Sometimes he had glimpses of a different reality, when he came across a photograph taken of her in years past, when he would be taken aback by an unexpected image of a plump, pudding-faced child staring stoically and solemnly at the camera. But then he would present this to himself as amusing, and he would quite forget how that photograph in its time had served, like its successors, as evidence to him of her loveliness.

Cohen glanced at his watch, and gazed out of the window at the cars beside them, all caught in the congestion of rush-hour traffic emerging from Regent's Park. Rachel would be at school now, safe and sound, and ready for a new week. He must call the Headmistress once more to arrange for some extra music lessons for her. Private lessons.

A shabby-looking man with a walking stick was tapping his way along the wide pavement outside Baker Street Station, and, for a moment, Cohen thought it was Mariss Steiner. Then the man turned, and he saw, to his relief, that he was a stranger.

Such danger in Steiner now, he thought. He appears to the world as a lunatic, but it's easy to underrate him. These days, there's a *Kamikaze* aura about him. Much more so than before. Age had not mellowed him in the least.

As the car moved away from the traffic lights, Cohen looked with satisfaction at the elegant dove-grey of the driver's jacket collar and cap, and his clean, soft hands on the leather steering wheel. Cohen had a great taste for luxury.

He mused on the difference between his life and Mariss Steiner's. Both of them arriving in London from Buchenwald as stateless refugees, and both exactly the same age. Fifteen years old, the pair of them – the most ancient, hardened fifteen year olds in the world. And with no family, no friends, no contacts, no advantages in England. They had both started together from that position. And now one of them was sitting in a Daimler, and the other living in rankest squalor in a bed-sitting room overlooking Paddington Station. Why was it? Neither one nor the other at that stage had been demonstrably the more intelligent, nor the more physically presentable . . . so why did it happen? Why was Mariss where he was, and he married to the daughter of Lord Rosenberg, and living in St John's Wood?

The chauffeur politely asked Cohen the arrangements for the day, and whether he would be required for the evening. There was a client to collect at Heathrow and to bring for lunch at the Connaught, and before that various meetings, and memoranda to read and write and discuss with his partners. Then, in the evening, he was due in Cambridge for dinner at a college he was assisting through his charitable Foundation.

They discussed all this as the car came down through Grosvenor Square, and Cohen glanced across at the ugly, assertive hulk of the US Embassy across the gardens on the other side. What in God's name, he thought, could the Americans have made of Mariss, when he was working for them? Was he ever useful – even marginally so? Did he ever have access to a single piece of information or contact that they were able to use?

And now Joseph Hermann was apparently under threat from this incompetent, muddle-headed, amateur revolutionary. Mariss wasn't really trying to avenge anyone, Lewis decided. He was simply attempting to make something of his life in one last great, public splash. He'd been thrown out of every Intelligence agency he'd ever tried to join, and was without contacts now. His work as a journalist was finished, and had been for years. He was mistrusted and ignored by everybody, and frozen away from access to any of the privileged information he craved, except for that which was spoon-fed to him by people who were doing so for their own reasons. Like Jacob Bergdorf was doing now, telling him about Hermann as if it were a privileged secret. The fact was that Hermann was part of an official delegation. There was nothing secret about his visit to England in any way! But Bergdorf had fed the news to Mariss in pretended confidence, and then had picked up the telephone to tell him, Lewis, that he had done so, and how dangerous he considered him. God knows what reasons he had for doing that.

When they drew up outside the office, Cohen gave the driver a letter to deliver to a client in the City. There were instructions over this, and more about his lunch arrangements, then Cohen climbed out from the rich leather seats, and went into the building, nodding

Tim Waterstone

and smiling at the saluting commissionaire as he walked through the lobby.

And now this absurd nonsense over a gun, he thought, as he pressed the button for the lift. Mariss is naive to the point of lunacy. It's almost as if he placed an advertisement in *The Times* for it. He's extremely fortunate that the contact he made was with Levinstein, who of course came straight to me the moment that Mariss first spoke to him. Anyone else would either have blackmailed him, or turned him straight over to the police. Both, probably.

Cohen smiled to his assistant as he walked into his room, and shut the door behind him. He sat down in the leather armchair in the corner, and chuckled to himself. One gun for hire please, he says, and you can have it back the next day. Mad as a hatter! So Levinstein tells him he can have whatever he wants, just to get rid of him. And then comes straight over to me. And most sensibly too.

The telephone rang, and as Cohen answered it, sitting on the desk's edge, he found that he was doodling on a sheet of paper. He shut his eyes, pulled his concentration together and completed the call, then looked back at the paper and at what he had started to write. A vertical line bisected the sheet into two half-columns, on one side headed by the name *Hermann*, and the other by *Steiner*, with *Bronowski* interposed in a bubble between the pair of them, and then, as an afterthought, *Edel* as well. There were still fifteen minutes to go before he was due at the partners' meeting, so Lewis continued with his little game.

Now he wrote, and beside it *Then*. Under both he marked *Advantages* and further below that, *Disadvantages*. Then he went from one to the other, listing down points as he went.

It was a question of whether to stop all this charade with Steiner now, or just before the final moment. Cohen had an instinct to let it run a few more days, but he needed to think through clearly whether it was safe to do so. Certainly it would be easier in many ways to leave it until just before Hermann arrived. Give Steiner his gun, explain it to the police at that very moment, and get him locked up. Permanently. For his own good and everyone else's. Certainly until Hermann was safely out of the country again. Less complicated to do it then. Much more difficult now.

But there was all this business with Bronowski too. His *Sunday Times* articles, of course – but what else was he up to? So better perhaps to leave the whole affair to run just a little, and see what else emerged. Was Bronowski merely the idealist he presented himself as? The researcher, beavering away for the 'truth'? That was difficult to believe, given the history of the man. There must be more to it than that.

There was a knock on his door, and Cohen's assistant came into the room, holding in her hands a folder of that morning's mail. She had already sorted and notated it, and removed the inconsequential material amongst it to be dealt with by someone else. She glanced down at the paper in front of him as she put the folder on the desk, and Cohen only just stopped himself in time from making the suspicious gesture of covering it with his hand.

'You're due down in the boardroom now, Mr Cohen,' she said, and Cohen watched her as she went, folding the piece of paper, and tucking it in his pocket. He got to his feet and set off for the door, then walked along the passage to join his partners.

I must be careful in this, he thought. Look out for my own interests. I've too much to lose, if anything goes wrong. Much too much to lose. Then, a yard from the door of the boardroom, he suddenly stopped dead, and smacked his hand against his forehead. He almost shouted out in delight. What a marvellous idea! How could he have missed it! What a chance there was in this to sort out the Bergdorf situation! Sort the man out once and for all! Put him in a trap. Trap him with Steiner! Compromise him, once and for all.

Chapter 30

Miranda had no idea who it was when she first opened her door. She thought initially that the small figure standing there in his overcoat, smiling broadly, and now, astonishingly, reaching forward to her and kissing her on the cheek, was some sort of religious proselytiser – a Jewish Jehovah's Witness, were such a thing possible.

But then he said, 'I can see that you don't remember me, my dear! I'm Mariss. Mariss Steiner. From a hundred years ago!'

He held out his hands again, and fearing that he was once more intending to kiss her, Miranda led him through into the sitting room and offered him a cup of tea.

'So many years, my dear! And you look so absurdly young! And so pretty! You shame us all!'

Sensing that his conversation was going to get stuck at this level for some time, Miranda set off again for the kitchen to make the pot of tea. All the while, to keep him where he was, she kept up a stream of talk while she collected her thoughts. When she went back into the sitting room her first impression was how awkwardly he was sitting. His jacket was immaculate, but his trousers were stained and dirty, and he had positioned himself on the very edge of the sofa, as if aware that he might leave marks behind him.

'It's so nice to see you, Mariss,' Miranda said, as if mimicking Steiner's hyperbole in her own delivery. 'But what a surprise! You must tell me why you're here, and what I can do for you.'

She poured them both their cups of tea, then looked at him, smiling still, poised for his response.

'Just some chatter, my dear,' he said. 'A little chatter, and some reminiscences perhaps. Of those good old days when we were young. Though you look so young still that—'

Reflecting that she wasn't sure she could take very much more of this, Miranda did not this time return his smile. There was a silence, and then Steiner said, now in a quieter voice, 'I need a little help from you, Miranda. You asked me why I've come – well, that's the reason. I'm very pleased to gather from Amos that he's seeing you again. I always thought it was such a pity that the pair of you split up all those years ago. I sensed somehow that one day you would be together again. It brought me great happiness when I heard that it was happening.'

Miranda coloured, and there was anger clearly beginning to surface in her as she said, 'No, Mariss. That's not the way I want to discuss my personal affairs. I don't want to be inhospitable or rude. It was very nice of you to call in to see me. But I don't want to talk about these things. I really don't.' She wondered what she could do now to hurry him with his tea, and get him out of the house.

'Oh, Miranda, I'm so sorry,' he said. 'I live too much alone. I do apologise to you. I'm so clumsy and insulting, and I really don't mean to be. I need some help from you, and I'm going quite the wrong way about it.'

'Just tell me. What do you want from me?'

'I want you to approach Amos on my behalf, and suggest to him that it would be a very good thing if he and I, and you, arrange—'

'No, Mariss. I'm sorry, but no. We're just beginning to get to know each other again, and in any case he's his own man, and he does what he wants. I'm not approaching him for anybody on anything. I'm not in a position to do so, and I don't want to do so. Whatever it is. *No!*'

There was a dead silence for several moments as Steiner stared at her. Then he replaced his cup on the tray, pushed himself to his feet and stood there resting for a while, leaning on his stick, his eyes on her still.

'I'm not sure that's quite how it'll be, Miranda. Because I'm determined that you *will* help me.'

He started to make his way to the door, and as he went, he said over his shoulder, 'The baby, my dear. The son you had by Amos, after he'd left you. I know what happened to the boy. I know too that Amos is not even aware of his existence . . .'

She stood absolutely still. The shock hit her, as if in a physical blow, and her breathing shortened. But she willed control of herself. She would not display to him what he had done to her. She'd keep herself in check.

'It's better that you help me, Miranda. I wouldn't ask you, unless it really mattered to me. We must work together on this. For both our sakes.'

Chapter 31

Cohen sat at his desk, and smiled his thanks to his assistant as she laid the coffee tray down before him. He made a dumbshow of offering milk and sugar to Bronowski, then poured their coffee, and looked down again at the thick pages of the brief he had prepared for the *Sunday Times'* article.

'Libellous obviously, if any of it's untrue. But your backing research . . .' He leafed through dozens of pages of appendices to the brief, then looked up and nodded his head. 'Well, that's formidable without doubt. I studied it at home last night. I recognised many of your sources and most of your data, as you can imagine. A great deal of the material, actually. Coming as we do from the same side of the tracks.' He made an expansive gesture of inclusion to Bronowski, as if was not just him but a group of them all there together.

'I'm seeing the newspaper's lawyers tomorrow morning,' he continued 'but I've already given them my preliminary opinion over the telephone – that the evidence is sound and the thrust of the material accurate and responsible. I've no doubt that they'll publish. It'll be a great coup for them – and most of all for you, of course. The two articles – and the book that follows – will together form an extraordinary achievement. I congratulate you from the bottom of my heart.'

Bronowski had very little experience of London lawyers, and when the paper wanted him to have someone on his side whom they could refer to over matters of copyright and libel, he had asked Edel for his advice; Gareth had immediately suggested Cohen. Now that Bronowski was with him again, he reflected that for all their years of occasional acquaintance he had never felt entirely comfortable with Cohen nor certain he could follow his motives and interests.

'Thank you, Lewis,' he said now, flippantly almost. 'It's been a long journey for me, but I'm at the end of it.'

He patted his knee a couple of times as if in indication that the conversation was completed, and started to move in his chair to depart. But Cohen was saying now, 'Yet I do wonder about the wisdom of it. I'm speaking now as your friend, Amos. As a lawyer I believe you're safe from successful libel proceedings: the statements you make are, as far as I know, true. Look – there's still time to stop the articles. The first is in ten days' time. I can still call a halt to it.'

He smiled, and tapped the folder to his side. 'I do think there's a case for second thoughts. Consider this for a moment. This report is going to have considerable impact. Of the twenty-five people you centre on, around nine or ten of them are in positions of influence and respect in the world.'

He turned the papers over until he found the summary page, ran his eye down the names listed and said, 'Singer, of course. Hermann is a prominent academic and writer. Bruch is a lecturer at Heidelberg. Siegel a well-known banker. Fiedel a Fifth Avenue physician in New York . . . And so on. I'm not at all sure what good is going to accrue to our community or to anybody else by blowing these people's lives open in the way that you're proposing.'

Cohen paused, but Bronowski said nothing, so he continued, his voice now almost supplicatory, begging him to take the point.

'You were at Belsen; I was at Buchenwald. You know as well as I do how we all had to behave in order to survive. None of us who went through that experience could, in any honesty, romanticise what happened. All of us fought like primitive animals for our own existence.'

He gestured, encapsulating the pair of them in a wider world. '*All* of us. Look – at the end of the war I was still a boy, and you're eight or nine years younger than me. Even so I'm hardly proud of my own memories of how I survived as a young boy in the camp, and I don't imagine that you are either. We were—'

Bronowski started to interrupt, but Cohen held up his hand. '*No!* Hear me out. What I'm trying to say is that for an adult, the dilemmas were far, far worse. The understanding of what was happening very much greater. The temptations, no doubt, more extreme. The hardships incomparably more appalling to bear. And, in the Buchenwald Communists' case, which so much of your report centres on, there were issues of political positioning as well. The Communists provided leadership in that camp when someone had to, or life would have come apart even more than it did. These issues are by no means simple, Amos!'

He was silent for a moment, fiddling with his pencil on the desk. 'There's the issue of selectivity, too. The business of picking these people out, and exposing them to the world, just because they have a certain position in life. Arguably, done so at random, from whatever motives that you . . .' He leafed through the thick papers in front of him.

'The illustrations you produce, and the stories you tell . . . Jews taking the opportunity to humiliate, bully, murder other Jews. It's as if at that time, a shadow of darkness and evil hung over the whole of Germany, evil in that time and in that place so great that it permeated everybody living there. *Everybody*. All of us who were there, to a greater or lesser extent. Nazis. Ordinary patriotic Germans. Jews . . .' The sentence trailed away.

'It's a story of horror,' he murmured. 'But I still don't want to see it published, because it's so destructive. So deliberately, wholly, wantonly destructive.'

'Buchenwald, Lewis,' Bronowski said quietly. 'You mentioned the Communists at Buchenwald. Do you remember the *Kapo* in Block 46? Arthur Dietzsch – the man who supervised the experiments with the SS doctor? The pair of them took healthy men and used them as typhus carriers. Do you recall that? And the time when he injected those men with a toxin that was to have been used in poisoned projectiles?'

He got to his feet. 'You're fooling yourself, Lewis. You want a quiet life and a prosperous one, and all the rest of it, and I can't blame you for that. But you don't want to look at the facts. And that's what I'm going to lay out for the world to have a look at. That's what we all should do with facts. Lay them out – look at them. Nothing else works for adult, responsible people. Certainly not—'

'Violence,' Cohen supplied flatly. 'If that's what you were going to say. Well, you're absolutely right in that.'

The two men stared at each other, then, as if they both knew simultaneously that it had gone on too long, there was a courteous process of leaving, as Bronowski was shown a bronze head Cohen had bought at Sotheby's the previous week, and the portrait of his daughter that hung on the wall opposite his desk.

Cohen saw him to the lift, and closed his office door behind him on his return. He went back to the window, and gazed out at the Thames beneath him, and, across it, the sun shining full on the Royal Festival Hall, bleached and pristine in the sharp light of the summer day.

Amos is not going to be stopped, he thought. It's all too late for that. So maybe I should consider instead how the situation can be used, perhaps, for the good.

Cohen looked out at the river for some minutes more, rehearsing, rejecting, exploring again the options and opportunities there might be in this. For himself. For others. Then, suddenly decided, he turned away from the window, and went over to the telephone directory on his desk.

The strange feature in this is Steiner, he reflected, as he leafed through the pages for the number he sought. Steiner, the great avenger. For were he a prominent man, like Bruch and Hermann and Singer and the rest, he too would have been exposed in this report. The man dreams of grandeur and heroics and divine retribution in that filthy bed-sitting room of his . . . and yet, to my certain knowledge, he spent most of his war working directly for the SS. In and out of the camps, acting as their messenger boy. Their plant. Their catamite.

That's an odd history for a man bent on moral outrage and revenge, Cohen thought, tapping one by one the dialling keys on his telephone. But it does give one an opportunity, of course. A quite wonderful opportunity. There's no doubt about that.

Chapter 32

After weeks of erratic, showery weather, most Londoners had begun to despair that summer would ever come. Steiner, in his normal humour and his normal health, barely noticed the seasons one way or another. But when he awoke after a night of continual, racking pain, he could see cloudless blue sky through the half-drawn curtains, and it was warm, and even to him the morning felt and sounded different and inviting and full of sunshine. There was birdsong too. The window was hardly open, but the day seemed full and lifted by birdsong, and Steiner lay in bed for some minutes, arms behind his head, and listened.

Skittishly almost, he rolled his legs out from under the blanket, hitched up his shrunken, stained pyjamas, and went over to look out of the window at his familiar view of the railway tracks, and the red double-decker buses on the Harrow Road beyond. Then, scratching at himself, he made his way over to the sink, urinated into it, shook himself down, filled the electric kettle from the cold tap, and made himself a cup of tea.

Beside him on a small metal table was the cardboard box which Steiner used as his bread bin. Opening the lid, he found in there the crust end of a stale brown loaf, which he spread with the last scrapings of some butter that he had stolen from the corner shop the previous week. He pinned his *yarmulke* into his hair, and then he prayed. As he always did each morning. In an amalgam of Psalms, and formal prayers of entreaty, and confession, and absolution, and pleas for Divine intervention, and vengeance on his foes, all of it in a form and order that over the years Steiner had himself evolved. He muttered in Hebrew, listening still to the birdsong of the summer day, clutching his mug and the crust in his hand.

'*Let mine adversaries be clothed with shame,*' he concluded, '*and let them cover themselves with their own confusion, as with a cloak.*

'*As for me, I will give great thanks unto the Lord with my mouth: and praise Him among the multitude.*'

The clothes he had worn the previous day were scattered on the floor beside the bed. The vest with the coffee stain down the front of it. The underpants that he had worn for at least a week. The cotton shirt with the fraying collar. The black linen trousers with the concertina creases in the crotch. All of these looked good enough for one more day, so he put them on, discarding only a pair of woollen socks, both with gaping holes in their heels. It was too hot for socks today anyway, he thought, so he put his feet directly into the scuffed black shoes, then wiggled his toes at the unfamiliar coolness and looseness of its feel.

Taking up his stick from the floor, he set off for the door, pausing as he passed the two suits hanging side by side in their plastic coverings. He fingered their sleeves, brushing and flicking at the mostly imaginary marks and stains he found on them, then, pushing out his foot, he straightened the single pair of highly polished laced walking shoes in trees that stood neatly beneath them.

He opened the door, and shut and locked it behind him, pushing into the jamb the sliver of wood that he kept hidden under a torn corner of the lino flooring. Sticks out like a railway sleeper, he thought. Lewis told me that it sticks out like a railway sleeper and, although he was already two or three steps down the stairs, he turned again, pushed himself up them, and adjusted and swivelled the telltale so that it was hidden by the frame of the door. Then he set off down the stairs once more, even in this weather wearing his raincoat, which hung loosely about him, as always flapping around his ankles as he went.

Standing out in the street, he was suddenly uncertain whether he was in the mood to go down to the corner store to get his milk and butter. The day, now that he was out in the fresh air, was so overwhelmingly lovely. He would leave the store for now. First he would go to sit on a bench in Porchester Square Gardens, and watch the lovers lying there together on the grass.

He crossed the road, and chose a bench. Brushing off the newspaper and empty cider bottle that were lying on it, he sat down, his raincoat gaping open on his chest, the zip of his flies undone, his bare feet white and blue-veined in his scuffed black shoes.

Seventeen days to go until Hermann arrives, he thought. I've only got seventeen days to go. I don't know enough about his movements, but the seminar will be the perfect occasion for it. I couldn't have organised anything better, even if I'd had a free

131

run at it. And I needn't worry about guards all over the place, either. Hermann's only an academic. There'll be no problem. I'll easily get in.

Steiner's mind turned to recollections of other events he'd attended uninvited. The list was long and most pleasurable to recall. It was one of Mariss's favourite pursuits, and one he was very good at. There was something so persuasively authoritative in his bearing and manner when he was playing the part, dressed in his pressed suit and the starched white shirt and the polished black shoes. The middle-class accent and vocabulary, the directness of his gaze; all of this making him into a figure who more often than not could convince security staff of the nonsense over the lost invitation, or the muddle over the appointment struck that very morning with the private secretary.

There would be no problem with Hermann, for heaven's sake! Not at some piddling academic conference or seminar or whatever it was. He'd get them when they were both together. And that was all he needed to do to complete the job.

Through the trees he caught a glimpse of a courting couple, and when they lay down and wrapped their limbs around each other he moved to the next bench so that he could get a better view. Put your hand on her leg, he willed the young man. Put your hand there, then move it up. Slide it between her thighs. He felt the void of excitement in his stomach, but then the two young people pulled apart, sat up, laughed together, and the moment had passed, and the promise of eroticism faded. Steiner got up, and turned back into Gloucester Terrace, and the direction of the corner shop. Even the modest heat of the day was beginning to make him feel faint. Also, to his fear, he caught a familiar if momentary surge of pain in his stomach, and he wanted to hurry now, and collect his groceries and get back to his room.

I'll do this because it's the will of God, he thought. It's too easy to stand aside. This is an act for God. And for all of us. It's a statement for my people. It's the culmination of my life.

And there it was now in his mind. The image of his childhood. A boy of twelve, lying in a pile of staring corpses, pretending that he himself was dead. At twelve years of age having the wisdom and the self-control to stop his breathing, and hold himself limp, and his face still, so that the guard prodding around in the bodies would think that he was dead, as the others were dead. He lay amongst them, his hands touching their hands, his face against their faces. As a child of twelve he did that.

Twenty guards with machine guns were lined up that morning in front of a thousand Jews waiting to be killed. Those who were shot dropped down into the pit, others jumping down after them to escape the bullets. They themselves dying in their turn as others fell in on top of them and suffocated them.

I saw them. The staring, empty eyes of the dead. The stiff, pointing limbs. The obscene exposure of their bodies. I was a twelve-year-old boy, each day twisting and turning and going with life this way and that and whatever way I was taken. Just to stay alive. Doing what I had to do to survive, as everyone else did. All of us, trying to live for one more day.

'In thee, O Lord, have I put my trust: let me never be put to confusion, deliver me in Thy righteousness,' he muttered, gazing down at the pavement in front of him. 'Bow down Thine ear to me: make haste to deliver me.'

Steiner looked up, and there he was now at the corner shop, and the elderly Indian behind the till was staring at him.

I've done nothing, and been nothing, he thought. I'm ready for this now. There's so little time left.

Chapter 33

The day after Cohen had been with Bronowski, Bernie Levinstein came to see him at his office.

He had been told to be there at half-past six, but he was waiting in the reception area outside his door fifteen minutes before that. One or two of the partners, emerging from Cohen's room after a meeting, looked curiously at the sharply dressed young man sitting there, but he kept his eyes down and studied a newspaper and avoided eye-contact and attention. Then Cohen came out to look for a file on his assistant's desk, and, seeing Levinstein, immediately beckoned him into his room. He shut the door behind him, a little sensitive about the impression this young man might have made on his colleagues.

That black hair in its ponytail, and the olive skin, the gleaming teeth and flashy handsomeness of him – like an old-fashioned ballroom gigolo. He assumed that was why that tour company employed him. Social & Entertainment Director, indeed! Taking coachloads of American widows around Europe, charming the socks off the lot of them. One sight of Bernie, and the poor creatures must think they've had a glimpse of paradise.

'I've done what you asked me to do,' Levinstein said. 'I telephoned Vienna once more and spoke to Mr Bergdorf. I said that you felt that the business of this gun was more his business than yours – Hermann being a friend of his, and so on, and both of them living in Vienna. He was very interesting about it. He said that maybe we'd all be a little better off with Steiner out of the way, rather than Hermann . . . that he was capable of ruining the lives and families and reputations of a great number of people, he said. People who should be left alone. So maybe we should ensure that they are. That's what he said. He's a direct man is Mr Bergdorf.'

Cohen sat there staring at him, as his words unrolled with such chilly fluency. He wished he'd never been obliged to have anything to do with Bernie Levinstein over this business. He'd not had much choice of course, because Levinstein had come to him in the first place when Steiner had approached him for a gun. But he'd gone at it too quickly. He had suddenly had this idea about entrapping Bergdorf, and he'd rushed it. And now he was stuck with Levinstein whether he liked it or not. The snare he was setting for Bergdorf was one of the best ideas he had ever had. Hermann was the bait. Mariss would make a fool of himself, but he'd come to no real harm, of course, Lewis would make absolutely sure of that. Hermann would be untouched, but Bergdorf would be trapped in the middle of it. Red-handed. His reputation and his hold on Hermann destroyed for ever. All very satisfactory. He should have handled it differently. And now he'd lost control. He would have to be careful. Levinstein was not to be trusted. Particularly with Bergdorf.

'Mr Bergdorf wants to consult you,' Levinstein was continuing. 'But he won't come to London personally, because he doesn't want to be seen to have travelled here at this time in case it's finally decided to take action against Steiner. He says he wants to talk to you about Bronowski as well. He won't telephone you, in case the lines are insecure, but he's keen to sound you out on it. He did go on at great length about Steiner. And Amos Bronowski. Bergdorf has all these contacts in the US Intelligence, apparently. And they've given him a considerable briefing on Bronowski.'

Cohen continued tapping on the desk with his paper knife, still staring away from Levinstein as he listened. Then he looked up from the desk and said, 'Bergdorf can be a bit of an old woman sometimes. Mariss is quite probably a physical threat to certain people, including Hermann. But *Bronowski*? He's no assassin, though I too have heard rumours, of course.'

Again there was silence between them. Then Cohen looked up and said, 'So how was it left? What am I supposed to be doing?'

Levinstein got up from his seat, flicked some specks of dust off the sleeve of his dark-blue silk suit, then ran his palms over his hair. 'Mr Bergdorf will be in touch with you, Mr Cohen. In touch with *us*, I should say.'

The assumption of intimacy and ranking in this hit Cohen once more with a jarring irritation. But he concealed it, and showed Levinstein out of the office, and along the deserted corridor to the lift.

'I'll wait then,' he said pleasantly. 'Or, as you say, *we'll* wait. Goodbye, Bernie. We'll stay in touch.'

As Cohen went back into his office, he told himself never to underestimate Bergdorf. He did seem to be reacting exactly as he had hoped he would, but one should never underrate the man's capacity.

As for Bernie Levinstein, his thoughts were on Bergdorf too, but in a rather different light. He's making a monkey of old Cohen, he reflected. I'd like to know exactly what he's up to. But so would the rest of us, of course, I'm sure of that. Joseph Hermann included.

Chapter 34

Cohen received his message from Jacob Bergdorf the following morning. The letter came via a special courier, who had waited for an hour while Cohen was in the boardroom with a client, and refused to release it to anyone else. Having at last put the envelope personally into Cohen's hands, he had then insisted on waiting for his written reply to it on the bottom of the original.

The letterhead showed a Vienna address, and was written in a careful, spidery hand, which Cohen recognised immediately from the several other notes that Bergdorf had sent him over the years. He went into his office to read it, purposely leaving the door open behind him, so as not to give the sense to his assistant that the letter had any particular importance or secrecy. The letter read:

My dear Lewis,
You're becoming so famous and well-connected that I hardly dare trespass upon your time. Only the great celebrities may do so these days, as my friends here in Austria tell me. How cleverly you choose your friends! Such a babykisser is Herbert von Karajan these days!

But I take my life in my hands, and write now to the great man, and request a meeting. There are one or two little matters of common interest between our respective law firms that need tidying up. A young friend of yours, whom I had the pleasure of speaking to the other day, said he thought you would be in Geneva on the evening that you read this note (June 23). By the purest coincidence I shall be there as well. I have a suite at the Hotel du Rhône, and would like you to join me there for a few moments, if your schedule permits. Shall we say at 6.45 p.m.?

With my warmest compliments,

Jacob Bergdorf.

137

Cohen scribbled his acceptance on the bottom of the letter, put it back into the plain envelope and sealed it, then returned it to the messenger, who immediately bustled away to the lifts. He telephoned Elizabeth to say that an urgent meeting of one of his client banks would require him to be in Geneva that evening, told his assistant the same story, and arranged for his driver to pick up an overnight case for him from home. A flight was booked, and a room for the night, and by mid-afternoon Cohen was on his way, carrying, for the sake of appearances, an attaché case containing the firm's current files on the Swiss Bank he had said he was to see. As a precaution, he rang from Heathrow to arrange a visit to them on the following morning.

Cohen arrived at the Hotel du Rhône with thirty-five minutes to spare, so he sat in an armchair at the very back of the lobby to pass the time before going up to Bergdorf's suite. He had been there for barely two or three minutes, when the door of one of the main lifts opened, and a man he recognised immediately came hurrying out of it and made for the side door leading to the car park. Cohen knew that he was mostly concealed by a group of tall plants, and doubted whether he had been seen, but just in case anyone else emerged from the lifts over the next few minutes, he moved to another chair even better hidden than the first, and waited to see what would happen. It was two or three minutes to seven before he went over to the house telephones in the corner and called through to Bergdorf's suite.

Bergdorf told him to go straight up, and was there at the door waiting for him, all affability and courtesy. Cohen watched Bergdorf as he poured him a whisky, and thought how much he had aged since they had last met. Cohen was almost sixty-five, but Bergdorf, at sixty-nine or seventy, looked at least ten years older. His hair was now completely white, and his tall frame, normally upright and commanding, was now quite distinctly stooped. Yet Cohen knew that Bergdorf was still a formidable man. He remembered with embarrassment his sneer of the day before. For all the fussiness of the man, Bergdorf was anything but an old woman.

'Thank you for coming, Lewis,' Bergdorf was saying, 'so good of you. Please forgive the cloak-and-dagger way I communicated with you in London. But as I grow old, I have an increasing obsession with the privacy of my life.'

He sat, raised his glass and took, what Cohen recognised from great familiarity in these things, an entirely dissembled sip at his drink.

'You didn't recognise him, from what I'm told, but the messenger I sent you was my very own son, Emmanuel. You last saw him when he was a boy of eight or nine or so, if I recall. I wondered if you would remember him!'

There were apologies then, and laughter, and questions about Cohen's Rachel, and Bergdorf's grandchildren, and Cohen knew the rituals of this, and for how long it was required of him to continue it.

Then Bergdorf, still smiling, said, 'But there is a problem I think – don't you? Your young friend Bernie Levinstein was very direct over it. I hope you don't mind that I suggested he came straight to you when he needed help. He told me the full story – of how Steiner had approached him for a weapon, with which to attempt to kill Hermann when he is in London in ten days or so. It does sound a quite extraordinary way to behave, but knowing Mariss Steiner as we do . . .'

Bergdorf gave a little laugh, as if the whole matter was nothing more than a schoolboy prank. Cohen nodded in response, and went on doing so, smiling, encouraging him to continue.

'Do you know, I doubt you and I are very far apart from each other on this,' Bergdorf went on. 'Over Joseph Hermann. I'm not sure either of us would choose him as a holiday companion exactly. There's the Buchenwald business of course, and all the controversy that generates. He has his reputation in academic circles quite certainly, and one has to respect him for that, though there have been some quarrels recently that make one wonder . . .' Bergdorf smiled at Cohen contentedly, as if the pair of them were used to performing together this sort of character and career assassination of their acquaintances.

'He's not well,' he continued, 'and one should give him allowance for that. But that's not quite the point. Mariss Steiner is proposing to attempt to kill him. I use the word "attempt" as Steiner couldn't be relied upon, in my opinion, to change a light bulb. But we should not take his intentions lightly.

'Well, does it matter so much, we may ask ourselves? Why not let Steiner try whatever he wants, and if he succeeds, so well and good, Hermann's a pain in the neck and Buchenwald has left him with a host of enemies, and deservedly so. If he fails, then Steiner will either have managed to shoot himself in the foot or he'll have been arrested. All good news, whatever happens.

'But whatever his enemies feel about Buchenwald, and who can blame them, Hermann must be left alone. Once you start this sort of ball rolling it's disastrous. And contagious. It puts into play matters that are better left undisturbed.' Bergdorf paused, then looked at Cohen, and smiled.

'Steiner's an old friend of yours, isn't he, Lewis? Or rather, he *was* a friend of yours at a certain stage of your life. Many years ago. Many, many years ago.'

Cohen recognised the invitation to deny Steiner in this statement, and followed it.

'Yes, as young men we did know each other. Once upon a time.'

The two men watched one another, then Cohen continued, 'Look – let me be frank with you. It's not just Steiner. I imagine you know of the material Amos Bronowski is about to publish in the British *Sunday Times*?'

Bergdorf nodded.

'Well, like you, I would prefer that didn't go ahead either. But it's going to. There's nothing I can do to stop it. The newspaper's lawyer asked my opinion of the material as a matter of form, but I was aware he'd taken advice elsewhere, and that he knew it wasn't libellous. They are all set to publish. Let's say that Bronowski's report will do damage to certain people . . . Singer perhaps, Bruch, one or two others maybe . . . Hermann, of course. Yes, there are men named in the report that one would prefer were not exposed in this way. But Bronowski has been cautious on the whole. He's tended to stay in the comparatively safer areas.'

Bergdorf nodded again. 'Yes, I agree. I've seen what he's written, and not too much harm is done, in the first article anyway. But you said you wanted to be frank?'

'It's this, Jacob. The reason why we both found the initial report blander than we had feared – perhaps more trivial than we'd feared – is because we haven't seen it all. He's held back his real meat for the book that follows. And when that is published, there will be stories there that will ruin certain of our clients. I'm sure I'm correct in this. There can be no other explanation.'

Bergdorf sighed. 'So there's Steiner, and there's Bronowski. Both dangerous, in their different ways.'

He moved in his seat, then was silent for some moments, lost in thought, picking absently at his fingernails. Cohen said nothing, watching him. Then, as if he'd forgotten entirely the previous three or four minutes of the conversation, Bergdorf continued, 'It's easy to underestimate Mariss Steiner, in my view. He's such a strange man. The clothes. First a tramp, and the next time you see him he's looking like a chartered accountant. Those extraordinary late night telephone calls, threatening anybody and everybody. Gatecrashing everyone's weddings and funerals. Wild letters to the newspapers. All those things. But the truth is that he's much more dangerous than that. He's far more threatening than he appears.'

Bergdorf went over to the window and stood for a moment or two staring out across Lake Geneva.

'Steiner's dangerous because he won't come to terms with the way his life has turned out,' he said slowly. 'He's resentful of me and you, and all those like us. He hates us! And with his knowledge about our lives, and our histories, and everything about us, and the camps . . . well, I don't think we can allow it to continue – do you? I gather from Levinstein, rightly or wrongly, that that's your view too. Is that correct? So we'll have to find a way of dealing with Steiner before any more harm is done. I would prefer a solution that was not too extreme, and I'm sure you would as well. But . . . we'll have to consider what's possible, and what isn't. It may be that an attempt at a halfway course would do more harm than good.'

The two men looked at each other, reluctant to mention directly what was waiting there to be defined. Then Cohen, feeling some response was demanded of him, said, 'I'll give some thought as to how we might get to the end result without any unpleasantness or involvement. I'm sure you will as well.'

Hands were shaken, compliments exchanged, and it was not until his hand was on the door handle that Cohen said, 'And then there's the other business, Jacob. As I said – Amos Bronowski. He's not by any means in the same category as Steiner, but from what I've heard about the new material he wants to release . . .'

He shrugged, and as they gazed at each other it was the complete coolness and composure of Jacob Bergdorf that struck Cohen. He had neither flinched, nor coloured, nor showed the slightest reaction to what had been said, nor surprise at its timing.

'One more issue to consider,' he said, smiling, and put his hand affectionately under Cohen's arm as he opened the door and saw him on his way.

All very well to make plans as far as Mariss is concerned, Cohen thought. Bergdorf is falling over backwards to paint him in the most lurid colours. But what is he planning with Bronowski? For it was Amos that he had seen hurrying away out of the lift that hour or so before. And what dealings has Bronowski got with Bergdorf? Why did they need to talk together before I arrived? And why was that conversation then kept secret from me?

141

Chapter 35

Cohen left his hotel the next morning shortly after nine o'clock. He was on his way to the meeting he had arranged at his client bank, and had he not been so immersed in thought, he might well have seen Bronowski once more, for he was sitting in a coffee shop a few hundred metres from the hotel, exactly on Cohen's route. Bronowski saw Cohen though, and it gave him a shock to do so. Bergdorf had told him to be sure not to be seen by Cohen in Geneva, and he had had no idea that he was likely to come to this part of the town.

He watched Cohen go safely through the doors of the bank. Ten minutes later, he was in Bergdorf's suite at the Hotel du Rhône, drinking some of the coffee that remained from the breakfast table, and waiting for Bergdorf to finish his telephone call.

'But it's not as simple as you suggest,' he was saying. 'I have no means of preventing Hermann from going to London. He's travelling in an official delegation from his University, and he's a lead speaker at the conference in Oxford, as well as the other dates he's got in London. He's in excellent health, and both his hosts and his colleagues are expecting him to be there. How do I stop him? By telling him that Steiner is planning to assassinate him? He'll simply inform the police, and carry on as before. Quite right, too.'

Whoever was on the other end of the line now spoke for some moments, then Bergdorf replied, 'No. I have no power to do so, even if I thought your suggestion was a good idea. Hermann will be perfectly safe, in any case. Yes, I can guarantee that to you.'

There appeared to be a further interjection from the other speaker, then Bergdorf continued, 'Yes. I agree with that. I will certainly have a conversation with Lewis Cohen about this. It's most wise of you to suggest that he should be involved. I'll speak to him today if I can reach him in London, or wherever he is, and I'll confirm to you subsequently what his advice is in this matter. Not at all. Not at all. I'll hope to speak to you tomorrow.'

Bergdorf replaced the receiver, then came across to join Bronowski at the table.

'One longs for time in these things, Amos. Hurry and rush lead to bad decision-making, in my experience, but unfortunately time is ticking away too fast on this, and we'll have to decide very soon now exactly what is to be done. Look – Hermann is in London in a couple of weeks, and, according to what Levinstein tells me, he is due to deliver this ridiculous gun to Steiner a few days before that. If he doesn't deliver it, then we're not sure what Steiner might do next. And that's a most unsatisfactory position for us to be in.'

The waiter came into the room to remove the breakfast table, and was treated with elaborate courtesy by Bergdorf as he did so. A tip was pressed into his hand, enquiries made as to his health, and the weather, and the door held open for him as he left.

'I think we should decide once and for all that Steiner should be tidied away permanently,' he resumed. 'Would you agree with that?'

Bronowski was picking absent-mindedly at a croissant he'd saved from the waiter. He'd felt a chill come over him as he heard Bergdorf's words, but remained gazing at his plate, feeling somehow that he should avoid a histrionic show of shock, and draw Bergdorf out further. There was a pause, then he looked up and said, 'Is that what Lewis Cohen wants?'

'Let's just say that Lewis and I are still at the preparatory stage in our discussions. But I would be surprised if such a course was entirely outside his thinking.'

'So – how would it be done?' Bronowski asked, keeping his voice as flatly disinterested as he could.

Bergdorf leaned forward. 'Here's one way – just thinking aloud, of course. Homosexuals of Mariss Steiner's age are in notorious danger from young men. And, as you know, the police are loath to get too far involved. It's very difficult for them to trace leads, and there's the problem all the time about what was in the nature of consensual activity and what wasn't. And somehow a feeling that these deaths are not within the public domain one way or another. Given that . . .' He gave a little shrug at the ways of the world.

Bronowski stared at him. 'And who would do it?' he asked.

'An outsider could be hired, perhaps. That's one option. But I doubt that the risk would be worth it. Which suggests a different category of person. Not a hired hand, but someone who would *enjoy* the task, perhaps. Steiner has had a very specialised sexual history, you may recall. We might have someone in Austria who would fit the bill. I think I may have heard of someone amongst a certain circle who might be suitable for this. It could be the ideal solution. But, as I say, I'm just thinking aloud.'

Bronowski got up, and went across to the window in his turn. Below him, the blue waters of the lake were at their summer best, but he stared out unseeingly at the hills beyond, his hands in his pockets. Then he turned around and said forcefully: 'This has all gone too far, Jacob. Much, much too far. I came here to Geneva because you asked me to come, and because you've been kind to me in the past, getting me the job at McGill, and that year as a visiting professor in Mexico, and the grant from the Liebenbaum Foundation. You pulled strings for me with great effect when I asked you to, and I'm very grateful for it.

'But you know what I did as a young man, and my time in London, and the Zionist work, and all of that. And the people I mixed with. Gareth Edel obviously, and Mariss Steiner too. Surely you must know I would *never* act against any of those people – including Mariss! And I agree with him about Hermann. Not in what he proposes for him, but in the principle of it. Whatever his subsequent life may have been, Hermann presided over certain atrocities at Buchenwald. In the camp infirmary particularly. That's beyond dispute. So I agree with Mariss in one sense: it should be avenged. But not in his way. Not by violence, but by public exposure. And that's exactly what I'm going to do.'

He paused, gazing at Bergdorf, measuring his reaction. Then: 'Mariss has bungled this anyway, as he always does. Approaching Levinstein was a crazy thing to do. I did try to get him to help me with my own project, but he wouldn't take it seriously. He's totally impossible – but that's not to say that I want him killed, because he's an inconvenience to us. You propose that he should be introduced to someone whose sexual violence is more extreme than even Mariss is used to, though all of that is news to me. And that we should then invite the other person to do what he wants, and sit back and see what happens. Well, I find that quite repellent! I'm *amazed* that you could believe anything else of me. I find it beyond belief, quite frankly. How could you have got me so wrong?'

They looked at each other for a moment, alert and thoughtful. Then Bronowski said, 'What was the real reason you asked me here, Jacob? Why did you bring me to Geneva? You know that

I don't want to get involved in this in any way. I want Mariss Steiner left unharmed, and I want Joseph Hermann left unharmed as well. So why are you telling me about it? Why in God's name am I here?'

Bergdorf leaned forward, and there was a new edge in his voice now. 'Amos. None of this must continue. *None of it!* That's why I've asked you to come here. Hermann must be left alone. Fiedel must be left alone. Singer must be left alone. I have a whole series of clients and friends who must be LEFT ALONE. All this is the completest nonsense. Don't you understand that? Steiner must be tidied away, because he's a lunatic, and we've discussed that. But you too must bring your activities to a halt, not because you're a lunatic, but because you're obsessed. You're on the wrong track. It's all too late for this. It's too many years ago, and no one cares. I think Lewis Cohen has told you that already, and he's right. Help me with Steiner. And come in line yourself. I want you to leave your obsessions alone. And I want your help over Steiner now, Amos. Now.'

'Do you know something, Jacob?' Bronowski said. 'I don't believe you care a fig about Fiedel and Singer one way or another. Nor any of the other Buchenwald Communists. You don't want Hermann protected from Steiner or anyone else. The whole of this conversation is a sham.'

Bergdorf shrugged, and gave a most charming smile. 'A sham, you say? Perhaps I want Joseph assassinated instead?' He laughed uproariously, and patted Bronowski on the knee. 'But I won't be cross with you. You've such a sense of humour, my dear. And you're too clever for me! Whatever can you mean?'

'Hungary is what I mean, Jacob,' Bronowski said, getting to his feet and moving to the door. 'The Hungarian Jews. *Himmler's Treasure*. There's only one thing you're interested in – getting your hands on that.'

Chapter 36

Back in Vienna, Bergdorf joined the airport taxi-line, and looked at his watch. There was still time to go to the office for an hour or so, and after that he'd go straight home.

This Hermann business really would have to be worked out over the next forty-eight hours or so, he thought, as he climbed into the back of the Mercedes cab. He'd reach him tonight by telephone, and find some way to charm him into a discussion the next day. They could walk perhaps in the Schwarzenberg Garten. Hermann was such a difficult man to approach, these days, as he grew older – seventy-four wasn't he, or seventy-five? He seemed to be able to concentrate on nothing, apart from this Foundation he was setting up. The Hermann Scholars. It would never lead to anything very much, of course, especially if he was expecting to attract public funding for it! And Hermann himself had no money, as far as one knew.

How different Hermann is from myself, he thought. I'm starved if I don't have access to the world I know – restaurants, and clubs, and little supper parties, and Embassy receptions. International conventions. Places where you can deal with several things at once. Like that weekend in Oslo last month. The US Senator worried over a little problem with his business friends in Bogotá. The Israeli politician with certain rumours about his early years appearing in the Press. The French diplomat to tidy up out of trouble, after the unfortunate incident with those adolescent boys in Sri Lanka last summer. Matters of that kind. Little affairs that require from me access to my range of contacts, and my influence, and my tact, and my judgement. And experience of what can be made to work in the world, and what cannot.

Bergdorf paid off his fare, and went in through the office entrance lobby. The understated design and décor of the place pleased and amused him, as it always did. The firm had occupied this building from their early struggling days to the time of their present, revered

146

status. The senior partners liked to keep the appearance of their offices as simple and bleakly functional as could be. They knew their position in the profession. They didn't need the pretensions of fashionable interior design to make flatulent statements of prosperity and good taste on their behalf. Bergdorf nodded at the stout, moustached lady behind the Reception desk as he passed her, and reflected, pleasingly, that she was a woman whose appearance and dress were ideal for the impression the firm wanted to convey. Quite perfect. They couldn't have found a better match if they had gone for the purpose to a theatrical casting agency.

He walked on down the half-lit passage leading to the rear of the building, ignoring completely a junior lawyer who had pressed himself against the wall to allow him to pass.

'Maria! Thank you for waiting. Are there messages for me?' he said to his assistant as he passed her into his office.

Maria had seldom seen Bergdorf so convivial after a long journey, and blushed at his attention, passing over to him a sheet of paper on which she had printed out a list of callers.

He ran his eye down it, and when he saw Joseph Hermann's name there he had an immediate and absurd instinct to conceal it with his hand. There was no harm in the fact that Hermann had called, nothing in the least surprising in it. If Hermann wasn't exactly a client of the firm, then he was the sort of person who might need to talk to Bergdorf occasionally about some matter or another. Maria would have thought nothing untoward about his call whatsoever. How dangerously edgy he was over all this business!

Hermann was probably getting into contact over something perfectly inconsequential. A request for a donation to one of his academic charities, perhaps. He knew there were a number of those. But it worried Bergdorf not to have the initiative in this. Life, whenever he could make it so, was worked to Bergdorf's agenda, not to that of others.

He went over to a steel cabinet in the corner of the room, turned its dial to unlock it, and took out a file from a section marked *Miscellaneous Commercial and Mercantile*. He glanced through the encoded material in it, then took another file out, and looked for some minutes through that too. Then he replaced them both, closed the heavy doors once more, spun the lock, and stood gazing out at the evening traffic as it streamed over Schweden Bridge, and up Tabor Strasse beyond.

This mustn't become muddled, Bergdorf told himself. There

are several separate issues for me in this business, and they mustn't become entangled. Even by my standards this is all most uncomfortably complex. Control and calm are essential if the whole affair is not to spin comfortably away from me.

He would settle down comfortably at his desk right this minute, and list each individual problem that had to be dealt with. That was the way to do it. List all the things to be dealt with, and think them through one by one.

First, and certainly the most important, was the Hermann business. That was now at a point where a number of unresolved matters could be brought to a head. All in one. Hermann needed to be charmed and lulled into providing the final pieces in the puzzle. He was ready to do it now – he just had to be helped over the last hill. Now was the opportunity to do that. It couldn't be left any longer. Then he and it must be brought to an end.

There was Hermann. There was Steiner. There was Lewis Cohen. The three of them suddenly, and most unexpectedly linked. Cohen was a minor player and always had been, but in recent weeks he had become – well, more formidable than before. In fact, he'd become a little bit of a pest. This plot of his trying to compromise me with Steiner so that he can turn me in! How obvious it was! But when you had someone floundering around like Steiner was, intent on mischief of one sort or another, you should never miss the opportunity to put all that energy to your own use. All that business with the gun! Bergdorf chuckled to himself.

And then there was Gareth Edel . . . The problem with trying to steer Edel in any direction whatsoever, as Bergdorf knew of old, was that one had thereafter not the slightest idea how many uses he had put the journey to. Or how many other services he was providing simultaneously to other people, behind one's back. Edel was best kept well clear of, in normal circumstances. But these weren't normal circumstances. And he no longer had any practical choice in the matter: Edel knew exactly what Bergdorf was doing, and had offered to help him. Bergdorf was uneasy why that should be, but it had happened, and he'd have to go along with it. Taking Edel into one's camp was better than leaving him outside, looking in.

As for Bronowski, Bergdorf was more than a little uncomfortable after their conversation together that morning in Geneva. It was not so much a question of using Bronowski, as discovering what he was really up to. Those articles of his were surely no more than a front. There must be more to him than that, with so much else going on. Of course there was. Why else should he have made those unexpected and unsettling remarks about the Hungarian bank accounts?

And then there was the Levinstein boy. Useful and loyal in his own way – he'd shown that over the last two or three years. But dangerous. There were some unpleasant matters to deal with, and it would be a pity to lose him. Still, he'd watch the situation over the next few days, and make his mind up over young Levinstein then.

But it was the Lewis Cohen issue that had immediately to be resolved. Cohen was stumbling his way through to the very centre of things if he did but know it, though one doubted that he did. What a buffoon the man was – trying to lay on this trap for him! Wildly inadequate sparring partner as he was, Bergdorf reflected comfortably that he was fond of Cohen. It was difficult not to be. And it was a pity that he had to be brought up against him in this way.

Yes, thought Bergdorf. I really do like Lewis Cohen. I don't know him well, of course. But that's a good thing. It makes it easier in the long run. Life is difficult enough as it is, without getting one's affairs cluttered up by personal loyalties and affections. Particularly when the stakes are as high as they are in this . . .

Chapter 37

Professor Hermann limped into his study and settled heavily into the leather chair drawn up to his desk. His rooms were on the second floor, and these days he found the climb up the stairs to be slow and tiring work. It was some minutes before he felt strong enough to open his briefcase and read his papers, minutes he spent smoothing with his fingers the petals of the single yellow rose that he kept there most days in the summer, placed in a silver flute vase he had been given on his sixtieth birthday by the University History Society.

But now he reached for his case, and took from it the file that the President of the Société des Banques de Genève had given him earlier that afternoon. He leafed through it once more, then went over to the filing cabinet in the corner of the room and came back with another file, also under the Société des Banques de Genève marking, and sat for forty minutes or so with both before him, marking them simultaneously with a red ink pen.

Completing his task, he reached across to a sidetable, and pressed an ancient brass electric bell that sat there on top of an enormous atlas of the world. Immediately a stout, late-middle-aged woman came in to the room, holding a shorthand notebook and a sharpened pencil in her hand. She had come to Hermann on retirement from a post as a senior secretary in the Civil Service, and prided herself on her rigid efficiency.

Hermann nodded to her, passed over the files, and pointed to the chair on the other side of his desk.

'Here they are at last, after twenty years of asking! I've annotated them for you as well as I can, but you'll need to go over them once more. Then you can make up a master file of these together with the similar lists that we've been given both by the United Bank of Switzerland people and last year by the Bank of Zurich. How long will that take you? Three days? Four?'

She pursed her lips, and leafed through the files. 'Is this basically the same material, Herr Hermann? A listing of East German and Hungarian families, plus a few from Poland and Czechoslovakia, and the state of play on the redemption of their accounts?'

'You make it sound too trivial, my dear,' Hermann reproached her gently. 'I repeat, this has been twenty years in the asking. More than that – forty-five years since I first became involved. But it's twenty years since I was promised by the President of the Bank himself the data you have before you, and only now has he released it. That's a disgracefully long time. Now that we've got it, we must move on it as fast as we can.'

'Of course,' she said. 'Of course.' She leafed through the files once more. 'Two days – no more.' At the door she paused, and turned. 'One thing I've always wanted to ask you, Herr Hermann. Why did you get involved in this? I don't mean to be inquisitive, but . . .'

Hermann shrugged, rather touched that she should have stepped outside the formal protocol of their relationship for a moment. 'I'm a Jew. I knew so many of these families at Buchenwald – German and East-European Jews like me. These bank accounts contain all their savings, and they should be released to their owners. It's a disgrace that they've been held in Switzerland for so long. I was sufficiently well known and well connected in my political days to know what strings could be pulled and how best to keep the pressure on the Swiss. That's what I did, and that's why I got involved. But it's been a very long haul. I wish I'd done it better,' he told her with a sigh.

'How on earth is it that the Swiss banks have been able to hold the money for so long?'

'They've made it difficult – that's how. These accounts were set up before the war in great secrecy; code names, secret numbers, dummy addresses, that sort of thing. Then, after so many of these families had died in the concentration camps, the Swiss refused to let the money go. They made it virtually impossible for any of the families' descendants to prove their claim. So most of it is still there. Seven billion dollars, or thereabouts. That's a great sum of money. The Swiss have done very well out of it indeed.'

'Is it all in cash?'

'Mostly. There are also works of art and jewellery, that sort of thing. But it's mostly money – building up, as you can imagine, into tens of thousands of million dollars of compound interest – all unpaid.'

She came back, and sat once more in her chair. 'May I ask more?'

151

she said, deferential to him as she always was, and Hermann nodded and smiled patronisingly. 'There's another thing. I don't understand what happened immediately after the war ended. I thought that the whole world was legally obliged to declare all assets that the Germans had deposited with them. And working through these files it's clear that as well as the families' deposits, there are also some accounts set up by the Nazis. Secret accounts, opened with the Swiss in just the same way. Isn't that right?'

She looked up for an answer, but then immediately proceeded, 'I know of course that the Swiss introduced their new banking secrecy laws in 1952, which tightened things up for them completely, but that was seven whole years later. Seven years. What happened before then?'

'Nothing,' said Hermann. 'The Swiss did nothing at all. They sat on what they'd got, and kept very quiet indeed. And then in 1952, as you say, they introduced their new regulations. Since that time, any attempts to open their books up, whether the money there in the accounts was deposited originally by the wartime Jews, or the Nazis, or organised crime, or anybody else – all those attempts have been vigorously opposed by certain sections of the banking community. They want to be as tight and as secret as can be. The Swiss Bankers' Federation made that farce of an announcement a few months ago that as far as they were concerned, the problem of the Holocaust anonymous accounts had been "solved", as they put it. Some solving. As they later had to admit, there were still huge sums sitting there in these dormant Holocaust accounts, all unaccounted for. The Association admitted to forty million dollars or so, but that, I can assure you, is a fraction of what's really there.'

'Well, I must get straight to work on them,' she announced. Then, hesitating, 'But please can I ask my question once more. You're a historian. You're a teacher. That's what you do with your life. I understand that you feel an affinity with other Jewish people who were in Buchenwald with you and so on, but this has taken so much of your time over the years. Why can't you leave it to the lawyers to do the job? People like Herr Bergdorf. Why can't he do all the work with the banks himself?'

'Bergdorf?' Hermann echoed. 'The banks would never work direct with him. They're prepared for him to do work for me, on my behalf, but they would never deal with him direct. They don't trust him. Nor do I. I just feed him the clients' cases to work on one by one. What he does, he does very well. But the banks don't trust him. They don't trust anybody very much. Neither do I.'

'But they trust you, Herr Hermann!' his secretary cried, clearly proud of her employer.

'Yes,' said Hermann, turning back to his briefcase. 'They trust me. But they know where I'm coming from. They understand the sort of person I am. They know me from Buchenwald.'

Chapter 38

Edel was always the last person in the building, sitting at his desk working on the catalogues, nodding and smiling his goodnights as the Burridge & Edel staff set off one by one on their way.

Soon the last of them had gone and, as he was expecting, at twelve minutes past six precisely there was a rap on the outside door of the stockroom. A narrow alley, along which the delivery men trundled their boxes, ran up to the back of the building. Going over to the window, Edel was able to look down into it to see who was there at the door, and also whether there was anybody else lurking at the farthest end, where the alley angled off into the adjoining street.

Bernie Levinstein stood back sufficiently to allow Edel full sight of him, and jerked his head impatiently for the door to be opened. When Edel let him in, he undraped the fawn cashmere overcoat from off his shoulders, threw it down on to a packing bench, and then, with laboured suspicion, picked a carton to sit on, first brushing at it to ensure that his mohair trousers would be safe from any dust. Stretching out his legs, he gave an expansive yawn, then smoothed his hair with the palm of his right hand – a gesture that Edel found as irritating as Lewis Cohen had before him.

'The situation has a certain neatness about it, I'll give you that,' Levinstein drawled. 'Symmetry, as my father used to say. In the first corner we have that disgusting old fart Mariss Steiner. In the second the fading, incompetent Amos Bronowski. Both going off in different directions, but still at the heart of them failed revolutionaries. In the centre of the ring we have the master Intelligence agent. *You*. With his handsome young assistant. *Me*. And in the other two corners we have a brace of manipulative old scoundrels, both of whom would sell their grandmothers for a pint of milk. Half a pint. The celebrated and devious Bergdorf. And, beside him, the charitable and pig-thick Cohen. What a cast it is!' he sniggered. 'And don't let's forget Miranda Bronowski, our

Dark Lady, or dreary old Hermann. I suppose he'll be the body. Unless someone unexpected turns up on the library floor.'

He laughed briefly and unpleasantly, then took from a box at his feet a copy of a new literary novel, a favourite for the Booker Prize. He flicked through its pages for a few moments, before, holding it between thumb and forefinger, he dropped it disgustedly back into its box.

'Christ! Well, say something. Tell me a good read.'

Edel sat down on the edge of the packing bench. He'd been surprised by Levinstein's sharpness and wit a moment ago. That speech was plagiarised from somewhere, Edel thought. Coarsened but plagiarised. The names were fitted in by Bernie, but the thrust of the text was someone else's. Rattigan possibly? Would Bernie know of Rattigan? William Douglas Home?

'The situation's not quite as neat as you put it,' he corrected him. 'There's too much loyalty and connection between us all for that. That's what breaks up the symmetry, as you call it. It all interlocks. Mariss to Cohen. Miranda to Amos. Amos to Mariss. And me. Loyal and connected to most of them. So there's no symmetry, not really.'

Levinstein grinned at him. 'I like the last bit,' he said, 'the bit about you and loyalty! You shopped poor old Steiner the moment he woke up and had the great idea. Sending him to me for his gun . . . A stroke of genius, yeah, but not exactly the last word in loyalty, eh?'

Edel got up from the bench, and went to pick up some loose delivery notes that had been abandoned on the floor. Still bending, he said mildly, 'What makes you think it was me who sent Steiner to you for the gun? Is that the sort of thing that I would do?'

'Yes,' Levinstein replied. 'Of course it was you. It's just the sort of thing you'd fucking do. As you were saying – you'd do it as a mark of your loyalty. To Mariss and Amos, and all the rest of the gang. Breaks my heart. Makes me cry. Now tell me what I'm supposed to do next. I haven't got the first fucking idea.'

'Well, why not this?' Edel said. 'Leave Mariss to run on this one for a few days more, so that we can see what else he unearths for us. Leave him thinking that he really will get his gun. He's not going to, of course, so he's never going to hurt anyone. At the end of the day he's not going to be able to do any harm to himself or to anyone else. But something may come to light if we let him run on a bit – don't you think?'

Levinstein looked for a moment as if he was about to argue. Then he shrugged his shoulders.

'Just as you say, Gareth, if that's what you want. But I'll tell you something else. I'm not comfortable about your friend Amos. He's more difficult than anyone to pin down, in my opinion. I don't know what he's capable of, or what he really wants. I suppose you've got him under control, but I even prefer Steiner to him, the nasty little shit.'

There was a silence between them, then Edel got to his feet, and threw Levinstein's raincoat across to him.

They agreed their time to meet later in the week, and as Levinstein set off down the alleyway he heard Edel lock and bolt the heavy metal doors behind him.

I wonder if he genuinely fails to grasp what the position is with Steiner, Levinstein thought. If he doesn't, he's a fool. If he does, he's concealing it from me. Either way I don't know where the hell I am with him. Devious fucking git.

Chapter 39

'You're such a cynic, Amos, you really are,' Lewis Cohen complained. The two men had met in Lewis's office, at Bronowski's request.

Bronowski grunted. 'I thought it was my famous energy and enthusiasm you always admired, Lewis. Nothing about cynicism. The wild Zionist lad browbeating the mob into ecstasy and revolution. *You're* the cynic, Lewis. I've never met your Machiavellian match in all my days. Actually, perhaps I have, now I come to think of it. Jacob Bergdorf. You and he are made for each other.'

Cohen offered Bronowski a drink, and put it down beside him. 'Ah, Bergdorf,' he said smoothly. 'I'm glad you mentioned him. Do you see very much of him these days? Are you and he friends?'

God, that was crass, Cohen thought. What on earth's the matter with me? He tried again, more subtly this time.

'I tell you why I ask,' he continued. 'He could be helpful to you in your research. He's a mine of information, you know, *if* he's prepared to let you tap it.'

Bronowski stared at him for a moment, but made no reply, seemingly in contempt for the banality of Cohen's approach.

Then he said, 'For heaven's sake, Lewis! You're hatching some plot over Bergdorf. I can hear it coming and see it coming. What the hell is it?'

He gazed at Cohen's expression of bewilderment, and laughed out loud. 'Lewis, you're impossible to be angry with. Let's try to cut through all this. I haven't got the time or the energy for it.'

Cohen once more started to assume a look of injured, forgiving innocence. Grimacing, Bronowski said, 'Lewis – for heaven's sake. For once in your life, play an open hand! As I was saying – Bergdorf. He called me over to see him in Switzerland, one day when he was there on business. He wanted me to keep my trip secret from Gareth, so I did so. But I told him immediately afterwards, of course. I hate that sort of duplicity. Life's too short.'

Lewis was watching him now with genuine concentration. I'm telling him something that he wants to know about, Bronowski realised.

'So I met Bergdorf in Geneva, in his hotel. I'm not sure, even now, if I really understand what he wanted from me. He presented it as a request for me to help get rid of Mariss Steiner, but I refused in no uncertain terms though at the same time I didn't believe that Bergdorf really meant what he was proposing. So then he said he knew all about various operations that I was involved with in my younger days.'

He looked across at Cohen. 'You know about that side of things, Lewis. We don't have to go through another farce of double-talking with each other, do we, for God's sake?'

Cohen caught Bronowski's eye, and said nothing.

'I came back to London that day wondering what Bergdorf was up to with me. He must have known full well that however much a clown Mariss might be at times, I wouldn't lay a finger on him. I've known him too long. *You've* known him too long as well, Lewis. Too long to harm him.'

He fiddled around with his drink for a moment. 'Leave him alone, Lewis. What you should be doing is protecting Mariss from himself, because he certainly needs it. But don't do anything to harm him. And make sure that nobody else does either.

'Actually I would tell you to be Mariss's guardian, except that I myself would never want to be thought of in that role. All I want to do is tell a story that should be told. To tell the truth. I'm an archivist. I'm an historian.'

'Oh come on, Amos!' Cohen threw up his arms in mock exasperation. 'You're not the only person who's ever written about the concentration camps! Are you suggesting that all those other journalists and writers, the whole tribe of them, haven't chronicled the truth of it all, in just the same spirit as you? And another thing – you talk about your personal experience of Belsen as if you had an adult's recall of it. But you were a small child. Gareth was barely more than a toddler. Your memories are those of infants, not those of reliable, mature minds.'

Bronowski shrugged. 'But we were there. And I've examined every existing source on the subject, and talked to hundreds of other survivors. Of course there's a literature surrounding the camps, and the Holocaust, and much of it is highly valuable. It can take its form sometimes as social history, and at others as romantic fiction or allegory, and however it's presented it's none the worse for that. All of it has something to say. It's all fine. But no one, *no one*, has told quite the story that I'm going to tell, nor traced out the same thesis. The report presents some facts that, for "our community", as you would put it, are harsh, and uncompromising, and uncomfortable. Some people are featured in my research who no doubt would much prefer not to be.

'But, and I say this one last time, I'm not publishing the report in order to be a sensationalist. I'm publishing it because I'm a chronicler of the truth. And I believe that the Jewish people are wise enough, and strong enough, to know that truth is very much better expressed and exposed, than suppressed and withheld. In the interests of history, and as part of the narrative of the Jewish people. They are your real "community". The Jewish people from the beginning of time. Not the clients of your law firm. Nor those of Jacob Bergdorf's, if it comes to that.'

Bronowski looked at Cohen, and half smiled, as if aware that his vehemence had been overdone and that his tone had been pompous. He paused for a moment, mumbling some comment which Cohen, only half hearing, construed to be a little joke of self-mockery, and got to his feet, wandering over to the bookcase, hands in pocket, running his eyes along the shelves. Then, his back to Cohen, he said, 'I went to Gateshead, Lewis, as you suggested. I'm not quite clear what fresh research material you were under the impression I would get from it. But I went. I traced the man whose name you gave. Ledelmeister. He's dead. Did you realise that? He's been dead for eight years. So has his wife. I found the records. I looked at his grave. Gustav Ledelmeister.'

Cohen, whose briefing from Edel on this he guiltily recalled having made more mysterious when relayed to Bronowski, coughed, and was still wondering what to say in reply, when Bronowski continued, still with his back turned.

'It was Gareth who put you up to it I assume?'

Cohen, floundering now, trying to remember exactly what he had said to Bronowski in the first place, heard himself saying, 'Well – I think he had in mind that—'

Bronowski cut in on him.

'Forget it, Lewis. You can never resist a hint of intrigue. It's not such a complicated story, though Gareth always thinks I have more up my sleeve on it than I do. Ledelmeister was at Belsen. He was a *kapo* there. He killed my father. If he hadn't, no doubt somebody else would have. Belsen was a nasty place. End of story. End of Ledelmeister. God knows how he ended up in Gateshead, but he seems to have done. He was an old man. And now he is dead.'

Chapter 40

Bergdorf sat at an angle to his desk, sprawled in his chair, gazing out at the neat, rectangular garden at the front of his house, and the elderly gardener in his green apron, raking patterns in the gravel of the drive.

He turned as his wife came into the room, putting down on his desk a mid-morning tray of coffee and cakes. She smiled and said something which, as usual, he ignored, then watched her as she set off again from the room. Her colourless hair was drawn back into a bun, her broad back encased tight within her habitual buttoned cardigan, and her swollen feet enclosed, as they always were when she was in the house, in her comfortable, plaid felt slippers. He had given them to her for her birthday the previous year, in a mood of not entirely affectionate irony, and he had seldom seen her out of them since.

'*Danke schön*,' he cried out after her, on a sudden impulse. Then, '*Liebling*,' he added, after a pause. She turned, surprised, her hand already on the door handle, simpering a pink, dimpled smile at him. She looked as if she was going to say something, then changed her mind, and padded soundlessly on her way. Bergdorf shook his head in a mixture of tired dismissal and momentary guilt. He poured his black coffee, added a thick dollop of cream, and allowed himself a few reflections on his marriage, specifically wondering for a moment if he was paying his wife quite sufficient attention these days in the assuagement of her physical needs. Then he put all further thought of her out of his head, swung his chair around once more to face the garden, and returned his mind immediately to its previous concerns.

The difficulty, he thought, was how best to contact Steiner. He could write, of course, and Emmanuel could be despatched with the letter, in the normal way. Then they could be certain that the message had fallen into the right hands, and that it had been read.

160

But somehow a letter was unsatisfactory. And a conversation by telephone would be worse.

He finished his coffee, bit at a cream cake, wiped his fingers clean with the little starched napkin that his wife had left for him on the tray, then got up from his chair, and went to stand at the open window, his hands locked together behind his back. The gardener caught sight of him, and made an awkward salute, then resumed his raking, much more vigorously than before. Bergdorf made a slight wave, then resumed his stare out to the two chestnut trees by the far wall, and the straggling, gloomy shrubs planted under them.

It would be better to talk to him direct, no question about that. But that would mean flying to London and meeting him in an hotel or in that disgusting room of his. The trouble was, it would be next to impossible to visit England without his presence there being traced, if anyone was minded to do so. It was dangerous enough to send his son. A false passport was possible; he'd done it before. But if it ever subsequently came to light . . . And Bergdorf didn't like disguises. He never had. If you are caught, you look an absolute clown, and automatically guilty of whatever it is you might be suspected of.

Bergdorf sighed, went back to his desk, and took a full mouthful of another thickly iced chocolate cake. He dabbed at his lips with Heidi's dainty napkin, then took one final mouthful and finished it off.

And yet to bring Steiner here to Vienna would be worse, he mused, shuddering at a mental picture of Mariss clumping his way through the airport with that ridiculous stick of his, calling out Bergdorf's name to all and sundry . . . And Vienna was so small and provincial and impossible to hide someone away in. Steiner spoke perfect German, even after all these years, and he would have the sense to impersonate a Viennese accent and vocabulary. But the appearance, and the very style of the man would be quite impossible to conceal and hide away. There were still too many people in Vienna who would recognise him from the old days, when the US Intelligence people were making such a big thing of pursuing him around the place looking for those files of theirs that he had walked away with. Like a shoplifter from a back street bazaar, Bergdorf grinned. Walking away with their files like an old lady stealing half a kilo of bacon, and stuffing it under her skirts.

No – I'll have to go to London and see him there, he decided.

161

Perhaps I'm making too much of the security dangers. There are always legitimate reasons for me to go to London. I'll get the office to arrange some meetings for me. There's some Embassy business I can attend to quite openly, now that I think of it, and some things to tie up for the Öestreicher Bank as well. I'll make sure there's a meeting with Lewis Cohen in my diary too. There, written into my diary, for anyone to see, who wants to see.

Bergdorf picked up the telephone, suddenly decided. As he leafed through his address book to find Joseph Hermann's number he reflected that it was a pity, for security reasons, that it was written there. But to remove it now . . .

'Joseph? Jacob here, Jacob Bergdorf. I have been meaning to be in contact with you for weeks. That note you wrote a couple of months ago with two more briefs – just what I needed. And your letters of introduction. You're very kind. Very helpful.'

He listened for a moment, then cried, 'Why, you say? Why should I want to contact you now?' He laughed, more loudly in his nervousness than he would have wished, and because of it pushed his wife's best silver coffee tray irritably across the desk and out of his way, as if the act of that, and the rudeness of it, would punish her, and make him feel the stronger and more resolute and more masculine for it.

'You're teasing me, Joseph – it's what you've always done. Why shouldn't I want to be in contact with you? After all our years together, and the experiences we've shared?' What was it about this man? he thought. Of course he'd been formidable. As a young man he was astonishing. Buchenwald and so on. But these days . . .

Calm down, Bergdorf told himself. He's an old man now, and I'm the most famous lawyer in Vienna.

'Look – you called me, and here I am returning that call,' he said, trying to inject into his voice now a certain cold, competent professionalism. 'What can I do for you, Joseph?' Then, suddenly irritated, 'Or, more specifically, what can I do that your own lawyers can't?' He had remembered, his calm returning, that the libel suit Hermann had recently instigated against a fellow academic, and on which he had won out of court a most substantial settlement, had been conducted by some partnership from Linz, or somewhere equally galling and provincial, whom no one had ever heard of, and never would again.

He listened now for some minutes as Hermann spoke, murmuring occasionally to indicate his attention. Once, during this, his wife peeped her head around the door, mouthing in dumbshow her question as to whether she could now clear away the coffee tray. She was met only by a violent swing of Bergdorf's arm, indicating her immediate and furious dismissal, and the door closed hastily behind her.

At last Bergdorf said, 'I understand, Joseph, but I can't comment on the accuracy of the rumours. Yes, I've heard them as well. No, I have no reason to suspect that they're any more true than those sorts of things ever are. No . . . No . . . I have no more information than you as to the intentions, or the state of health and mind, or indeed the whereabouts of this man Mariss Steiner. When did I last see him? When did I last speak to him? Oh, several years ago. Decades ago, more likely.'

The sweat was now beginning to bead all over Bergdorf's forehead, and he patted at it with his handkerchief, which he then ran around the inside of his collar. As he pushed the handkerchief back into his pocket, his face assumed an expression of soft, ironic amusement, as if the two of them were in the room together, and Bergdorf was putting on a show of professional *gravitas* and expertise. He gesticulated with his free hand, holding the palm up as if in amused, tolerant surrender.

'Joseph, Joseph. Enough of this. Someone has come up with a ridiculous rumour that neither of us should give so much as house room to, and we're quarrelling over that? It's ludicrous – laughable! Would I allow you to be injured, Joseph? Would I not rush to your aid if I thought you were in peril, after all that we've been through together?'

He listened more, and this time his face pulled itself into a stagey grimace of horror, as if Hermann was there in the room with him.

'*I* would do harm to you? You've heard a rumour that *I* am planning something of that sort? This is preposterous. This whole conversation is insane, it really is. If I wasn't an old friend . . .'

He listened now to Hermann for some further moments, then burst out furiously: 'All right, Joseph, now you listen to me. I won't be threatened and insulted in this way. If you continue in this vein for very much longer, I can assure you that I will take action to— No, no, not that: *Legal* action. But there'll be no need for that, because you're going to calm down and listen to me.' It flashed through Bergdorf's mind that a few years ago, he would no more have made such a remark to Joseph Hermann than to the President himself, but he continued.

'I'll tell you what I'm going to do. I'm going to drop everything, and go immediately to London. When I'm there, I'll move heaven and earth to find where Mariss Steiner hides and . . . you say he's in the telephone book? . . . well then, what could be better? I'll call him when I'm there, and arrange for him to come to see me, and I'll find out exactly what, if anything, he's up to.'

He listened some more. 'Yes, all right, if it will make you feel easier. Yes, I'll make sure he's behind bars, and safely out of danger's way for the entire period of your visit. I'll ensure that the Ambassador and the British police and all the authorities are made fully aware of the nature of the rumours. And of the fact that Steiner shouldn't be dismissed as some type of harmless crackpot. He is dangerous, and I'll make sure they're told that.

'As far as the other issue is concerned, my hands are tied. I was aware of these newspaper articles that Amos Bronowski has written, naturally – and I want them to appear as little as you do. I haven't seen them in advance of their publication, because I have nothing to do with Bronowski whatsoever, but it sounds as though they're going to be thoroughly destructive and mischievous. Maybe they're actionable and libellous – if that's any comfort to you,' he concluded, attempting some sort of suggestion of a joke, and wincing at Hermann's furious response.

As Hermann launched into another tirade, Bergdorf stared out of the window at the chestnut trees, no longer interrupting him, lost now in thought. It continued for some time, then, when Hermann was finished, he said, 'Yes. Yes – I'm still here. As I've told you, Joseph, I'll fly to London tomorrow to try to sort some of these difficulties out. Steiner will have to be dealt with. Bronowski must be curbed, if that's possible. But there's one other person I must warn you about. In the strictest confidence. This other man will do you more harm than either of them. He's out to destroy you, as a matter of fact, and unless you protect yourself he will most certainly succeed. In a sense it's none of my business. From the point of view of my own safety, I would be much better advised to stay out of the way, and leave this to others. But we're old friends, you and I, and I can't simply turn a blind eye.'

He paused, enjoying the dramatic silence on the other end of the telephone. Then he said, 'It's Cohen, Joseph. Lewis Cohen. That's who you have to look out for. The others are a nuisance, but it's Cohen who is the real danger to you. He's the man you really have to fear. I must advise you – do be on your guard with him. Better than that; have nothing to do with him at all. Refuse his calls, and return his letters. Have nothing to do with him whatsoever.'

Chapter 41

Once Bernie Levinstein was gone, and the doors out on to the back alley were padlocked and secure, Edel went over to the packing bench, reached inside his jacket, and took out an envelope, checking once more the address he had been given. Then, reaching with difficulty up to the top locks of the front doors to turn them behind him, he went off down the street.

He decided to walk the mile or so to the coffee shop off Victoria Street where he was to meet Lewis Cohen. Edel was a man of compulsive thrift; the pound or so saved on this fare would make his evening drink at the *Princess of Wales* taste all the sweeter. And since he was going to walk, he decided to take a small detour through St James's Park on this pleasant summer evening, past the roses in their wide beds along the lakeside.

It was typical of Cohen to choose this as the place for them to have their talk, he thought, for the street was a deserted turning behind Westminster School and the Abbey, and the coffee shop was next to a dingy little ecclesiastical and legal outfitters – just the sort of establishment, in its dusty Englishness, for which Cohen had a taste. The man's hardly your standard Holocaust survivor, Edel thought. You'd think he'd been born in a country parsonage, or a Cathedral Close. Matins at St Paul's. Christmas Carols at King's College, Cambridge.

Cohen was already there, sitting on his own at a back table, staring and frowning at *The Times* crossword puzzle. Edel pulled out a chair, and Cohen looked up at him, tapping the heel of his propelling pencil up against his lower lip, frowning in thought.

'*Cow goes straight into the marshy area.* Eight letters, the fourth letter *e*. Or just possibly *g*. Quite infuriating. I'm losing my touch. I think it's because of the muddle over the *g*. Hello, Gareth. How are you?' he finished, without the slightest interest in his voice, and went straight back to the crossword for a few more moments. Eventually he flung the paper down on to the

166

chair beside him, cursed and sipped at his glass of mineral water.

'The greatest moment of my life,' he said. 'I'm going from here to a dinner party at the Bishop of London's house, just around the corner.' And although the remark had been laboriously ironic, Edel wondered what Cohen really felt. 'The Anglican League for Jewish Reconciliation,' Cohen explained. 'I'd never heard of it before last month. The dinner's a thousand pounds a plate! I've never known one of these things priced in that way before. It's as if we were on the primaries trail in the US Presidential elections. I don't imagine they've sold a single seat, except to me. I bought two, for Elizabeth and myself, because I couldn't bear the thought of the poor Bishop coming into his dining room to find not a single Jew there to meet him.'

'Who's reconciling whom? And why?' Edel said.

Cohen waved a hand in vague, irritated disapproval at Edel's sarcasm. 'Mutual. We them. Them us. And a very good idea too.'

Edel stirred some sugar into the cup of coffee that Cohen had ordered for him.

'It's all right, Lewis. You can call a halt. Forget the Anglicans. You wanted to see me.'

Cohen took another sip from his mineral water before replying, then sat for a moment in thought, fiddling with the clip of his propelling pencil.

'This article in the *Sunday Times*—'

'Is nothing to do with me,' Edel said immediately, interrupting him in mid-sentence. 'It's Amos's article. And as far as I know it's going out as planned. The first next Sunday.'

'Of course it is,' Cohen said. 'I accept that. I said to Amos what I felt I had to say about it, but I didn't win the day, and that's hardly surprising. You know my view. I don't have to go over the same ground all over again.'

'No,' said Edel, 'you don't. And that's not why you've brought me here.'

Cohen looked over at him, and hesitated for a moment. 'Life does twist around for us, Gareth, does it not? You, and me, and Amos. And however it twists, we never can disentangle ourselves from each other's lives. We go for months or years without seeing one another, but the thread is still there between us. We only have to give the thread a twitch, and we're back together again.' He held up his hand as Edel, shaking his head in irritation, started to interrupt. Cohen said, 'You must let me finish! I mention the thread between us, because I need, not for the first time in my life, to pull at it a little. Put more simply, I need a favour from you, Gareth.'

Edel said nothing, but sat there watching him, an expression of fleeting, mocking irony in his eyes.

'I can guess what it is, Lewis,' he said finally. 'I know what you want. You want me to help with the business over Mariss Steiner. Tuck him away out of sight while Joseph Hermann is here, in case something unpleasant happens. Or is it the reverse of that? You want Marris to launch an assassination attempt on him, so that you can be Hermann's heroic rescuer. Is that it? So that you win his confidence and can then get involved in his affairs?'

Cohen blushed violently, then, pulling himself together, shook his head and made an attempt at a smile. 'No, that's not it. Mariss is a bore, certainly, and I hope we can persuade him to drop all this nonsense over Hermann, and settle down at home to write his memoirs, or something like that. Actually, that's rather a good idea.'

He chuckled, and Edel smiled courteously in response, still waiting.

'No, it's nothing to do with Mariss,' Cohen repeated. 'It's about Bronowski and his articles. Gareth, Amos is due to deliver the second article to them on Tuesday of next week. I believe that he'll be putting the finishing touches to it over the weekend?'

Edel shrugged. 'You'll have to ask him. But that's right, as far as I know. That's what he told me.'

Cohen hesitated, then said, 'Look, Gareth, Amos is going ahead with these articles, although I advised him against it. The *Sunday Times* articles are going to happen, I realise that. But if they're going to happen, I want them to be fair. I'm sure you do as well. My view is this; if Singer, to take one example, is going to have his world knocked out from under his feet, then we should ensure that he has not been singled out arbitrarily. I believe that Singer's story is one that Amos gives great prominence to in the second section of his report. Is that right?'

Edel watched him closely, and nodded, cautiously. 'As far as I know.'

'If Singer, why not others?' Cohen demanded reasonably. 'Why shouldn't others be exposed in exactly the same way?'

'There *are* others, Lewis,' Edel replied, slightly impatient and still suspicious. 'Plenty of them. You know that – you saw the original working draft. Singer, certainly. Hermann again, of course, which will please Mariss Steiner no doubt. Bruch, Amos deals with at some length. There are several more case histories – particularly of those amongst the Buchenwald Communists. It's Buchenwald that's the main thrust of this, as you know, and particularly the rôle of the Communist leadership there.'

He gazed at Cohen. 'You're changing your tune, Lewis, aren't you? How many more people do you want exposed, for heaven's sake?'

Cohen suddenly struck his palm on his forehead, and reached for his newspaper. He scribbled some letters down on the crossword puzzle, then turned back to Edel.

'FRIGHTEN. *Cow goes straight into the marshy area.* FRIGHTEN. You know – marshy area; fen. The cow's right in the middle of it.'

Edel looked blank.

'"Right" in the middle of the word,' Cohen explained. '"Fen". *F* is the first letter in the word *Frighten*, and *E* and *N* are the last two. Ingenious of course, but that's the game, and it was stupid of me to take so long at it. It was that muddle over Seven Across that put me off.'

He picked the paper up again and immediately scribbled letters across the final uncompleted boxes.

'It's obvious,' he said triumphantly. 'There we are. TOGETHER. *Combined to irritate the lady.* To irritate the lady. TO GET HER. Combine it, and show the meaning of the whole word. TOGETHER. That's it. Finished.' He flung the paper back on to the chair beside him, and beamed across the table.

'I was asking,' said Edel, 'and with a certain sense of bewilderment, how many more people you wanted Amos to include in the article?'

'Only one more, to be honest with you, Gareth. Just one for now, and that only for the sake of justice being done, and fairness. There is one more name that should be brought into this with the others.'

They sat looking at each other, both waiting for the other to make the next move.

Then Edel said, 'Who are we talking about, Lewis?

Cohen glanced at his watch, picked up the bill, and threw some change down on to the table. He, stood up then turned to Edel.

'Bergdorf, Gareth, that's who. Jacob Bergdorf. Use your influence, there's a good fellow. Amos would never do it for me, but he would for you. Remember – Bergdorf.'

Edel stared at him.

'Bergdorf?' he repeated eventually, his voice mocking. 'What do you have on him? He was at Buchenwald, of course, but I've never heard a whisper of gossip about what he did when he was there. None whatsoever. So what's Bergdorf got to do with all this?'

Cohen hesitated.

'It's not so much Buchenwald, as what happened afterwards,' he said, beginning to move off towards the door. 'Let me see what I can provide for Amos to consider. I'll do that. It wouldn't be right to let Bergdorf get away with it, and see the other people exposed. That wouldn't be fair at all.'

Chapter 42

Lewis Cohen settled his wife into the front of the Daimler, and closed the door after her with a gentle courtesy. He walked around the car to climb in to the driver's seat, then looked back at his daughter behind him, already with her homework open on her knees. He smiled at her, then leant over to peer more closely at the notes she was writing in the margins of the text. He turned to the front again, and started the engine.

'Such work they give you these days, Rachel!' he said, the delight obvious in his voice.

They drew away from the kerb, and he ignored, as if oblivious to it, the enraged shout and the long blare on the horn as he pulled out directly in front of a taxi.

'A child still,' he continued, 'and they expect you to read Bunyan! At eleven years of age!'

He turned to Elizabeth, glowing in his pride not only in the demands on Rachel from her academically precocious school, but in his private pleasure that the author she was studying was so much part of the fabric of English culture. Of course he was proud of their Jewishness, he told himself. From the time his daughter was a toddler, he had been emphatic in his insistence on their familial observances of Jewish life. But *Bunyan* . . .

The three of them chattered all the way down to his parents-in-law's Georgian house, tucked away in the green, folded hills of the South Downs. As the Daimler swept up the long carriage drive, the good fortune of his marriage into the Rosenberg family struck Cohen all over again. Of course he was still in love with Elizabeth. What nonsense to think anything else. Of course he was, and in a sudden burst of affection, he laid his hand on her thigh, in doing so reflecting that it was a gesture of familiar and easy physical intimacy that he hadn't made to her for a very long time. But today he felt so happy with his life. He had with him his precious daughter and his lovely wife, and all was well with the world.

171

Cohen looked across at the parkland stretching out before them, and the ancient walled gardens beside the simple, elegantly proportioned house. This, he thought, was exactly as he himself wanted one day to live. His own house in St John's Wood was fine, of course, and well in keeping with the image he required of himself and his family. There was nothing wrong with his house. But *this* – and, as he got out of the car he looked around him once more – this was as good as you could get! As English as you could get! And maybe . . . after Felix had died . . .

But now he was swept up, if vicariously, in a flurry of activity and familial affection. The Rosenbergs ran out from the house the moment he had drawn up the car, and rushed forward to seize both Elizabeth and Rachel in delighted embraces. Cohen stood to one side, laughing in his pride as his daughter was picked up into her grandfather's arms, and thrown up in the air as if she was as dainty and light as a feather, eleven years old as she might be, and tall and big for her age. He hugged her to him, then set her gently down on the gravel. Cohen beamed at this overt, unaffected love for his daughter. This was Felix Rosenberg, no less. Rachel was his own flesh. His daughter, Rachel Cohen, was Felix Rosenberg's flesh. And then the moment was over, and his father-in-law turned to him, and shook him pleasantly by the hand, though, as he did so, his gaze was over his shoulder at Elizabeth, standing there alone.

A servant, picking up their suitcases, crunched his way across the drive to the porticoed front door. Sadie Rosenberg, who had ignored Cohen to that point, craned her painted face up now for him to kiss, and he did what was required of him, in what he hoped was a seemly show of appropriate, if decorous enthusiasm.

'It's so sad that you can't yourself stay down here for the week-end with Elizabeth and Rachel!' she cried, then, opening her arms in a theatrical gesture of dismay, she turned away, reaching out to pinch her granddaughter on the cheek. Cohen noticed, and hoped that her grandmother hadn't, that Rachel flinched perceptibly as she did so. But Lady Rosenberg was continuing, in her customary harsh, raucous caw, 'So sad! When we have so many happy treats planned for them both! You should stay! You work so hard at your blessed law firm, Lewis! Too hard! Weekends even!'

It was a shock quite disproportionate to the action when Lord Rosenberg touched Cohen lightly on the arm, and said he would like to have a word in private before he left. There was something in the pitch and tone of his voice that was immediately discomfiting, and, as he was steered into Rosenberg's study, his mind raced over the various possibilities of what the conversation was going to be about.

His guess, and his fear, proved to be correct. Now they were alone, there was a coldness in his father-in-law's eyes and voice that was chilling. It appeared that Rosenberg knew only a tiny fraction of the story from his sources, and what he did seem to know was mercifully slight and undamaging, but Cohen felt horrified at the realisation of even that. To be humiliated like this by a man as distinguished as Elizabeth's father . . .

But, surprising himself by it, he found that he was able to keep calm, and lucid, and coolly articulate. And, he mused, as he at last was able to get out of the house, and into his car, and safely away from the place, he had succeeded in being persuasive as well. Rosenberg seemed relieved and content with the story in explanation that Cohen had weaved for him. He had shown him out of the house and returned to his daughter and granddaughter with a pleasantness and warmth that signalled he now regarded the matter as closed.

But despite Lewis's self assurances, the matter was far from settled in Felix Rosenberg's mind as he settled down at his desk later that day. He flexed his writing hand, pulled his concentration together, and reached into a drawer for several sheets of paper. Taking out his fountain pen, he began to write.

Darling Elizabeth

Absurdly, I'm writing you this letter on Saturday afternoon, hidden away behind the closed doors of my study, and you're in the garden somewhere with your mother, not two hundred yards from me. But I have various matters to tell you about that I know I would find very hard to do face to face.

I've done this so many times before. Those problems you had at school the year before you left; the incident over the borrowed credit card when you were a student; that sadly ill-starred engagement of yours with that melancholy boy you met on the kibbutz. On all those occasions, and others, I wrote to you, rather than had the courage to talk to you direct. And the result, of course, was that we never did discuss, on those occasions or any others, what should have been matters of responsible dialogue between us. And, consequently, our relationship has never matured in the way that it should have done. But there we are. And here I am. Doing the whole thing all over again.

My dear, I've watched your marriage over the years with nervousness, but, at times, not without hope. The age difference between you and Lewis was – is – unorthodox, and there's no hiding from that. But I've seen in my life partnerships before where these age differences have been there, and in many cases the marriages have been the more successful for them. Or is that too glib? How are any of us to know, as outsiders, what makes this marriage work, and that one fail? And how can we see for sure where contentment exists, and where it doesn't?

Outsiders would think of Lewis as being nothing less – nor more – than a brilliantly successful lawyer; one with the most extraordinary reputation as a fixer and a solver of his clients' problems. And not just his clients' problems actually; he always seems to me to be the sort of person who cannot resist tinkering with everything that passes his nose. His dabbling in other people's affairs is actually almost disinterested. It's interference, and manipulation, for the joy of the skill of it.

I'm sure you haven't the slightest idea what is going on in Lewis's professional life, and that you never have done. I'm fairly certain that you don't have that sort of marriage. But Elizabeth, my dear, I find, or rather I am informed by others who reliably know about these things, that Lewis is in the middle of an initiative that may bring considerable problems to those of us who have become his family. You, and me, and your mother, and Rachel. The initiative – I will call it that, for at the moment I don't want to become, in my cowardly way, more specific in the description of it to you – appears, as always with Lewis, to be part romantic, part dabbling in other people's affairs, part a deliberate attempt at the protection of his clients' interests. And part pure naughtiness. All the hallmarks, in fact, of Lewis's conduct in anything and everything, so that, in itself, should not bring us any surprise. But, in this case, there's a difference. I've been led by the evidence to believe that there's another element to it too. Something which creates a problem to the members of our family. I believe that it's my duty as your concerned if morally cowardly father to tell you what the position is, so that between all of us we can decide what it is to be done. It's this. I've discovered something in the last few days that I never before suspected or had reason to fear.

Elizabeth, Lewis has no money whatsoever. None at all. His debts are, believe me, wholly overwhelming. One or two of his creditors are pressing him now to the point of bankruptcy. I know it will come as a shock, but I'm afraid it's true.

I'm not at all sure how Lewis has got into this position. I don't believe that there is anything lurking in his life that would provide the usual explanation in these cases. He doesn't gamble, it appears. There is no record of his having been improvident or grossly unfortunate in his investments, though perhaps there has been some incident or other of which I am unaware. His personal tastes do not look to me to be those of a man of absurd and inappropriate extravagance. Your house is nice, of course, and I'm grateful to him for that, but the furnishings are not over-lavish, and the pictures are pleasant enough, but not those of an obsessively driven collector. The car is very grand, but I imagine is provided by his firm. Rachel, and again I am grateful to him for it, is at a good and no doubt expensive private school, but the education of a single child should be well within his range.

So I don't know what's happened. And I'm particularly bemused as his firm has to all accounts been a most successful partnership, and they've always had as many clients as they wish to handle. Or so it has always been believed, by those of us in the profession. So I don't know the reason for the collapse in his affairs. But I do know that what I've told you is true, and I'm distressed that it is. As you can imagine. I want for my daughter a happy and secure life, and financial insecurity on this scale is a hard fate to deal with.

Your mother and I are comfortably off, as you know. But only comparatively so, and most of what I have saved from my inheritance and my working life, after making suitable provision for Sadie, has already been tidied away into the family Trusts of which you and Rachel are the beneficiaries. So, with the best will in the world, there is not very much that I could do for Lewis, even if I was of a mind to do so. You, my dear – and, as if I have to say it, Rachel – are a different proposition. You can depend on your mother and me to provide you both with everything that you need, and at any moment, and at any time. You know that, of course.

Well – the worst would appear to be about to happen. It seems inevitable that Lewis is to go into bankruptcy, and I'm sure you know that bankruptcy will deal him the most terrible blow. He will be debarred from practice quite automatically, and of course from his charitable Foundation as well. And for Lewis that will seem to him like the end of his life. He depends on what his work brings to him: influence, reputation, contacts with the great and famous, the good opinion of his peers. He'll lose that – all that – and it's hard to see him recovering from the blow of it. Would you not agree?

Which brings me back to the 'initiative', as I'm afraid I'm going

175

to continue calling it. The operation in which Lewis is currently engaged. I imagine he regards it as a make-or-break chance to repair his fortunes, and to put his affairs on their feet once more. All I can tell you is that I have only in the very last few days grasped the magnitude of what is going on. It is a business of potentially great danger, and I must now do everything that I can to put an end to it. And stop it I most certainly will. Too much is at stake. Other people's lives and reputations are endangered by what Lewis seems determined to complete. Not least, by reasons of our family connection to him, those of ourselves. And therein, of course, lies my concern. We Rosenbergs must stay together, my dear, and we will. You can depend on that.

Elizabeth – you must of course decide for yourself the degree to which you wish to share with Lewis the weight of his burden. You are his wife, and it would be wholly improper for me, or for your mother, to attempt to persuade you in any way, or to influence you as to how you conduct your relationship with your husband. That is entirely your affair, and that is how it should be. But I think I can allow myself to say this. It cannot be a surprise to you if I was to admit that neither your mother nor myself have warmed to Lewis over the years. We've never said that to you before, but I'm afraid it's the case, and I suspect you're too clever a girl not to have sensed it.

It's hard to explain the reasons for our lack of affection for him, and I'm not sure I really know them anyway. We know nothing but the broad outlines of his family background of course, and that may be a part of it. It is perhaps shamefully unfeeling and cruel of me to have quarrels over that, given the horrors of the poor chap's early childhood in the concentration camps. But, without being boastful about it, though to my own daughter I feel I'm allowed a little of that, the Rosenbergs have been at the forefront of the Jewish community in England for many generations. The family firm was not unduly profitable perhaps, and its takeover ultimately unavoidable, but it was a dignified, fine, celebrated business, and, most importantly for the family, it more than played its part in securing our position and needs. In particular, in paying for our education. My grandfather – your great grandfather – was a Fellow of All Souls, and a member of the Royal Society. His brother was a High Court Judge. My father was a Member of Parliament, and a distinguished journalist. And so on. The family has been amongst the most professionally and intellectually accomplished of any in the country where we came to make our home. You've been aware of that all your life. I am proud of our achievements, and I am proud too that I have not myself let the Rosenberg name down.

So, given this background, I have to say that we did not view Lewis's arrival on the family scene with quite the enthusiasm that we might have done. There was no doubt either about his cleverness of course, or his achievements. But we didn't know about him. Or rather what we did know was not entirely encouraging. His father was a merchant, we learned, whatever that may mean, and for all the tragic circumstances of his death, it must be deduced that the Cohens were a Warsaw family of no distinction of any kind. A million miles from the Rosenbergs. The truth of it was that Lewis married you, your mother and I believe, and here again you will forgive the frankness of what I say, because he saw in you a most advantageous match. A Rosenberg, for a guttersnipe of a Polish merchant's son, was a match of quite extraordinary distinction. And the daughter of an ennobled Rosenberg, a Judge, then later a Law Lord no less, must have seemed to an ambitious lawyer to be like a bride from providence. I don't say that Lewis didn't love you. He may well have done. But it was you as a Rosenberg, I'm afraid. That was what he loved. Not you for what you were.

So we must be rid of him, my dear – don't you think? There is about him now – actually there has been about him all his life, whatever the appearance of things in recent years – a most dangerous instability. The clients that his firm handles are not entirely the sort of people I would wish our family to be associated with. On top of that, there is – unmistakably – the whiff of danger about his Foundation, and there is the whiff of danger about Lewis himself. The Rosenbergs do not trust their lives and reputations to people such as those. That's not a remark that I would risk making outside the privacy of my own family; but you are my family, and my lovely Rachel is too, and I have nothing in my heart more deeply held than my determination to shield you both from dangerous situations and dangerous people. And your husband, never more than now, is one of those.

Read this, my dear, and think about it, then come down to me here again and we'll decide what is to be done. Divorce will not be difficult. I will make certain of that. Certain contacts of mine have cast an eye over Lewis's life, and although I can assure you of his physical fidelity to you – my research on this is clear – there are other aspects of his record that, when brought to him for discussion, will persuade him of the wisdom of an immediate severance of his links with our family. I'm sure of that.

I've been here in my study since before teatime, and now it's time for dinner, and both your mother and you are calling for me to drag myself away from what I am doing. Little knowing, of course, what absorbs me so. I will finish now, and give the letter to Harris to hand to you when he drives you and Rachel to the station tomorrow morning. And then I will await your call.

With love to both my angels, from your most adoring – and concerned,

Papa

Lord Rosenberg sealed the envelope, and tucked it into a drawer of his desk.

Even the most well-meaning and honourable of men were obliged, on occasions, he thought, to conduct a game of necessary duplicity with those around them. Otherwise the processes and dealings of daily life can never be satisfactorily conducted. Duplicity is too strong a word. Practicality. Pragmatism. There has to be a certain wordliness in it all. A certain . . . artificiality. Otherwise one's affairs never come to a conclusion.

At that moment his wife looked around the door, and he noddded and smiled at her as she shook her head in mock exasperation at his delay in joining them for dinner.

'Coming my dear,' Rosenberg said. 'On my way . . .'

Chapter 43

Bernie Levinstein peered down at the Army blanket on Steiner's bed, and cleared a spot to sit on it by brushing away with the back of his hand some pieces of fluff, and crumbs of what looked to him to be ginger cake.

'Christ,' he muttered, his face contorted with disgust, and with the toe of his gleaming shoe he poked out of sight the stained, crumpled pyjama bottom lying before him on the carpet.

Steiner lifted a pair of mugs unwashed from the sink, and offered him coffee.

'Not bloody likely,' Levinstein said, then gazed around the room as Steiner, seemingly quite unabashed, sang and whistled to himself what sounded to be a Yiddish music-hall song. He pottered around at the sink with the kettle and a gleaming new jar of Nescafé, shoplifted only that very morning from the all-night grocery store recently opened two or three streets away, and to which he had now transferred his custom.

'You're cheerful, Mariss,' said Levinstein. 'I can't think why, living in this hole. Look at the carpet, and the bedclothes. These mounds of paper stuck all over the walls. Fucking pigsty. How long have you been like this, for Christ's sake?'

Steiner waved his free hand around him in a gesture intended to indicate pride in the wealth of the treasures around him, then lowered himself into his armchair.

'I'm used to it, Bernie,' he said. 'It's my home. And – as you can see – I have all my bits and pieces around me. My whole collection. I know where everything is. That's the great thing. I've thrown so little away in my life, that it's important to know just where everything is.'

He laughed, and drank noisily and with apparent content from the filthy mug in his hand. 'It's not that bad,' he said. 'A little untidy maybe, but I'm happy enough with what I've got. My friends too.

Your father often came here to see me, I'm glad to say. And *he* drank my coffee.'

Steiner laughed again, and Levinstein reflected that he was mysteriously lacking in stress, for someone who was about to perform what, in his own eyes at least, would be one of the century's more dramatic political assassinations. There was a most odd sense of flippancy about the man – wholly out of character for one normally so angry and self-pitying.

'Well – today's the great day, isn't it?' Bernie said. 'Now's the moment when you hand me my five hundred quid, and I hand you your nice shiny new gun. It was today, wasn't it? Because that's why I'm here – for the five hundred quid.'

'Bernie, you're just like one of those actors from a 1940s' Hollywood B-movie – a poor man's John Garfield. I can't be the first to have told you that. Your clothes – particularly the camelhair overcoat draped over your shoulders like some caricature of a dancehall pimp . . . your accent even changes completely when you're in this mood. Your vocabulary too. Brilliant! What a parodist you are!'

Unmoved, Levinstein looked at Steiner more carefully. He's a dangerous little sod actually, he thought. A buffoon of course, but brighter than one tends to allow for. Lewis Cohen was right to be guarded with him, though even he sentimentalised him, for some reason. The guy's a right fucking weirdo.

'Yes,' he said. 'I can hardly get to sleep at night for laughing at myself. Now – where's my five hundred quid?'

Steiner shrugged, and sipped again at his coffee, then wiped his hand across the back of his mouth, and placed the mug down on the floor beside him.

'And where's my gun?'

Then, as soon as Levinstein started to speak, he held out his hand to stop him, laughing uproariously.

'You knew I was having a little game with you when I came to see you that day. A practical joke on the great parodist. And now you're letting it run on, you naughty boy. It's just the sort of thing that amuses you. Well – *touché!* But no gun!' he said, throwing up his hands in theatrical rejection of the idea. 'Please don't give me a gun! Don't take the joke that far! I'd be terrified even to touch the thing! Even a toy one!'

Levinstein gazed at him with overt dislike. 'I haven't got a gun, you cunt. And I don't imagine you've got five hundred quid. Hysterically amusing, isn't it? I was passing, and I thought we

could have one last go at it. With Hermann due here in only a
week, we'll need to find something new to kid each other along
with. So ha ha. And now I'm off.'

He got to his feet, slapping vigorously at the back of his trouser
legs to remove any lingering traces of Steiner's bedding.

'I'll see myself out,' he said. 'Give me a call again sometime.
When you need a good laugh, try me out.'

The door closed behind him, and as he started down the stairs,
he could feel the metal of the little handgun he'd brought for Steiner
rub along the inside of his thigh, uncomfortably sharp in the place
where it had loosened itself from the webbing in which he had
secured it. He reached into his trousers to adjust its position, and
shook his head.

That complicates matters, he frowned. I wasn't expecting that.
It never occurred to me that Steiner might chicken out. Last week
he seemed obsessed with his plan to get at old Hermann and kill
him. And now this mysterious jollity. What's going on? I had
better keep an eye on Steiner. I won't feel happy until I know
what he's up to.

I don't trust friend Mariss. But then I never did. The nasty
little tit.

Chapter 44

The bank manager poured Cohen a cup of tea, and sat back primly in his chair. He patted at his brow with a folded handkerchief, his regulation frock-coat, still imposed by Chapman & Co on its employees, straining tight and wrinkled against his armpits.

'I'm afraid that it's impossible for us to give yet more help, Mr Cohen. Quite impossible. Thank you for your most informative letter, containing an estimate of your likely earnings over the next few years. We were all most impressed with that, as you can imagine. But the Bank has already gone further than the original arrangement we agreed with you, and there's a lack of satisfactory security over any further drawings. We already have a charge on your house, and that is now fully borrowed against. Apart from that, you have not been able to put up for us anything very substantial. You have a small portfolio of shares, certainly, but these are already charged, and in a declining market . . .'

He sipped daintily at his own tea, and looked across at Cohen with a smug, pink satisfaction. For a moment, Cohen wondered if there wasn't a hint of anti-Semitism in there as well, but he quickly dismissed what he told himself was a paranoid response. He smiled at the man with a breezy show of self-confidence, reached across the table to retrieve the sheet of paper, and got to his feet to leave.

The manager got up too, almost reluctantly, Cohen thought, as if sorry to lose his sport so soon. He pointed to the sheet of paper and said, 'And one more thing. I'm afraid the answer has to be "No" on those, Mr Cohen. Your daughter's school fees, your life insurance premiums and the Harvey Nichols' bill. I'm afraid that in the circumstances we will not be able to clear those. So please don't embarrass us by writing cheques that we will not then be in a position to honour. I must be absolutely clear on that score. If you draw them, the cheques will be returned.'

Cohen hesitated. 'I wouldn't ask you unless I was obliged to do so,' he said, 'but I would be very grateful if at least my daughter's

school fees . . .' The manager was shaking his head even as he
spoke, and Cohen let the sentence trail away.

'Under no circumstances, Mr Cohen. We cannot honour any
further cheques from you at all.'

He let this sink in, then cleared his throat, and gazed contentedly
at Cohen once more.

'The final point I have to make to you is this. The overdraft
was granted to you on the basis that it was repayable on demand.
Well – we've decided to foreclose on it, Mr Cohen. We require it
to be repaid in full. Let's say within seven days. I will write to you
tonight confirming that formally. But please make arrangements
now for the account to be put into credit. Within one week, Mr
Cohen please. A week today.'

Lewis stood quite still, willing himself to look calm and in control
of himself.

'That's a little hard, Mr Johnson. You granted me the facility to
the end of the calendar year. I explained to you when we last met
that there are substantial payments due to me from my firm at that
point, and that these would enable me to clear my borrowings in
full. You made the arrangements with me on that basis. It's a little
hard of you now to say that—'

'Within seven days, Mr Cohen, if you please. Those are the
instructions I've received,' the manager said, somehow suggesting
in his intonation that such was his seniority and standing that no
one in the Bank, from the Chairman down, would actually presume
to instruct him on anything, and that the form of words he had used
was a politeness only, and that the decision to foreclose on Cohen
was a personal act, done for reasons of private certainty of his lack
of integrity, let alone solvency.

Cohen set off for the escalator, nodding and smiling his thanks
to the reception staff as he went, determined to reach the street
outside without showing in his body posture the slightest signs
of dismay. And when safely outside he continued the affec-
tation of it, whistling a cheerful tune, though hardly a sound
emerged from his parched lips. He felt oddly calm and at ease,
as if the Bank's foreclosing on him meant that there was no
longer a need to fight on in a battle that he was always certain
to lose.

What's the worst that can happen anyway, he thought. Let's look
it in the eye. Bankruptcy. He would be obliged to resign from his
law firm, from his clubs, and from the Foundation. Those would
all be gone. His house too, because the Bank would sell it to recover

their debt. His car, his pictures, his furniture – all of those as well. All gone.

But . . . how much did the loss of these things matter? Was there any real pain in that at all?

The sort of car that I drive, Cohen thought, the house I live in, the school that Rachel goes to, the restaurants in which I eat, the arts and charitable institutions that I serve – most of those I put there for other people to judge me by. And me too. Caught up in it, judging myself by those things as well. But inside of me, I've always been playing a part. The show of wealth never truly entered my soul. It was a disguise, that's all, but a pernicious one. It disguised me from myself.

As Cohen turned into the Strand, a woman in a doorway, sheltering a small child under her arm, held out a filthy hand and asked him for money. He felt in his pocket, pulled out a five-pound note, put it into her palm, nodded to her, and continued on his way.

More rich man's gestures, he thought. They become addictive. But that child . . .

He stepped out into the road, then sprang back when a taxi, brakes squealing, hooted at him in rage. For a moment Cohen felt quite faint with the shock of it, and rested, leaning against a lamp-post until he had recovered his breath and calm.

Work matters to me, he thought. Work, and Rachel. I may lose my work, I suppose, but I can't lose Rachel. Nothing that happens to me can take Rachel away.

The very thought of his daughter being taken away from him, unlikely as it was, impossible as it was – on top of the fright with the taxi – suddenly made Cohen feel that he was about to burst into tears. He put an arm across his face, and held it tight against his eyes, until in a moment or so he felt quietened enough to drop the arm and continue on his way.

Nothing touches at the heart of me, he thought. Nothing touches my soul. Everything inside of me remains untouched, and undamaged, and whole. My imagination, my affections, my soul. Everything that's real remains in there untouched. This is just a crisis of the moment. I'll get through this, as I always have before, and I'll come out the other side, and I'll be the stronger, once again, for the experience of it.

God knows why this business with the Bank should have blown up right now. I had it under control, just about, and certainly by the New Year I could have paid off the debt, as I had told them

I would. And the other creditors as well. But this extraordinary foreclosing on me, with seven days' notice, creates a very tricky position indeed. And all at the same time as the business with Bergdorf and Hermann. And the others. Steiner, and Bronowski, and Edel, and Levinstein. All six of them. Plus the Foundation. All different situations, and different stories, and different things to be done. Done quickly, too. All that, and suddenly this unexpected problem with the Bank.

Everything together in one fell swoop, Cohen muttered to himself. Then, suddenly, in a flash of optimism, he felt entirely restored. As he ran up the steps of his office building he had a smile on his face, and laughter within him. Of course there was a way through this! *Of course there was.* What was all the gloom about? The firm would have to make him an advance, so that he could pay off his overdraft. Something of that kind. That could be arranged. The other partners would understand. They were all good friends. And then the quicker he got to the Swiss accounts the better. With Hermann's help preferably, but without if necessary. That was the way through! It would all work out.

Now Cohen chuckled out loud in his relief, and as he did so he had a sudden irrelevant thought about the bank manager. He knew who it was that the man reminded him of, in his frock-coat straining at his armpits. It was the broker's man in the pantomime he had taken Rachel to when she was six or seven. The one wearing the tails. The one who had the custard pie smacked into his face.

Chapter 45

Edel stood by a news-stand at Heathrow, holding a magazine up in front of his face, so close to him that he looked like a man of unusually severe short sight with inadequate spectacles.

It was, he told himself, the pose of an amateur detective hiding behind the curtains in a bedroom farce, and he was ashamed of it, but doing this sort of business in international airport terminals always discomfited him. Every third person a security guard of some sort or another, and nothing and nobody quite as they seemed. Or so he suspected, and in doing so recognised the instinctive fear of a man who himself has spent his entire adult life being by no means quite what he seemed.

But now he could see Bergdorf coming out from the immigration and customs hall, his thick white hair showing up like a marker in the crowds of passengers hurrying on their way out to the taxis and car parks. Edel put the magazine back on the shelf, by force of habit turning his head away from the cashier so there would be no eye-contact that she might later recall. Then he made his way across the crowded floor to the florist's shop, tucked into the rear of the hall, well outside the immediate gaze of any but the most tenacious observer. Facing into the tiny shop, Edel pretended to look over the various bouquets of cut flowers that stood there in buckets, already wrapped in stiff, crinkly cellophane. Bergdorf was beside him almost immediately, ostensibly engaged in a similar task, picking and fingering at the several small bunches of violets laid out in a water-filled tray.

'You look grey, Jacob,' Edel said. 'But then I've never seen you look anything else when you've just got off a flight. Why don't you give aeroplanes up, and go everywhere by train, for the love of God?'

'Because people like you don't allow me to,' Bergdorf replied. 'You never give me adequate notice of anything. It'll be the death of me, of course. The stress of it, at my age . . .'

186

Bergdorf went up to the counter, and paid for a double bunch of the violets, which the assistant tied for him in a pretty bow of golden ribbon. He came back, put his hand on Edel's shoulder, and the two of them walked away and stood in an area concealed on most sides by a screen, behind which some workmen were clattering and knocking around with hammers and drills.

Edel reached into the inside pocket of his raincoat, and handed Bergdorf an envelope. 'I don't like being put in the position of a messenger,' he said. 'It makes me feel too exposed, carrying bits of paper around with me like this. But here we are – the names you wanted, the ones that have been held back for later. You've got the full list now, and beside them you'll find a brief summary of the information we've got about them.'

Bergdorf opened his briefcase and put the envelope inside, then redialled the lock. 'No names withheld?' he asked. 'Everyone there – including the one or two suggestions that I asked you to . . . to research specially?'

Edel nodded, made a slight smile, and started to move away. 'Everyone's there that we know about at this moment,' he said. 'We'll get more, but it'll take time. Look – I feel happier back in the crowd. And anyway, the job's done. I must get back to the shop. I don't think we should see each other again on this visit of yours incidentally, and telephone contact is out – particularly on the mobile number. If you need me, wait until you're back in Vienna, then get to me through the normal route. But keep well away while you're here.'

'If I wasn't so exhausted by the perfectly dreadful experience of that flight, I might well object to your tone,' Bergdorf replied. 'I've come here today simply because I have to do something about Mariss Steiner. I don't believe any of the rest of you realise that the circumstances surrounding that man at the moment are extremely dangerous for the whole lot of us. This other business of yours is important, but nowhere near as urgent. You summoned me here today to take this list of yours off you, and I've done so, but in fact I had already decided to make the trip myself.'

Edel turned, and grimaced. 'Not now, Jacob. None of that. We had a talk. I told you I had a list. You asked for it. I've given it to you. Now I have to go.'

Bergdorf caught up with him, and laid a hand on his arm. 'Gareth, my friend, calm down. I told you I would help you, and I will, but I don't want to be diverted from my most pressing task – of dropping Mariss Steiner into the Thames with a gigantic block of concrete around his neck. Quickly – before the blundering idiot does more harm than he could possibly realise.'

But Edel's mind was suddenly on something else, and while Bergdorf was speaking he motioned for the briefcase to be opened up once more, and taking back the envelope, he wrote on the back of it an address, and then, after a moment's hesitation, a telephone number.

Ignoring what Bergdorf was still in the course of saying to him, he put the envelope back into the case, shut the lid, spun the locks, and muttered, 'I've given you there a name and a telephone number that you might possibly need if you get yourself into trouble. If matters go . . . very badly wrong.'

'And what exactly does that mean?' Bergdorf replied. 'Are you suggesting that I'm personally in physical peril?' He looked incredulous at the thought of it.

'I'm a man of peace, Gareth, you know that,' he continued. 'A lawyer, engaged in my professional responsibilities. My only consideration is the welfare and protection of my clients. I wish only for those things that are in the interests and the good of the people and institutions that I have the honour to serve. And that of my family, of course.'

Edel smiled at him without warmth. 'I've known you too long, Jacob. It's wasted on me. I can read you like a book. Perhaps I'm the only person who can.' And he set off once more into the crowds milling around the Terminal floor.

Bergdorf watched him go, then picked up his briefcase, sniffed at the bunch of violets that he still held in his hand, and presented them, with a theatrical show of charm, to a little girl passing him at that moment.

Bergdorf patted her on the head, and said to her mother, 'She's a delight, Madam! That little face! Those won't be the last flowers she's given!' Then, making a courtly little bow to the baffled woman and the silent, blushing child, Bergdorf went on his way, following Gareth Edel's path across the terminal to the taxi rank outside.

Edel was a man who had seen too much grief, Bergdorf brooded, climbing awkwardly into the back of a cab. First there was Belsen, and the loss of his family there, but then there was that wife of his. He abandoned life, or the prospect of life, at the moment she died, or so it seemed.

How odd it was, Bergdorf reflected, as the vision of his own wife flitted across his mind, that a man should live with a girl for just nine months or a year, and spend the rest of his days in mourning for her. Most people mourn, then move on, but Edel was like the mynah bird, who pairs once in his life, and then, on the loss of his mate, looks only for his own death. As if the whole meaning and purpose of his existence has faded on his partner's passing.

That's not right, Bergdorf told himself. Life has more in it than women. Much more – for those who know what they're looking for.

Chapter 46

'It's nice of you to see me, Professor,' said the American. 'I appreciate your time.'

Hermann appraised him across the desk. He didn't much like the look of this young man. His initial conversation had not impressed him in the least. If he was, as he'd claimed to be in his correspondence, a Doctorate student finalising a thesis on the Jewish influence on German Communism in the thirties, then Hermann doubted whether he would have passed muster at a decent European University. The statements he'd made so far had been too drearily obvious and one-dimensional. Not an original, interpretative thought about him. A third-rate mind, and, remembering from where he claimed to come, a typical product of a third-rate college.

Harrison, or whatever his name was, had now headed off on an interminable question – or was it a statement? – on the pre-War demographics of the Jewish people in Hungary. What on earth was the point of this? Hermann looked at his watch, and with no particular effort at concealing the fact. He wanted to get on with the article he was writing for *Foreign Affairs* – the first they'd asked from him for years. The editor had allowed him up to 7,000 words on the post-Soviet Empire prospects for voluntary, free-will Communism in Eastern European and there was scope for him to develop an original, thorough piece of work. He'd get rid of this young man as soon as he could, however far he might have travelled to see him. He was a timewaster.

But there must be courtesy in these things, so Hermann pulled his concentration together, and studied the young man more closely. At least he looked neat and tidy and healthy, he thought. Not a hint of the hippy degenerate that one so often saw in the undertalented who clung on too long to student life. Button-down white shirt, and short hair, and striped tie, and a blue, department store suit. There was order about him, at least one could say that.

Now he caught, guiltily, the drift of the young man's last sentence or two. But what was he saying? He wanted to spend time with Hermann himself, completing his research? Hermann shrugged, and gave the young man what he hoped was a smile of courteous but firm dismissal.

'That would be very pleasant,' he said, 'but not practical, I fear. My writing, my teaching . . . my various duties around the University itself . . .' He threw his arms open in a gesture of defeat, then looked at his watch once more, this time with actorly dismay. 'Now – you must ask me one or two specific points on which I may be able to assist you, and then I must hurry on to my next appointment. I'm running hopelessly behind this morning already.'

'It's this final section of the thesis – what's happening sixty, sixty-five years later that I find so interesting,' the American said. 'Maybe I can persuade you to allow me to work with you on it. I can complete my work on the thesis while helping you in whatever way you like, as your research assistant – unpaid of course!'

'Research assistant?' Hermann repeated. Perhaps he had misread the original letter that Harrison had written to him. If he *had* needed someone for that task it certainly wouldn't have been Harrison that he selected. 'I have my own students for that, I'm afraid,' he said, 'though for most of the time I do my research myself.'

Harrison smiled, and Hermann felt suddenly uneasy. The man was uncomfortably self-confident, as if holding back some matter that he knew would give him the overwhelming advantage when he chose the moment to let it free.

'What I had in mind is the Hermann Foundation. And what a wonderful vision that is!' Harrison said. 'The Hermann Scholars and all the rest of it! I could help you on that – on how the Foundation can be properly funded. Researching how we can raise more money. A very great deal more money. That's what I would like to do.'

Hermann sat at his desk, his head buried in his hands. Harrison was standing in front of him now, smiling and still holding up the sheet of notepaper that Hermann had refused to look at.

'It doesn't matter, Joseph,' he said kindly. 'It's only me who has this information, and I haven't told anyone else whatsoever. Believe me! It's your secret and my secret. No one else knows.'

He stood there for a moment or so, gazing down at Hermann, then shrugged, and threw the paper down in front of him. In time

Hermann took his hands away from his face, and looked Harrison in the eyes.

'You're CIA,' he said heavily. 'They must have a reporting system, just like any other organisation has. Whoever it is you answer to, you'll have given him the detail of what you've found. So it *isn't* a secret between you and me. Other people in the CIA must have it on file now as well.'

Harrison shook his head, and smiled. 'Let me say it again. Tracking these Swiss bank accounts has been on the CIA's schedule for years. There's a lot of money there, and some day it's going to be on the move, so we watch it. At the present time *I* watch it, and I've become aware that you've had some of it. There's the proof of it, in front of you.

'No. I haven't reported to my superiors to that effect. That's what I'm saying to you. No one else knows apart from you and me. Hang on to that. No one knows except for you and me.'

Whistling cheerfully, Harrison went into the bathroom, and urinated loudly into the toilet. Still zipping up his fly he came back into the room, retrieved his sheet of paper from the desk, folded it, and pushed it into his trouser pocket. 'The thing is, Joseph, I can't see that you've done anything wrong. You've taken five million dollars. But it wasn't for yourself, for Christ's sake! You needed financing for your new Foundation. What could be more worthy and altruistic than the Hermann Scholars – Jewish boys and girls from Eastern Europe, winning scholarships and going in their droves to Cambridge and Harvard. That's a wonderful idea. That's true philanthropy. It's the best way of using these funds anyone could possibly think of. Because whose were they anyway? You found two accounts that were never going to be unlocked properly, because they were Nazi accounts, set up by one of Himmler's people, now long dead. And what did they have in them? Jewish money that the Nazis had stolen from God knows how many Hungarian-Jewish families. No one could possibly trace who those families were, or what was taken from each. The Swiss would have sat on the lot for ever. So you did something very sensible. You popped in front of them some papers that you'd borrowed from somewhere else, laid a false trail on the identification of them, fooled them one hundred per cent on the verification of a deposit receipt, and the money was yours – or rather, the Foundation's. Except the Swiss didn't think it was going to be the Foundation's. They thought it was going back to Hungary.'

Harrison laughed. 'You're very good at it, Joseph. It's because you're such a puritan. You wanted the money so much, and for such a good cause, that you must have exuded integrity and determination at them. I'm not surprised they handed it over!'

There was a silence, and for some minutes Harrison let it continue. Once or twice Hermann started to say something, then shook his head, and stopped, burying his head again back into his hands.

'Forget about the guilt, Joseph,' Harrison said roughly. 'You took the money for a very good cause and I respect you for it.'

Hermann looked up, and stared at Harrison searchingly. 'So what do you want from me?' he asked. 'I don't understand.'

Harrison smiled benignly. 'I simply want to be your research assistant – remember? And I also want to help you raise more money for the Foundation – from the same sources . . . Much more money. But this time I want a commission on what you raise. Sixty per cent for the Foundation, and forty per cent for me.'

'You're blackmailing me,' Hermann shot at him. 'And like all blackmailers, it won't be long before you're asking for more.'

Harrison pulled a little face of contrition. 'That's true, alas. That I can't deny. But for now, sixty for you, and forty for me. Correction. Sixty for the *Foundation* and forty for me.'

The two men stared at each other, then Hermann got to his feet, and went to the door.

'Forget about the guilt, Joseph!' Harrison called after him. 'You've no need for it. You can leave the guilt to me!'

Chapter 47

Miranda returned Steiner's telephone call during the morning school break.

He had rung the Secretary's office at St Peter's earlier in the morning, leaving a number where Miranda should call him back. He gave the Secretary a false name, and told her to be sure to tell Miranda that he had an urgent message for her from one of her relatives. Miranda, when she saw the note in her pigeon-hole, was wholly bemused by this, as, to her knowledge, she had no relatives alive of any sort. Still trying to work out who it could be, and, despite herself, intrigued and excited by the mystery of it, she took a moment or two to recognise Steiner's voice when he picked up the phone. When she did so, she immediately protested at it.

'A harmless little subterfuge, my dear,' he said. 'You mustn't be angry with me. I was concerned that if I gave my real name you might refuse to speak to me, and that would have been such a pity. All I want is to be your friend, Miranda. That and a little bit of help with a task I've set myself. As I mentioned to you when we had tea together in your lovely house.'

'Mariss, I don't want to see you or speak to you again. You know that. I have no intention of allowing myself to be bullied or blackmailed by you.'

'My dear,' he said, his voice now full of soft persuasion, 'you have nothing to fear from me. Really you haven't. I spend too much time these days in my own company, and that makes me awkward with people. I come across as aggressive, when that's the last thing I want. It leads me to be misunderstood, and that's what happened with you. I—'

Miranda had half a mind simply to put the receiver down and cut him off. 'Mariss – I'm afraid I have to go back into class almost immediately. I'm very pleased that you've got in touch with me again after all these years, but I really was offended by what you said to me when we talked together, and I don't think

194

another meeting would be a good idea.' Her tone had as much definition and firmness as she could force into it. 'So, Mariss, no more meetings. I want to make myself absolutely clear on that. And now I must go.'

She was about to replace the receiver when she heard his voice continuing to speak, and after a moment or so she brought the telephone back to her ear so that she would catch his final comments.

'. . . and I don't believe you're that sort of person. Women like you have more sense of loyalty and . . .' He hesitated, and there was something in his voice; a new directness, that made her hold her concentration on what he was saying.

'Hello? Miranda? Are you there?'

'Yes,' she said, after a pause. 'Yes. I'm still here.'

'I'm never going to threaten you again in the way that I did then,' he told her. 'Nor do I believe that I will have any reason to threaten you, in order to persuade you to do what I ask. Amos needs your help. You may no longer be his wife, and you may have no intention of letting him back into your life. I don't blame you for that. But you're the mother of his child. His son. And I do assure you that he needs your help. He's become involved in a situation which he's very ill equipped to deal with. He needs you. You have a great capacity for love, and for loyalty and connection, Miranda. Anyone would sense that of you. You're incapable of letting love go. You won't this time, any more than you have in the past.'

There was a silence. Then; 'All right, Mariss. I don't promise anything whatsoever, but I will listen. What do you want? Why is it you're pursuing me? What is it you want me to do?'

Chapter 48

Jacob Bergdorf sat in the Palm Court Lounge of the Waldorf Hotel, his deep armchair and the extravagantly profuse foliage around it protecting both him and his companion, he hoped, from the gaze of a casual observer. He sipped, miserably, at his tea, then felt in his pocket for the tiny tin box that contained his dyspepsia tablets, and slipped one under his tongue.

'Your father always used to insist on having tea with me here,' he said. 'All Earl Grey and cucumber sandwiches, like a couple of English tourists in an hotel in Cairo, stifling in our linen suits and solar topees and clutching fast to our *Baedeckers*. I've never been able to understand the English passion for tea. I don't normally touch the stuff. But somehow, with the thought of you coming to join me, I remembered your father, and . . .'

Bernie Levinstein glanced surreptitiously at his watch. If the old boy doesn't come to the point in a moment, he thought, I'll . . .

'There is a look of your father about you, Bernie,' Bergdorf was continuing. 'Somehow that gives me confidence in you. It's not a misplaced confidence, is it? No? Can I be sure of that? And your dependability? You're not still harbouring violent thoughts about Professor Hermann?'

Levinstein had a range of facial expressions and masks at his disposal. With women he could be any one of several things. A charming, beautifully mannered, endearingly cheeky lad on the town; a straightforward physical pick-up; an earnest young man with his way to make in the world. With Steiner he was, invariably, unaffectedly discourteous. With Edel, moodily communicative at best. He knew him too well, or thought he did. But for Lewis Cohen and Jacob Bergdorf, both friends of his father, he would perform in certain moods someone entirely different. The intense, determined young professional. A chip off the old block, and then some. It was one of his favourite roles.

Frowning to display not rudeness but incredulity, he said,

196

'You're not suggesting that I would ever let you down, Mr Bergdorf? I always do just what you say. I have the strongest sense of duty and loyalty. Responsibility is at the heart of my being.'

Levinstein paused at that, taken aback for a moment by the resonance and flow of his own rhetoric. The final two sentences sounded vaguely familiar to him. He knew he had borrowed them from somewhere, but couldn't place where it might be. He continued in a much more understated style.

'No – really, Mr Bergdorf, I understand. You will only work with people in whom you have the fullest confidence. I don't blame you – not in our line of work,' he concluded, then cursed himself inwardly as he saw the look of disdain cross over Bergdorf's features. He doesn't like anyone to suggest that he's in this line of work at all, he thought. Particularly me. Silly old queen. He looks this minute like some dowager at the tenants' annual tea party, catching one of them fart in her presence.

Bernie tried again. 'May I summarise at this time, Mr Bergdorf? *Overview*: Hermann is due in this country next week. We know he's in danger from Steiner. *Fact*: Steiner tried to borrow or buy a gun from me to do the act, then pulled out of the arrangements in suspicious circumstances. *Supposition*: he has secured a weapon from another source, and wishes to separate his actions from ourselves. *Fact*: Hermann has heard that he is in danger from Steiner, from source or sources unknown. *Fact*: he has a suspicion that you are in some way responsible for Steiner's plot. *Supposition*: parties unknown are spreading rumours to this effect for reasons of their own interests. *Supposition*: their interests demand that there is a rift in the trust pertaining between you and Hermann.'

He paused, and Bergdorf nodded at him vaguely, his eyes indicating that Levinstein's speech had set off in him some line of thought on which he was now bound. Levinstein waited a little longer for a fuller acknowledgement, but none coming, he went on.

'That's one side of the equation. On the other we have Bronowski. His newspaper articles, supposedly damaging to various of your clients, and Hermann in particular, appear in the *Sunday Times* as from this weekend. As I understand it, there's no action that can be taken to stop the publication of these articles. You've examined the possibility of taking out an injunction against the newspaper, but you believe that the courts will not permit such an injunction to be raised. There is, therefore, no further legal action, or any other action, that is possible under these circum-stances.

'Finally, we have the conundrum of Mr Cohen. We are uncertain exactly what he's up to, and to what degree, if any, he is involved in the promulgation of the false rumours linking you, Mr Bergdorf, with Steiner's plans regarding Joseph Hermann. You tell me that you suspect him of it through reasons of professional and competitive jealousy. But you have no certain evidence of it, nor of his general disposition in this matter. You want me to try to find some.'

Levinstein stopped, and watched for Bergdorf's reaction, but his mind seemed still to be preoccupied elsewhere. Eventually he started to move in his chair, as if ready to summon the waiter for their bill, in preparation for leaving.

'Shall I run over the options for our game plan, Mr Bergdorf?' Levinstein offered, but Bergdorf held up his hand, and the shake of his head was clear in its determination.

'No, thank you, Bernie. Not now. Just do two things for me, if you would. First Mariss Steiner. Go back on to the street, or wherever you get your information, and try to find out a little more about what he's up to. The weapon, for example. The one that he either has or hasn't got. But also – listen to the quality of the gossip about him generally. That first.'

Bergdorf studied Levinstein for a moment, as if deciding whether or not to trust him with any other tasks at this stage. Then he said, 'And you're going to think about Lewis Cohen, of course. There's that.'

For a moment it seemed that he was going to say something further, then he changed his mind, made some pleasantry or another, and soon he had succeeded in getting Levinstein on his way. As he watched him go, his hair pulled back in its ponytail, his glistening black shoes tapping their way across the black lacquered floor, he wondered how safe he himself was with him.

It was different with Lewis Cohen. No one could be as physically unthreatening as him. With Steiner too, oddly enough, dangerous as he might in the end prove to be. And emphatically different with Edel.

But this boy was straight off the street, for all the fact that he is David Levinstein's son. Not a finished thought in his head. He's like a Mafia foot soldier. I used to think that all you had to do was win his allegiance, and he'd do absolutely anything for you. Jump through hoops. Beg for biscuits. Die for the Queen. Now I'm not so sure. I'm no longer certain that he's mine. I assume I put him on Hermann's trail when I saw him in Vienna. I wonder if I did. I wonder if I know him at all.

It was a pity if that was true. Bergdorf didn't have access to that many people to do his bidding in London. For all his faults, the Levinstein boy was the devil he knew. He would have to let him run his course – at least for just a little bit longer. Just another few days. But not a moment longer than was required.

Bernie Levinstein's thoughts, as he made his way up to the Aldwych, were, had Bergdorf known it, strangely similar. He had insufficient access to the sort of people he admired; men at the centre of affairs, men of influence and action. Old Bergdorf was a fringe figure these days, in Bernie's opinion. All that poncing around the world to conventions to make sure he's seen with the right people. Then, to attract attention to himself, whinging about how frightened he was of flying. Fat old queen. He could never sit still where he was. None of the big league used him now for anything of importance, these days. But, for all that, he was up to something, if Bernie read the tea-leaves aright. Something significant. It was well worth stringing him along for the time being.

So . . . Bernie would work with him for now, and see what came from it. Networking, that's what it was. *Touching base*. Checking out who on the street was up to what. He would certainly ditch the old twat without a moment's hesitation when the chance of a more direct line of attack came up.

He was on the trail now, getting closer and closer. He'd get his revenge for his father, and that was for sure. But it was more than that. It was not just going to be a killing. Bronowski would see to that. Hermann would be killed, but Bronowski would tell the world *why* he'd been killed. That was the real revenge. No one messed around with the Levinstein family. Hermann's a dead man. And the world will know why.

Chapter 49

'But that's all that I wanted, Herbie,' said Bergdorf. 'No more than that. I'm not a greedy man. Not someone who bears grudges, or who stores up a lot of unpleasant jealousies about people. I just want to help – that's all. And be treated fairly, as part of the family.'

He beamed at Harrison, who stared back unsmilingly. 'Which is the reason you called,' he said.

'But of course,' Bergdorf nodded. 'Just to remind you that I was part of it all as well, and that I wanted to go on doing my bit. The Swiss banks are rogues. Absolute rogues,' he added.

Harrison laughed, for the first time in the hour that he and Bergdorf had been together. 'So that's why you called,' he said again, and he studied Bergdorf without warmth. 'And that's why you tried to threaten me.'

'Threaten you?' Bergdorf chuckled. 'It would be a brave man who attempted that, Herbie! All I was doing was reminding you that I've given the CIA a helping hand on and off for nearly fifty years – ever since the war – and I knew how concerned you all were to keep an eye on what's happening to these Swiss bank accounts. And that I was part of your team, whenever you needed me, and that I didn't want you to forget that. That's all it was!'

'No. That *wasn't* all it was,' Harrison said angrily. 'You tried to suggest that unless I handed you money, then you had a tale to tell – and you would tell it. The story was about the means by which Joseph Hermann had provided the seedcorn finance for his Foundation. And that I was encouraging him to help himself to more from the same sources. That's what you said, Jacob, and that sounded like a threat to me.'

'Don't let's play with words, Herbie. Perhaps I was a little tactless, but I'd never dream of telling tales to anyone. I'd be too afraid that someone might start telling tales about me in return.'

Although the remark was delivered in the Bergdorf style – all

200

rubicund charm and humour and dismissal of the unpleasant – Harrison could see in him now a certain caution, a certain *respect*. He'd waited for that to come, as he knew it would. He was forty years Bergdorf's junior, or thereabouts, and Bergdorf would have underrated him. He'd not had sufficient dealings with him yet to have tasted Harrison's strength. But he could see it now. And, like everyone else, was wary of it.

Harrison allowed a silence for a moment or two. Then he said, 'That's right, Jacob. We wouldn't want that. Tales in return.'

They looked at each other, and Bergdorf was the first to turn away. He got up from his chair, picked up the coffee tray and took it into the other room, fussing around like a bourgeois housewife while, as Harrison knew, he cleared his mind and prepared his tactics. Then, returning to his chair, he said, all smiling gone: 'I don't want money from you, Herbie, but I do want a stream of business. I'd like your assurance that Hermann will pass me a steady flow of accounts to work on – much more than he has in the past. And good ones, Herbie. *Fertile* ones . . . I think you know what I mean.'

Harrison made no reply, nor indicated any response. Bergdorf continued.

'It's the Hungarian accounts that I really want to have a look at, Herbie. The Nazi ones – Himmler's Treasure. The ones that Hermann has had a go at himself – for the Foundation,' he added, as if an afterthought, a hint of sarcasm in his voice.

Harrison smiled, picked up his raincoat, which he had thrown down on the sofa beside him, and made to get to his feet.

Bergdorf watched him, then continued, 'There's something else you should know before you go. Bernie Levinstein – that unpleasant young man you came across in that incident in Brussels. I think you should know that Levinstein is after Hermann, because of some tale he appears to have just picked up about what did or did not happen to his father in the Buchenwald Infirmary. I believe the rumour I've heard is correct: Hermann should be careful. Bernie Levinstein is a very violent and disagreeable young man.'

As Harrison set off for the door, Bergdorf called after him, 'I simply want to work with you as a colleague, Herbie – that's why I'm telling you these things. You and I and Hermann should all be together as one family. No one else should be allowed to trespass on our territory. And there are people who do plan to trespass, you know. Well – I exaggerate. Not people – one person.'

Harrison paused, and turned back to face Bergdorf, pulling his raincoat on as he stood.

'Who's that, Jacob? Whom do you have in mind?'

Bergdorf beamed at him, his bonhomie restored.

'I wonder if you know him? It's Lewis Cohen, the London lawyer. But of course you do! Like me, he does the occasional task for you folks, I believe? Well, Lewis, bless him, is on the trail as well. He's got himself into financial trouble, and sees the Swiss accounts as the way out. Particularly the Hungarian ones.

'But don't we all!' he cried out after Harrison. 'Don't we all!' The smile faded from Bergdorf's lips, and he remained staring at the door Harrison had slammed shut behind him. It's best to get Bernie Levinstein out of the way, he thought. It was probably a mistake winding him up with that story of his father. I was very confused by his attitude when we met together at the Waldorf. Steiner's the man for the job. He'll do it. It's just a question of organising him properly for the task.

Chapter 50

Steiner made his way through the crowds of Oxford Street, whistling as he went. When an old lady turned and crossed immediately in front of him, instead of ritually knocking at her stick with his, which in normal circumstances he would certainly have done, he paused, and said to her some words of caution about watching out for the traffic. A tourist asked him the way to Buckingham Palace, and Mariss despatched him in precisely the right direction, which was something he hadn't knowingly done for years. These would each have looked to the world like agreeable little encounters, and so they were. There was a smile on Steiner's face, and a tune on his lips. Anyone who observed him as they passed must have thought that here was an elderly man with peace in his heart, and a good digestion too, and the spirit and the good humour and the kindly humanity to withstand the cruel, bent rigours of his arthritic condition.

But these same people would have been surprised indeed to have known from where Mariss's good humour had arisen. Three hours earlier, he had been sitting in a deserted warehouse in Deptford, being taught the procedures for priming and detonating a bomb.

It was a small device to Steiner's untaught eye, but enough for the job, he was assured, provided he followed the instructions exactly. And so, for nearly four hours, Steiner and a man whom he had never before met, and who would speak to him only in German, sat on packing cases and rehearsed together the simple five-part exercise that he would in due course be performing for real. Five simple, unchanging, repetitive tasks, that, the German said, anyone of the least intelligence could learn to do, and, were their nerve to hold, be sure to perform reliably and faultlessly each time they were called upon to do so.

While Steiner was being instructed, Gareth Edel sat deep in the shadows, silent and well out of Steiner's line of sight. He heard the German instructor, for the umpteenth time, correct Steiner in the way that he held the wires, and Edel wondered if, in any circumstances, this whole arrangement would ever have worked. One wasn't used to seeing Mariss exposed to the demonstration of his nerve. His manipulation of people, his perception, his tenacity – all those were familiar enough to anyone who had spent their lives in contact and business with him. But his composure under stress had never been observed.

It was possible, thought Edel, that Steiner himself had little idea how he would behave when the time came. There might have been occasions in his younger years, at the time he was working for the Americans, when he was involved in physically perilous tasks, but somehow Edel doubted it. That was not Mariss's style; then, as now, he had been the plotter behind the scenes, the catalyst for conspiracy and revenge. Never out there in front, as far as Edel knew. How strange it was that he was so anxious to get himself out there in the front line now.

Edel climbed down off the packing case, and wandered across to the window. He stood at an angle to it and stared at the street outside, then, looping back into the space behind him, and well out of sight, he crossed to the other side of it, so that he could have the same view down across on the opposite angle.

There was no one out there in a position of observation, as far as Edel could tell, but if there were they could easily conceal themselves, if they so desired. There was that abandoned building-site opposite, its mud and brick mounds and hollows half covered in dense clumps of brambles and wild buddleia; the locked and shuttered old warehouse at the end of the street; the battered van, half drawn up on to the pavement, one wheel removed, the curtains in its back window open a couple of inches . . .

'I wouldn't describe you as a natural at this, Mariss,' he commented now.

Steiner was enjoying himself so much with the technical business of playing around with a genuine bomb that Edel's criticism quite passed him by. He smiled his dirty, yellow-toothed grin, then bent his head once more over the jumble of leads and metal clips that he was attempting, under continual instructions from the German, to sort and connect.

'I'm all thumbs, I'm afraid, Gareth,' he said. 'But I'm getting the hang of it now. *Damn!*'

Steiner sucked at the pad of his finger as the blood beaded on the surface of a little cut, then wrapped his grimy handkerchief around it, and tried once more to get his clumsy, arthritic fingers to pick out and hold the lead he was fiddling to secure. He had the look at that moment of a naughty, but guileless urchin. Edel reflected that there was one corner of Steiner's personality that was probably exactly that. Within the murk and the shadows there lurked a small boy; worldly, complex, damaged, but a small child nonetheless. And as prone to hurt, and the need for admiration and encouragement as any small child would be.

But then Steiner broke the spell. 'This is going to be a great moment, Gareth,' he gloated. 'For too many years Hermann has been allowed to go free and unpunished. He's had this coming to him, and I'm going to be the one to blow him to smithereens. I can't tell you how much pleasure that's going to bring me.'

'That's not what professionals are supposed to say, Mariss.' Edel forced a smile on to his face. 'And you're a professional now. You're supposed to be dispassionate, if I remember my movies correctly.'

He put his hat on his head, and raised his hand to them both as he went. 'Don't hate, Mariss!' he called out, walking towards the cavernous stone staircase that led down to the street. 'Hatred gets you nowhere. Nor does it help those people who for one reason or another have agreed to help you.'

'That's exactly what I'd like to ask you,' Steiner called after him. 'Why *are* you helping me, Gareth? Why are you setting me up for this?'

The device trailed its wires as he held it, in tenderness almost, and again the image of a small boy came to Edel's mind. A small boy with a broken toy.

'That's what I don't understand, Gareth,' Steiner shouted, the child desperate for acknowledgement and recognition. 'Why me? Why now?'

But Edel had gone, and Steiner was left staring after him, listening to the tap of his shoes on the stairs as he hurried down and away into the filthy, littered streets of abandoned, East End London.

Chapter 51

Miranda stepped on to the down escalator at Earl's Court station, clung to the handrail, and as she did each morning, turned her head to gaze at the advertisement panels on her immediate right. She was determined not to look down. She had travelled on the underground, and on this route, for more than thirty years, but she still feared this moment every single day she came to it. There in front of her would appear a descent of what she imagined to be, on the few occasions when she had dared to peep, a drop of fully one hundred feet. That was an unthinkable distance to fall. If she dwelt on it too much, she would find it next to impossible to step on to the escalator at all.

Down on the platform, she squinted at the big poster advertisements across the tracks, noticing that her eyesight had declined now to the point where she would shortly be obliged to wear glasses all the time. She had been putting this off, unwilling to appear to look different in front of her pupils.

I only feel safe as I am, she thought disgustedly. If I change one tiny aspect of that I feel threatened.

'Christ!' she muttered out loud, aghast at her lack of self-esteem. What an astonishing coward I am too, she thought. In front of a class of eleven-year-old schoolgirls, I'm too frightened to wear spectacles.

She had spoken more loudly than she had meant, and the man now sitting at the other end of her bench had turned to look at her.

Normally Miranda would have flushed at this, and turned away. But he was such a good-looking young man, with his dark, modish hair, and his olive skin and white teeth, that Miranda felt unchallenged by him, and at her ease. Young men as expensively and stylishly dressed as this were completely outside her range.

'First sign of madness,' Bernie Levinstein said, 'talking to yourself!' And he reached across for her elbow, to help her to her feet as the train rushed its way into the station.

The two of them stood crammed together in the middle of the carriage.

'Now I have the advantage on you,' Bernie said, turning back to Miranda, 'and my mother always said that when you have the advantage on someone you must always let them know it. It's good manners to tell them. That's what she taught me. I've always remembered that.'

Miranda looked up at him and nodded brightly, wondering what on earth he was talking about, and who he was and now desperately looking forward to finishing her journey, and arriving at Hammersmith underground station. Surely he couldn't be going there too?

'The advantage on me?' she said, feeling she had to say something. 'What do you mean by that?'

'Well, I know who you are, you see, and you don't know who I am.'

Their bodies bumped together as the train gave a sudden lurch, and, Miranda realised to her surprise that she had not found the experience of it to be as disagreeable as she would have expected. A distinctly wholesome smell wafted from him, and Miranda registered the fact that masculinity of this type did appeal to her.

'Excuse *me*,' he murmured, and Miranda thought for a moment that to amuse her he was pretending to play the part of a stage cad in an amateur theatrical, so she smiled brightly in response. He gave a flicker of a wink. 'Miranda, isn't it? Amos's wife. Your name's Miranda Bronowski.' He smiled down at her, then gave a little squeeze to her elbow. 'See? I told you I had the advantage on you. But let me introduce myself. I'm . . .'

But, before completing the sentence, he bent down suddenly to peer out of the train window, apparently to identify what station they had now arrived at. At this level, his tanned face was no more than an inch or so from Miranda's chest, and she pressed herself back a fraction, away from him. But then he straightened once more.

'Baron's Court,' he said. 'One more stop to go. I thought we'd got to Hammersmith already, I was so busy talking.'

I can't believe it, Miranda thought. He *is* going to Hammersmith. And how did he know that I was going there?

'I'm Bernie Levinstein,' he introduced himself. 'I recognised you straight away, the moment I saw you.'

'How?' said Miranda, baffled.

'Oh,' he said brightly, 'from photographs that Amos has. He keeps them in his wallet. He shows them to everybody.'

Bernie turned to glare at a businessman whose umbrella had touched his foot, and pushed him away from him with the back of his hand. Watching him, Miranda wondered how many more ludicrous untruths she would have to hear from people about Amos's relationship with her. Why this extraordinary conspiracy?

She and Amos had slept together again, for old times' sake maybe, then three or four times more, and then he had disappeared. None of that could be considered an unusual occurrence between two people who had once been lovers – who had once been husband and wife! – and who were now each alone and unattached. That's all it was. Or, that's all it was to her at her least considered moments. But Amos seemed determined to persuade her into some web of deceit, and everybody else seemed to be in on the act as well. This nonsense with Mariss Steiner. And now this odd young man too. What on earth was going on? What is Amos trailing around with him?

I'm going to find out the answer to this, Miranda told herself. I really don't appreciate finding myself being propelled out on to the platform of my very own Hammersmith underground station with this ballroom gigolo's hand under my arm. As if he was a dutiful nephew steering his elderly aunt off for her annual birthday lunch . . .

'Well – we're both early birds, and that's for sure,' he was saying, as they walked together up the staircase and towards the light shining down from the street outside. 'You schoolteachers work too hard, that's what I always say.'

'Oh, I enjoy my job very much,' she promised him.

As they strolled along the pavement, exchanging pleasant if meaningless banalities, Miranda's mind flew ahead to a vision of the St Peter's staff common room on a normal day. Last week's Education *Guardian* dropped on to the floor, laid open at the Appointments page. Dirty coffee cups and ashtrays and elderly magazines littered around on the tables.

To Bernie, as she walked by his side, Miranda's expression seemed to be one of docility and feminine trust – just as it had been when he had first spoken to her. All in all, everything had gone very well. She clearly hadn't seen him follow her from her house. He had feared that he could hardly have been more obvious, as he hung around in the empty street for her to emerge from her front door. But it seemed that all was well. She didn't appear to be in the least uncomfortable that he was with her.

Now they were almost at the gates of St Peter's, and Miranda turned to Bernie and held out her hand.

'Goodbye, Bernie,' she said. 'How kind of you to come all the way to the school with me. It must have been a considerable distance off your route to wherever it is you're going. It really was most courteous of you. I appreciate it very much. Many thanks!'

He took her hand, and as she started to withdraw it, she found to her dismay that he was continuing to hold it within his grasp. She reached out with her left hand, and play acted at the business of rescuing her right from his hold, then wrung her hands together in mock hurt at the power of his grip. She smiled her farewell, and turned in through the school gates. Suddenly, she felt she wanted to be away from him very badly indeed, and had to make a conscious effort to stop herself from running up the steps of the front doorway and into the safety of the entrance lobby.

Bernie hitched the camelhair coat more securely on to his shoulders, winked intimately at a flushed-faced young woman in a tracksuit whom he guessed to be the games mistress, and set off once more for the underground station. Bernie liked girls' schools. He particularly liked the idea of girls' schools' games mistresses. He wondered if he might come back to St Peter's that evening to meet Miranda as she set off for home.

But instinct warned him not to hurry Miranda so much that he put her off. Make friends, he told himself, or she'll be suspicious, and she won't cooperate. Miranda was his only route to Amos, the only way he could get anywhere near him. And Amos was the only way he had of getting the Hermann business in the public eye.

So, reluctantly, Bernie decided against making contact with Miranda again that night. Give her time enough to think about today, he concluded, and brood about what he'd been up to. And hope it was what she thought it was.

Bernie laughed out loud, and, in his good humour, made a pretence at swinging a smack on to the bottom of a seventeen-year-old pupil bending over to do something to the chain of her bicycle.

But I mustn't leave it too late, he thought. Hermann's arrival is in no time at all. And then there's the business with Steiner. We can't have him buggering about at the last moment. That must all be sorted well before Hermann arrives. And so it will be. I'll make sure of that. By God, I will. The fucking little prick.

Miranda's trials for that day were not over. In the evening, at home, Mariss Steiner phoned her. She had hoped that the conversation she had had with him earlier in the week, when he had rung her at St Peter's, had been conclusive enough to put him off further contact with her. But it was soon apparent that she had been wrong.

'I'm like a bad penny, my dear,' he said, immediately she had picked up the telephone. 'You can't get rid of me. Every time you look, I'm back in your pocket. And I must say, now I come to mention it, your pocket sounds to me like a very nice place for me to be. Very warm and cuddly! Very nice indeed!' He laughed, the tone of it a caricature of a smutty saloon-bar bore, complete with the requisite prolonged, agonising smoker's cough at its completion.

'Mariss,' she said wearily. 'Please stop. Please stop this business of telephoning me, at school and here. I don't intend any insult to you at all – but please, Mariss, stop pestering me!'

Why do men always assume they can treat me in this way, and why do I always let them do it, she thought wildly, as his voice droned on down the telephone. Bernie Levinstein picking me up at the Underground station as if I was some sex-starved widow; easy pickings for whatever it was he was of a mind to extract from me. Mariss now; utterly imperturbable in this drivelling flattery and cajoling of me.

She realised suddenly that there was a silence now on the telephone, though she could hear from a background rustling noise that Steiner was still there.

'Mariss?' she said. 'Mariss?'

She was about to put the telephone down when there was a knocking sound as he apparently dropped his receiver, then a muffled curse. Then, 'I've got them,' he panted. 'Miranda? Are you still there? Half the papers fell down from the wall when I unpinned them.' He laughed. 'You've never seen my room, have you? You'd love it. A journalist from the *Guardian* interviewed me here once for an article on Holocaust survivors. She used a picture of this room as an example of how the survivors' lives in this country had turned out. She imagined that all of us lived like me!' There was a long, wheezing chuckle from him.

'What is it you're talking about, Mariss?' Miranda knew that a blow was about to fall. 'You've got what? What have you taken down from the wall?'

210

'The birth certificate, my dear. Or rather a certified copy of it, and I'm sorry that I was laughing, as it's a serious matter, I know that. The mother is named as you – Miranda Bronowski, *née* Thomson, daughter of Donald Thomson, Methodist Minister. And the child's father is shown as Amos Isaiah Bronowski. It's all signed and sealed and here in front of me. I've had it for years. And the death certificate too.'

Miranda gripped the table and closed her eyes, willing herself to stay calm.

'I'm determined that you should help me, Miranda,' Steiner immediately continued, 'and I'm running out of time. The alternative is that I take these two certificates and show them to Amos. And I know that that's not what you could possibly want. After all these years of concealment from him.'

Suddenly, an odd sensation of relief ran through Miranda. The threat doesn't work on me any more she thought, with surprise. I actually *want* Amos now to know about Michael. The years have gone on, and Amos is what he is, and I'm what I am, and I want him to know about his son. But not in this way: that's the only part of the threat that bothers me. I don't want Mariss going anywhere near Amos over this. That would be a disaster. *I'll* tell Amos myself – as soon as I can reach him.

'Look – let's meet, Mariss, and you can tell me more of what you want,' she said. 'I don't promise anything whatsoever, but I'll come over to your house tonight, if that's what you want. I'll come later tonight.'

Chapter 52

Miranda spent some moments walking up and down the street outside Steiner's front door.

Now that she was here, she was uncertain whether she could face going through the whole business of it. But eventually she gathered her resolve, and strode up the steps and into the front hallway, passing an old lady on her hands and knees, scrubbing away at the floor with a thick brush and hot soapy water, her blue plastic bucket beside her.

Miranda took off her shoes and, to avoid leaving dirty marks on the wet stone floor, tiptoed across it in her stockinged feet. At the bottom of the staircase was a wooden notice board, and on this was shown, by a rack of sliding panels, the name of the resident of each of the rooms, and an indication of whether they were in or out.

Steiner's panel declared that he was out, but Miranda guessed that it had shown him to be out for as long as he had lived there, so she went on up to his room on the top floor, and knocked on the door. There was a pause of perhaps half a minute, the staring, fish-eye of Steiner looked out through the peephole, and then there was the sound of the security chain scraping and rattling as he withdrew it from the lock.

'My dear!' Steiner cried, standing before her in the open door and gesturing her inside. Miranda noticed immediately that the fly zip of his baggy, stained trousers had been left pulled down to its limit, leaving the underpants showing; for a moment she wondered if he was attempting to expose himself to her in sexual display, then told herself that this was probably how he normally dressed when at home.

As Bernie Levinstein had done just a few days before, but with none of his disdain, she selected for herself the edge of Steiner's bed, but before she sat down she straightened the bedspread that was thrown across it, as if, in her courtesy, she was afraid that she might crumple it.

Steiner had hobbled over to the sink, and all the traditional business was under way there with the filthy coffee pot, and the stained, becrusted spoons, and the curdling milk sitting in a half-finished bottle. Without asking Miranda what she wanted, Steiner returned some moments later with two brimming mugs in his hands, both of which slopped on to the linoleum as he made his way back across the room. He handed Miranda one of them, then sat down heavily in his armchair, more coffee spilling out and down on to his trousers as he lowered himself laboriously into the cushions.

Once sitting, he sighed exhaustedly, reached up to straighten the *yarmulke* on the crown of his head, then sipped at the mug, and said, 'You would like me to be direct, my dear, you've made that very clear, so I will be. I won't go through all that business of threatening you all over again, because I know I made a mistake in doing that. It was unintelligent of me to underrate you in the way that I did. So I've looked them out for you. There they are.' He pointed up to a portion of the wall, and Miranda, following his finger, saw there the two certificates of Michael's birth and death pinned side by side.

'May I?' she said, and got up from the bed to take them down. Sitting once more, she laid them side by side on her lap, stared at them for a moment or so, then reached down for her handbag, and, folding them in two, slipped them inside.

'Yes,' he said after a few moments. 'You take the pair of them, and we can forget the whole business of it. So that's that. Now we can just have a chat about more pleasant things, and you can drink your coffee, and we can spend the evening together as friends. Shall we do that?'

Miranda took a sip at her mug, then put it down gently on the floor beside her. 'Well, we could talk about Amos,' she suggested. 'I don't understand what you originally wanted from me, nor what it is now. Why were you threatening me? What did you want me to do?'

Steiner was momentarily silent, and Miranda felt the beginnings of disquiet and physical fear. She knew the reasons for it, and she wanted to have a moment or two to rationalise herself out of it. Several things were frightening her – the gay magazine most of all, perhaps. She had seen it laid out on the carpet in the corner of the room. It was opened at a centrefold page, and showed the flagrantly naked body of a bronzed male model, his hips and engorged penis thrust out to the camera, his arms folded behind his head.

213

In a sense the evidence of Steiner's homosexuality should have quietened any alarm in her, and yet it had done the reverse. It had served to awaken it. It wasn't so much the sexuality of it, as the fact that he had left the magazine so artlessly unconcealed for her arrival, and was so entirely unconcerned, or apparently so, for the niceties of conventional reticence in these things before women of her age and type. All that, and, of course, this room of his too. The bizarre, flaunted dirt and unkemptness of his accommodation was a statement of contempt for conventionality and a rejection of it. It was this which so disturbed Miranda.

But then Mariss started to speak again, and she was able to put these thoughts aside, and follow him in what he said.

'I get a little cross with Amos sometimes, Miranda – that's all it is. One or two incidents between us over the years do jar a little in my memory. And, sometimes, probably when I'm overtired, I feel I'd like to put those things to him. With you there as well. That's what I want. The three of us together.'

'With me there as well?' Miranda said, trying to keep the distrust out of her voice. 'Why that? And why all these threats? Why all the business over our son?'

Steiner scratched at his groin, pulled up the zip of his fly, then made his way over to the table in the corner of the room, and leafed through the scraps of paper and letters and bills that covered the surface of it. Eventually he found what he seemed to be looking for, and squinted his eyes down to read it.

'I've been stupid, my dear. I've told you that. Let's forget about it all now. And let's talk about something more pleasant. Amos's seminar at the Queen Elizabeth Hall. Amos is the first speaker, then a Rabbi that I've never heard of, then old Shlimovitz, and finally . . . now, who else was it?' He patted at his pockets for his glasses, found them, put them on his nose, and peered down once more at the crumpled newspaper cutting that he had picked up.

'Ah yes – the last speaker is Joseph Hermann, who was the political leader of the Communist group at Buchenwald. Four of them. It should be a good evening.'

Steiner put the cutting back on the table, then scrabbled around in a drawer for something else. After several false alarms, he came up with a ticket, which he held aloft and waved in mock triumph, then dropped into Miranda's lap as he made his way back to his armchair.

'So there we are, my dear. Use my ticket, and have an enjoyable time. I know I'll never actually go to the thing myself, when

Monday comes around. The seminar, or whatever they call the thing, is all about this article of Amos's in the *Sunday Times* this weekend. I imagine the purpose of it is to try to drum up a bit of controversy and thunder and lightning that night so that everybody buys the next week's issue as well. I can tell you exactly what'll happen. Amos will hint that all the best bits are not in the *Sunday Times* at all, but are being kept for his book, so save your money up for that, and the Rabbi will preach the usual stuff about *forgiveness* but not *forgetfulness*.'

Steiner said this with heavy, theatrical sarcasm, then sniggered heartily.

'Old Shlimovitz will quite certainly be drunk out of his mind,' he continued, 'and wholly incoherent, as he invariably is. As for the Buchenwald Communist – Hermann – God knows what *he's* there for, except to protest that it's all a misunderstanding, and really he and his friends were just cuddly old bears.'

He scratched once more at his groin. 'I bought the ticket to be loyal to Amos, but to be honest, my dear, it's not exactly my cup of tea.'

'That's very kind of you, Mariss, to give it to me,' Miranda said, getting now to her feet, and pushing it into her handbag. 'I shall certainly go to the evening. But why don't you come as well?'

'I may do,' Steiner promised, pushing himself up on to his feet once more, and moving with her to the door. 'Now that I know that *you're* going, I'll get another ticket just in case. We can sit together and laugh at the Rabbi. And take a drink afterwards off the triumphant Amos. Suddenly the whole evening sounds like much more fun to me.'

Miranda turned at the door. 'You do keep on saying that you want me to do something for you. I thought that's why I had come tonight. Something about Amos. Well – what is it, Mariss? What do you want me to do?'

Steiner laughed. 'It was just a trick, my dear! Just a trick to get you here to see me. No – there's nothing. I've changed my mind. Nothing you can do. Or rather there is – but we'll talk about it another time. When we've got to know each other better.'

Miranda nodded, and was through the door now, and already waving her goodbye as she set off down the stairs.

'We'll go together on Monday,' he cried after her. 'What a wonderful idea! We'll go together! We'll give them all a surprise!'

Chapter 53

Miranda, deliberately, was several minutes late. She had been nervous all morning about the arrangement, but knew she couldn't now cancel it. Amos had been as persistent in her pursuit over the last couple of days as he had been at the time of his first arrival in London. Now that she had agreed to see him again it would be fruitless to try to cancel it. And better by far to meet here in Kensington Gardens than at her house.

As she came up the hill towards Kensington Palace she could see him already there, sitting on a bench beside the Round Pond, the watery sunshine of the early evening reflecting on the puddle before his feet. He saw her too, immediately, and got to his feet to walk towards her, smiling and waving his hand. She didn't know how to react, unwilling to seem too enthusiastic about their meeting, and embarrassed that they were at least a hundred yards apart from each other, but she waved back, and smiled as pleasantly as she could, then turned her head in the pretence of interest in a pair of dogs, barking and chasing at each other on the other side of the pathway.

He put out his hands and kissed her on both her cheeks. She suggested that they walk down in the direction of the Serpentine, and to break his hands from her waist she ducked down to pick up a stick, which she threw, in a markedly unathletic movement, for the dogs to chase.

'Well done with the *Sunday Times* piece,' she said. 'You must be delighted. The correspondence columns have been full of letters ever since. You've stirred up quite a controversy. Which is what I assume you wanted to do.'

Amos shrugged, then grinned, and Miranda glanced at him and could see the pleasure and pride in his eyes. He's so puffed up with the importance of what he's done, she thought. I suspect he has it quite out of proportion – pathetically so, almost. All this going underground now, moving himself on to some hidden address, in

216

the grand expectation of some fearful retribution from the people he has exposed. It is really all so significant? Is he producing anything of interest or originality at all?

'Controversy?' he said. 'Perhaps. Surprise more than controversy probably. Few people now, apart from the survivors like me, know anything much about the camps at all, apart from the obvious things – the gas ovens, and those images of hollow-eyed, ruined people in their striped uniforms. That's why I was particularly keen to expose Joseph Hermann. There are many, particularly in Germany, who still consider him something of a folk hero – the man who kept Buchenwald from complete disintegration, and all the rest of it. That's a travesty, of course. That's why I was at such pains to write his case up at length in this first article. To set the tone for the other stories to follow, most of them in a similar vein. There are other parallel cases, you know. I'm not talking about the so-called political and organisational leadership Hermann was supposed to have shown. I'm talking about how he was corrupted by his power over the other inmates. And what he did with that power. My God – what he did with it!'

Miranda glanced at him again, then looked away. He protests the point too much, she thought. There's too much rhetoric about it. He's obsessed with Hermann – but I wonder what the truth about him really is? Was he as Amos is so determined to paint him? Or was he, as everybody else seems to think, an effective leader at a time when those in Buchenwald would have collapsed without him? Why is there this zeal in Amos to present him as something else?

She wondered what else she could find to talk about, without misleading Amos into thinking that she wanted to indulge in intimate reflections. She cared about the concentration camps – of course she did. Who could not be moved by the horror of them? Those archive pictures of staring, emaciated children? Those naked bodies heaped up like broken toys, the white, angular limbs thrust out at angles from the piles, like sticks? But although she cared, and at one time in her life, when first she had fallen in love with Amos, she had wept, night after night, at the thought of his suffering as a small boy, there was no longer in her any focus to the emotion. Nor, she thought, was there for him. He cares now only for the hunt, and the desire to see men like Professor Hermann humiliated and exposed. But – and as the reflection came to her, she felt a momentary pang of tenderness for him, and guilt – that's because he sees himself as a defeated, unfulfilled man.

217

The researcher whose efforts had never before been seriously considered; the minor academic whose reputation as an historian barely transcended the narrow boundaries of McGill.

Amos had stopped now to tie the laces of his shoes, and as he bent down to the ground Miranda looked down at the crown of his head, now balding, but furtively so, the hair combed carefully across it. He cares for the research, and he cares for the exposition of it, she thought. He cares, he thinks, for 'truth'. But that's all there is. He's become bloodless; the arrogant, proud young man has dried up and withered. Perhaps what he perceives as a lifetime of professional underachievement has done that to him. Perhaps he's been unhappy with his women, whoever they may have been. Perhaps . . .

'I'm sorry Mariss has been bothering you, Miranda,' he said, straightening up. 'He left a message for me at Gareth's house. Giving me some odd story of how we should all meet up together once more. You, me and him, as a threesome. And how he thought he had persuaded you that we should do that. I can't believe that's the case. As far as I remember you hardly met the man when I was with you. Did you?'

Miranda hesitated before she replied, suddenly frightened by what had happened to her. She'd lost her privacy the moment that Amos had set foot in London. She hadn't realised how much she drew from the safety and security of it; she liked to be alone, and left in peace. Amos had bludgeoned his way through all of it, and she wanted now nothing so much as to be left on her own, in control of her own life. Mariss Steiner and his weird, theatrical menace. Amos and his puzzling, persistent demands on her. The threat of Michael being thrust out into the spotlight in an uncontrolled, brutal fashion. When would it all stop? How could she be rid of them all, and back where she was before, secure and at peace once again? 'Go, Amos,' she thought, articulating the sentence in her mind. 'Go, for God's sake! Leave me alone!'

But she left it unsaid. Instead she looked at her watch and muttered, 'I'm sorry, Amos. I want to go home now. I've work to do,' she concluded, but without definition in her voice, so that the excuse sounded hollow, and empty, and despairing.

Amos stopped too, and shrugged, then smiled. 'We'll try again!' he called after her, as she turned, and retraced her steps. 'I knew it would take time. Of course it will.'

And then, a moment or so later, 'We should have had children,

Miranda, you and I! I would have loved to have had a child with you! We both missed so much by that!'

Miranda continued on her path, as if she had failed to hear him, her hands deep in the pockets of her raincoat.

What made me say that? Amos thought as he watched her go. What's happening to me? What was the point of that cruelty? Why have I done to her the things that I have? Why did I walk out on her, after two years of marriage, in which she had done nothing but try to make me happy?

God knows what drives us. God knows what drives me. God knows why I picked up her life, and held it my hands, then threw it in destruction to the floor. Such cruelty. Such disloyalty. And then – such pain.

Chapter 54

Lord Rosenberg sat in the corner of the residents' drawing room at the Connaught Hotel, sipping unhappily at his lukewarm tea. He looked over his shoulder to reassure himself once more that they could not be overheard, then interrupted Bergdorf in the middle of a sentence.

'No, Jacob. No. That's not the point, if I may say so. Too many issues are being confused into one. You have your own agenda in this, no doubt, and I suppose I have mine. But we can be helpful to each other as long as we keep our lines uncrossed.'

He studied Bergdorf for some moments, then continued, 'We've known each other long enough to be clear and open with each other, surely to God? I'll be straightforward with you, and you must be the same with me. That way we can move ahead. At the moment we're going around in circles.'

Bergdorf started to reply, but he was cut off in mid-sentence yet again. Rosenberg was self-inflated to the point that he was preposterous. Emerson's aphorism came to Bergdorf's mind. The more anyone told him that they were about to be open and straightforward with him, the more he was on his guard for them to do the exact opposite. '. . . *the louder he talked of his honour, the faster we counted our spoons.*'

'I have only a single interest in this, Jacob,' Rosenberg was saying, looking sternly at him. 'My one and only concern is for the welfare of my daughter and my grandchild. That's all. If that means that I'm put under certain obligations in the protection and support of my son-in-law, then so be it.'

The old humbug, Bergdorf thought. The sanctimonious old prig. 'Too many issues being confused into one', indeed! He called me here. He summoned me to his presence. He wants to get the knife into Cohen as quickly as possible, so that his reputation is destroyed, but he's too steeped in hypocrisy to admit it right away. So we have to go through this act.

'Of course, Felix. How true that is,' he said. Then, listening to himself, and reflecting that the two of them were beginning to sound like a pair of dull old men on a park bench, platitudinising about the world and its troubles, he reached into the inside pocket of his jacket, took out a cutting and passed it across to Rosenberg.

'This is what you asked to see. The Foundation for Philanthropy and Humanitarian Patronage. FPHP as it's referred to. Founded by Lewis five years or so ago, and backed by his law firm. Read this. It's a most remarkable concept. I'm not surprised it's been so successful. You'll see there how it works, and who's put money into it. The Van der Baum family. The Anderschs. The Schmidt family Trust. Dozens of others – *hundreds* of others, counting the small people in with the big.'

He paused to give Rosenberg time to read it, then went on, 'But that's what so misleading about it, Felix, as I want to explain to you. There *are* some well-known philanthropists involved – of course there are. Lewis *did* initially attract some famous names amongst the givers. I'm not sure that he was necessarily intending to be fraudulent when he did so. In fact, knowing Lewis I would suspect that fraud and deception were the last thing on his mind. *Initially*. But the scheme ran away from him. These things can do that.'

Bergdorf stopped again, seeing that Rosenberg was reading the cutting once more, as if he hadn't entirely succeeded in picking up the sense of it the first time around.

'Let me explain it to you myself,' Bergdorf offered. 'Somehow media articles, like the one in your hand, always make it more complex than it is. This is the situation. The essence of the Foundation's message is that help should be given only to those who have the courage and drive to help themselves. No more free handouts to charities who do no more for themselves than sit up and beg and ask for other people's money. All very 1980s, you might say, and in a way you would be correct. But the whole thing's spun out of control, whether Lewis realises it or not. Actually he must realise it, but I suppose he thinks that at the end of the day something will turn up.'

He reached across, took the photocopied cutting from Lord Rosenberg's hand, and started to draw a simple diagram on the back of it.

'Look. It's like this. Charity A approaches Lewis's Foundation, and he says to them, "Go out and do something for yourselves, and *we'll* do something for *you*." So Charity A goes out, and starts an Appeal, and raises, let's say . . . two million pounds. They lodge the two million with Lewis, or rather with FPHP, and their reward is that Lewis says he has people on his books – generous, wealthy philanthropists, all of them known only to Lewis – who admire people who put their money where their mouths are, and, if they approve of the charity, they will match what the charity has raised for itself, pound for pound. Leave the money with us for six months, he says, and that gives me time to talk to my people, and show them what you've done, and I can promise you – I can *promise* you, he says – that at the end of that six months you'll get your original two million pounds back, and a matching two million from my philanthropists. As a gift from them. You'll have doubled your money, and these are not easy times. Most charities are floundering deeper and deeper into trouble. Well done! Virtue rewarded! We'll match whatever you're prepared to do for yourselves!'

Rosenberg stared at the diagram, and nodded his head slowly. 'I see,' he said. 'I see.' He looked up. 'And has he done that? Have all these charities got their money back, and a matching amount with it? Has Lewis really managed to double their money?'

Bergdorf nodded. 'Absolutely. There have been no hiccups whatsoever. Every charity that Lewis has dealt with has been delighted with what he has done for them. Every single charity that he has taken on, bar none, have got from FPHP exactly what they were promised – their own money back after six months, with one hundred per cent matching funds from the Foundation. An amazing achievement.'

Lord Rosenberg nodded again, and pulled a wry little face, then shrugged his shoulders.

'So what's the problem? It sounds to me as if my son-in-law is providing these charities with a marvellous service. There can't be any other institutions offering a matching programme of this sort.'

Bergdorf nodded again. 'That's right. There aren't any.'

Rosenberg was still bewildered. He began to show signs of exasperation. 'I just don't understand what all this is about. Or indeed what's in it for Lewis.'

'Interest on the deposits,' Bergdorf replied simply. 'The Foundation keeps the interest on the money that the charities lodge for six months, which is the period that Lewis says he's out there finding individuals to match it. The Foundation takes no fees, but gets what interest they can on the deposits, and they say they need that to cover their expenses in locating the matching philanthropists.'

Rosenberg shrugged. 'Seems fair enough to me,' he said. 'No percentage commission on funds raised, or any murky business of that kind. And you say that Lewis has never failed to find the people to put up the matching funds. If all he has is the interest on the money while he's working on it, that sounds quite reasonable.'

'Yes,' agreed Bergdorf. 'But the sums are very large indeed. So far the Foundation has been operating for rather less than eight years, and in that time Lewis has raised matching funds for about sixty million pounds' worth of charities' deposits. If the funds have been on deposit for the full six months, and that is presumably what has happened, then that represents an interest income of around four million pounds over the whole period of it. Perhaps a little more, with interest rates so much higher in the early days of the Foundation's life. Say five or six million. That's a good deal of money.'

'Yes,' said Lord Rosenberg, but with an air now of indifference. 'Yes, that's a large sum, and yet he's done what he's promised for these people, and no doubt his expenses have been high. He travels a good deal. No doubt a lot of that moving around the world is for the purpose of persuading these anonymous philanthropists of his to release their money for these matching funds programmes. That must take a good deal of time. There's the preparation work. The explaining to them about the needs and operation of each of these charities individually. Not to mention all the hours spent on the wining and dining and timewasting that goes with that. He must have a good deal of work in it all. I'm surprised his partners allow him to spend what must be a large part of his time in this way. Goodness knows how he can be allocating so much of his life to it, in a busy practice such as that.'

Bergdorf smiled. 'They get the fees,' he said. 'It's as simple as that. Indirectly, it's true, but over the years all that interest earned on the Foundation's deposits has effectively gone through to the firm in the form of fees. One hundred per cent of it, or thereabouts.'

Lord Rosenberg grimaced, then paused for a moment, staring at Bergdorf, as if off on a different train of thought. Then he said, 'But the Foundation's expenses . . .?'

'There aren't any. Or practically none. One secretary perhaps, who wouldn't be there otherwise. An office room. Some postage stamps. The odd small professional bill . . .'

'And the donors? The individual philanthropists? The . . .' Again Rosenberg paused, the sentence trailing away to nothing.

'I remember this happening once in the past,' he said eventually. 'Or rather, I remember reading about the case, and my father talking about it. It was just after the First World War. The story took place in Boston, Massachusetts. I remember the man's name – Charles Ponzi.

'He was a quiet-living, unobtrusive sort of fellow, if I remember the story right. Nothing flamboyant or extravagant about him. He appeared to be quite uninterested in wealth or show. But he became a folk hero in Boston, when it seemed that everything he touched for his investors there turned to gold. He gave the Boston people who followed him the sort of returns that Lewis has done. Doubled their money for them, and appeared to want to take very little of it for himself, in the form of fees, or commission, or anything else. So he doubled what they gave him, they gave him the money back again, and he did it again. Doubled it up once more. Back it came, and the same thing happened.

'It was like magic,' Rosenberg said, warming to his theme. 'It seemed that Charles Ponzi had reinvented the concept and meaning of money and wealth. Give him a dollar, and a month later he'd give you two. Give him the two back again, and he'd come back with four. The four turned to eight. The eight turned to sixteen. No one need be poor ever again. No one need work ever again. No one need be hungry and without food, or be sick and without medicine, or be in rags and without clothes. *Ever again*. All you had to do was to give what money you'd got to the wonderful Mr Ponzi, and your troubles would be over. Mr Ponzi would make you rich. Mr Ponzi worked miracles.

'He never said he was able to turn bread into wine, or put fish into empty nets. But what he *could* do was more than that. He could make money – real money, masses of money – come out of thin air. Like a magician. Every time. And not for himself, because all Mr Ponzi wanted was a little smidgen of interest on your money while he looked after it for you. The riches weren't for him; they were all for you.'

Lord Rosenberg rummaged in his pocket and eventually pulled out a scarlet handkerchief with a Winnie-the-Pooh motif on it; Bergdorf guessed quite correctly, that it was a present to him from his granddaughter. Rosenberg gave an extravagant trumpeting solo of blowing his nose, and vigorously wiping it thereafter. Then he continued.

'You know what it was, of course, that Ponzi had invented. It was the Pyramid. He was the first; occasionally there are imitators, but Ponzi invented it. The notorious financial Pyramid.'

Bergdorf said nothing and waited for Rosenberg to continue. He had to endure a further round of nose-blowing and wiping, but the older man resumed his story.

'Ponzi made the Pyramid stand up for quite a long time, before it toppled down around him, as these things must ultimately do. You know how a Pyramid works. Or rather, in the end, how it collapses.'

'The cash came into Ponzi's hands in waves. Citizen A put in his dollar, and Citizen B did as well. That made two dollars on which to collect interest. In time Ponzi gave A his dollar back, and gave him B's as well. Two dollars. Double his money. Citizen B got his two dollars from Citizens C and D. C from E and F. D from G and H. And so on. And so on, and so on.'

Rosenberg leaned over and jabbed his finger at the diagram Bergdorf had drawn. 'There – the sharp point on which the Pyramid stands. That's the first investment in. Citizen A's investment. Each round of money coming in was used to repay the earlier investors, and then that round was paid out by the people coming in after them. And so on, until it seemed to everyone in Boston that it need never stop. But it did stop eventually, of course. One day it crashed in smithereens to the ground. The amount of money required to double the money of all the investors got larger and larger as the Pyramid widened. It got so wide that there weren't enough Boston citizens to deal with the sheer volume of money required. So – *crash*! – the party was over. All the people who had put their money in during the final weeks lost the lot, every single cent. Their money had gone on paying out to the previous people and there were no more investors left to follow them.'

Lord Rosenberg smiled across at Bergdorf. He appeared newly invigorated by the telling of the tale.

'Boston was played out for Charles Ponzi, and the party was over. No more double your money. It was finished, and devastation followed. Complete devastation.'

There was silence then as the amusement in the telling of the tale died away from Felix Rosenberg's eyes. He stared at Bergdorf for a moment or two, as if wondering how to continue. Then, 'And that's what is happening to poor Lewis, is it?' he asked. 'His charities are played out for him; he's run out of people. Am I right, Jacob? Lewis is running a Pyramid, and now it's all over for him too?'

Bergdorf nodded his head, and opened his hands, palm up, in a gesture of disinterested assent. 'Yes,' he said. 'That's what it looks like to me.'

'And the Andersch family,' Rosenberg persisted. 'And the van der Baums and all the rest of them? Did they ever exist? Did they ever really invest in Lewis's Foundation? Were real philanthropists of their sort ever persuaded by this – or is that all nonsense too?'

'No – it's not all nonsense, as far as it went,' Bergdorf said. 'The philanthropists were real enough, as far as I can discover. But they invested only a single time, it seems. The van der Baums helped with the Great Portland Street Hospital Appeal, for example – and generously too. The Anderschs did something with Devonshire House Hospice. The Hampton Family Trust were benefactors of Prince's College, Cambridge, when they heard that their money would be going in on a matched basis from the College itself.

'All that happened most certainly, and there were other instances too. But there was not enough of it, and it was all too slow, and probably before he knew what was happening, Lewis was paying original depositor charities off with the later charities' money. Perhaps he thought it was just a temporary measure. Perhaps he was so excited by the sheer volume of money being generated that he really didn't think about it at all. Whatever.

'But the result . . . well, the result was that the Foundation began to snowball away completely outside Lewis's control. The moment he first used a later depositor's money to pay an earlier one, he was hooked. It had suddenly become too easy. It could go on for ever and ever. And there was all that interest money flowing into his law firm now, in the pretence that they were fees . . . and the delight of his partners at what was happening . . . and his own cut of the fees, of course. That had grown to be enormous.'

Bergdorf paused, as if embarrassed to proceed.

'I don't want to be offensive, Felix, but it does seem that Lewis did manage to spend an extraordinary amount of money – by almost anybody's standards.' Bergdorf allowed the sentence to trail away, regretting that he had allowed the issue to have been raised at all. It was pointless to risk losing Rosenberg's goodwill at this juncture.

It was Lewis's wife of course, not him, who spent all the money. Felix's daughter. You could see that from the most cursory glance at the bank statements and the credit-card summaries and the rest of it that the security search people had included in their report to him. Harrods, Harvey Nichols, couture clothes, fashionable charities, shopping trips to New York . . . all those. Massive personal expenditure.

But there was something else as well. Odd, and almost surreal . . .

For the largest payments Cohen had made had been to his wife's mother, *Lady Rosenberg*. Well over one hundred thousand pounds had been routed through to Sadie Rosenberg over the last two years. By any family's standards, these were very generous gifts.

No wonder poor old Cohen was not averse to the receipt of substantial personal fees. Given those sorts of demands on him, that was hardly surprising. But FPHP was a registered charity, and for a Trustee of a charity to receive benefit from it on this scale of things was risking far more trouble than it was worth. There would be a public scolding from the authorities at the very least, if they got wind of it. And a published reprimand, for a lawyer of Cohen's standing, would be extremely humiliating. And socially damaging. For both Cohen, *and* his wife, the Law Lord's daughter.

How odd this conversation has turned out to be, Bergdorf mused. I know why he wanted this information. He wants Cohen ruined, and out of the way, although neither of us is allowed to say this openly. I also know he wants to make me a personal proposition. Why doesn't he get on with it?

'Why are we here, Felix?' he asked suddenly. 'What is it you want from me? You said you had heard from some source or another that I was making enquiries about Lewis on behalf of one of my clients. In deepest confidence, and with respect for our friendship, I was able to confirm that. But you asked me to join you today for what you described as an exchange of views. What we've discussed so far has not really been that at all. We've established that we're both concerned that Lewis may have become entangled in a Pyramid finance scheme that could well bring him down. You'll do what you can to help him, and I will too. But that's not what I thought you wanted from me today. You told me you had your own agenda to cover. Shall we move on to that? Can you tell me what it is?'

Lord Rosenberg smiled, and turned away for a moment to pick up a bundle of papers from the chair beside him. He began the laborious process of forcing himself up to his feet from the oversoft cushions.

'My agenda? Why – the protection of my daughter, that's all. That, and . . . Do you know, Jacob, I believe I need to think this through a little more, and then we might have another word perhaps. But you *have* been helpful. You're a very good friend to us all – the sort of man whom people naturally turn to when they're in trouble or need advice. No wonder your client list is so impressive! You're just the man to have on one's side in moments of difficulty. I'm sure that's why you've taken so much interest in poor Lewis. You've been trying to see how you can best help him. You're a very good friend, and I'm sure he knows that.'

Rosenberg was struggling with his raincoat as he spoke, and there was a pleasing little scene with the elderly waiter who rushed across the room to help him. 'Thank you, my Lord. Careful of your shoulder, my Lord. Very good to see you here once more, my Lord,' he said, and Bergdorf rose to his feet as well, smiling and helping to collect the papers as they fell from Rosenberg's hands, watching with admiration the waiter's *legerdemain* as the bank note Rosenberg found for him disappeared up his sleeve as he bowed.

'Do you know what finally happened to Charles Ponzi, Jacob?' Rosenberg called, turning back for a moment as he set off for the main lobby. 'Do you know what he did, the very morning that he disappeared? No?

'Well, I'll tell you. He had over one hundred thousand dollars in his personal account – every penny he had saved from the whole affair, and in those days a decent sum of money. That morning, Ponzi closed the account and gave everything in it to a Boston orphanage. The lot. He gave it all to the orphans and left himself penniless. And he was never, ever seen again.'

Chapter 55

Bernie Levinstein was a man who enjoyed his own prejudices, but knew it was expedient to keep them under control. He despised the weak, of course, physically hated them, but in normal temper could walk past a huddled, blanketed figure in a lonely doorway without kicking it.

Today was different. Whatever the reason, the sight of the youth drunkenly lurching towards him along the pavement aroused the violence within him. Perhaps it was the weather, for the grey, dark drizzle had fallen now for days on end, and was enough to depress the mood of anyone who craved the summer sun as much as Bernie did. That, and the stress of the times too, for Hermann's arrival was now only a few days away. He was near Miranda's school now, and the prospect of seeing her again cheered him considerably. He was approaching her for a reason, of course – if anyone knew where Amos was at that moment it would be her, and that was why he had set all this business up in the first place. But it wasn't just that. She was a real lady. Gentle, polite, and dignified. Rather like the Queen Mother. She didn't know he would be there at the gates waiting for her, and that was all part of the fun. She would help; he knew she would if he asked her nicely. He'd explain at least some of it to her so that she understood how important it was. Amos was definitely the route through.

But for all this in his mind, and his pleasant, almost romantic anticipation of the evening ahead with Miranda, there was something about the way the ragged young man stumbled towards him that was too much for Bernie. He was scum. He was everything that Bernie hated. He was a degenerate, dirty animal, and the moment Bernie saw him, he knew he was going to hit him. The anticipation of it gave him a breathless excitement, as if he was about to have sex.

But the moment the first blow had landed, he knew at once that it was excessive. The fixed band of heavy rings that Bernie had pushed on to his fingers as the young man approached, smashed into his face as sweetly as if he was punching an over-ripe, giant tomato. He could feel the nose click and snap as the youth's head jerked back, and his jaw drop, and his eyes swing upwards as his body crashed down on to the ground. Bernie quickly looked around to see if there was anyone in view, but the little side street was completely empty. The youth's features were now completely covered in blood as it pumped out rhythmically from the centre of his face, where previously his nose had been.

'Fucking sod,' said Bernie, feeling the need to establish to himself a sufficient reason for why he had hit the youth. It made him feel better, so he said it again, and again, and *again* . . . and as the kicks rained into the boy's face and temple, the blood pumped more, and the groans and the convulsive jerks ceased, and Bernie knew that the boy was dead.

'Fucking sod,' he muttered once more, panting now with the exertion of it. 'Fucking sod. Fucking, fucking scum.'

Then he pressed himself back against the wall, slid the band of rings off his fingers, and looked up and down the street. Still there was no one there that Bernie could see, so he turned his coat collar up, and started to move away. But as he did so the doors of the nearby pub burst open, and two middle-aged women came out, cackling together with laughter. Bernie's first instinct was to swing around so that his face remained concealed from them, and retrace his steps in the other direction. But to do that would mean walking straight past the boy's dead body again, so he continued as he was.

'Do you have such a thing as the time, dear?' said one of the two women as he passed them, winking lewdly as she did so. At this the other screamed her laughter once more. Bernie stared at them vacantly, all his bounce and energy lost for the moment in the aftermath of what had taken place with the young man.

He looked at his watch. 'Twenty-five to seven,' he said, then smiled uncertainly as their laughter broke out again. He looked from one to the other as the two women stood there, tipsy, wiping their eyes, arms around each other's shoulders for support. So he chanted now, to show willing:

> 'Twenty-five to seven,
> But at *half past nine*,
> You can hang your knickers
> For me *on the line*.'

But his heart wasn't really in the schoolboy smut somehow, and he made a gesture of coarse dismissal to them and turned away, their whoops of delight following him down the street.

'Fucking cows,' he muttered. 'Randy, fucking old cows.' There was nothing that horrified Bernie more than sexual immodesty in females of mature, maternal years.

It was a moment or so before Bernie realised that the women had crossed over the intersecting road, and would shortly be passing the boy's body. He wondered now how far into the alleyway he had pushed him, and whether, if they saw him, they might think that he was a sleeping vagrant, and pass on their way. But the sudden, terrible scream gave him his answer.

For a moment he was completely confused. First he started to run back the way he had come, and then, on a whim, he swung off down to the right at the crossroads. A middle-aged woman was walking ahead of him, well dressed and holding a leather attaché case. She stopped, turned her head towards where a second scream had come from, then, as they started again stepped firmly into a telephone booth.

Bernie's heart lurched. He stared at the booth. She was going to ring the police. He ought to stop her. But he'd left it too late to turn away, for the woman, telephone to her ear, had swung around to peer up at the name of the little side street where the screams were coming from. She said some final words, and replaced the receiver, but all the time now, ever since she had seen him standing there staring at her, her eyes were on him too. For a moment or two she remained in the booth, as if that would give her safety and concealment, but then she reached down for her bag, and stepped out again into the street, her eyes all the time locked on to his.

Bernie gave a little movement of surprise, as if to indicate that she was familiar to him, then forced a smile on to his face and stepped forward. He reached out, bizarrely, to shake her hand, and as she glanced down he realised, with a sudden blow of horror, that he was still holding the thick band of linked rings there in his grasp. And, worse, that his raincoat had come open, and in the fading light of the summer evening, the cuffs of his white silk shirt and his fawn linen suit could be seen to be stained dark with blood.

Levinstein had been cooped up in hiding for three days now. He hadn't so much as been out of the door the entire time he had been in the little hotel, existing on packets of food he'd brought with him from the all-night supermarket on the Finchley Road, and the breakfast which was delivered to his room each morning by the teenage Irish chambermaid. He didn't know if the police were out there searching for him or not, but it was better to be on the safe side. Better to lie low.

Now, for lack of anything else to do, he went over and stood in front of the full-length mirror beside the wardrobe. Tightening his hair back into its ponytail, he turned the collar of his starched, open-necked shirt up at the back, thinking to experiment for a moment with a more *sportif*, weekend look. He wet a finger, and smoothed the line of his black, full eyebrows to make them straight and sleek. Rather liking what he saw, he tried out a new smile – intimate, confident, sexy – before moving his attention to the presentation of his groin. He tugged up the waistband of his underpants, put his hand inside to bulk and thicken himself, then spent some moments studying his virility, both in profile and face on to the mirror. He'd have a go at the chambermaid when she brought up his breakfast the following morning. Give her a glimpse of what he'd got. Nice little redhead. Cheeky little thing. It would kill some time, if nothing else.

It was six o'clock – perfect. If he left now he would be just nicely in time to be at the main gates of St Peter's at six forty-five. Miranda always came out at six forty-five on Friday evenings. He'd rung the school and asked, pretending to be a hire-car driver. It would have to be tonight, he thought. With Hermann arriving in only a few days, there was no further time to spare. He had to talk to her. He had to tell her the story about Hermann and his dad. She'd understand. She'd listen. Bronowski would never take it from him – he'd never even replied to Bernie's letter and the telephone messages. He wouldn't have anything to do with him. But he'd listen when Miranda told him. She was his wife. And then, when he'd got Hermann, Bronowski would give the story to the world.

Bernie pulled the net curtain back with his finger, and glanced out into the street. It seemed to be clear. He went back to the wardrobe and took out the only jacket he had brought with him from the hurried trip he'd made to his flat – the sharkskin with the black suede collar. He would have preferred the black cashmere for this really, considering it was Miranda he was seeing, but that was back at home, so he would have to make do with what he'd got. He undid another couple of buttons on his cream silk shirt and admired the effect, as he did so nestling the gold chain more subtly amongst the chest hair. He bared his front teeth to rub at them with his handkerchief, centred the gold buckle of his belt precisely under his navel, then looked down to check the fall of his black linen trousers on his alligator-skin shoes. Crossing to the window, he slipped his shoes off and spat on their toes, then polished them vigorously with a handful of the curtains, leaving there on them a copious smear of shoe polish.

Now he was ready to leave, and almost forgetting to go through the motions of checking up and down the passage, he was soon passing through the lobby and on his way. Sussex Gardens, after all those days locked away in the hotel bedroom, had never looked so welcoming. He was grateful for the little band of straggling, mangy flower beds and the noisy traffic of seedy, transient London. He was about to disappear through the glass front doors, with the stick-on badges of a clutch of credit-card companies and cut-price travel agencies festooned upon them, when he heard the cry from behind him.

'Mr Rapier! Mr Rapier! One moment, if I may!'

Bernie took a moment to recognise the name under which he had made his registration. Beaming his widest, handsomest, little-boy smile, he raised his hand and waved to the youngish woman who had shouted after him; she was the deputy manager, he recalled.

'Miss Blenkinsop, isn't it? How lovely to see you. I must have walked straight past you!'

Bernie made his way up to the desk and stood there in front of her, all charm and good humour and bubbling good spirits, as if she was a hostess at a club, and Bernie was on a night out with the lads. She pinkened a little at the self-confidence of him, gave a nervous bob of the head in response, then, to recover herself, assumed a frown of officious, businesslike expertise, and tapped emphatically and rapidly at the keyboard of the computer in front of her.

'Here we are, Mr Rapier,' she said. 'You booked for the four nights. We haven't seen you down here, and we wondered if everything was to your satisfaction. And to remind you that tonight is the final night we can take you; we shall need your room tomorrow morning for the weekend reservations. Check-out time is ten-thirty a.m.,' she concluded, the final words delivered with rather less of the *hauteur* she had managed initially, as she was subjected once more to the full display of Bernie and the little-boy charm.

'I'm sure you can find me a room, dear, for another night or two,' he said. 'Now that I'm here and so comfortable and nice.' He reached into the inside pocket of the sharkskin jacket, and emerged with a sheaf of banknotes, secured with a gold money-clip. 'You prefer cash, don't you? I quite understand that.'

He winked, holding out the bundle of notes, and in the gesture was somehow the implication that it was not only for the room that he was paying. Miss Blenkinsop blushed once more, and instinctively started patting and fluffing up her hair. But then the Manager himself appeared from the dingy little back office behind her, a cigarette in his hand, his cardigan hanging open in front of a crumpled flannel shirt. He raised his eyebrows, as if there to deal with an importunate but familiar scene.

'What's all this?' he asked, drawing deep on his cigarette and exhaling it in a single, astonishingly protracted stream. 'What's going on?'

'We were only able to accept Mr Rapier's reservation for four nights,' Miss Blenkinsop said. 'He now wants to stay longer, but that Irish coach party have booked us out for the whole weekend.'

'So that's it, then,' said the Manager, taking another pull at his cigarette, and continuing to stare at Bernie. 'You heard the lady. We're booked up. Full. Tonight's your last night, my son. Savvy?'

Bernie let the charm and innocence fade away from his face, and the knuckles of his right hand tightened up into a fist as he gazed at the flabby paunch, and the lined, smoker's face of the man before him.

'You want to watch your manners, Grandad,' he said. 'You've got a bit of a lip on you. You want to watch that – or I might watch it for you. Know what I mean? *Savvy?*'

Bernie flexed and bent his neck from side to side, as if loosening himself up for combat, his dark eyes staring all the while into the manager's as he did so. Then, with a final, overt wink at Miss Blenkinsop, he turned away and set off once more for the door, whistling cheerfully as he went, theatrically standing aside and pressing himself back against the wall as an old lady came past him.

'Fucking Yid,' said the Manager, dropping a large cylinder of cigarette ash on to Miss Blenkinsop's keyboard. 'Fucking Jewboy. Never could stand 'em myself. "Mr Rapier" indeed. Some chance. Got a good mind to call the fucking police, I have. They'll "Mr Rapier" him all right. Stick it up his backside!'

Muttering still, the Manager wheezed his way back into his office, and, allowing herself an overt look of disgust, Miss Blenkinsop delicately blew the ash away.

*   *   *

234

Edel had sensed that Bernie Levinstein would come for her too; he'd disappeared for a day or so, but Edel had been certain that he'd be there, outside the school, that evening. There were so few days left. He wouldn't be able to leave it any longer.

And Edel was right and so relieved that he had come. There was Bernie, lounging against a fence, a hundred yards or so away to the right of the school gates. Edel himself had approached the school indirectly, by way of a narrow little side street that ended in a small area of park space in front of the main gates. By coming from this direction, he himself had remained concealed, but with a full view of the area. He could check that first, and then he could watch Miranda come out of the main building, and observe what happened then. Without himself being drawn until such moment as he chose.

Thank God for Bernie Levinstein, Edel thought. Thank God it's Bernie there, exposed and waiting and vulnerable. Thank God it's him, because I know where he, at least, is coming from. Edel pushed himself a fraction deeper into the shadow of the great London plane tree under which he stood, then continued to search for who else, less obvious than Bernie, might be waiting too.

There were cars parked up and down the road, but at infrequent gaps, and all of them seemed empty. There were no parked vans, or little goods lorries, or any other of the conventional vehicles so beloved by surveillance teams. A hundred yards or so over to the right a gardener was forking at the soil of a flower border, and Edel watched him. But the man's back was towards the school, which suggested that he was not there to observe who was passing in and out of it, and then a second gardener, coming out of the plant store, greeted him in cheerful acquaintance. They looked harmless and genuine enough. Even so, Edel continued watching them for a few moments more, and then turned away to follow a young couple, who had appeared at that moment from around the corner, walking slowly towards the school gates, hand in hand, scuffling their trainers along, kicking languidly at the sticks and leaves they came across on the pavement.

God knows, Edel thought. Those two there; the classic operators in these situations, all youth and innocence and beguiling love. The gardener – both the gardeners. The postman just getting out of his van to empty the letterbox. The drunk over there on the park bench gazing vacantly, stupidly about, lager can in his hand, wiping his forearm over his stubble. The two young women at the end of the green, knocking up together on the tennis court, laughing, chattering, showing off their tanned, athletic legs to anyone who was there to admire them. The elderly man clipping his hedge. The over-dressed, over-anxious old woman coming along the street now with her snapping, cross little terrier in her arms. The nanny with the two toddlers climbing on the playground swings. Any of them. Any of these innocent-seeming people might be there to watch. Or to follow, or to photograph, or to kidnap, or to waylay.

Or to assassinate, he told himself, then shook his head as if to dislodge and banish the thought from his mind. Not Miranda. Please not Miranda. She knows nothing whatsoever about anything. Don't let her get pulled in. Let Miranda come out of this unharmed.

He allowed several more minutes to pass, then, just as the first knot of anxiety for her absence formed in his stomach, the front door of St Peter's opened and swung back, and Miranda came out into the light, her arms folded across her body, the strap of her plain leather handbag passed over her shoulder. She turned once to raise her hand in farewell to someone calling to her from the hall behind, then came down the steps, apparently lost in thought.

For a moment it seemed to Edel that Bernie was going to remain leaning there on the fence, and let her go. Initially he made no movement towards her at all. Then, when she had walked fifty or sixty yards, he moved off after her; once more Edel looked up and down the street, watching for anything and anybody that might arouse his suspicion. But there was nothing, and emerging now from beneath the tree, he went to stride across the grassed park area at such an angle that he would intercept Miranda as she turned into the main road.

And then Edel saw him.

It was the odd gait of the man that first struck his attention. It wasn't so much his walk, as the manner in which he clutched that stick of his to him. He looked like an amateur actor, handling a stage prop with which he felt self-conscious. Whatever it was, Edel knew immediately that there was something false, and inappropriate, and strange about the man, and all the experience of his clandestine life screamed caution and peril at him.

He stopped dead in the middle of the grass, his heart pounding in his fear as he watched Miranda and the man draw nearer and nearer to each other. Although a shout of warning had formed itself on his lips, Edel realised that he could make no sound come out, and now both his hands were held to his head, his face puckered into a grimace of terror.

The man was there. He was passing her. Edel was too late.

But nothing had happened.

Miranda, still hurrying along, head down, had not even glanced up as the two of them passed each other. In a moment she had turned the corner at the end of the street, and was gone.

And then Edel knew. It was Bernie the man was after. Not Miranda. And when they reached each other, Edel saw what happened as clearly as if the action of it was being performed specifically for his personal observation.

The man approached Levinstein, and held out a London map. He appeared to ask some question or other. Bernie paused for a moment, there was some activity between them, and then he suddenly pushed the man away, and set off after Miranda once more. But now the previous nonchalance of his pursuit had given way to a madcap, frenetic run . . . that lasted only ten or eleven paces before he started to stagger, and then fell, and tried to rise, and then went down again.

It was a re-enactment of the Georgi Markov killing on Waterloo Bridge seventeen years before, as Edel realised straight away. The man had stuck the map out right in Bernie's path, and Bernie had raised his hand to brush it away. As he did so, the point of the stick had been scratched against his wrist. Bernie had looked at the mark, put it for a moment to his mouth, then started, desperately, to run.

Edel shouted, and set off into a sprint towards them. Always hopelessly unfitted to any form of physical aggression, he knew that he made a ludicrous sight as he came at the man, his fists waving in the air, his shouts more like the hysterical shrieks of an angry child than an adult.

But anyway he was too late. The motor bike had already whisked the man away before Edel could reach him, and he was left running after it, screaming his curses, before he slowed, and stopped, and stood panting on the pavement, the tears running down his face.

He turned back. Bernie was crumpled on the ground before him, and Edel knelt and took him into his arms. He smoothed his hair, held his head up close against his chest, and then, with thumb and forefinger, closed the lids of both his eyes.

He knew, of course, Edel thought, lowering him gently to the ground. Bernie was an assassin himself. He would have realised as quickly as I did what had happened. And I wish, at that moment, he'd known that I was there. Whatever he was as a man, or whatever he wasn't, he was part of my life. I wish he'd known that he didn't die alone.

Edel remained kneeling, his hand still on Bernie's head. Then he heard a voice; the two young women from the tennis court were standing there, pink in the face, eyes full of good, English, Girl Guide concern. He got to his feet, aware that they could see the tears on his cheeks.

'Is your friend all right?' one of them said. 'Shall we get a doctor or something?'

Edel wiped his forearm across his face, then continued the movement across his forehead as well, as if to suggest that the wetness they had seen was sweat.

'Heart attack, I think,' he said. 'I've no idea who he is. I saw him suddenly keel over and slump to the ground. I tell you what – could you stay here with him while I rush off to get help? That might be the best. Keep an eye on him, and let him have plenty of air, just in case he comes round. I'll be back as quick as I can.'

Chapter 56

Cohen sighed as the telephone rang on the desk behind him. He was tempted to leave it unanswered, but it continued remorselessly, and, giving in, Cohen picked up the receiver.

'Hello?' he said in an unusually mild and noncommittal voice, as if anxious to hold all his options open before finally confirming his identity to the caller. 'Can I help you?'

The wheezy chuckle on the other end of the line was immediately identifiable, and when Steiner announced himself, Cohen was already grimacing with irritation that he had answered the call and allowed the man to reach him in this way.

'This sounds most unlike you, Lewis,' Steiner was saying. 'Normally you bark down the telephone like a prison guard. You mustn't let this business get to you.'

Cohen could hear Rachel outside in the garden, laughing and fooling around with some schoolfriends. He took advantage of the telephone's extended lead to walk over to the window, and, replying in monosyllables to Steiner's opening banter, he watched the three children attempt their handstands on the swing he had built for Rachel in the pear tree. The sight of his daughter immediately acted to calm him, as it always did.

'. . . so I thought I should call you and ask if it's true,' Steiner was saying. 'The newspapers seem to have the story now and are busy investigating it, and you can expect the whole affair to break any moment.'

You can hardly blame him for the note of exultation in his voice, Cohen thought. *Schadenfreude*. He wouldn't be himself if he didn't take pleasure in the discovery of my difficulties. Not after the pattern his own life has taken. And his conviction that we have all defrauded him of a normal, successful career and position. No one has defrauded Mariss of anything whatsoever, of course. Except for himself. He's been at war with himself his entire life. Ever since Buchenwald.

239

'I'm not at all sure what you're talking about,' Cohen said. And the strange part of this is that now the moment has come, I feel quite calm, he thought. I've been living in dread of this, yet when the news is broken to me over the telephone by the most unwelcome source possible, I feel perfectly tranquil, and more in control of myself than I've felt for weeks.

Actually, he found it cathartic in a strange sort of way, like a Catholic confessional perhaps. Thinking of Catholics, Cohen's mind turned to Gareth Edel. He hadn't seen him or heard from him since their meeting in the coffee shop behind Westminster Abbey. Since then, the first article had appeared in the *Sunday Times*. It had carried no mention of Jacob Bergdorf, as Cohen had known it wouldn't. But the second article was due that weekend, and Amos would have had time to introduce the new material on Bergdorf that Cohen had passed him.

It was true that Edel had made no effort to reach him since then. He didn't know what he'd said to Amos. Certainly he hadn't been asked to read any new material for libel. But Amos was such an independent spirit. As was Gareth. Both went off and did things in exactly their own way. But he had by no means ceased to hope that he would find all the Bergdorf material out there exposed to the public eye, when he opened his newspaper on Sunday. Not at all.

Amos has gone to ground because he wants to avoid any further pressure from me, Cohen thought. Gareth too.

'. . . and you can count on my support, Lewis,' Steiner was saying. 'It's so important that we present a united front against the world, don't you think? So why don't I come around to your house this evening, and you can give me a drink in your nice drawing room, and I can meet your wife – for the first time! – and we can sit down together, all three of us as a team, and discuss what we should do next. Isn't that a good idea? Send your car down to me, and I'll come straight up to St John's Wood. The great thing is for your—'

Quite suddenly, Cohen had had enough of this. He wondered how he could have allowed the conversation to have gone on for so long.

'That's enough, Mariss. Stop there,' he said, cutting him off in mid-sentence. 'You've misunderstood the situation entirely. You're too curious and meddling, and you've dealt with journalists' tittle-tattle as if it was fact. Your conclusions from it are all nonsense. As I would have expected. You claim that you've got other motives in this apart from personal spite, but I haven't the time or energy to discover them. Thanks for calling, Mariss. But that's enough. Please leave it there.'

Yet as he put the telephone down, Cohen had a sudden vision of Steiner as he had been as a young man. Yes – there was opportunism and moral degradation in the securing of his survival at Buchenwald. What's more, there had always been in him an egotistical, self-absorbed isolation and remoteness. But as a young man . . .

Cohen stared out of the window at the three children, now sitting together safely side by side on the garden bench, absorbed in their conversation. He had a memory of a certain evening in a Soho pub, thirty years before. There had been a meeting of the political group, and then a number of the members had stayed on afterwards to entertain the guest speaker – some academic or other from Tel Aviv, as Cohen could recall it now. Bronowski had been there. Edel too, tucked away on his own in the corner of the room.

But Cohen's real memory was of Steiner. Full of good spirits, and good talk, and fluent, generous humour, he had dominated the evening. Cohen had never seen him like that before or since. He had charmed them all. He had told his stories, he had made his speeches, impassioned and aflame, he had performed his mimicry, especially for the Tel Aviv man, of certain famous figures of the Israeli establishment. He had made them laugh, and cheer, and think. He was a transcendent, triumphant figure. Burning with energy, and bustle, and intelligence.

At that time his personal history with the SS was unknown; perhaps it would have made no difference. Most of those who were in the Nazi camps had no real appetite for judgement on each other by that time. The War was long over; all of them were trying to build their lives in their adopted country; all trying to look forward to the future, rather than back to the past. Reliving Buchenwald or anywhere else would bring them no happiness They were bent on achieving hope, and light. For themselves, and for their children, and for their children's children.

This business of exposure about what happened or didn't happen in Buchenwald that Bronowski has devoted so much time towards is as irrelevant now as it would have been then, Lewis decided. As old hat now as then. But – shamefully maybe, pragmatically, whatever – it's done the trick for me. Hermann's under pressure. Bergdorf's under pressure in a different way. And that's going to do the trick for me . . .

*　　*　　*

Cohen remained gazing out into the garden, the sun of the summer evening shafting through the big Victorian drop windows, lighting his face, sombre, and lined, and heavy in thought. The telephone was still there in his lap from where he had placed it on the conclusion of his conversation with Steiner, and, forgetting its presence, he started in surprise when it rang so close to him.

He picked the receiver up once more, and his voice as he answered it now was firm and confident and in character. His conversation with Steiner had served to restore him. If that was going to be the sort of enmity that he was going to have to face, then Cohen felt now entirely ready for the fight to come.

The Foundation had swung out of control – there was no doubt about that. But so far, no one had got hurt. Nobody had lost any money whatsoever. All the charities that had lodged funds with him had got them back, twice over; exactly as he had promised. It had become a Pyramid, that was true, and he would admit that if he absolutely had to, and financial Pyramid schemes had an ambiguous position in law. But it hadn't started out that way. He could demonstrate that. All he needed now was a further tranche of genuine private philanthropists who were there to give, and wanted nothing back in return. Those people were out there. It was just a question of finding them and persuading them once again, just as he had done in the first place. That was all it was. Then, when they had put their money in, the Foundation would no longer be operating as a Pyramid. One small adjustment, and it would be back in the clear once more.

As for himself, if he could get some access to these Swiss accounts he would be all right as well. Back in the clear – just like the Foundation. Life was cyclical. You got your ups and your downs, and when you hit a down what you had to do was keep calm, and carry on, and wait for your luck to turn. It always does in the end.

'Lewis Cohen,' he barked, back now in full voice, and Edel, as always, was a clear three or four seconds delayed in his initial response, as if deciding whether or not to enter the conversation at all. But then he said his name too, and Cohen felt immediately pleased.

'It's good to hear you, Gareth. I imagine you're calling about the journalists' attempts to stir up gossip about my Foundation. Well, as always in these things, the truth is somewhat different to the—'

Edel interrupted him immediately, and at first, Cohen thought

Edel was trying to stop him from slipping into the banality of laboured explanations of half-truths and half-lies, all of them reducing and humiliating to both the giver of them and the receiver.

'Partly that,' Edel had leapt in to say. 'Partly that, and partly the other issue. The matter that you and I have discussed.'

He hesitated, and Cohen said, 'The line's clean – I can assure you of that. That's one advantage of doing occasional work for the Americans. The line's clean, and you can speak as freely as you wish.'

But Edel trusted nobody's telephone line, and Cohen's least of all, so he would do no more than arrange that they should meet together in the morning, at a place and time that he would specify only in a form of simple oral code that they both understood, and the conversation ended there.

Or almost there. As Cohen was about to replace his receiver, Edel said, 'I am sorry, Lewis. My mind's not really on the business of this Foundation of yours, and your other difficulties, but I *am* sorry about it all the same. I won't pretend that I haven't known about it, because the rumours have been around for some time, though I doubt you've realised that.

'You're an innocent, Lewis, however the world perceives you. A bit of a fool perhaps, and devious to the point of lunacy. But above all you're an innocent. I've always known that. Always.'

Chapter 57

His clerk came in through the door with the tray, and Lord
Rosenberg made a smiling show of trying to persuade Cohen to
change his mind, and have a cup of tea.

'At least you'll have a chocolate biscuit, my dear fellow,' he said.
'Rickson and I absolutely insist. Am I right, Rickson?' he said to
the clerk, who responded with a practised, sycophantic chuckle,
and thrust out the plate so close to Cohen's chin that the easiest
way for him to escape was to take a biscuit, and pretend to make
a show of nibbling at the thing, if he really had to, in due course.

The truth was that Cohen hated chocolate, and never ate biscuits
at any time. He also disliked the male institution common room
aura of places such as these Chambers. He felt that every joke
made in these circumstances was in some way aimed at him; so
was immediately on the defensive, and because of it awkward
in the way that he behaved. All of that made worse by the fact
that he distrusted the very appearance of the place. There was
insecurity in him for that too, as he well knew, but the pipe-smoke,
walking-stick, frayed-carpet stage set of it concealed, in his eyes,
a clubby, closed circle malice. And that closed circle was not one
to which Cohen, whether he wanted it or not, would ever be an
admitted party.

Cohen loved the idea of Felix Rosenberg; it was the reality
of him that he sometimes found dispiriting. When he saw him
in his West Sussex home, with the parkland, and the cerise
silk wall-papered drawing room, and the walled rose garden in
bloom, and the gardener's boy tying the hot-house peaches into
their individual muslin bags, why, all was well, and he glowed
at his pleasure at being married into such a household. There
were few, if any, Jewish families in Britain of such distinction.
No one would dispute that. The Rosenbergs weren't particularly
wealthy of course, and Cohen, despite the pressure of his own
circumstances, remembered, with no great malice, the numerous

'loans' he had made to his mother-in-law over the years. All of them, he had assumed, to deal with her quite prodigious appetite for horse-race gambling. If her past demands on his purse were any guide, then Sadie Rosenberg must be one of the most substantial and least successful players in the country. He could do with that money himself now – by God he could. And not for gambling. Dumping her little difficulties on him must have seemed to Sadie like a very sensible solution. A practical way of keeping an untidy little secret in the securest of hands. But however they behaved with money, the family's professional reputation was, of course, of the highest level. That was without doubt. And had been for generation upon generation.

All that time here in England, Cohen thought. For so long at the top of the tree. How fortunate the Rosenbergs had been to achieve that. How sad that Felix was capable of being as big a shit as he was no doubt about to show himself to be.

'Good of you to come, my dear fellow. Very good of you,' Rosenberg said, and came around the desk, beaming his welcome. 'Rickson . . . would you kindly . . .' He nodded in dismissal at his clerk, who immediately left the room, making as he went a pointed statement of shutting the door behind him, as if to emphasise to Cohen that although Rickson himself was fully briefed on every detail of what was to be said, as far as the rest of the world was concerned there was to be complete privacy and security.

Rosenberg went to fiddle around on his desk behind him. He picked up a sheet of notepaper, glanced at it for a moment or two, then sat down in his swivelled chair, and looked at Cohen from across the polished desk top.

He smiled vaguely, as if keen to indicate kind and familial concern, then said, 'Not to beat about the bush, I can confirm that I have definite information that your affairs are by no means in order. Neither your personal affairs, nor those of your Foundation – FPHP or whatever it is. I'm most sorry to hear about it, of course. These must be worrying times for you. Very worrying. I'm sure there must be something I could do . . . do to . . .'

Cohen stared at him. Make him work for it, he told himself. He feels guilty over the way his wife has behaved, and so he should. But there's more to come. Let him do the talking. Sit still, and let him come to me.

Then Rosenberg blushed, as if aware that he was the loser in the initial struggle of will.

'Sadie and I are not so wealthy as people no doubt think we

are,' he began. 'We live pleasantly, of course, but we were very fortunate to pick Priory Place up well before the inflation in the property market got under way. That's been a real blessing to us. And since the point must be on your mind, let me say that Sadie's . . . my wife's little problems are something that we are both learning to face up to and deal with. It goes without saying that the money you advanced to her will be repaid. Sadie's illness – and that's how we look at it, as an illness – is by no means an unusual one, and she's learning to handle it. But the Rosenbergs themselves have never been a family to throw money around. The family firm was never resilient enough for any temptations of that sort to have entered my father's mind, or my uncle's. And when the firm was sold, the money we got from it has been spent largely on maintaining the house, which will be Elizabeth's one day of course, and education, and charity, and . . . and . . .'

Horse racing, Lewis thought. Gambling, for the love of God. That's Sadie's 'little problem'.

'. . . and other things of that sort. Jewish charities you know, in the main. Mainly Jewish causes,' Rosenberg concluded lamely, as if the repeated assertion to Cohen of their mutual race would serve in some way to give the account of his domestic budgetary arrangements an additional dignity and decorum.

'So there we are,' he said. 'We'd like to give you a helping hand to help you out, but as things are neither Sadie nor I are getting any younger, and we're concerned as to whether we're going to have enough in our retirement to keep the wolf from the door.'

'Felix,' Cohen said, thinking that the time had come when he really had to make some attempt to correct the flow of the conversation. 'I don't understand what this is about at all. Let's start again. What exactly are you saying to me?'

After a dignified pause, Rosenberg removed his half-moon glasses and laid them down.

'The Foundation, Lewis. Some people have been briefing me about its activities. You meant well, my dear fellow, I'm sure you did. But the Foundation has got out of control, and it owes money all over the place. Way too much for it to handle. *That's* what I'm talking about.'

There was a schoolmasterly tone of pious disapproval in Rosenberg's voice; Cohen found, oddly, that he was amused by it. This was outrageous. He was being set up. Cohen knew why he had been brought here – and it had nothing whatsoever to do with Sadie's gambling debts, or the Foundation, or his own overdraft. But he bided his moment.

'I don't know who you've been talking to, Felix, but your description of things is not quite fair. The Foundation has had a difficult time in recent weeks, and I would be the first to admit it. We do need to find some more benefactors, and I accept that we should have got on to it very much quicker. But now we've got going, and I'm very confident of the result.

'So far, each and every charity that deposited money with the Foundation has received exactly what they were promised. They're all delighted, as you would expect them to be. There hasn't been one single default on that promise. Not one.'

'But it's a Pyramid, Lewis, isn't it? So far you haven't got into trouble with it, but you know as well as I do what happens to Pyramids before very long. They get too wide at the top; they owe too much money to too many people; they run out of sources of fresh money, and because of the sheer size of the new funds required each round, eventually they collapse. You can't go on doubling up until the end of time! Eventually the thing has to collapse. And when it does so, the last tranche of people in lose every penny they've got.'

There was a silence for a little as both men studied each other. Then Rosenberg went on, 'Pyramids can be a problem in law. You're a lawyer. You know that.'

'I don't accept your statement that the Foundation has been running a Pyramid,' Cohen objected. 'For a period – possibly – it might, technically, have looked like . . . But all that's in the past. We have a programme now that will bring a whole host of new donors into the Foundation. We'll be able to—'

'Look, Lewis,' his father-in-law interrupted. 'I must be frank with you. We can't allow this to go on. I have a position in life which dictates that every member of my family has to abide by clear rules of conduct and probity, and it does appear that you are about to be in rather severe breach of those. The affairs of the Foundation smack to me of a situation where the man in control of it has got completely carried away by enthusiasm, and perhaps even idealism, and has quite abandoned his sense of proper thrift and reality and integrity in the process. And the same applies – *exactly* the same applies – to your personal financial affairs. You're enthusiastic; you're a generous provider to your wife and daughter; you're even an idealist in the way that you do that; and – yes – you were most generous to my wife when she asked for your help. I say it again – you're a generous man. An affectionate man as well. The two are very much linked. But . . .'

He shrugged, and Cohen made himself nod pleasantly in response to the paternalistic approval that had been extended to him, before whatever ritualised punishment was then about to follow, 'for his own good'.

As he did so, a moment's guilt came over him. Was it really 'love', to allow his wife to lead the life she did – extravagant, empty, trivial. He was affectionate to Rachel – most emphatically so. But it wasn't Rachel to whom he was obliged to be financially generous. There were her school fees, of course, and he spoiled her with uncalled-for presents, whenever she would let him, which was surprisingly seldom. There was in Rachel a most surprisingly mature sense of modesty, when it came to money and show. Quite unlike her mother.

'To put it at its most crude, you're broke, my dear Lewis.' Rosenberg was continuing. 'Over the last few years, you've been spending on average more than half as much again as you've earned. So, naturally, each year your reserves have become depleted. In recent times you seem to have sustained yourself entirely by borrowings. But no one can go on borrowing more and more for ever and ever. Eventually the security runs out, and so does the money.'

That sentence carries the grammar and the banal moralism of a Dundee nanny, Lewis thought. And I'm beginning to find this scene offensively intrusive.

'You've a rather highly coloured version of the story, Felix,' Cohen said, trying to appear calm. 'Elizabeth and I will have to put our house in order. It's high time we did so. I wish she and I had been more open with each other before. But we'll do so now, and together, I'm sure we can—'

'Which rather brings me to the point, Lewis.'

Rosenberg got up from behind the desk, and as he walked around to sit once more with Lewis, he made a great play of picking up his sheet of foolscap, screwing it up into a ball, and throwing it into the waste-paper basket. Then he settled down in his chair, crossed his legs, and laid his hands down neatly in his lap. His expression as he looked at Lewis was one of deep, sincere humanity and compassion. Lewis gazed back, and wondered how much longer this was going to continue.

'As I say,' said Rosenberg, as if reading Cohen's exact thoughts. 'That brings me to the point I feel I have to make to you. Lewis

– with your personal affairs in the order that they are, and with what I do greatly fear, whatever you say, is likely to be the most unpleasant scandal over your Foundation . . . Lewis, I'm going to ask you to . . . I'm going to ask you to leave the family.'

Cohen looked at Rosenberg with complete bewilderment. This wasn't what he was expecting at all.

'Leave the family?' he echoed, 'What do you mean – leave the family? I'm not *in* the family. At least,' he said, quickly, sensing that he had phrased this in a way that weakened his position, 'I'm not a member of it in the sense that—'

'Exactly. That expresses it very well. Lewis – I've been as straightforward and as frank with you as I could be. You didn't have the easiest of starts in life, and you've had a most successful and determined time of it. We all of us applaud you for that. It's a great achievement. But in recent years the fortunes do seem to have conspired against you, as sometimes happens, and the fear is that you're on the brink of being exposed in a major scandal. Whether it's your fault or not, I have to think of my daughter's welfare, and her happiness. Elizabeth is a Rosenberg. You realise what that means, of course – and I'm sure, when you think the situation through, that you'll make this sacrifice.'

For a moment, Cohen almost felt like laughing. You didn't settle other people's lives this way! You didn't simply call your son-in-law into your Chambers and tell him, just like that, to 'leave the family'. I assume he means that I should agree to being thrown out in disgrace, and being divorced by Elizabeth, Cohen thought incredulously. Before any financial scandal breaks that might embarrass the Rosenbergs. Christ! He says all this, and it's *still* not the reason why he called me here in the first place. I can't take much more of this.

'This is completely preposterous,' he said in a low voice. 'This is insane. Listen to me. One – I don't want to leave my wife. Two – I don't want to allow myself to be divorced. And three – I certainly don't want to be deprived of my daughter. None of those things. Absolutely not. Yes – there are difficulties at the moment, but I believe that's what marriages are about. That's when marriages really come into their own. Mutual support and succour in times of distress. These are stressful times for me. I want my wife at my side, and I want my daughter there too. I have no intention of agreeing to your idea. None whatsoever.'

Cohen got up and started to move towards the door. He was about to ask if Rickson could be summoned to show him the way out of the maze-like building, when Rosenberg said, 'I think you will actually, Lewis. When you've had a chance of hearing me out.'

Cohen hesitated, then swung around.

'Stop this, Felix,' he said. 'Stop it! What happens between me and Elizabeth is between us, and us alone. I'm going to tell her now about my difficulties, and discuss with her what we're going to do. We're husband and wife. We're staying together. Leave us alone.'

Flushed with anger, Cohen slammed the door shut behind him, and Rosenberg watched him go.

Elizabeth will do what I ask her to, he thought. Lewis's creditors will foreclose on him, he'll be driven into bankruptcy, and the Foundation story will appear in the press. That will finish him in Hermann's eyes once and for all. Which means that Bergdorf and I can have a free run at the Swiss accounts from the British residents' end of things. It's a pity all this has to include Bergdorf, but I need him. At least I think I need him. That too could be thought about.

You'll have to keep your wits about you, Felix, he told himself, playing, as he often did in his private moments, a childhood game of self-dialogue, frivolous in its tone, and naughty in its language. Think it through, and find the way, and get on with it, my dear. Get on with it.

You're a Law Lord, in case you've forgotten. You can work anything out. You're the *crème de la crème*, my dear. You're a fucking Rosenberg.

Chapter 58

Cohen whistled as he made his way home along St John's Wood Terrace. Cohen liked people who remained unfazed and cheerful when faced with danger – and here he was, doing it himself. He was proud of that.

Sod the old bugger, he thought. May a curse descend on the Rosenbergs, and render them impotent, infertile, and plagued by sores. Felix particularly. Pompous, manipulative old sod.

Outside his neighbour's house, a small boy in T-shirt and jeans stood forlornly waiting for his mother to come out to the car. He was kicking at the ground with the toe of his trainers, his violin case trailing from his hand, the picture of discontent. As he passed, Cohen patted him affectionately on his curly head, then turned and shaped up, as if inviting him to spar.

'Cheer up, Jakie!' he said. 'It'll soon be over!'

Cohen went whistling on his way, and a few yards further on he was at the steps leading up to the front door of his own house; he ran up them two at a time, fumbling in the pockets of his trousers for the key.

As he turned the lock, and walked through the door, Cohen's mind flitted for a second to Steiner's chip of wood stuck in the door jamb of his unspeakable room. Clumsy it might be, but it did at least serve its purpose.

Something was wrong. It was the way that the letters lay on the floor. The angle of the fall was too wide, and the spread of it too deep. It looked to Cohen as if someone had picked the pile of envelopes up, sorted them through, then tossed them back on to the ground deliberately at random, but in doing so failing to re-create their normal dispersal.

There was the picture too. The picture was always, quite deliberately, hung with a slight leftwards angle off the true. The bottom corner of it was kept precisely in line with the second and third from the right of the apparently random pinpricks with which

Cohen had marked the wallpaper. This was the only picture that mattered. Behind it, under the paper, was a concealed spring; when pressed, it released the safe lock in the dining room, on the other side of the wall.

Cohen stayed absolutely still, and listened. It was several minutes before he felt comfortable that he was alone. Bracing himself, he walked through to the dining room. He knew exactly what he would find there. And he did.

The safe had been tampered with. It had been opened, and shut again. Without question, someone had been there.

Cohen went back into the hall, pushed the picture to one side, pressed the spring pad, and came back to the safe. The door swung open, and, at one glance, he could see that the files were in their correct order. But that wasn't the point. Someone had been there. The question was, what had they read, and what had they taken?

There was very little there that a passing thief, or even a passing security person, would find of value on a casual basis. Bank statements going back for years. A bundle or two of love letters from different women, but all from so long ago – well before his marriage – that his possession of them was not in itself directly incriminatory. Embarrassing perhaps, were they to fall into Elizabeth's or Rachel's hands, but only mildly so. Some more recent letters from creditors, and some of them aggressive; these, possibly, might have been photographed by someone with trouble to make. Correspondence recently with the Inland Revenue; that too. Old school reports of Rachel's. A letter from her one year when he was travelling in the US on business. A large manila envelope containing her birthday cards and Christmas present tags to him as a small child. These he spent some moments looking through, then put them carefully to one side.

Files covering the general correspondence of the Foundation were now in the strongroom at the office, and Lewis blessed the day he had taken them there. A good job he had been prudent in that.

Cohen crossed his arms, and gazed out of the window, absently watching the summer breeze toss the vivid green leaves of the lime tree that stood up against the garden wall. He felt so calm. Ever since the conversation with Felix Rosenberg, he'd had a sense of peace, and resignation, and acceptance of whatever fate was to deal him. But the truth was that fate was not going to deal him anything very much. He was going to be all right, personally, and so was the

A Passage of Lives

Foundation. He was certain everything would settle down again. There was absolutely no point in panicking, and screaming at everybody, and rushing around in circles. He had very practical plans afoot for ensuring that all went went. Plans in which Joseph Hermann was already playing a considerable part. And they were going to make a very considerable difference indeed.

Micawber was right, Lewis told himself. And in his present, serene mood he laughed in self-mockery at the thought of it, then started, one by one, to push the files back into the safe, each in its set position.

There was the business of the so-called divorce, of course. That would have to be sorted out. There wasn't going to *be* a divorce. That was something that would have to be made so clear to Felix that the suggestion of it would never be made again. Best of all Elizabeth should do it, rather than him. He'd talk to her the moment she returned from Cap d'Antibes at the end of Rachel's half-term. They'd sit down together and have their first real conversation for years . . .

He sat there staring at the files for several minutes longer, quite lost now in thought, knowing in his heart what it was that the interloper, or friend, or stranger, or member of the family, or whoever it was had been looking for.

It wasn't the creditors' letters, or the Inland Revenue file, or those bundles of old love letters, or anything to do with the Foundation. None of that. There was just one thing they were after. And he imagined they had got it.

They must have got it. They had signalled to him that they had got it. That's why the place was left in the way that it was. The letters thrown around the hall carpet. The picture left askew. They were signals for him. Him alone.

They'd wanted to see the list. They'd wanted to see the names and the addresses and the numbers on the list. The code they were written in was familiar to them. They knew what they were looking for. They'd found it, and copied it all down, and gone away.

Leaving their calling card, so that Cohen should know they had been there.

Chapter 59

Steiner sat at his table, spreading a piece of sliced bread with margarine from a grubby, half-finished plastic container.

A pigeon landed on the sill of the open window behind him and cooed, as if hinting that it would like to share the meal. Steiner immediately turned to watch, then pushed himself upright, bread in hand, and laid it down on the sill. As if in irritation with him that it had taken so long, the pigeon started to peck at it, and Steiner leant forward, as gently as he knew how, and stretched out his hand in an attempt to stroke the bird's back. But at the first touch the plump pigeon stiffened, and dropped off the window sill in flight, curving in its fall to land down on the roof of a small shed that faced on to the backyard of the building.

Steiner gazed down after it, then, making chirruping noises in encouragement, he picked up the slice of bread from the window sill, and threw it down after the bird, aiming to drop it down beside it on the roof. But the throw missed of course, and by a distance, and the bread fell neatly at the feet of the janitor, who was emerging from the shed just at that moment, clutching an armful of brooms to his chest.

The man stopped dead in his tracks, then looked up to see where the bread had been thrown from. On seeing Steiner peering down at him, he grimaced, and shook his head, and waved his fist up at him.

'You filthy old bastard,' he shouted. 'I've told you about this God knows how many times before, you Yid git. Don't fucking throw your filthy fucking garbage out of your filthy fucking window. Get it? I'll tell you again. Throw your fucking garbage away in the right fucking place. And don't fucking throw it out of the fucking window. Nor anything fucking else. Not now, not never. Is that in your thick skull? Or do I have to fucking say it once fucking more?'

And with a final wave of his fist, the janitor kicked the bread over to the side of the gutter, and continued across the yard. Steiner shouted down some insult or other after him in response as he went, but his heart wasn't in it somehow, and it was for form's sake as much as anything else, and the oath lacked bite. When Steiner withdrew his head from the window and went back to the table to spread himself another slice of bread he found that he was chuckling, and in very good spirits, and most untypically appreciative of the theatrically farcical nature of the scene he had just initiated.

He hadn't felt so cheerful for a long time. Everything was falling into place for Hermann's arrival, as smoothly as the jam-stained margarine he was now eating straight off his knife. He'd planned it so well. He'd taken such care to get all the people in the drama set up to do what he wanted. Everything was in place, and everyone organised, if they did but know it, and it was all going to work.

But, in the middle of these thoughts, Steiner suddenly felt a stab of sharp, jagged pain. He was all too familiar with it these days, and he bent double, grimacing, stricken with fear, knowing what was coming. Each time this had occurred, and the remission periods in recent weeks had been shorter and shorter, the savage horror of these attacks had been past his imagination.

He remained where he was for a minute or two, face bleached of colour, sweat pouring down from his brow. And then it came again, and each time the pain came Steiner screamed, then, as it ebbed, sobbed, as a small child would sob, waiting for the balm, and peace, and haven of his mother's arms.

At last it was over, at least for the time being. Steiner straightened up, waited a few moments more, and limped his way over to his bed.

'Gott zol mir heiten,' he said. 'God protect and keep me.' Terrified in case the pain would hit him again if he made any sudden movement, he carefully lowered himself on to the filthy, stained coverlet. Incongruously, he noticed, perhaps for the first time since he had stolen it from a famous Chelsea department store some ten years before, that the cotton of the coverlet was in a pretty pattern of rich cream buttercups and crimson and cerise primroses, and that cute Disneyesque baby animals danced amongst the meadowgrass in which the flowers were nestling.

'Like Aunt Sara's house,' he said aloud. 'Like the furnishings there.' And as he settled fearfully to rest, his memories were of a comfortable, bourgeois villa in the outskirts of Charlottenburg, and the curtains in the nursery, all kitsch, and sentimental vulgarity, and his aunt's cook cursing and clattering in the kitchen, and the butler in the hall, and his uncle's umbrella, as tightly furled as a sergeant-major's marking-stick, standing bolt upright in the crested porcelain umbrella-stand in the hall.

'What happened to those days?' Steiner muttered. Despite his insults and contempt for the doctors in the cancer clinic the previous week, he knew he was terminally ill. Now, frightened and alone, his memories were all of Passover in the family house in Berlin. Uncle Isaac standing by the menorah candelabrum, and lighting the candles one by one. The sweetmeats in the silver dish on the sideboard. His cousins looking demure and respectful halfway down the table. His mother scolding his older sisters for their giggles. His small brother, only just old enough to attend the feast, sitting opposite him, and trying to catch his eye, and trying to make him laugh as his father chanted the ancient liturgies of the festival.

Steiner turned his head, and looked over towards the opposite wall. Pinned there, almost at ceiling height, was a large group of faded photographs of his family. His father was in most of them, as starched-collared and as rigid as a rising young Berlin lawyer could be. But in one of them, tucked away a foot or two from the rest, there was a photograph of him in an open-necked shirt and hiking clothes, bronzed and happy, and strikingly handsome. Beside him, standing about as tall as his father's waist, was a little boy of perhaps six years old, also dressed in his country clothes, holding his hand up to clasp his father's. But the expression on the child's face was one of fathomless melancholy. As if he, Mariss, and only he, knew what the future held, and what unspeakable tragedies were about to unfold.

Steiner lay quite still, staring at the photograph. He remembered the day on which it had been taken. He remembered his father's joy at the prospect of a few days' holiday, and his small brother bounding around in the garden in his excitement at their departure, and the family Alsatian, Nico, running about him in his anxiety at his high spirits.

Steiner remembered that day so clearly, as he had throughout his adult years. And the next memory too.

Kristallnacht. Smartly dressed women applauding and laughing and holding their babies up to watch the scene as the Jews were kicked and beaten by youths with lead piping in their hands. The sacking of his school by the Nazi stormtroopers. His jump from the upper-storey window into the bushes below, and then hiding behind the barrels in the school outhouses for two whole days, until it was safe to come out.

The family house empty and deserted. The window in his parents' bedroom swinging, creaking in the breeze, and the net curtains puffing and flapping in and out, as forlorn and purposeless as the sails of a shipwrecked schooner. His mother's underclothes, shockingly, lying crumpled and scattered all over the floor and the unmade bed. His brother's toys dumped discarded in the hall, looking as if he had attempted to take them with him, and, at the last moment, had them torn from his hands. Nico, dead there on the kitchen floor, shot through the heart as, with his usual simple loyalty, he had leapt, perhaps, at the throats of the intruders. The slats on the side of his sister's cot for some, inexplicable, horrific reason broken and stark and jagged. Surely they couldn't have torn her out of the cot through the bars of it? Surely they must have lifted her out? Surely to God they can't have smashed the sides of the cot to get at the child, as she lay there in it, clutching her favourite woollen blanket? Sucking at her rubber comforter. Smiling at the strangers no doubt, as was always her way.

Steiner folded his arms tight across his eyes, as if to force the image back into the recesses of his mind.

'Schluf in shalom mit Gott. Sleep in peace with God,' he muttered, then turned his eyes now to the open window, and his own curtains flapping in the breeze, as those in his parents' bedroom had done that afternoon, almost sixty years before.

He realised that he was not in the least afraid of dying. In fact the more he brooded on it, the more welcome it appeared. Provided he could go without too much pain. These attacks were becoming unbearable. He could be given morphine, as that impertinent idiot of a doctor had told him, but to get that he would have to be in hospital, and the thought of those tarts of nurses laying their incompetent hands all over him, and messing him around, and clanking about with their thermometers and bedpans and disgusting meals and all the rest of it . . .

He would rather be here, amongst his own possessions and in his own surroundings. Where he could at least look at his photographs, and read his old boxes, and do whatever he wanted to do.

And be on his own. He was happier by far on his own. He always had been. Ever since that afternoon when he had gone back to his parents' house, and knew that he would never see his family again.

'Schluf in shalom mit Gott,' he said once more, and put the

257

memory of those things away, as he had grown used to doing, and tried to compose himself to rest.

But then, suddenly, he chuckled at the recollection of the janitor. 'Fucking garbage on my fucking head,' he mimicked, aloud, the intonation of the man's histrionic pique as startlingly accurate as could be, as it always was in Steiner's copy of any accent or any language. Then he plumped his pillow, glanced at his brand new, shop-lifted watch, and, smiling still, settled himself to sleep.

Just a couple of days to go, he thought, as he felt himself drift away, exhausted by the pain of a few minutes before. And then it's done, and the man's dead, and it's all finished, and I can be on my way.

As his sleep started to sink in on him, he recited in his mind his father's talisman psalm.

'Thou, O Lord God, art full of compassion and mercy: long suffering, plenteous in goodness and truth.

'O turn then unto me, and have mercy upon me: give Thy strength unto Thy servant, and help the son of Thine handmaid.

'Shew some token upon me for good, that they who hate me may see it and be ashamed: because Thou, Lord, hast holpen me and comforted me.'

His eyes opened for a moment, and he stared out once more at the curtains flapping out through the open window, and the patchy, dark grey clouds now beginning to gather and come in from the west. 'Shew some token upon me for good,' he repeated, then settled himself once more.

Chapter 60

Cohen flopped down into the armchair, and smiled up at Edel as the glass of iced Stolichnaya was put into his hand. He drank half in one draught, then put the glass down on the table beside him.

'I haven't been in this house for years,' he said. 'I'd like to have been, but you've never asked me. You're such a recluse, Gareth, you really are. You shouldn't spend so much time on your own.'

He contemplated him cheerfully. 'And where's Amos? I haven't seen him for days. He never showed me the text of the second article for libel reading, and it's too late now anyway. But where is he?'

'I don't know,' said Edel. 'Somewhere.'

He stared at his glass and said no more, and Cohen, waiting for him, shook his head, and smiled.

'All right. We won't enquire about Amos. So let's move on to Bergdorf. It *is* Bergdorf you called me here to talk about isn't it?'

'Very well,' Edel declared. 'Bergdorf. You're right. We'll both get to the point immediately – most unlike us.'

He went over to a battered little leather attaché case lying on a chair in the corner of the room, and extracted a computer printout, and some handwritten notes on several sheets of plain white notepaper. He sat down again in his chair, and laid these out on his knee.

'These are yours, Lewis,' Edel said. 'They're from your safe.

Cohen sat back in his chair and gazed at him. 'How on earth did you get them?'

Edel took off his heavy hornrim spectacles, polished them with his handkerchief, and put them back on his nose. 'How did I get them? How do you think, Lewis? I took them. I walked into your house, and took them. I didn't want anybody else involved, for reasons that I'll explain in a moment. So I took them myself.'

Cohen gave him a look of incredulity. 'How did you know where they were?' he demanded. 'How did you know where the safe was and what was in there? And the combination lock. All of those things. And how did you get into the house in the first place, if it comes to that?'

Edel gave a slight smile, and a faint shrug of his shoulders. 'Come on, Lewis, you know more about me than that. And I have to say that the traps you set were not exactly original. That business of lining up pictures with pin marks, and so on.' He burst out laughing.

'Lewis – don't think that I'm being flippant. I know the serious-ness of your financial position. I appreciate how worried you must be, and the stress you're under. I've got a solution to that, which is why I've brought you here. We'll talk about it in just one moment. But I do promise you that that house of yours is childishly easy to break into and find one's way around. It's all gimmicks and tricks, and not a single modern electronic device in sight, apart from a bog standard burglar alarm. Seven minutes at most after I'd come in through the door – and the lock incidentally took me less than a minute to release – I was able to leave . . .' he held up the papers '. . . with these in my hands. You can have them back now.'

He reached across to Cohen with the printout and the sheets of paper in his hand, and, after a moment's hesitation, Cohen took them from him, riffled them through, and laid them down on the table beside him.

'Just some names and addresses. And some other bits and pieces,' Cohen muttered, then hesitated. 'Account numbers. Pass-port details. That sort of thing,' he concluded uncomfortably, and looked away from Edel's gaze, reaching for his drink.

Edel said, as if to put him out of his misery, 'Don't worry, Lewis.' He reached into the inside pocket of his jacket, and pulled out a tightly folded package of stapled sheets, perhaps six or seven in all. He opened them up, glanced through them one by one, then tossed them across, so that they landed on Cohen's knee.

'Here's some more from my own collection,' he said. 'That's why we're here tonight.'

Cohen flicked through the pages, but made no response.

'One hundred and ninety there,' Edel told him, 'and sixty in the ones I took from your safe. As far as I could see, about twenty-five or thirty names were on both lists, but that still leaves us with well over two hundred names. Some with their bank account numbers, some with other details. That's enough to work on. More than enough.'

'I didn't realise that you were on the same trail,' Cohen said, 'that you yourself had an interest in these accounts. Personally,

'I only became fully aware of them two or three years ago, when my firm advised one of our clients, a Swiss bank. At the time they were under some threat of action being taken against them by a Dutch lawyer. It came to nothing, but it did make me realise the scale of the opportun . . . the scale of the problem.'

And Edel's laughter at what he took to be the slip of Cohen's tongue was so delighted that Cohen found himself not only irritated, but humiliated now, and tired and defeated, and finished. He had never seen Edel in a mood of this sort before, and he was in no condition himself at that moment to appreciate it.

'I'm sorry, Lewis,' Edel said, the levity gone. 'I really am. Let's start again. The total sum involved is over four billion pounds. That's the total value of the cash that's been sitting there in Switzerland since the end of the war. Count in the works of art, and the jewellery and so on, and it comes to around seven billion dollars. And it's impossible to get out, except in certain circumstances.'

'It's impossible,' Cohen broke in, 'unless one has certain information – and that's what I was in the process of acquiring, and adding to this list,' he said, prodding at it with his finger. 'The one you took from my safe.

'You can see what I've got, and you can see what I'm still missing. Before the banks will take any notice whatsoever, you need to have the original contract drawn up when the money was first deposited. If that's not available, and with these accounts that's almost always the case, for obvious reasons, then one needs to be able to give the cover name that the account-holder used. Assuming that they didn't use their real name, and as you can imagine very few families did that. Plus of course the account number itself. Then you have to prove your relationship with the dead account-holder, so that means you have to be able to produce birth certificates and notarised statements. You need documents from any other banks that might be involved. You need a death certificate. You need a will, or failing that some other proof of inheritance. You need the lot. And these were people who died in concentration camps, for heaven's sake. Not nice and neatly in a government hospital bed.'

He paused, then said, 'Or you *used* to need the lot. The Swiss now say that they'll make it a little easier, and at least start their search on the basis of a reasonable claim, and demand all the documents only if something is found. Until that you couldn't even get them started without handing across a fee, which for most of these families was well outside their pockets. So that's progress of some sort – *if* they mean it. But I doubt that they do. This money has been there in Switzerland for a very long time. It's extremely profitable to house. They're going to be very reluctant indeed to hand it over.'

Edel smiled at him. 'You've done your homework,' he conceded. 'I wasn't sure if you had. What were you proposing to do with it?'

Cohen hesitated before he answered. Then he said, 'The Berlin Wall coming down made a lot of difference, as you will be aware. The families of Jewish victims previously living under Communism were then free, and their documents with them. It's possible now, on hundreds and hundreds of these accounts, to provide a good deal of the evidence that the Swiss require. So for me . . .'

He shrugged. 'I'm a lawyer, Gareth. There's a wonderful opportunity in this for some lawyer or other, and I want to get in there first. I'm going to get behind these families, organise their papers, sort out all the information that they need, represent them to the banks, and help them get their money out. I'm turning myself into a specialist in it. And I'm going to persuade the banks and the Swiss authorities to see that they can convert the whole affair into a massive publicity benefit for themselves. They need the world to feel that they really are trying to help, or they'll never be left alone now. They've set up an ombudsman, but that's not enough. They need more than that, and they know it, in their heart of hearts. They're going to have to hand the money over sometime. My brief will be to persuade them to do it now, with a pleasant smile, and a press photographer snapping away at their elbow.'

He looked across at Edel, and smiled. 'And with *me* there to pick up the fees! Large fees, I hope. And from both sides of the transaction, if I play my cards correctly.'

'Just one thing, Lewis,' Edel said. 'Where did you get your list of names? And the details that you have on them?'

Cohen nodded, and studied Edel for a moment or two before he said anything in response. He shifted in his chair, and the discomfort and guilt in the action made Edel warm to him all over again. Cohen was the most transparent of men. How he had ever managed to persuade people about the Foundation in the way that he had was beyond Edel's understanding. The charm of him, in Edel's eyes, lay very largely in precisely that transparency. It was as if one was dealing with a naughty, but furiously affectionate, and very clever child. Well meaning, and without a drop of malice in him for anybody, but up to every single trick in the book, and then some. Was it only Edel himself who saw that in him? Were others bamboozled by the Daimler, and the law firm, and the St John's Wood house, and the Rosenberg wife? Did no one else see him for what he was? And enjoy it as much as Edel did?

'The detail? The names? Where did I get them?' said Cohen, openly playing for time while he thought through his next move, and Edel had to restrain himself from breaking out in laughter once more. Edel held up his hand.

'No, don't say it,' he cut in. 'Don't say anything. I know where you got them from. Lewis – the names came from Hermann, Joseph Hermann. Please don't attempt to lie about it. But Hermann himself didn't give them to you, did he? Someone else did. Yes?'

Cohen nodded his head, at first grudgingly, then, as if realising that he might as well make a virtue of the truth, with a bold, cheerful confirmation of it.

'Yes. His secretary did. I bought them from her. Last week it cost me rather a lot of money. She doesn't come cheap.'

Edel was glancing quickly through the pages once more as Cohen was speaking. 'I don't know what you paid for them,' he said, 'but I can tell you that what she's given you is genuine, and up to date. No, she hasn't let you down.'

Cohen studied Edel for a moment. 'So why did you break into my house, Gareth? Why didn't you simply *ask* for it? You don't have to steal things from me. And, anyway, how did you know that I had it?'

'I knew you had it,' Edel said. 'I doubted that you'd give it to me, or even admit to its existence. So I walked into your house and took it. And now I'm giving it back.'

'You haven't told me how you knew,' Cohen persisted.

Edel shrugged. 'You know who I am, Lewis. I don't have to spell it out to you. I have an interest in watching over this, and I'm doing so. I knew that Hermann's secretary had sold you a list; I didn't know what was on it, and I wanted to see it. Let's leave it like that.' There was a silence, then Cohen too shrugged his shoulders, and looked away for a moment, fiddling with the papers.

Then he said 'You said you wanted to talk to me about something, or tell me something or whatever it was. You confirmed it was to do with Bergdorf. What is it?'

Edel nodded. 'Yes. Bergdorf,' he said. 'Well – how do I start?'

'I told you earlier that I'd been working on this for many years,' he began. 'Well, so I have. We wanted to build up enough data to unsettle the Swiss, and we've done so. They weren't taking Hermann seriously enough. We knew we could do more. You've seen how the publicity has mounted in recent weeks. Largely that's our doing, behind the scenes, as well as in the open. There's nothing complicated about what we're trying to do. We've got one very simple agenda. We want the families who have a rightful claim to these accounts to be paid their money, and quickly. We've achieved a handful of successes in that already. And we want what remains, and it will be a lot, to be given to the State of Israel. Lock, stock and barrel.'

'We?' said Cohen.

'The World Jewish Council. You know that perfectly well.'

Cohen smiled. 'When you and I have had our little conversations together in the past I rather had the impression they were on behalf not of the World Jewish Council but somebody else. Didn't you hint that . . .'

Edel interrupted, a flicker of irritation crossing his face: 'What I want to do now is include you in the knowledge of some research we've been carrying out on Bergdorf. Here we go. This is what's happening. Hermann has been closer to this than anybody, due to his old links with the Eastern Bloc. I've followed along in his path, but wholly independent from him. But it's not just me and Hermann; Bergdorf is on the same trail. Hermann gives him bits and pieces to do, but that's not enough for him.

'You told me why you're doing it, Lewis, and I believe you. You're there for the fees. By your standards, that's reasonably straightforward and above board. But Bergdorf has been there before you. Many years before you. For a time he did all that Hermann could have wished from him, and that at a time when East Germany was still a nation state, and it was all so very much more difficult. Hermann gave him a brief or two, and he worked on them, and succeeded in getting money out for a number of families, some of whom were connected with Hermann's own family in one way or another – acquaintances of his parents, and that sort of thing. I imagine Hermann was perfectly satisfied with what Bergdorf had achieved. But as the years went on, he started to behave rather differently. We do have evidence that in at least one case he stripped the account out completely, and pocketed all the money for himself. In several more there's clearly been an element of his having skimmed quite a large amount off the top for himself before the families ever knew it was there, and then, on top of that, charging fees for what he'd done. He's deep into this business of milking the accounts now, and although I don't believe Hermann has the same evidence as we have, I'm certain that he's begun to be suspicious.'

'Do you think Bergdorf realises that Hermann has grown suspicious of him?' Cohen said.

'I imagine so,' Edel nodded. 'He must have had some inkling of that.' He tapped his fingers on his knee, as if hesitating how best to introduce his next point. Then he said, 'But in any case, I think we should stop him, Lewis – don't you? It's in all our interests if Hermann is made fully aware of what Bergdorf's up to. Though Hermann's own hands are not exactly . . .' His voice tailed away, and he paused in thought. Then pulling himself together, he continued. 'Anyway it's gone on long enough now. It's time it was all brought to an end.

'So I've been thinking . . . and what I decided we should do is to lay a little trap for Bergdorf. A sting!'

He grinned at Cohen. 'I think we should catch him redhanded, Lewis. You and I together. Don't you think that's a good idea?'

So they talked, and they planned, and an hour or so later Edel and Cohen had agreed what was to be done, and how the trail would be laid, and how they could ensure that the juiciest plum of all would be there, right in front of Bergdorf, sitting seductively before him on the bough, too delicious for him to refuse.

But both of them kept their own little confidences from each other of course, more from force of habit than anything else. It didn't matter very much in the greater scheme of things that Cohen thought it better not to volunteer at that moment that he had known for months what Bergdorf had been up to with the Swiss accounts; and hoped, by discrediting him with Hermann, to take his place. For his own part, Edel thought it wiser not to mention that he had deliberately fed that information to Cohen in the first place, while he was still thinking through his tactics. Via what he had affected to believe had been a confidential, under-no-circumstances-tell-Cohen conversation with Mariss Steiner.

Chapter 61

Lord Rosenberg looked across the desk, and tried to keep his expression full of appropriate disappointment and sober, considered responsibility. He knew the man just sufficiently to carry off the strategy he had embarked upon; that of the concerned father of an only, treasured daughter, wrestling with his conscience and duty, and deciding that he had no alternative but to bring her husband's transgressions to the notice of the proper authorities.

The Inland Revenue Commissioner nodded sagely, took out his fountain pen and made some careful notes on his pad, which he then read through and underlined.

'I understand absolutely, Lord Rosenberg. A man in your position. This must be the most unpleasant conversation for you. You have my respect and sympathy for the dilemma you've been presented with. But you did exactly the right thing in coming here to me. As you say, it's for Mr Cohen's own good. And that of all your family.'

'Before any more harm is done,' murmured Rosenberg, in reprise.

'Of course,' agreed the Commissioner and looked back again at his notes. 'For the last five years, you say?'

'At least that, I'm afraid.'

'And the money charged to the Foundation in false expenses and charges perhaps half a million pounds over that period?'

'That is the approximate sum.'

'This leading to fraudulent accounting in his firm as well, and subsequent major misappropriation of funds?'

Rosenberg nodded grimly. 'I've nothing more to say. Your Inspectors must find their own evidence and conduct their own searches. It's now entirely in your own hands. But I would ask you to act immediately now that I've brought this to you. Before any more harm is done.'

'For Mr Cohen's own good,' said the Commissioner and got to his feet.

'And for the good of the family,' Rosenberg murmured, and turned away.

'I appreciate this very much, Lord Rosenberg,' the Commissioner said, as he showed him to the lift. 'We will, as you suggest, act immediately. My Inspectors wil be on to the case straight away.'

As Rosenberg walked out into the street he found that he was swinging his umbrella in an unmistakably perky manner, and glanced quickly behind him to check that he was not being observed. That had gone most remarkably well! What a success! Perhaps he should try to find a way of getting a story into the gossip columns . . . A piece in the *Evening Standard* perhaps, and another in *The Times*. Plus *Private Eye*, naturally. That would be ideal.

The tax people, and the news of the divorce breaking, and the bank foreclosure – all that should do the trick. Any credibility Lewis might have with Hermann would be entirely obliterated. He'd not met the man yet, but Bergdorf had said that he was a considerable puritan. Rosenberg knew the type. Those left-wing academics were all the same.

Overkill almost. Perhaps he'd arranged too much. But Bergdorf had now said that the opportunity with the Hungarian property – 'Himmler's Treasure' as he so invitingly called it, the paintings and jewellery and money that Himmler had removed from the Hungarian Jews and shipped away to be hidden in Switzerland – the opportunity with that was immediate, and whether one liked it or not it was Hermann who held the key to it. Also to those hundreds of potential British claimants too; and Felix knew from Bergdorf that Lewis had started to have his eye on them as well. Those British families might well be Rosenberg's best chance of getting in on the action in this.

Lewis must be removed as a rival. If there was overkill in his efforts to discredit the man, then so be it.

'This is business, you cunt,' Rosenberg murmured to himself, reverting joyfully to his nursery game. 'There's no time to lose. All's fair in love and war.'

Chapter 62

'Why not?' Harrison asked. 'Why can't we have a go at these two accounts in just the same way as you did before? As you explain them to me, they look identical to the ones you've already cracked. You know the code numbers; you know at least part of the code names; you have sufficient of the deposit documents to be able to match them up convincingly with others you can borrow from somewhere else – so what's the problem, for Christ's sake?'

Hermann made a gesture of despair. 'I've told you why I don't think we can do it – because of the Hungarians! I got away with it once, but that was on two accounts that I selected as being the easiest and safest I could find. None of the money nor the other assets in them were traceable to any family or any institution whatsoever. I spent months of my time checking that through.'

There was no response from Harrison, so he went on, 'Persuading the Bank to let me take title to the accounts was one thing. The documents I put up persuaded them of that, and I was confident that they would do so, or I would never have risked it. The Hungarian Trust I . . . invented, and so on. All that business. That's one side of it. But the other side is the risk one runs from the Hungarians themselves. As I told you, these accounts that Himmler and his people set up contained not just cash, but works of art, and other valuables. The galleries and museums know exactly what went missing, and what everything looked like. Do you think I want to be caught in possession of a picture that a museum curator can identify as his? Or found trying to sell something which every half-baked dealer can find listed on the security files? My Foundation has no use for pictures! My Foundation needs nothing more at all, as a matter of fact. We needed cash to get our scholarships up and running, and we got it. Now we're on our way. I can't risk trying to get any more. I've got enough.'

Harrison sprawled back in his chair, his hands locked together behind his head.

'Well, I haven't,' he said at last. 'If you're not going to get the money for me, then the best thing for me to do is to turn you in, and get the credit for being the ace operator that I am. And don't think that you can tell any tales about me, if that's in your mind. I'd counter it with this – that all I was doing is flushing you out so that we can see how these things can be done. And when I'd had enough, that I was planning to turn you in. And your goddam Foundation. That's what I'd say. I've got the proof of what you've been up to, remember, but you've not got a thing on—'

Suddenly, so fast that Hermann had time for only a momentary flash of shock and fear, Harrison had sprung on him, thrown him to the ground, and was wrenching at his clothes, pulling at his shirt, ripping off his shoes, emptying his pockets, running his fingers down the seams of his suit. Hermann, stiff with his arthritis, was crying with the pain of it, but Harrison left him there on the floor when he'd finished, standing over him, panting with the exertion of what he'd done.

'You're clean, I'll give you that,' he said. 'I suddenly thought you might be wired. But from now on, all our meetings are in my hotel room, like this one, or somewhere else that I choose. And we'll meet often. I want that money. So get on with it!'

Hermann straightened himself up, and tried to get to his feet, but his clothes were so entangled that he gave up, humiliated, his trousers and underpants around his thighs, his old man's body white and crooked.

'There's something you'd better know,' he muttered, gazing down. 'That London lawyer, Lewis Cohen, has appeared on the scene. He bribed my secretary to let him have copies of one of our files. She told me about it afterwards. She couldn't live with her conscience, and she told me about it.'

Chapter 63

'Most of it was put there in the 1930s,' Bergdorf said. 'All of it of course before 1945. The biggest tranche of the money still unclaimed is probably attributable to the East Europeans – the old Communist bloc people. But according to the Swiss Bankers' Federation, in their new mood of sunny generosity and openness, there's a good number of British account-holders as well. Dead British account-holders, of course. But if the Swiss are genuinely prepared to cooperate, the surviving members of the families have a good chance of proving their claim, given the fact that the original account documents are more likely to be traceable.'

He paused, and gave Felix Rosenberg an encouraging smile.

'Well – as you can understand,' he continued, 'it's difficult for me to find a way of getting through to these families. A lawyer I may be, but a foreigner nonetheless. The English would be most suspicious of that. It's an ideal opportunity for an English lawyer of the right background, certainly. Lewis Cohen, for example. I imagine you'd be very pleased about that. A member of your own family. And someone who could do with a helping hand at this juncture of his life.'

He paused, and sipped at his tea with a barely concealed grimace. 'Or for you, my dear Felix. A Law Lord, no less, and a Jewish one too, acting as the sponsor of a Campaign which the whole world would support!'

The slight sneer on his face irritated Rosenberg. It was more than a little patronising. But he knew as well as Bergdorf that the reason they were there together that afternoon was that there was indeed an opportunity in this for Rosenberg. A considerable one. The sneer gone, Bergdorf smiled charmingly. 'Be assured, Felix,' he said, 'that there's nothing in this to cause you any reservations. Believe me, if I thought that one whiff of scandal would arise from it . . .'

Allowing himself to appear won over, Rosenberg nodded once

more, this time accompanying it with a smile of conviction and acceptance. 'What would you like me to do?' he said.

As Bergdorf drew from his case a file for him to look at, and a letter of agreement for him to sign, then a further document opening a bank account for him in Liechtenstein, under a nominee's title, with a five-figure deposit already there in place as an advance, Rosenberg's heart was already thumping at the excitement of it all. As Bergdorf had said, he was doing no more than lending his name and his prestige to an appeal of the highest possible motives and aims. What could be more worthwhile than to help these unfortunate families retrieve their lost inheritance from these Swiss bank people? British people too. His own countrymen. He owed it to these families. He would do it.

So they shook hands on it, and Rosenberg signed his papers, and Bergdorf too, and the first programme was drawn up for the passage of the British Appeal, and the Press launch for it, to be chaired by Rosenberg at the House of Lords. And as they left the hotel lobby, Bergdorf's hand under Rosenberg's elbow in pleasing, fraternal intimacy, they would have appeared to anyone who observed them to be what, in a way, they were. Two elderly men of accomplishment and stature. At peace with themselves, and at peace with the world.

Chapter 64

Bergdorf burst out laughing, and threw the package up into the air so that it landed on the bed beside him. Mariss Steiner smiled pinkly from his chair, looking both embarrassed and surprised.

'Mariss – Gareth Edel gave you this thing? Why – it's a toy, my dear, that's all it is! You're pulling my leg, surely? You couldn't have been serious when you told me that you had a bomb? And this was it? You believed it?'

He laughed once more, uproariously now, gave the package a little prod, then recoiled from it in a pretence of terror, all the while Steiner gazing at him with a fixed, dull grin on his face.

'My dear, Edel has been playing a joke on you. I'm no great expert in these things, but I've been on courses, you know. Over the years. And I can tell you that this thing wouldn't blow up if you stuffed it full of dynamite and put a match to it. It's a dummy. Just a load of wires, three torch batteries – probably dead – and . . .' he smelt the little clingwrapped plug of a grey, putty-like substance '. . . tile cement, I think.'

He picked the package up, and tossed it across the room for Steiner to catch. 'Naughty Gareth Edel. Goodness knows what he thinks he's up to.'

'Up to?' said Steiner, still trying to recover from Bergdorf's greeting of his bomb, which he had been gazing at in admiration ever since the German had delivered it to his room the previous evening, rehearsing in his mind all the instructions he had been given at his training session in the warehouse. He put it down on the table beside him, still so gingerly as to make Bergdorf wonder if he had believed what he had said of it.

'Up to?' Steiner said again. 'I told you what he's up to. He got in touch with me and told me that he thought getting rid of Hermann would be a very good idea, but that I shouldn't trust Bernie Levinstein to get me a gun that actually worked. He said that Bernie would cheat me, and that anyway I would be much better off to use a simple explosive device, and that he would provide one and teach me how to use it. He said . . . well, he said . . . he wanted to help me,' he concluded, so miserably that Bergdorf again broke out laughing, though after a moment he did try to stem this, remembering that he should be careful not to offend Steiner too much. He had his own agenda with him that afternoon, and Steiner was not only incapable of self-mockery, but had a notoriously eruptive temper.

'So he wanted to help you kill Hermann?' he said, to keep the conversation alive while he thought out his next move.

'Three times,' said Steiner, suddenly flushed red in the face. 'Three times I've told you that. Do I have to make it four? *Edel wanted to help me to kill Hermann.* Do you have it now? Edel – wanted – to—'

Bergdorf held up his hand, and pulled a face of contrition and apology.

'I'm sorry,' he said. 'I ask the question rhetorically in that way, because I'm confused, and I'm thinking my way through it. So – Edel told you he wanted to help you kill Hermann. He stopped you from accepting what was probably a perfectly good weapon from Bernie Levinstein to do so, and fitted you up with . . . a void device. Now why should he do that?'

'Because he *didn't* want me to kill Hermann,' said Steiner flatly.

'That's right. He wanted you to *think* that you were going to kill Hermann, but he didn't want you to do it. So he gave you a . . . void device.'

He said no more for a moment, staring at Steiner, deep in thought. 'I tell you what we should do, Mariss my dear. *I'll* give you the bomb. I'll get you something to kill Hermann, because I too think it's high time he was dead. Buchenwald, of course. A complete disgrace,' he said, inadequately, furtively. 'The Communists at Buchenwald. All the Infirmary business, and so on.'

Bergdorf caught a gleam of irony in Steiner's eye as he tailed away. I needn't go through all that, he thought. Not with Mariss. He doesn't believe a word I'm saying, but it doesn't matter. Mariss is so determined to do what he wants to do, that the last thing he's going to worry about is why I'm anxious to get the same result.

'You'll get me another bomb?' said Steiner.

'Absolutely,' Bergdorf replied. 'I can arrange that. This time, it will be a real bomb. I'll get it to you by tomorrow evening. With the simplest possible instructions about how you make the thing go off. As simple as can be.'

'Simple instructions, eh?' echoed Steiner, staring now at Bergdorf as thoughtfully as Bergdorf previously had at him. 'Let me show you something, Jacob,' he said, laboriously unpinning some old papers from off the wall. 'Two birds with one stone is what I've been thinking of now, and I think you've been as well. And why not? Two birds with one stone.'

And half an hour or so later, as Bergdorf made his way towards Paddington Station to find a taxi, it occurred to him that all was sometimes not as it seemed. You expected twists and turns with people like Gareth Edel. Lewis Cohen too, in his way. Rosenberg you could see thundering his way towards you a mile away, beaming his greed at you like the headlight on an express train. But Mariss Steiner . . . Steiner was an example of a man seemingly so dim that the world and his dog could lead him wherever they willed. Edel and his bomb was a good example of that! But the truth of it was different. Steiner was actually not like that at all. Not now at least, when the man was dying.

Chapter 65

Hermann went over to his desk, turned the key in the lock, and took out from the drawer a large manila envelope, which he brought back and handed to Harrison.

'There we are,' he said wearily, and lowered himself down once more into his chair. Harrison opened the envelope, flicked quickly through the banknotes, then pushed them back into the envelope, and dropped it into the attaché case at his feet.

'And that's on account,' he stated. Hermann nodded. 'For the main payment no later than four weeks' time,' he concluded. Hermann nodded again, then turned his eyes away, and sank into brooding, preoccupied silence.

Harrison watched him for a moment or two. 'It's Edel,' he said then. 'That's what worried you. Don't get yourself in a state about it. You've known all along that he was concerned with this business, acting on behalf of the World Jewish Council people. He's been harrying the Swiss for years, but has never got very far. Forget about him. So he called you up. He's done that before, you told me, and there's nothing surprising about that, given the fact that you've been involved with the banks over this business for forty years or more. He's called you before, and he's called you now. What's the matter with that?'

Hermann looked across at him, and when he spoke Harrison was struck by the quiet certainty of his tone. 'There's no point in deceiving ourselves. Edel knows what I've done. What he does with that information is another thing. But he knows. I'm absolutely certain of that.'

'Did he say so directly?'

'No. But don't deceive yourself. He knows what I've done.'

Harrison took note of the phrasing of Hermann's statement. He's consumed by guilt, he reflected. He'll never get over it. But he's hooked. He's given me the money. He's thought about it, and he's decided that he must do what I say. He cares more about his Hermann Scholars idea than anything else in the world. He's not going to risk his new Foundation being disturbed, just when he's only set it up, and his career is on the wane, and it's the only thing he's got left. He'll allow himself to be pressured. He's mine, and he'll remain mine. But Edel is a complication. Edel I'll have to think about.

He left Hermann then, doing so in a manner that was as calming and unaggressive as in the circumstances was possible. He'd have to do that from now on. They'd got to the point where Hermann needed a family around him. The bullying had done the trick, and now was the time to switch it off. So he put his hand on Hermann's shoulder as he passed his chair, and before he left placed a tray of coffee on the little table beside him.

But Hermann barely noticed, or heard Harrison's departure. For fifteen or twenty minutes he was completely still, staring at his bookcase, his hands thrust into his trouser pockets. Then he went to his desk, checked a scrap of paper from his pocket, and dialled a number. His life was probably finished. What he'd most wanted would never now come about. But Edel – gentle, honourable Edel – was the person to turn to. He'd go to him. Now.

Chapter 66

Jacob Bergdorf stepped out of the taxi, under-tipped the driver, and walked into the bank, his attaché case in his hand. This was one of the few Zürich banks in which he had never been before, and, free from the risk that the lobby security staff would recognise him, he wrote a false name for himself in their register. Bergdorf always did this. He greatly disliked lobby security registers. He had never in his adult life given his real name to anyone, when an assumed one would serve as well. He couldn't imagine why anyone would.

He stepped briskly into the lift, lest one of the guards looked at the book and challenged him, and went up to the executive offices on the topmost floor. The attaché case was bulging with the documents that Hermann had sent to him for the meeting, though in the end they had been delivered to his house only the previous evening. It was so unlike Hermann to be late in anything of this sort that Bergdorf had attempted to reach him at home, only to learn that he had already left for London. As far as his housekeeper knew, he was at that moment uncontactable.

But he had Hermann's documents now, although it was a pity that he hadn't had more of a chance to master them, even though he had been up into the early hours reading them through as carefully as he could. However, Bergdorf had attended dozens of these meetings with Swiss bankers in the past, and he knew exactly how to handle them. Seldom smile, never joke, and speak with rigid, glacial formality. Hand the papers across one by one, and only as they are individually demanded. Present the impression of a lawyer who, when possible, retains all he can and offers the minimum to achieve his ends. Require receipts for all documents that are handed over. Refuse to accept any certificates that are given in return, unless they either be originals, or properly certified and notarised copies. If the latter, take them, but only after a show of irredeemable suspicion as to their provenance. Read every line of every fresh document immediately it is tabled, and do so pedantically, meticulously, and several laborious times over, displaying sublime indifference to however long the process of that might take.

Bergdorf glanced at his watch as the lift slowed, and saw, to his approval, that he was precisely on time. Neither thirty seconds early, nor thirty seconds late. Nine-thirty, Herr Strauss had said, and nine-thirty it was. The eighteenth-century clock over on the corner table struck the half-hour precisely at the moment when he handed his card across to the unsmiling black-suited, black-tied steward, and he was shown into a small drawing room along the corridor to await Herr Strauss's entry.

But when the door opened, it wasn't Strauss alone who came into the room, and at first this took Bergdorf aback. Normally these meetings were held in private with the banker with whom the original correspondence had been conducted. But Strauss had brought two colleagues with him; both vigorous, athletic, fair-haired young men in dark suits, gleaming white shirts and wire-rimmed spectacles.

All four men straightened their shoulders, nodded, shook hands, made stiff little bows, then sat at the oval mahogany table, pads of white crested paper before each place. Bergdorf looked coldly at Strauss, and waited for him to make the opening statement. It came straight away.

'I am indebted to you, Herr Bergdorf, for the letters of introduction you arranged for me to receive from the Bank of Geneva, the Swiss Canton and Federal Bank Corporation, and the United Bank of Switzerland. They were very helpful. Thank you. Your passport, now, if I may. For standard verification procedures, of course.'

He held out his hand, and Bergdorf reached into the inside pocket of his jacket, removed the passport, and handed it across the table. He was accustomed to this. What he was not accustomed to, however, was to see it handed immediately to another party, and the young man who took it straight away left the room, returning a few moments later with a receipt, which he handed to Bergdorf without further explanation or comment. Then Strauss spoke again, so quietly and slowly, sadly almost, that Bergdorf had to move forward in his chair to ensure that he could hear him.

'Our correspondence,' he was saying, 'has been in connection with certain accounts held on deposit at this Bank. Your suggestion to me was that there is held here part or all of the assets of some Hungarian-Jewish families who were unfortunate enough to be interred and dispossessed during the war. I cannot comment on that. Your further suggestion was that a proportion of these assets were forcibly acquired from those families by the German military, and deposited here by them as if under their own legal title. I cannot comment on that either, and you would not expect me to. You requested this meeting however on the basis of a test case. You have told us that you are able to exhibit to us such evidence as would establish beyond doubt right of ownership to assets held by this Bank. Substantial assets, as it happens. You have indicated that you have all the documents, including the original account certificates, which we would require to release those assets to *you*, Herr Bergdorf, acting as an agent for your client. The documents include such security codes and devices as we and the depositors decided to adopt when the accounts were opened, for our mutual protection; this including cover names. Is my understanding of that correct?'

Bergdorf nodded, reached into his case, and took from it four or five of his files, which he stacked neatly before him on the table.

'I wish at this meeting to establish preliminary title to two accounts,' he said. 'This is an important case. These two accounts hold a series of deposits made by the German military over a period of four months during the summer months of 1944. I will be able to demonstrate to you, and any other parties that you may require, that all the assets in these two accounts were seized by the military from the Budapest family of Razhedensky at the time of their imprisonment, and later their murder at Natzweiler. I have available for your inspection a full inventory of the assets deposited, which include cash, securities, jewellery and paintings, some of the latter of considerable value. I have sworn statements from witnesses. I have the account numbers that were used by your Bank and the depositors. I have the coded cover names that were originally utilised by the depositors under your mutual agreement. I have wills, and I have original documents of claim.'

Bergdorf paused, and remembered just in time neither to smile nor to give the appearance of a flippant triumphalism.

'I believe that I have what you will require of me, Herr Strauss,' he continued, then decided to say no more than that.

Strauss nodded, and over the course of the next hour and a half Bergdorf laid out the papers before him one by one. But, document by document, as he related their content, and demonstrated their provenance, and displayed the sworn affidavits and the statements of claim, he sensed, inexorably, where he was heading. None of Strauss's reactions felt right, nor those of the two young men with him. Bergdorf was used to impassivity in these meetings, but theirs had an emotionless, poker-faced quality that he had not encountered before.

He began to look more closely at the documents as he exhibited them, but could see nothing there to arouse his suspicion. Indeed, he thought to himself that Hermann had on this occasion quite surpassed himself. The Budapest family's papers were in such good order that it looked almost as if they willingly cooperated with the Nazis when the assets were taken, what with the inventory, and the documents of claim, and the wills all there neatly filed together. Goodness knows how Hermann had unearthed such a gold mine as this. And managed to secure such trust and dependence from the surviving members of the family.

Now the final certificate was there on the table, and his presentation of his documents was over. Bergdorf sat back in his chair, and looked at Strauss, who stared back at him, still silent, and by all appearances unmoved. Bergdorf said, 'Well – there we are, Herr Strauss,' and then, allowing himself the barest suggestion of a pleasantry, 'my case rests. Perhaps the members of the jury could—'

'Members of the jury?' said Strauss. 'Why do you say that? Why do you suggest that a jury might be interested in what you have told us?'

Bergdorf spread his arms, and smiled. 'A joke, Herr Strauss. Unamusing perhaps, but just a little attempt at humour.' He held his smile, nodded at Strauss's two companions, and started to gather his papers together, as if the meeting had come to an end, and he would be on his way.

But then Strauss said, 'Let me ask you a question or two more, Herr Bergdorf. We have to be so very careful – you know that. First this. For how long have you known the family who are making this claim through you? No – let me restate that; can you assure me that you personally have spent sufficient time with the Razhedensky family to have confidence in the authenticity of their claim, and the documents on which their case will rest?'

Bergdorf knew he had no option. 'Absolutely,' he lied. 'I can confirm that. I knew you would require that of me. They're fine, honest people. I've got to know them well. I'm convinced of the legality of their claim.'

Strauss nodded. 'Thank you. As you know, we do depend in these cases partly on the conviction and integrity of the lawyers handling them. That's why we will deal only with lawyers who come to us with impeccable references and reputation. We two have not dealt with each other before. That is why I asked you to obtain letters of reference from other banks, and to give me permission to follow up those references afterwards in personal, private consultation. I've done so. The references were indeed immaculate, Herr Bergdorf, as were the consultations afterwards. We were given full reason to have confidence in our future dealings with you.'

He paused, glanced at his two colleagues, then turned back to him.

'Which is why the events of today are surprising to us, though I must confess we had in the end some warning of it. You have made a fool of yourself, Herr Bergdorf.'

Bergdorf felt the blood run from his face, but he stared directly into Strauss's eyes, willing himself not to flinch, waiting for the next blow to fall.

'Or let me put it another way,' Strauss continued, and for a moment all Bergdorf could think of was the quiet, undemonstrative, even tenor of the man's voice. 'Perhaps this is more to the point. Someone has made a fool of you.'

As Bergdorf felt his hands beginning to shake, Strauss explained: 'The account numbers you gave us have nothing to do with the German military, or the Nazis, or war-time booty, or the Razhedensky family, or anything of the kind. The numbers are those of dummy accounts set up three or four days ago with our connivance by the security officers of the World Jewish Council. Similarly, the cover names you quoted. They are theirs also. As arranged three or four days ago. Then the documents. Most of the ones you showed us have already been accepted by this bank in the settlement of another account: the Razhedensky family's account. They have already received full reclaim of the assets deposited by their relatives just before the war. It was an easy case to prove because every document and certificate was to hand and in good order. As you've shown us today. We released the assets to the Razhedensky family immediately we came across the case. Through the agency, once more, of . . .'

He nodded, as Bergdorf swallowed, and tried to hold his stare. 'Yes. The World Jewish Council.'

There was dead silence. Then Strauss said, his voice not unkindly, 'The only papers I had never seen before were the two or three you produced relating specifically to the German military. Those may be forgeries of some kind, but I don't think they are. My suspicion is that they're genuine enough, and have been "lent" to you for this case by whoever supplied you with the rest of the documents. Who I can tell you, incidentally, is not who you think it is. I have a feeling that I shall be seeing those German military papers again, this time assigned to their proper home. When next we have dealings with . . .'

He shrugged, and a wintry, awkward smile came across his face. 'With the World Jewish Council – don't you think? I would say so. I would guess that that will be the case.'

He got to his feet and nodded to Bergdorf, pleasantly enough, who pushed himself upright in obedient response. The two young men came quietly across to him, and stood silently by his side.

Chapter 67

Cohen leaned back in his chair in the small office at Burridge & Edel, folded his hands behind his head and grinned contentedly at Gareth.

'You're a master, Gareth, you really are. But I still don't understand how you pulled it off. How did you know that Bergdorf was in contact with Hermann over that Razhedensky account? And how did you ensure that Hermann didn't give the game away accidentally, through ignorance of what was going on?'

'Not so difficult,' Edel replied casually. 'You make it sound more complicated than it really was. We planted the seed with Bergdorf some time ago by pretending to work with him. I said that I was dismayed at how slow Hermann was being over the Swiss accounts, and that I thought Bergdorf would get on with it faster. So I met him at Heathrow and gave him a list of names to get on with. Particularly flagging the Razhedensky family. Then we simply wrote to Bergdorf from an imaginary member of the Razhedensky family, asking him for his help in retrieving their assets. Painting a colourful tale about how they had been sequestered from them by the Nazis, and what their value was. And making sure there was more than a little hint in it that the trail would lead from their account to the "Himmler's Treasure" business that has always bewitched Bergdorf so. We said in the letter that he should arrange an immediate meeting with the Associated Bank of Zürich, and that Hermann had all the material on the case, and that he would send it to him. Though we had it, of course. We sent it to him ourselves. We had to use the papers from a real case, or Bergdorf would not have believed them.'

Cohen nodded thoughtfully. Then he said, 'How did you know when the meeting with the Bank had been arranged?'

'That was hardly a problem,' Edel replied. 'We had already briefed Strauss, who was working with us. He informed us when the meeting was to be.'

Cohen sat there, nodding still, his hands remaining interlocked behind his head. 'I still don't see how you ensured that he didn't contact Hermann in the meantime. That would have blown the whole thing apart, surely?'

'Because Hermann wasn't there to be contacted. We were looking after him. He's got himself into a good deal of trouble and fallen into unpleasant hands. So we have him now under our care. Bergdorf would never have been able to find him in a month of Sundays. All he could do was to sit there and wait for his files to arrive. Even if Bergdorf had found him, it wouldn't have made any difference. We'd briefed Hermann by then. He knew what was going on.'

'Look, Lewis,' Edel went on earnestly. 'All that's one thing, but I got you here for something else. It's this. I want to help you. I want to help you get out of this mess with your Foundation, and also see if I can help to save your skin in your personal finances. First the Foundation. So far you've honoured every promise you've made – is that right?'

'Yes,' Cohen replied, somewhat wearily. 'Everyone has got their money.'

'And if you stopped the thing now, took in no more money from any more charities, and paid off everything that's due, how much would you need to find?'

Lewis braced himself to tell the truth. 'Four million pounds,' he said. 'If the Foundation never took in another penny, but honoured the promise to pay out double, we would need four million pounds.'

Edel nodded. 'Right. And on the other side – if we can keep your creditors quiet for a little, how much do we need to keep you going, to solve the immediate crisis? A hundred thousand pounds? Two hundred? More? How much would we need?'

'Five hundred thousand,' Cohen muttered, and Edel turned his eyes away from him when he saw how he had coloured in his embarrassment. He allowed him to collect himself for a few moments, then said,

'Hm . . . Four million for the Foundation, and five hundred thousand for you.' Edel looked at Cohen. 'That's a frightening sum of money. I'd hoped it was a very great deal less.'

They were both silent for a moment. Then Edel continued, 'Tell me, Lewis – are there formal contracts between the Foundation and the charities? Obviously you give receipts for the funds deposited, and they're dated for repayment, but what I'm asking is whether there's a formal, legal obligation for you to *double* their money? Surely they can't have expected you to contract to double their funds in six months ... A statement of intent, maybe, in the narrative. A "best endeavours" clause, or something of that sort. But a formal contract?'

Cohen looked increasingly miserable, but Edel pursued the point.

'Please, Lewis. Let's deal with this once and for all! Let's have it all out on the table. Tell me exactly what the position is. Is there a formal, binding contract to double their money, or isn't there?'

Cohen shook his head. 'No. A "best endeavours" clause, that's all. But I did give these people my word. I'd find it very difficult indeed to go back on that. I just couldn't do it, to be honest with you. I couldn't bring myself to do it.'

Edel gazed at him. 'You have no option, Lewis. Yes, you do. You can go to prison. You can carry on with this thing until you reach the stage when it's past saving, and the depositors lose the lot. And then you've had it.

'Grow up, Lewis,' he said forcefully. 'I'm trying to help. And answer this question. If you simply returned the money tomorrow, didn't double it, but gave a conventional, orthodox rate of return on it, as if it had been in gilts, how much would you have to find?'

Cohen hesitated, and now it was Edel that flushed, but in a flare of irritation.

'Lewis. For heaven's sake. Work it out. Work it out now.'

Cohen reached into his pocket, took out his pencil, and started to do some calculations on an envelope. He looked up.

'Most of it hasn't been there very long. It comes to two point two million, or thereabouts. A bit less. Probably two point one.'

'Two million two hundred thousand. Let's say two million three to be on the safe side,' said Edel, automatically assuming, as Cohen realised, that he was being unduly optimistic. He stared at Cohen for a moment, then shrugged, and said, 'Well – here's one way by which you might be able to deal with that.

'The World Jewish Council have identified three hundred million pounds that the Associated Bank of Zürich is going to have to hand over to the State of Israel. There'll be more from them, and more from other banks of course, but that's what's been accepted by the Associated Bank people as their total for now – the aggregate of the deposits made by Holocaust victims which Associated have been sitting on. Not including the money they know they're going to have to hand over to families who can prove their claim. I know the sum. I did the research, and I did the negotiations with Associated. It's definitely three hundred million pounds. They've agreed to hand it over to Israel, on certain conditions, one of which is that they have control over the consequent publicity. Our conditions were simple – that they hurried it up and handed it over. And picked up not only our historical costs, but those to come on completing the legal aspects of it all. They've agreed that, with a ceiling on present and future legal costs of five million Swiss francs. Two and a half million pounds, or a little more.

'This is what I suggest. Your firm can apply to be the World Jewish Council lawyers. If you succeed – and it won't be me who makes the decision – you can *earn* the fees. Associated would then agree no doubt to advance against them. What you need to find is two million three hundred thousand pounds. Whatever you get from Associated will have to go straight away to the Foundation to put towards the replacement of the charities' money. Their principal, plus interest. Only that – as if they had been in gilts. The shortfall your firm will have to borrow. And then that's the end of it. The Foundation calls it a day. Everything is wrapped up and brought to a halt. And no doubt you'll get your knighthood. "Sir Lewis Cohen." It sounds very well.'

He smiled, but then immediately said, 'And the money *will* be used in that way, Lewis. We'll require formal undertakings from you and your partners. And don't think incidentally, that you'll have any trouble with them. We'll be pointing out to them certain aspects of their own conduct in the acceptance of fees from the Foundation over the last few years. They'll be only too glad to accept, I can assure you of that.'

Cohen watched him, tapping his fingers on the arm of his chair, then Edel turned away and, reaching up on to the bookshelf behind him, he took down a sealed envelope and handed it straight across to Cohen.

'That's a contribution towards your personal debts,' he said. 'Don't open it now. I wrote the cheque before you came. It's made out to you personally, for fifty thousand pounds. Take it. Pay me back one day. When you're safe. When you're back on track.'

Cohen took the envelope, gazed at it, then shook his head, and handed it back.

'Not for me, Gareth. I can't let you do this. I'll find the way. I'm determined to sort this out myself.'

Chapter 68

Elizabeth held out her hand, and Cohen passed her father's letter back to her. He stared at her for a moment, then broke out into a smile. But there was little humour in it. Cohen was tired. His mood over the last few days had fluctuated hour by hour between one extreme and another – flushes of euphoria, as he felt his problems were there to be faced up to, and beaten, as when he had been with Edel, then moments of darkness, when all seemed too much to bear. Felix's letter was a travesty. In another state of mind it would have angered him very much. Just then it wearied him. There was a snobbery in it, and a self-regard, that defied description. Felix was a monster. But Cohen, the forces of enmity gathering around him, felt at that moment too much in despair to take him on.

Then Elizabeth broke the silence, reaching her hand out to him again as she spoke. 'Hang on, Lewis. Don't give up. I'm here. I'm so sorry all this has happened. We must talk about it now. We never do talk, and now we must. Tell me everything. Tell me what's happened. I'm your wife.'

So Cohen told the story, angrily at times, shouting at her even, as Elizabeth persisted, cross examining him point by point. But at last there was no more to tell, and in the relief of that his spirits lifted a little. There were definitely rays of hope; of course there were. He realised, now he'd thought about it, that the firm would not be able to give him personally a loan; but some of the partners themselves, if they realised the extent of his plight, probably would. So far he'd bounced no cheques because he'd written no cheques. There was a day or so in hand on that. Elizabeth herself thought that she might be able to persuade the Trustees of a particular family Trust, from Sadie's side of the family, to release some funds, though the sums would not be large. She had jewellery, some of it quite valuable, and she insisted, despite his protestations, that all of this should be taken to sell the very next day. Some furniture and pictures as well. Five hundred thousand pounds – it had taken considerable tenacity on Elizabeth's behalf to wrest the true figure from Cohen on this – was beyond them. Three hundred thousand was a possibility. Maybe they could find another bank to allow him a facility on the shortfall. Maybe Elizabeth herself could borrow the money. Maybe her mother could be shamed into helping them, if approached without Felix's knowledge. Maybe Felix himself, were Elizabeth to appeal to him, might change his tune. Elizabeth, now that she had the truth, was frozen in her horror at the life she had been leading. She – truthfully – had never suspected the position they were in. She cursed herself, aloud and, for a minute or two, incessantly, for not having tried earlier to follow the course of their circumstances. It was something to do with the fact that Lewis was so much older, and apparently so professionally established. Something to do with that perhaps. But something to do equally with her own temperament and upbringing.

Then, calming, she got up from her chair and put her arms around Cohen's neck. 'I love you, Lewis,' she said. 'I'm so glad we married each other. You're the most charming man I've ever met.'

And Cohen, his arms now around her back, reflected on that. He knew about his charm. All his life, even in the Buchenwald days, he had been aware of his power to attract people to his side. That's what had carried his life through. He'd traded on charm, and it had never let him down. Old Mr Robert Rubinstein, a little in love with him maybe, unable to do him an injury, quietly replacing the money Lewis had stolen from the firm's petty cash box. Rachel's headmistress, flushing with pleasure at the sight of him, overruling a punishment that a member of her staff had imposed. The clients wooed from other, equally effective firms. The secretary who had been with him, underpaid and overworked, for the whole of her professional life. The Foundation. The money charmed into that from the great philanthropic families; not enough of course, as things turned out, but significant sums, nevertheless.

But now, his arms still around Elizabeth's back, he felt the fleeting optimism drain out of him. Perhaps now he would really not be able to cope, as he always had before. Perhaps the run of good fortune that had carried him through his entire life, even through the War years, was at last exhausted. The Foundation, his personal insolvency, perhaps now it really was all too much. He had never in his life seriously worried about what the future held in store. Things always turned out for the best, if you kept calm. Something always turned up. But now maybe – at last – it was all too late.

He disengaged from Elizabeth, gently and affectionately, and went to switch on the porcelain table lamp on his writing table. The glow of the walnut veneer, and the sheen of the silver dish he kept on it, polished daily as he liked it to be, served to provide him with at least a marginal lift of his spirit. He loved the little artefacts of his life. The books. The table, bought with Elizabeth one happy day when they were first married. The dish, given to him by her at about that time. He loved his home. He loved his wife. He loved his daughter, and the untidy clutter of her schoolbag and belongings in the hall. Perhaps all would be well. Perhaps they would find a way. There was so much to lose if they didn't.

'I tell you what, Elizabeth,' Cohen said, turning to her, and smiling. 'If we ever do get out of this we'll do something together. Something entirely different. A complete switch in our lives. We'll do something useful. We'll open a hospice. Or a shelter for homeless people. Or – why not? – an orphanage. Yes, we'll disappear from sight. We'll open an orphanage! We'll give them the lot!'

Elizabeth tried to smile too. She had meant exactly what she had said. She *did* love him. She *was* glad she'd spent her life with him. He *was* the most charming man she had ever met. But can I go through it all again, she thought? Can I go through one more wave of plans, and bullishness, and boundless, childlike energy? And idealism of course. But an idealism mixed with a dangerous, subversive contempt for playing an open hand. Maybe I can. Maybe there really is a new future for us. Maybe this time it will work.

Chapter 69

Lord Rosenberg first heard of Bergdorf's arrest through the columns of *The Times*. The shock in his face as he read of it, and the sudden pallor of him were so acute that Lady Rosenberg, entering the dining room for her breakfast, stopped dead in her tracks, gave a little cry, and rushed to his side.

'Felix, darling. Whatever can it be?' she whispered to him, and peered over his shoulder to see what he was reading. She even wondered, for the flash of a second, if her beloved daughter and grand-daughter had been injured or killed, and that somehow the news had failed to get through to them before he'd read of it in the paper. But she could see nothing there to bother him. Dr Stuttaford's medical column. Had Felix suddenly realised he had some dreadful disease? An interview with a Welsh opera singer. Something more about the French and their nuclear tests in the South Seas. An Austrian lawyer in trouble in Switzerland on some fraud charge or another. What could there be there to upset him so?

Rosenberg got to his feet, patted his kneeling wife on the back and set off out of the room, saying as he went, 'Nothing, my dear. Nothing at all. I suddenly remembered that I had quite forgotten to do something. Enjoy your breakfast.'

But the smile on his face as he turned to raise his hand to her at the door was as strained as she had seen it, and she spread the newspaper out on the table to go through each of the stories once more. It *must* be something in the medical column that had worried him so, she thought. She was halfway through an article on warts and verrucas when the telephone rang in the hall and she went out to answer it.

It was Lewis. Sadie Rosenberg was immediately thrown on to the defensive. She was at least two weeks late in paying the interest on their loan, and the moment she realised who it was she started on a garbled account of how she was going to rush up to her room that very moment to find her chequebook and get something in the post to him and how sorry she was but she had been so dreadfully busy. Indifferent to that, Cohen cut across her and asked if Felix was available. But she had already heard the bathroom door locked shut behind him, so she said the first thing that came into her mind; he had already left for London, but would be home that evening, and might he return his call then?

'Absolutely,' Cohen said. 'But can I leave a message? It's this. I've been asked to pass on to him a rumour that Jacob Bergdorf is being a little fantastical with the Swiss police. So much so that in his panic he's spinning some elaborate fable to them about Felix, and his rôle in the affair – whatever that may mean. What affair? It all sounds pretty odd to me. I can't think what it's about. But give him the message, would you, Sadie? And lots and lots of love to both of you from all three of us! Lots of love. And Sadie . . . are you still there? Forget about the interest cheque this month. Keep it for yourself. Choose a horse. Live dangerously.'

Chapter 70

Miranda could see Bronowski coming from right along at the other end of the street. She had been out for a few minutes to buy milk at the local store, and as she walked back along Britannia Road towards her house she saw him come around the corner and approach from the opposite direction. His head was bowed as he gazed at the pavement in front of him, and Miranda stopped in the shadow of a tree as he came towards the house, watching his characteristically splay-footed walk, reflecting how hunched his shoulders had become as he had grown older, and how tired now was the posture and the bearing of him.

All of that ought to attract my love and my sympathy, she thought. Most women in my position would look at him now, and want only to help him and settle him into a comfortable, conventional decline into old age. But whatever my fear and inadequacy at the time, it was his vitality and his exuberance that I fell in love with, when he was a young man. The passionate, animal youth. But that was then. I don't want to be with him now. I never had a chance to reduce my feelings for him slowly down in the normal way, to the point where everything was quiet affection and mutual, comfortable dependence. We never did that, and now we've been too many years living apart.

I no longer want Amos in my life, and I no longer want to tell him about Michael. I couldn't do so without the story of Michael's life being coarsened and sullied by the description of it. So I'm not going to tell him. Which means, no doubt, that my guilt for what I fail to feel for him will build up in me all over again.

Miranda stepped out from the tree and called to him. He looked up, smiled, and raised his hand.

'I was coming round to see you,' he said. This meaningless ritualised opening remark was one that he would never have dreamed of making as a young man. There seemed to be next to none of the old arrogance in him now. She would have much

292

preferred it if there had been. A failing, defeated Amos, mumbling and cursing and railing his way into a spiteful decline was not what she wanted to see. Yet those newspaper articles of his – shrill, vengeful, impotent – showed him exactly in that light. When she'd read them, she'd been surprised that they had been published.

She wanted at that very moment no more than to exchange one or two mild pleasantries with him, and go on her way, and shut the door of her own, private, personal home on him, and be left alone. With not so much as a moment's pang for his departure, or his physical ageing, or his happiness, or his lack of it, or whether or not she would ever see him again.

But now he was pointing at her door, and had set off towards it. She turned the lock, and led him in, and offered him a drink, and poured that for him, and before she knew what had happened they were sitting together in her kitchen. And unless she was careful there would be yet one more of their pointless, loveless visits to her bedroom. No, not loveless. That was wrong. When she and Amos were making love it had each time now felt like that. Love. The fear of her youthful years had gone and she wondered at it. She could caress him now, and move her body, and respond to him, and direct him, and say those words of sexual awareness and daring she had, throughout her life, fantasised of doing. And watch him. And hold him in her arms. When they were making love now, it felt like love. It wasn't love, but it gave the illusion of love, so long as the act of it lasted. Who can explain that?

'Why are you staring at me?' he said. 'What is that look in your eyes?'

She turned away, and made some trite response, as mechanical as his had been earlier. She knew then, for a certainty, that she would help him in whatever he wanted her to help him in. The whole business of it was mad; she knew little or nothing of what was going on, but sensed that it was some deadly charade in which he and she and all of them had become ensnared, and compromised, and threatened. But she would help him in it, if that was what he wanted her to do. And needed her to do. It was because she still, after all these years, even now, was grateful to him. Amos had married her. No one else ever would have married her, however long she had remained alone. And Amos had given her a child. Without him, she would have been childless all her life.

In all her days, she told herself, she had never done anything for Amos at all. Not one thing. She recalled that she had not even given him a wedding present, so dazed she was that the event had ever actually taken place. On her wedding day, she hadn't even found the confidence to give her husband a gift. She'd been married, but she'd never been a wife.

It wasn't Amos who had failed. *She* had failed. She had never believed that he could really have wanted her for a wife, so, in self-protection, she had never allowed herself to become that. To the extent that she had kept from him the knowledge of her child. *His* child. She'd never allowed him to know that he had fathered a child, even though, as far as she knew, the rest of his life had been childless. How was she empowered to assume that she had a greater need and longing for a child than he had? Why should his sense of incompleteness be any less than hers?

Confirmed in her comfortable, familiar sense of inadequacy, when he had left her she had resumed the life she had all along assumed was ultimately to be her lot; loneliness, hard work, solitude, reflection. All this confirmed by the fact that she now had in her life a child of her womb, but a child cursed by a mental malfunction so severe as to make contact with any human being outside herself an impossibility. An impossibility even with herself perhaps. Michael may never have known that he had a mother. Could she, even now, face that truth? Maybe there never had been the spark of life in Michael that she had so insistently tried to identify. Maybe there never had been anything there at all. Maybe that was the truth. Maybe Dr McCready had been right.

'Miranda? Miranda? Will you help me?' Bronowski was saying, leaning forward in his chair towards her, as if to attract her attention better that way.

'What do you want me to do?' she said. She'd hear him out, and she'd do what he wanted, and then she'd bring the whole of this conversation and this affair to a close. For ever.

'I'm doing a seminar shortly on various issues surrounding the Holocaust survivors,' he at last blurted out. 'Issues arising from my *Sunday Times* articles, primarily. Various people are on the panel with me, amongst them a man called Joseph Hermann. You may remember the material I revealed about him. The Communist leader at Buchenwald, and the camp infirmary and so forth.'

Miranda nodded, and waited, the suspicion coming to her that she was being pulled yet again into an intrigue in which she had no place.

'I want to get something to him before the seminar,' he was saying now. 'I can't send it through the post, and it's too precious to have delivered by a stranger. I can't take it myself, because I doubt that he'd see me. I've heard that he's very angry about the *Sunday Times* article, and because of that I don't somehow think that he's likely to be prepared to talk to me, except under the formal circumstances of the seminar. I can't ask anybody else, so I'm asking you. You could refuse of course, but . . . Miranda? Would you be prepared to help me?'

Miranda gazed at him. 'What is it?' she asked. 'What do you want me to take to him?'

'A letter, that's all it is. Well – more like a small package.' He flushed suddenly. 'For Christ's sake – just that. A little package. I wouldn't ask you to take something of any size. You need do no more than take this thing to him and leave it there. It's only twenty minutes from your house. Is that too much to ask?'

Miranda knew that his sudden burst of petty aggression was a cover for something else, but she was in no mood to look for trouble. Surely there was no violence in him? Why not do this task for him, if that was what he wanted, and get it out of the way.

'Yes. All right,' she said. 'I'll deliver a letter to Mr Hermann, if that's what you want.' She held out her hand. 'I may as well take it now. Tell me where he's staying and when I'm to deliver it. I'll do whatever you say.'

Bronowski got to his feet. 'Thank you, Miranda,' he said. 'I do appreciate it, I really do. I'll bring it to you tomorrow – at eight o'clock in the evening, say? Would that time suit you? And then you can take it straight around to him. As I told you, he's only a few minutes away. He's staying at a little hotel in Cranley Gardens, and I know he'll be there then. He's seeing someone I know.'

Again, as Miranda met his eye, she was irritated by the look of pink, schoolboy guilt on his face. Too much detail and explanation. Too much feeble excuse for why he wasn't able to deliver his package himself. She'd ask him one more time.

'Why can't you take it to him yourself, Amos? Tell me again. You're seeing him the next day, so why can't you take it to him yourself, or give it to him at the seminar?'

Again he flushed, this time, as she could see, with a quick rush of anger, which he immediately tried to control and camouflage.

'I told you why not! Because he's full of hatred for me for what I wrote about him in the newspaper, and will only see me under the formal circumstances of the debate at the seminar, when he is able to publicly return his fire. I asked him to see me, and he wouldn't.'

You didn't say that before, Miranda thought. That's new. And it's not true.

'It really is important that he sees this material I'm sending him before the debate,' Amos went on hurriedly. 'I don't trust anyone else with it. I want it handed over to him personally. You're the sort of person that the hotel will trust, and he will trust.'

She shrugged, and got to her feet. 'Fine,' she said. 'See you here tomorrow evening, then. Eight o'clock.'

Bronowski moved forward, and put his arms out to embrace her. She kissed him quickly on the cheek, then put her hand under his arm, and led him out into the street.

Chapter 71

Harrison sat on the bed, having refused the chair, turning away from it when he saw a patch of what looked like partially dried mushroom soup spread ringed all over its seat. He shook his head again when Steiner brought across to him a glass of red wine.

'Changed my mind, Mariss. I'd forgotten the way you do your washing-up. You have it instead.'

Steiner laughed delightedly, and sat heavily on top of the soup patch, sipping at the wine.

'Some nonsense about me not being able to drink with these drugs I'm taking, but to have you here once more, Herbie, after – what? – three years at least, and to be able to swap our tales together like we used to, why, that's worth drinking to.'

Harrison nodded, and leaned back against the wall. 'Yes,' he said. 'I remember. The last tales we swopped together were when I came here to tell you that unless you stopped going around London announcing to all and sundry that you were a CIA man, we would have to chop your legs off.'

'I still am a CIA man.'

'No,' said Harrison. 'You're not. Thirty years ago you were – or on the fringes of being so. Before I was born, almost. But now you're not.'

'It's like being an Etonian,' Steiner replied. 'Or an Army officer. Once you're a—'

'*No!*' Harrison said once more. 'It's not like being an Etonian. You're not a CIA man. But that's not why I'm here, as you know.'

'Just teasing you, Herbie,' Steiner chuckled. 'Just a joke. So why *are* you here?'

Steiner took a gulp of his drink, then immediately went into a prolonged and increasingly desperate fit of coughing. Harrison watched him from the bed, at one stage straightening up as if he was about to go over to help him, then drawing back again as he saw the spittle hanging loose and slimy from out of Steiner's mouth. In time the coughing stopped, and Steiner leant back in his chair, ashen-white, sweat beading all along his forehead. Harrison let him rest for several minutes, until eventually Steiner wiped the sweat off his face with his sleeve, and smiled across at him.

'Good to see you, Herbie,' he said.

Harrison nodded. 'How ill are you, Mariss?' he asked. 'People tell us that it's bad. How bad?'

Steiner shrugged. 'What does it matter? Yes, I'm ill. That's why I want to get this thing over and done with as soon as possible. While I'm still able to, and not cooped up in some hospital.'

Harrison nodded again. 'I understand. But what thing, Mariss? That's why I'm here. That's what I want you to tell me. What thing?'

Steiner started to say something in reply, but Harrison put his hand up to stop him.

'You see, it's not Hermann, is it? Edel thought it was, but you've got nothing against Hermann, have you? He never did you any harm. Bergdorf gives you an explosive device, for you to hand to Hermann, having pressed its activating switch, and then stand well back. Right? I know why Bergdorf wants to be rid of him; that's simple. But I don't understand why you do. I don't believe you could give a damn one way or another as to what Hermann's rôle was. He looked after your sort of people perfectly well at Buchenwald. So why should you want to kill him? What are you really up to?'

Steiner, lying right back in his chair now, eyes half-closed, gazed at him through his lashes. 'What's it all about, you ask? Ask Bergdorf maybe. Or somebody else. I'm tired.'

'I'm asking *you*, Mariss. It's only you who knows. Come on, share it with me. OK, you're a CIA man – is that better? You're CIA through and through. Always have been, and always will be. Now – share it with me. Tell me what you're up to.'

Steiner first volunteered nothing, then as Harrison pushed himself forward, threateningly, he shrugged and said, 'You're right, of course. I've no real intention of hurting Hermann one way or another. Why should I? But I do have an interest in some-one else.'

Harrison supplied: 'Amos Bronowski – right? The man who drove you out of the CIA when he told some of our people that you were doing bits and pieces for Mossad as well, behind our backs. Now, after all these years of brooding on it, you want to

have your revenge on him. One last, glorious explosion. Killing
you both, maybe. And Hermann too. Because that way, because
of who he is, you'll get the headlines.'

He watched Steiner for a few seconds, then continued, 'So you
wanted to do it at Hermann and Bronowski's seminar. The last act
of your life one of international newsworthiness. That's it, Mariss,
isn't it? That's your plan.'

Steiner lay quite still, then, after a moment or two, slowly nodded
his head.

Harrison smiled. 'Well – that wasn't so painful, was it? And you
know something? We think it's rather a good idea. You want to
be on your way, and feeling as ill as you do who can blame you,
and you want Bronowski to go with you, for what he did to you
in the past. Good thinking. I agree. He's a pain in the arse. Take
him with you. Hermann too.'

Steiner sat up in his chair, and looked at Harrison with an
expression of total incredulity. 'You're serious? But Amos is one
of yours.'

Harrison shrugged. 'Too wild these days. Too damned sanctimonious. Too uncontrollable. Show me Bergdorf's bomb.'

Steiner went over to the bed, gestured to Harrison to move to
one side, and dragging it away from the wall, picked up from the
floor a large padded bag, open at the neck.

'God – I've been sitting on it,' said Harrison, and taking the bag
from Steiner, slid out from it a narrow cylinder, covered in white
plastic. He faced towards the window, and for a minute or two
appeared deep in its examination. 'Yes,' he said, turning again to
Steiner. 'It's real. I know these things. You know how to set it up.
You press this bit here, and hold the pressure continuously for at
least four seconds. Not less than that. Four seconds. Count it out
when you do it. Slowly. One – two – three – four. Then get the hell
out of it, if that's what you want. Otherwise stay around. Is that
what Bergdorf told you?' He pushed the cylinder carefully back
into the bag, and laid it himself gently on the floor, moving the
bed back over to cover it.

Harrison laid his hand on Steiner's shoulder, then moved away
to the door to let himself out.

'Good luck, Mariss,' he said. 'You're right. What a gesture! You'll
be famous! What a way to go!'

Chapter 72

Miranda stood outside the little hotel, the package in her hand, the rain pouring down on her uncovered head. A car turned into Cranley Gardens from the Old Brompton Road, and, accelerating away from the traffic, ploughed straight through a deep puddle at the kerbside, throwing a great splash of water up against her legs.

She grimaced, bent to wipe it off the best she could with a crumpled tissue she found in her pocket, then, forgetting her earlier hesitancy, ran through the gate, up the marbled front path, and through the open double doors into the front hall. Before her was an enclosed, cramped little front desk, on which stood a plastic credit-card advertisement, some tired flowers in a chipped white vase and a brass bell. Miranda rang this, then, nothing happening, did so once more, and, after some banging and shouting from behind a closed green-baize door, a woman of middle years came through and stood in front of her.

'Yes?' she said. 'I'm afraid we're full, dear. No rooms tonight, I'm afraid.'

'No – I have a package to deliver,' Miranda said, and the woman looked first at Miranda's sodden coat, and then at the rain-stained Jiffy bag in her hand, and for a moment seemed as if she was about to send her packing with it. 'It's for Mr Hermann,' Miranda continued quickly. 'One of your guests here. Professor Joseph Hermann.'

The woman reluctantly put her hand out to take the bag from her, but Miranda held it fast, and shook her head.

'No – I'm so sorry,' she said. 'I do have very specific instructions on this. I have to give the package directly to Professor Hermann himself. Might I do that? Could you possibly ring through to his room to see if he's there?'

There was a lengthy process of looking at the register, taking two outside telephone calls, and having an argument with the chef, who had suddenly stuck his head out from the baize door in rage at something or another, before Hermann's room was called.

The woman was about to replace the receiver, when at last she got through.

'I have someone to see you, Professor. With a package. Someone called . . .'

'Miranda from Mr Edel's office,' she said, exactly as Amos had told her to.

The message was given, then repeated in a louder voice. 'From Mr Edel's office,' she shouted, then listened for a moment and replaced the receiver. 'He's with somebody, dear,' the woman said, getting to her feet, and clasping to her bosom a large black cat, which had jumped up on to the desk in front of her. 'He asks if you'd wait for ten minutes, and then he'll be down.'

She pointed towards a sofa in the corner, covered in imitation leather, and went out once more through the baize door. Miranda sat down, and pulled the package out from the protective bag she had put it in. She felt at it once again, as she had been doing whilst standing out in the street. The package was sealed both with staples and tape, and, as Miranda pressed and squeezed at it, she persuaded herself again that it seemed to contain nothing more than a simple rectangular box.

She looked up at the clock. Still at least eight minutes to go, even if he really did mean ten minutes and not more. What on earth was she doing here in this dreadful little hotel? What sort of fantasy was this, that she had to be a covert messenger for Amos in some stupid, dangerous clandestine business of his? All that nonsense about 'Miranda from Mr Edel's office'. And although she had kept on telling herself that Amos was by no means a violent man, nor Gareth, of course, what *was* this object that she'd brought to Hermann?

Suddenly she was tearing at the sealing tape, and scrabbling to rip the package open. Amos has gone mad, she thought, and knew the panic was mounting in her. He's gone mad, and he's trying to kill this man with a letter bomb, and like a fool, I'm taking it to him and putting it in his hand. She was ripping now at the tape and the paper, and now it was open and there was the object inside.

The two parts of the box came apart in her hands. She was half expecting the explosion to come at that instant, and she dropped the box on the floor, recoiling from the blast, but none came. There was complete silence. The box was sitting there open on the floor, and an obscenely grinning, tartan-coated, black-faced

301

doll was rocking back and forth on its spring. Fallen on the carpet beside it was a folded piece of paper, and Miranda picked it up to read it.

I can't kill. If I could, I would have sent something different. But maybe this is better. It's a mark of my contempt, and I wanted you to know that before we meet in public tomorrow. But it's also a warning to you, in your own interests. You have more enemies than you know. Some of them are dangerous. I do assure you of that. Amos Bronowski.

'Miss Miranda?' said the old man standing in front of her. 'Miss Miranda? You have a message for me? – from Mr Edel's office?'

Chapter 73

The following morning Miranda had calmed herself down, but her anger when she'd arrived home from seeing Hermann had been so violent that it had turned, mercifully, into a solitary, sobbing near-hysteria.

She was certainly enraged, but she knew that it was with herself as well as with Amos. She had allowed the business with him to run on unresolved – because she had been unresolved. They'd been to bed together, they'd talked together, but Miranda had failed either to decide definitely to let him back into her life or definitely to let him go. She recognised now that he did, genuinely, want to return to her. The responsibility for the future now was hers. But still, when it came to the point, she was irresolute.

And as painful as her indecision over Amos was her inability to address with him the issue of Michael. It had to be done now. She no longer could live with her excuses for not doing so. In one mood, she could assure herself that Amos had been an errant, absconding husband, and the child, morally, was hers and hers alone. At other times, softer, more sentimental, she would persuade herself that she had, out of affection, shielded Amos from the truth. In protection of him. Knowing the guilt he would feel that he wasn't himself looking after his incapacitated child. But neither of those are true, she told herself. They're both fabrications.

Then Amos was at the door, precisely on time as always. She went to let him in, muttering to herself that this time she would show some courage, and resolve the business between them once and for all.

She opened the door, and there he was, and she knew the moment she saw him what her decision was, and what she was going to say. The abrupt certainty of that cleared the fear from her, and she brought Bronowski into the house, and sat him down at the kitchen table, and when he started to make some remark about the previous evening, cut him short.

'Amos – listen to me,' she said, and felt so strong and calm and decisive that she wondered how it was that she could ever have felt afraid. Her certainty of will elated her. 'This is the end for us, Amos. Thank you for trying – and I do believe that you really did want to come back to me. But I don't want to come back to you. So hear what I'm saying. This is the last time we're going to see each other.'

Bronowski nodded, and for some moments sat there, motionless, and she could see the tiredness in him, and the defeat, but this, instead of moving her, made her all the more resolute.

'Before you go, there's one more thing I've got to tell you.'

She swallowed, and suddenly the fear was catching up with her again, and she willed herself to continue before her nerve went. She stumbled straight into it; immediately, as she did so, all the self-hatred for what she had done broke in her.

'We had a child, Amos,' she said. 'A boy. He died twenty years ago. He was severely mentally and physically handicapped.'

Still he stared at her, and she began to wonder if he had heard or grasped what she had said.

'He was nine,' she went on; the words now galloping away from her, the speech coming from a different voice. 'He died peacefully in my arms, without pain. It was an early summer evening. He knew me. We were together at the end.'

Bronowski grimaced suddenly, frighteningly, as if in a sudden shot of acute pain. Then he pushed himself to his feet, and stood staring down at her.

'He was nine years old, you say?'

'Yes.' Miranda wondered how it was possible that she'd held his son's life and death from him. Whatever he'd done. Whatever he and she had or had not been.

Bronowski turned away from her, and went to the door. Then it came. The rage – blind, breathless, wild – burst out from nowhere. She heard herself shouting at him, screaming at him, so shrill, so coarsely that it was if she was a madwoman.

'*Don't you want to know his name, for Christ's sake? Your son's name?*'

Then on and on, trembling now, screeching, brutal.

'*Your son, you bastard. Your son! His name was* Michael.'

'Michael,' Bronowski repeated, soft and flat, and opened the door, and went out into the street.

Chapter 74

Edel stood in the middle of Steiner's room, looking around him at the inimitable chaos of it, and reflecting, with a momentary pang of bizarre regret, that he would never see it again. He turned his back to the bed as the police and ambulancemen zipped the body bag tight shut, but too late to miss a final glimpse of Steiner's face, wide eyes staring, mouth open, a line of spittle partly dried on the side of his stubbled chin.

'Time of death ten forty-five, or thereabouts, Gareth,' the police surgeon said. 'Which squares with when the woman downstairs thought she heard a sudden big thump, or however she described it. Cause of death is for the coroner, but I'm pretty sure it was a massive heart attack, caused by the shock of this thing going off right underneath his bed. And he was dying anyway, I should imagine.'

He pointed to the bottle of morphine beside Steiner's bed. 'He was only given it this afternoon, for the first time, according to the chemist, who checked it on his computer. We'll talk to his doctor later on tonight, if we can succeed in reaching him. Cancer, probably. In its terminal stages, I would imagine. Bowel, liver, stomach . . . any of those. The poor sod must have been in devastating pain a lot of the time. Refused to go into hospital no doubt, and his doctor decided to let him go in the way he chose. Except he didn't. This firework thing went off first.'

Edel nodded. 'How powerful was the firework, Henry? The explosives man will tell us in due course, but you know as much as he does. Was it big enough to kill, if he'd been holding the thing?'

'Oh yes,' the police surgeon said. 'If he'd been holding it at the time it exploded it would certainly have blown his face off. I would guess it was like that one you and I dealt with four or five years ago at the airport. Big enough to kill whoever was holding it, and maybe the people immediately beside them. What happened in this case was that this bed has got these particularly low legs, and the pile of blankets and quilts and things the old boy was lying on at the time was sufficient to stun the explosion. The blankets burnt, as you can see, though they didn't catch fire. Death was virtually instantaneous, I would think.'

'Do you recognise the device, from what's left of it?' Edel gestured at the mangled remains of the bomb lying undisturbed by the police, a white chalkmark circled around it on the linoleum. The police surgeon made as if to prod at it with his foot, but stopped short.

'McGillivray will tell us when he gets here, but it's bog standard, I can assure you. Detonated by a simple push-button arrangement, on a pre-set timer. Somebody did just that. Pressed the button, having set the timer, and left it there to blow up at the time he'd set. Ten forty-five, I assume. What did you say his name was again? The old man?'

'Steiner,' Edel said, and went over to the wall, studying the various pieces of paper that were hanging there. 'Mariss Steiner.'

'And a friend of yours, I gather? Tomkins told me that your name was there on the computer in code as the contact officer in the case of accident to him, which is why they'd got you round here tonight. A friend, or simply someone you were running?'

There was a silence, and the police surgeon stood watching Edel, aware suddenly that he had asked the question in too flippant a style. Edel was upset, and he'd made it worse. He'd seen him like this before, on some most surprising occasions. Edel never took death well. He'd worked with him for almost twenty years and they'd experienced this so many times. Edel never could accept death. Even the deaths of people with whom he himself had been in direct conflict.

But then Edel said, 'A friend. A friend for many, many years. He knew that. And someone I was running – but that he didn't know. At least, I hope he didn't. Though with Mariss, one was never sure of anything, and that's the truth. Never sure of anything at all.'

The following morning was Sunday, and as Edel turned into the alleyway leading up to the dark, hidden little church, there was in him a profound longing for its tranquillity and peace and certainty. He was far too early for the service, but, exhausted to the depth of his being, he needed, more than anything he could think of, to be able to reflect, and pray, and remember, and heal himself in the familiar, dependable resolution and beauty of the Mass that had been his legacy from Maeve.

But he was still thirty or forty feet from the West door when he knew something was wrong. There was the slightest of sounds from behind him; for a moment he hesitated, then walked on, holding his pace, clenching the muscles of his back, as if in anticipation of the blow to come. He'd never carried a weapon in his life, and had no idea how to use one anyway, but at that moment he longed for protection. He was breathless with fear, and just as the panic hit him, and he started to run, there was a shout from behind him, then another, this time of a different voice, and Edel could hear the crack of the gun. He threw himself at the door, banging at it with his fists, wrenching at the handle, then swung around, his eyes starting in terror.

But the only person there was the elderly priest, Father Thomas, blood pouring from his face, standing, hunched-shouldered, his hands hanging down loosely to his sides. His face, invariably smiling, was at that moment completely blank, and as Edel recovered, and ran toward him, he saw that he was blanched white with shock.

It was a passer-by who later told Edel, and the police, what had happened. The young man in the tracksuit had come out from the doorway, pushed the priest aside, and, standing at the head of the alley, lined his gun at Edel's back. Before he could fire, Father Thomas had recovered himself, and lurching forward, smashed his walking stick down on to the young man's forearm. There was a struggle, a shot, Father Thomas was punched in the face, and then, suddenly he was alone. Staring down towards the church. Staring at Edel, pounding in his terror on the locked door.

Chapter 75

Edel fell silent for a minute or two, gazing across the Thames at the bright lights of the new Charing Cross Station on the North bank. Then, so quietly that Bronowski had to flex his head to hear him, he began to speak.

'Did I ever explain to you about Mariss? Did you know what he actually wanted from you? What he wanted Miranda to help him set up?

'It was something very odd. Odd, and vicious, and inhuman, and exactly within Mariss's character. He knew he was dying. And the nearer he got to death, the more obsessed he became with what you'd done to him all those years before, in discrediting him with his beloved CIA. That had been his only home. He had adored the glamour and self-importance those CIA connections gave him, tenuous and trivial as they actually were. All his crackpot idealism was actually subverted into a desire for personal vengeance. But not only that. He wanted something more. He wanted to curse you. Literally. A formal, biblical curse. And he wanted to curse you publicly, in front of the person most likely to be hurt by it. Miranda.

'There's a Psalm – Psalm 109 – that I saw lying open beside Mariss's bed each time I'd been to his room in recent months. It's an unpleasant piece of work I think. It's all about hatred of one's enemies, and the calling down of God's vengeance upon them. Very specific vengeance.

'*Let his days be few: and let another take his office.*

'*Let his children be fatherless: and his wife a widow.*

'*Let his children be vagabonds, and beg their bread: let them seek it also out in desolate places.*

'*Let the extortioner consume all that he hath: and let the stranger spoil his labour.*

'*Let there be no man to pity him: nor to have compassion on his fatherless children.*

'*Let his posterity be destroyed: and in the next generation let his name be clean put out.*'

Edel looked across at Bronowski. 'Mariss wanted Miranda to arrange a meeting at which all three of you would be there together. And then, before he killed you, he was going to . . . he was going to curse you. Like a Biblical Prophet. And tell you, for the first time, about your fatherless child. And tell you too that God had followed the path of vengeance, and that your posterity was destroyed, and that in the next generation your name had been put clean out. That's what he wanted. He wanted the three of you together, alone. You, Miranda, and himself. That, of course, is why I diverted him with the idea of the bomb. To make a bigger thing of killing you than that. To make it a big, newsworthy, political assassination, by bringing Hermann into it as well. All nonsense of course – all nonsense. But it strung him along, and for a man as ill as he was, that was all I was interested in doing.'

Amos was for some moments completely silent. Then, oddly indifferent, as if merely to make conversation, he said, 'Then Harrison killed him anyway. As he had killed Levinstein. As he tried to do to you. He certainly seemed devoted to keeping Hermann alive. But I still don't understand why he bothered to murder Mariss. He was a dying man anyway.'

'But still a threat, I suppose,' Edel replied. 'Harrison was probably not convinced that Mariss's interest in Hermann was as slight as he said it was. I'm not sure I was either. So – perhaps on the spur of the moment – he killed him. Just to be on the safe side. Harrison is completely dispassionate. The act of killing means nothing to him at all.'

Edel got to his feet, and Bronowski too, and the pair of them walked slowly towards the footbridge, their heads lowered, gazing at the shimmering gleam of the wet paving before them. Edel slipped his hand under Bronowski's arm.

'Why are you going back to Gateshead, Amos?' he asked. 'The seminar's cancelled, and all of that's over. Why not just rest? You know why I got Lewis Cohen to get you up there in the first place, though he made the whole business of it so much more complicated than it needed to be. You know who Ledelmeister was. Isn't that enough? You've seen that the man's dead now. That's all I wanted to achieve. I wanted you to have the certainty of that, and now you have it.

'So live your days out now, Amos. Buchenwald. Belsen. It was all so long ago. Let it go now, Amos. Let it be.'

Chapter 76

The rain blew in from the sea in gusts of fine, misty drizzle, and Bronowski wrapped his arms across his chest, huddling down into the warmth of his coat. He wiped his sleeve across his face, then broke away from the path, cutting across the grass to the far corner of the cemetery, where two yew trees, bent and misshapen, reached across to touch each other, as if elderly, infirm companions in mutual physical comfort and support.

Drawing nearer, Bronowski hesitated when he saw a figure, wrapped in headscarf and an old tweed overcoat, bending down, kneeling on a groundsheet, tending with a trowel and pair of handshears at the grass around what looked like a new headstone, a few feet away from where Ledelmeister and his wife lay. But the old woman looked up and smiled at him, and continued with her work, and Bronowski did what he had come to do, sitting on a bench shielded from the rain, gazing for what he had told himself would be the last time at Ledelmeister's grave. Remembering.

After some minutes the old woman tidied up her tools and the groundsheet into a basket, then got to her feet. Bending her back, she held her sides in stiff discomfort from the position she had been in, then turned to Bronowski, smiled, and came over to sit beside him.

'Sorry to disturb you,' she said, 'but I really must sit down. And I can't help asking; I saw you looking at the grave – did you know the Ledelmeisters? A relation or something like that? They were neighbours of mine, you know. Lovely people. Germans. Jewish, but they became Christians. Members of my church. They were concentration camp victims of course. Belsen. What dreadful stories they had to tell! We were all so fond of them. But you knew them, did you?'

Bronowski, often brusque with strangers, found himself replying to this perfect stranger with courtesy and warmth. She knew Ledelmeister. She was filling out the story for him, though in an

310

unexpected way. He found himself talking quite freely, safe in his privacy. She would never know his name, or who he was. Her face was kind, and she was resting from the rain, and he needed her. He needed someone to draw out from him the image that had remained there in his mind all his life. No one had heard the story before. He'd never told it to anyone. Not to Miranda, and not to any of the women who had come and gone from him over the course of his days. And not even to Edel, who knew only that there was within him a recurrent nightmare, and that its root lay somewhere in Ledelmeister's name.

Bronowski leant forward on the bench, and stared out over the wall at the grey, gaunt lines of terraced cottages, stretching down towards the docks, and the bleak, windblown beaches beyond.

'My father was a widower, you see. Before the War he had been a teacher, in a small village somewhere down by the Czechoslovakian border. He and I came to Belsen together. We'd only been there a few weeks when he was put to work in a quarry and, despite his age, he was made to dig out and carry great blocks of stone. He would always take what rest he could when the *kapos* – the Jewish Trusties – were out of sight. But one day he was seen by one of them leaning on his pick, and the man kicked him in the stomach so hard and so repeatedly that he fainted with the pain of it. I was there with him. They'd allowed me to go with him to the quarry. I was three years old. I knelt beside him, and held his head in my arms, but after a few moments someone pulled me away. They tried to get my father to his feet, but as they did so he died. He was still holding his pick. That's what I've never been able to forget. He was still holding his pick, and the only way the *kapo* could get it off him was to prise it, finger by finger, from his grasp. He had to force and break it away from him. As if the wooden handle that he held so fast was his final possession on earth. As if it was me.'

He grimaced, then got to his feet, walked forward to Ledelmeister's grave, and gazed down at it. 'The *kapo* was Ledelmeister.'

'I shouldn't have said,' the old woman called out from the bench. 'I'm so sorry. If I'd known, I never would have described him in the way that I did. He seemed such a gentle man to me.'

After a moment or so, Bronowski heard her get to her feet and gather her basket to her. He guessed that for a little while she watched him still, but then someone called out to her, and she made some reply, and he knew that she had gone.

My father, he thought, lying there under Ledelmeister's boot, dying in my arms. My dead child, whose presence I knew all his life, and wanted to acknowledge, but left too late to do so. The marriage I walked out on. Love affairs that came and drifted away. An obsession with revenge on Hermann, who had done me no harm. A career that never amounted to anything.

It doesn't add up to much. I wish it did. I wish it had. I wish my life had come to something. To anything at all.

The rain gusted in across his face, and Bronowski pulled his collar up once more. He shivered in the chill of the evening air as he turned to pass back under the two aged yews, entwined in their heavy, defeated embrace. 'That's all it's been,' he muttered. 'That's all it ever is. Just a random concurrence of people. Just a passage of lives.'